KINGS OF MORNING

PAUL KEARNEY

KINGS OF MORNING

This novel first published 2012 by Solaris
an imprint of Rebellion Publishing Ltd,
Riverside House, Osney Mead,
Oxford, OX1 0ES, UK

www.solarisbooks.com

ISBN: 978 1 907519 38 3

10 9 8 7 6 5 4 3 2 1

A CIP catalogue record for this book is available from the British Library.

Designed & typeset by Rebellion Publishing

Printed in the UK

This book is dedicated to the
finest man I have ever known;

my father,
James Francis Kearney.

HARUKUSH MOUNTAINS
MACHTIC SEA
SCANION
CARALIS
ISCA
BAS MATHON
GAN CRAS
GOSTHERE
MACHRAN
MINERIAS
AVENNES
ARIENUS
HAL GOSHEN
PONTIS
PLAETRA
IDRIOS
SINON
GAN SAKR
HANEIKOS R.
SARDASK R.
ASKANON
ASHDOD
SINONIAN SEA
KUPR
ANTIKAUROS
ESKIS
KUMIR
IRUNSHA
GYGONIS
KHULM
HAFDARA
TANEAN SEA
OCHOS
KAUROS R.
OCHIR
KORASH
ANARIS
KERKH
JUNNAN
OTOSH R.
JUTHA
JURID R.
THE MI
DADIKAI
GEMINESTRA
TAL BYRNA
ESIS
PLEN
TANIS
GADINAI DESERT
ABEKAI R.
ARTAKA
GADEAN HILLS
ISHT
BEKAI R.
BOS
ARTAN R.
N
0 100 200 300 400 500 MILES
0 200 400 600 800 1000 PASANGS
BEKAI R.
UM

KUF

THE EV-MERIDACH
PADRAN
HONAN
PASTIR R.
ANAMIR MTS
BEKAI R.
MOUNTAINS
UDRUK
CARCHANIS
KAIK
HAMADAN
ASURIAN GATES
ASHUR
MAGRON
ASURIA
ARAKOSIA
BOKOSA
ADRANOS MTS
YUE
OSKUS R.
MEDIS
KOSAN
PANJIR R.
IRGUN
KANDASAR
VIDEHAN GULF

PROLOGUE

THEY LAY IN the heather with the sun on their backs and stared east, the bees busy in the tangled fronds and roots about their faces, the scent of the birthing summer all about them, a fragrance as old and as new as life itself. They were perched on the tawny hillside like ticks on the flank of a great-backed hound, the land unaware of them, going about its existence as it had these thousands of centuries. They felt their own impermanence, the tiny pricks of their souls on the existence of the world, and they smiled as they caught one another's eye, attuned to that knowledge.

East again, their gaze turned, and they saw the huge blooming sweep of the world open out before them like a hazed cloak swung over oddments, vast beyond comprehension, and yet intimate, bulging here and there with hills, scabbing over with the blossom of forests. All of it blurred and lazy under a warm sunlight, a blessing in the air itself.

The younger of the two turned, lay on his back under the sun and stared up at the sky. He was a pale, slender fellow, but there was a golden tinge to his skin that answered the sunlight.

'He is not taking us seriously, Rictus.'

The other, an older man, lay watching, his grey eyes as pale as the underside of a snake. He rested his chin on his forearm, and the lumped flesh under his lip jutted out, an old scar. His forearm, too, was silvered with streaks of long-healed wounds, matching the badger-thatch of his hair. He was gaunt, austere, a man who seemed to have been peering into the wind all his life.

'Serious enough. It's as big a camp as I've ever seen.'

The younger man turned on his stomach again, shaded his eyes and stared across the sunlit plain before him.

'All things are relative, my friend. We look out here upon a sensible riposte to our enterprise. He has sent enough to answer the challenge; not enough to crush it.'

'And?'

'And –' the younger man's face darkened. For a second it seemed almost that the bones within it grew more pronounced, making him into something else entirely; a grim creature of humourless will.

'And he is not here himself. There is no Imperial tent. He has sent his lackeys to fight us, Rictus.'

Now it was the older man's turn to roll on his

back. He rubbed at the white scar furrowing his chin. 'Then they will be the more easily beaten.'

'Where's the glory in that?'

Rictus smiled, and for a second he seemed a much younger man. 'After everything we have done, Corvus, do you still need the glory of it?'

'Now, more than ever.'

The young man looked down on the older one. In some ways they were akin; the high cheekbones, the colour flaring in them, the scars they both carried. Corvus leant and kissed Rictus on the forehead.

'My brother,' he said, 'Were it not for the glory, I would not be here at all.'

PART ONE

HEART OF EMPIRE

ONE
MONTH OF FROGS

Imperial Ashur, greatest city of the world. The last of the spring breezes which swept cool and blue from the Magron Mountains to the west had sunk into the drying earth of the vast Oskus valley. Now the first true heat of summer was upon the city, and the sun glinted in painful brilliance off the polished gold tiles plating the ziggurat of Bel.

The dust was rising in the streets, and the striped canopies of traders and merchants were lowered against the growing heat of the year. Mot and Bel had finished their struggle for one more season; the rains had come and gone, the glittering grid of irrigation channels that spangled the earth for pasangs all around the tall city walls were gurgling and alive with frogs, which the local farmers brought into the city in baskets, as a seasonal delicacy. In old Kefren, this month had once been known as *Osh-ko-ribhu*; the Time to Eat Frogs.

Kurun bit into his with relish, tearing the delicate meat off the skewer with teeth as small and white as a cat's. He had a face like a cat too, all pointed chin and large eyes, and a small snub nose which was considered ugly by the high-caste Kefren, who preferred something more beak-like to enhance their long, golden faces. Kurun was a *hufsan* from the Magron Mountains, a small, wiry youth with the dark skin and eyes of his people, and black hair which, when it was not oiled, stood up straight and thick on his head like the pelt of a cat in a thunderstorm. He had a winning smile, and the man with the skewered frogs knew him well, and would not take his money, but stood tending his charcoal and listened as Kurun told him news from the High City, the words tripping out of his mouth between mouthfuls.

'And Auroc, the Kitchen-Master, he says that the Couch-Chamberlain has told him already to make preparations for the move to Hamadan. They have the Tithemen on the roads as I speak, Goruz, and are bringing in half the imperial herd from Bokosa. Twenty thousand cattle, Auroc said, and he is worried that the new grass is not yet high enough to keep them in flesh all the way to Hamadan.'

'Twenty thousand cattle,' the frog-seller said, shaking his grizzled head. 'At this time of year they will strip the land of every growing blade and ear. It will hurt the valley farmers.'

Kurun wiped his mouth. 'The Lord wants the roads clear before high summer – so they say in the Palace. I can't think why. Didn't the army already leave months ago?'

'Perhaps they want another army gathered,' Goruz said with a shrug.

'What need of another army? Surely one is enough.'

'I was at Kunaksa, Kurun, one of the city levy. I saw our left wing, thirty thousand strong, blown away like straw in the wind when those monsters crashed into them. They are demons – who is to say that they did not do the same to the army that left for the west?'

Kurun frowned. 'That is a story, Goruz, put out to frighten the common folk. Everyone knows that the demons from across the sea were destroyed by our Lord, chased back across the mountains and broken into pieces. He sent their heads to every corner of the Empire.'

Goruz shrugged again, the resigned shrug of the misbelieved poor. 'I know what I saw. It was near thirty years ago, but I do not forget that day. I remember it better than any day before or since – that is what war is like. The memory of it stays clear and cold in a man's mind.'

Kurun handed the old man back the hardwood skewer and tossed a tiny thigh-bone into the street. 'Well, whatever happens, Goruz, at least the frogs are good this year.'

'They are, at that, as plump and fine as I've seen them, Bel be praised. Are you back to the High City now, Kurun?'

'Where else?' The boy flashed a white grin. 'There is an audience this afternoon, Goruz. There are couriers due in from the Middle Empire. If I can wriggle my way to the platforms I'll have more news for you, by and by.'

'Mind you your station, boy – that skinny back of yours was not made to take a whipping!' Goruz called. But Kurun was already gone, darting through the crowded street like a minnow flashing between stones in a brown river.

He wore the purple stripe of the imperial household on his chiton, and tattooed on his shoulder was the stylised horse head that was the Great King's mark. He belonged to the man who owned everything. He was a creature of the High City, as the Palace ziggurat was called by those below. He knew the back ways up to the heights, the dark entrances which led to the bowels of the Palace wherein toiled legions of slaves from every race in the world. The ziggurat was more ancient than Ashur itself, a man-made tell as large as one of nature's mountains, a city within a city whose inhabitants numbered in the tens of thousands, slave and free, high and low.

Kurun had been born among the real mountains that lined the rim of the world far to the west, but he no longer had any memory of them. When the poor folk of the Magron could not pay the Imperial Tithemen on their yearly visit, they gave up their children to them instead, and these were brought to Ashur by the thousand every year, slaves of the King, to be reared in his service and then disposed of as he saw fit. They worked his fields, carried his burdens, serviced the carnal needs of his soldiers and officials, and generally oiled the workings of the teeming metropolis that was ancient Ashur, mistress of the world. It was the way it had been in all of history and memory. It was the way it would always be.

Kurun had been lucky, gifted almost straight away to the Household, his owner the Kitchen-Master of the Court itself. His earliest real memory was of turning a spit above a charcoal grill, his tears sizzling as they dripped upon the coals. Before that there was only a hazy impression of cold air, bright blue skies, and the blaze of sunlight on snow. He had never seen snow since, except on clear autumn days when one could make out the white-tipped peaks of his homeland glimmering on the horizon. When the Great King moved his court to Hamadan to escape the heat of the summer lowlands, Kurun had always been left behind, no matter how hard he tried to insinuate himself with his master. He was a *hufsan* slave, and there were thousands like him in the uplands of Hamadan.

He picked his way through the crowds with unfocused ease. The Oskus valley produced two harvests a year, and some of the more adept farmers of the floodplains were already in the city with their wares, stealing a march on their fellows with cartloads of rice, the first corn, pomegranates, and palm hearts. The dust was already thickening underfoot, and an inkling of the summer reek had begun to rise from the vaulted sewers that gurgled in every street. In the poorer sections, these were little more than brick-lined ditches; closer to the ziggurats, and they were massive underground tunnels which Goruz said a wagon could be driven through.

Kurun stopped to inhale the fragrance of a bunch of purple irises from a flower-stand. They grew like weeds across the Oskus valley, lining the irrigation ditches in bright borders. Here in the city, almost every house had bunches of them in earthenware jars to sweeten the air. The smell was as much a harbinger of summer as the stink of the sewers.

The city opened out before him as he entered the wide expanse of the *Huruma*, the Sacred Way, a massive thoroughfare some half a pasang wide which linked the Fane of Bel to the Palace. It ran through the city with the precision of a knife-cut, and was loud with the sound of running water, the air full of the spray of fountains. Here, the famed processions of history were held; Great Kings rode along it to be crowned on the summit of the Fane, and conquering satraps led parades. The Priests themselves blessed the fountains every year in a haze of incense, accompanied by the singing of the people and the tolling of ancient bronze bells. Folk travelled from all over the Empire to stand here, to look up at the ziggurat of Bel and that of the Great King, to dip their hands in the holy water and fill a flask which they would take back home to sprinkle on their fields and thus gain the blessings of the highest priests of the earth. The breath of God Himself, it was said, was in the waters of the Huruma, and Kurun paused, as he always did, to brush the surface of one of the pools and touch the cool liquid to his forehead. The water was too sacred to be drunk; it was even used to anoint the head of the Great King on the day he was crowned. Only he was allowed to sip it, thus ingesting the Breath of God, and rendering himself holy and inviolate, one touched by the Creator Himself.

Kurun felt a tug at the hem of his chiton, and looked down to see a dark, bright-eyed face, a shock of hair ragged as a cow's tail. 'Kurun! Bel kiss you and bless you!'

Kurun seized the child by the shoulder and hauled it to one side, into the shadow of an awning. 'You can't be on the Huruma, Usti. Don't you know anything? The waterwardens will cane you all the way to the gates.'

'I wanted a touch of the water, for luck.'

'A *nomoi* isn't allowed.'

'Who's to notice?'

'They always notice, Usti.' Kurun relented, loosening his grasp on the child's stick-thin arm. He thumbed the moist patch that remained on his own forehead and touched the filthy little face. 'There – I have given you my blessing from the water. Bel keep you.'

A grin, showing brown, gapped teeth. 'A blessing from you, Kurun, is worth more than money.'

'No it isn't. Don't try that with me,' Kurun warned the urchin. 'And keep your hand by your side. You've none to spare anymore.'

The child lifted up one arm, and the threadbare sleeve fell back to reveal a gnarled stump of flesh. 'This is my life, Kurun. I eat like a Priest this time of year; the farmers toss me all manner of things from their carts in pity at the sight of it. I will be fat before midsummer!'

'The farmers are kind-hearted fools,' Kurun said, with the condescension of the city-dweller. But he smiled, and dug into the folds of his sash. A copper obol flashed in the light, new-minted and barely tinged with green. The child's jaw dropped.

'Take this, and stay off the Sacred Way.'

He dropped the coin into Usti's palm, and the child clamped its fingers around it until the bones showed white through the dirt.

'You bless me twice today, Kurun. I shall buy a green frog and sacrifice it for you at the Garden Gate.'

'Don't be sacrificing frogs; buy a skewer of them off Goruz instead, while they're still to be had.'

The child backed away, eyes shining. 'My brothers will eat meat today, Kurun – we will sing a holy song for you at the –'

'Yes, yes – now get yourself lost before the waterwardens catch a whiff of you.'

In a twinkling, Usti was gone, as a mouse will vanish in sudden light. Kurun stood in the shade of the awning, the people here barely glancing at his purple stripe. His young face creased with momentary sadness. Then he shook his head, and yawned, and carried on his way to the looming ziggurat of the King.

THE KING'S STEPS soared up, a stairway to the sky. They were for the high caste, civil servants, diplomats, men high in the King's service. And they called for fit men, because there were three thousand steps, each wide as a ledge. The Great King rode his horse to the summit of the ziggurat, but for everyone else the climb had to be made on foot.

At their base the Royal Honai stood, like golden statues resplendent in polished bronze, with silver pomegranates on the butts of their spears. There were ten thousand of these tall Kefren, the finest soldiers in the Empire, the bodyguard of the Lord himself. A great army had been sent west the winter before, but the Honai had stayed behind, and the King with them. Whatever war was flickering out at the borders of the Empire was not considered important enough to warrant his personal attention. And why should it? This was the world that all people knew, and had always known. There was not a generation living that had contemplated anything else.

The Steps were not for the likes of Kurun. He padded quickly through the serried manifold maze of alleyways and mud-brick streets that congregated along the base of the High City like the breakers of a brilliantly coloured sea. In this babel of shouting, haggling, gesticulation and barter, the small merchants and traders of the city traditionally had their stalls, their carts, their shops and lean-tos. They sold small animals for sacrifice, sweet incense, flowers, bolts of cloth to be draped and cut upon the wearer in the street, sandals of plaited reeds, trinkets of every base metal and some precious ones, bright pebbles from the river polished to brilliance, and cuttings touted as sprigs from the gardens of the Great King himself.

One man, Arozian the gardener, had a stall covered with miniature trees which he kept small through constant pruning. They always drew an open-mouthed crowd from the provinces, and his stall was well known as a honeypot for pickpockets. Kurun pressed his fist to the belly of his sash as he passed, flashing a wave to the blue-faced old Juthan. There were few of his race left in Asuria. Most Juthans, slaves and free, had left or run away over the years to join their kin in Jutha under the rebel king Proxanon. Those that were left had become something of a curiosity, and one that was viewed with a certain suspicion. But here in the Long Bazaar Arozian was a fixture, and he liked to boast that the High Priest himself had made purchase from him.

A dark gateway loomed, many times Kurun's height, wide enough for two wagons to enter abreast. It looked like a door to the underworld, and in many ways it was. This was the Slave Gate, one of the entrances to the dark intestines of the High City. The traffic passing in and out was watched over by more of the royal Honai, but these warriors were not the gleaming legendary figures who stood at the foot of the King's Steps. They wore true battle-armour, and short stabbing spears with butts of iron which doubled as maces. Like their brothers, resplendent at the foot of the King's Steps, they were incorruptible – unlike almost every other gate-guard in the city – and were as quick with a blow as a query. Kurun bowed his head as he shuffled past them, as did the rest of the crowd, and the hubbub of the street was dimmed, so that it seemed the Slave Gate was witness to pulsing trains of penitents intent on their sins and the dust on their sandals.

The heat and light of the sun was blocked out, and at once the smell of the Slave-City engulfed Kurun.

Thousands of bodies, sweating and ill-washed and packed together. Animal ordure, soot, woodsmoke, and here and there the half-sick fragrance of perfume on a slave-girl.

Massive hanging lamps of clay added to the heat within. It was always lamplit night here, in the base of the tell. Higher up within the massive structure, stone-lined shafts were cut into the mound and admitted the light of Bel, but this was a subterranean labyrinth. No Honai here; the Great King's elite did not soil themselves with the streaming stink of the Slave-City, but instead *hufsan* guards in leather cuirasses stood in pairs at intervals, bronze scimitars on their hips and steel-flecked whips in their hands. In these worn, endless corridors of flagged stone, tens of thousands toiled unceasingly in the Great King's service, living out their lives and breeding and dying in the flame-flickered world that had been constructed by their own forbears millennia before.

Once, Kurun had feared the bottom tiers of the Slave City. This was where he had been introduced to servitude, and he vividly remembered the first time he had seen the sun cut off, and had felt his young head fill with the reek of the place. A world of caverns, it had seemed to him; a succession of nightmares. But he had been very lucky, sold up-city almost at once. He had not remained down here long enough to shun sunlight, as many slaves did. Hundreds of the Slave City's inhabitants could no longer bear the light of Bel in their eyes. They had been made into creatures of the dark, and needed no lamp to see their way within it.

But it was not a place to wander aimlessly. There were forgotten tunnels here, old antechambers and ancient passageways which had been bricked up and forgotten as the daily concourse changed its routes, like a river shifting its bed over centuries. Parts of the Slave City had been neglected and disused for generations, and it was said that renegade slaves had made a warped life in these abandoned districts, renouncing their servitude, and they preyed upon the unwary with bestial, unimaginable appetites.

So the kitchen slaves liked to say, gathered in their quarters with the day's work done, or drunk on palm wine in times of festival. One of the Undercooks who was Kurun's friend, fat, lubricious Borr, liked to tell of the time he had become lost in the lower levels as a youngster, and had seen them, the dark-dwellers. They had skin white as maggots, he said, and eyes as large as eggs.

An immensely wide passage ascended ahead, the incline steep, one half stepped, the other a ramp which slaves pushed handcarts up, sweat streaming off their backs. They toiled naked, *hufsan* from the highlands who bore the mark of the King, not as a tattoo on their shoulders but as a brand upon their faces. At their rear, one of their own race flicked a tongue of leather at their calves, and barked at them in common Asurian, the gutter-language of the Empire, leavening the tirade with some *hufsan* profanity from his own mountains. The slaves strained harder. In the handcart were baskets of Oskus clams, as big as Kurun's fist, and the massive silver sheen of river catfish, their mouths still opening and closing as they struggled, drowning in the fetid air.

Beside them was the flip side of the coin; gangs of more *hufsan*, rolling empty carts on the down-road before them, tugging on ropes to slow the clanking vehicles and keep them within bounds. They winked and nodded and exchanged ribaldries with their colleagues who were still ascending, and the guards raised whips at one another in salute.

Kurun felt inside his sash for the tiny, oilcloth-wrapped parcel that had occasioned his foray into the sun. Auroc the kitchen-master had entrusted him with the errand, only the second time he had ever done so, and it would not do to lose the thing now, so close to home.

Up, up, always up, the steep passageway becoming a sinuous thing, an immense hollow coil of stone within the ziggurat with passageways opening off on both sides, people joining and leaving it as they went their way about the Slave-City. This was the *Silima*, the Serpent Road, the main artery in the body of the ziggurat. It held the various levels together, and was the one concourse wide enough for vehicles which ran through every height of the immense structure. Many pasangs long, it was also meticulously maintained by gangs of road-slaves who cleared the detritus of passage day and night, and overseers who saw to it that traffic went smoothly.

When there were heavy crowds on the Silima, one could stand on a stone floor in the kitchens of the upper city far above, and feel the entire tell vibrate minutely under one's feet, like some gargantuan organism, a great animal whose insides were swarming with minute parasites.

THE KITCHEN LEVELS were close to the top of the ziggurat. Here, the shafts opening out on the sunlit sides of the tell made the wide pillared chambers within seem dazzlingly bright after the sweating lamplight of the Slave-City. There were pullied platforms upon which entire banquets were hoisted up to the summit above, cold rooms stacked high with ice brought all the way from the Magron, corridors lined with wine-jars a man could drown in, and cages of live birds singing their hearts out in the patchworked sunlight, heedless of the filleter's block that stood beside them.

Every possible foodstuff from across the Empire was represented here, when it was in season. Currently, woven baskets stood everywhere alive with the croaking of frogs, and such was the glut that the cooks paid no mind to thieving spit-turners who would snatch one from above the coals when they thought they were unobserved. Kurun had once been one of these grimy youngsters, and he remembered well the unending work, day and night, the furtive snatched meals, the fights, the rancid loincloths which were their only clothing, and the wit-stretching struggle to catch the eye of the cooks, to gain favour, to climb the ladder. It had taken him two years, he thought – he was not quite sure. He had seen boys kill one another for a comfortable place to sleep, their corpses tossed out in the morning without comment by the cooks, just more rubbish from the kitchens to be dropped down the garbage pits. Two years. It had marked him as deeply as war.

He touched the purple stripe on his chiton as if for reassurance. It marked him as a slave with a difference. The guards of the slave-city could not raise their whips at him, and he was spared the casual abuse meted out to the young in the lower levels. Not only that, but those who wore the stripe were marked for better things, the possibility of advancement. Not freedom, never that – even Auroc was a slave, bound to service in the ziggurat for his lifetime – but there were degrees of servitude. Kurun had even been allowed to accompany his superiors to the world under the sun above, when they were short-handed on feast-days, or sometimes simply as a forgotten afterthought. To breathe the same air as the Great King himself on the sacred summit of the ziggurat. For such moments he had strained and connived and laboured all his short life.

AUROC SAW HIM, raised a hand and barked at one of his assistants to mind the fish. Smoke hung in the air here, but not enough to sting the eye or taint the food. Ventilation shafts led out to the slopes of the ziggurat, and on still days the spit turners would be set to cranking on the massive wooden ceiling fans that hung below them, greasing their axles with olive oil that they licked from their fingers.

The heat was shattering, a shimmering vice that sucked the water from men's bodies. It rose from charcoal grills, radiated from the bread ovens, and seemed to be soaked deep into the very stone of the floor. Auroc raised a dripping gourd from one of the water-jars that were stationed everywhere and drained it dry. 'Kurun, you little brown-faced shit – you took your time. Follow me, boy.' A knowing look. Kurun nodded and patted his sash. Auroc closed one eye for a moment.

There were bakers of bread, butchers and fishcutters and poulterers, pastrymen, wine-mixers, choppers, slicers, kneaders, charcoal-lighters, and all manner of specialists strewn across the kitchens of the ziggurat. Each had apprentices, scullions, and every shade and shape of other underlings below them, as officers led men in an army. It was a caste system, based not so much on race or class but on expertise, and at the apex of this enclosed, stratified world were the cooks, men who received their orders direct from the chamberlains of the world above, in that rarefied fiefdom which was the Court itself.

Auroc was true Kefren, as tall and pale as a mountain birch, with the violet eyes and raptor's nose of his kind. He was lord and overseer of the kitchens, and on occasion had even been summoned above to be complimented on his work by the Great King himself. On especially important state occasions he needed the discipline and level-headedness of a general at war, and he demanded the same of those under him. Anyone who failed him was shipped with bewildering speed to the Slave-City, and a lifetime of toil in the dark.

He had taken a liking to the slim, otter-quick *hufsan* boy that was Kurun, noting his good looks, his quick mind, and the streak of ruthlessness in his nature which had made him leader of the spit-turners in two short years. Kurun had become something of an anomaly in the kitchen under Auroc's wing. He came and went largely as he chose, but worked hard, was good-humoured, and well-liked for the many small acts of kindness he performed for both high and low. Most importantly, perhaps, he had the capacity to keep his head even in the most pressured panics, when the bulbs in the sand-clocks were running empty and the Great King himself was waiting to be served.

'What did he charge you?' Auroc asked, holding out one long-fingered hand.

'Two silver surics, master. But I beat him down.' Kurun handed over the oilskin packet, and then added to it a clinking stack of coinage. 'It is all there. But I gave a copper to a beggar I know down near the Sacred Way.'

Auroc studied his palm, and then the taut face of the boy before him.

'You are very free with my money, Kurun.'

'You promised it to me for running the errand, plus I saved you more than that with my haggling.'

Auroc tilted his head to one side, like some huge predatory bird, a golden vulture with a shrewd eye.

'Your logic is sound. That works with me – but it will not do with everyone. To some it will seem presumptuous. Even the money you save does not belong to you. Your wages do not belong to you, unless I say so. Do you understand me, boy?'

Kurun lowered his head. 'I do, master.' He did not see the smile that flitted across the tall Kefre's face.

'Very good – another lesson learned. Now I have a further errand for you.'

'Yes, master?'

'Go to Ramesh the linen-master, and tell him you are to be clothed in something suitable for the Palace.'

Kurun's face snapped up, eyes shining. The questions danced on his tongue like bubbles of gold, but he said nothing, merely nodded. He bowed deeply to Auroc, then turned and dashed away as though afraid his master's mind would change. Auroc chuckled.

Fat Borr wiped his hands and paddled over to the Kitchen-Master. 'He's a likely sort, little Kurun,' he said. 'You spoil him, chief.'

'Maybe,' Auroc said. 'But mark me, Borr; in ten years that boy will stand where I stand now, or even higher. He has it in him.'

Borr snorted. 'He's *hufsan.*'

'He will not let that hold him down. I think it may be time to let him see a little more of the sun.'

Borr shrugged, his bald pate gleaming with sweat, his quivering jowls ashine with it. He had a pale, porcine face with surprisingly kind eyes. 'As you think best. But be careful, chief. Even this place has not yet taught him deference, and the folk above do not care for wit and spirit in a slave. I know.'

Auroc set a hand on the fat man's round shoulder. 'He who has not felt the flame does not fear the fire. I cannot watch over him always, Borr, but if he learns a little humility in the world above, it will be no bad thing. It will round out his education.'

THE KITCHENS GEARED themselves up for the daily frenzy of the evening meal. The Under-Steward had sent down a menu, and after looking it over, Auroc had hissed between his teeth and cursed softly. As the undercooks gathered about him he snapped out orders, then up-tilted the shortest sandclock and clapped his hands. Striding about the kitchens like a warlord inspecting his front line, he made the undercooks break into a storm of activity, and in turn those below them were shouted at and cuffed as they kneaded, chopped, stirred and seasoned at their stations. When the kitchens had broken into a purposeful cacophony, Auroc took his place beside the pulley platforms, reached into his sash, and broke open the oilskin package Kurun had brought him from the Lower City. He balanced some poppy-red powder on one thumbnail for a second and then sniffed it up, blinking, eyes tearing over.

Kurun appeared, now dressed in a snow-white chiton with a purple stripe of pure silk, his hair greased down and shining. Auroc looked him over.

'Ask Yashnar for some kohl – she'll put it on for you – and carmine for your lips. Lose your sandals; you will go barefoot above. Make sure your toenails are clean.' Auroc stared up at the sandclock. 'Be quick, Kurun. I will send you up with the first course.'

The boy swallowed, as nervous as Auroc had ever seen him. 'What shall I do up there, master?'

'Make sure no dishes get left behind. Stand still and keep your mouth shut. Do not meet anyone's eye. Be decorative, Kurun, like a footstool no-one uses. Do not stray from the platform, and count the dishes back in; we were short two platters yesterday. Those bastards above think I can't count. Do you mind me now?'

The boy swallowed again. 'Yes, master.' He raised his head and looked Auroc in the eye. 'Thank you for this.'

'Don't thank me just yet. And make sure you piss before you go up. It's going to be a long night.'

THE PULLEYS TURNED noiselessly, lubricated by fine oil that would command an absurd price in the Lower City. Kurun felt himself rising, leaving behind the world he knew, the steaming, sweaty, expanse of the kitchens, the firelight, the black cauldrons and long hardwood tables with slaves bent over them. Auroc caught his eye and nodded, and then was gone. Kurun was in a darkened shaft, the platform quivering under his scrubbed toes, a vast array of covered dishes and platters all about him. He rose higher, the smooth stone passing his nose. Looking up, he saw light above, the gold of the evening sun.

He stared at it for a long moment as it grew above him. Then, deliberately, he bent and lifted the heavy silver cover from one of the dishes beside him. From the fragrant, steaming interior he drew forth a black olive, dripping with a sweet red sauce. He ate it, chewing thoughtfully, tasting food fit for a King.

Then the light grew around him, the brightness of the sun flooding his eyes, and he could hear the sound of wind passing through the limbs of great trees, the trill of birds, and the silver music of many fountains.

TWO
THE GARDENS IN BLOOM

'SUCH A DRAB little bird,' Roshana said. 'And yet he sings as though he were the lord of all winged things.'

'In Artan's day they had them gilded while still alive,' Rakhsar said. 'Few survived the process, and those that did never sang again. The King was so angry that he strangled the survivors with his bare hands, and then poured molten gold down the throat of the man who had promised him he could make nightingales look as beautiful as their song.'

Roshana turned away from the cage and stared at her companion. 'I believe you make up these stories to vex me, brother.'

Rakhsar laughed. 'Not me! If you want stories of the excesses of kings, then there is no need to make them up – just go down to the Court Records and take out a scroll. Our family has a history of excess.

We are the lords of Kuf, Roshana. We define excess. If you think that was interesting, let me tell you –'

'No more. We will be eating soon.'

'You eat like a bird anyway.' Rakhsar tapped the cage, a beautiful, golden-wrought affair that was chased with enamels and inlays of lapis lazuli, bloodstone, ruby. The little brown bird inside went silent, and cocked its head to look at him.

'I think he likes me,' Rakhsar said with a grin.

'Leave him be. I'd rather listen to him sing than hear more of your stories.'

Rakhsar leaned back from the cage and reclined on the silk-cushioned couch that they shared. The sun fell on his face, and as the wind moved in the branches of the tall trees above so the shadows came and went, back and forth across his features. His skin answered the passing sunlight, a pale gold, almost translucent, and blue as a bruise in the hollows of his temples and nostrils. His eyes, bright and violet, seemed to catch the waning light and reflect it back at the evening. His long, rufous hair was tied back from his face in a topknot fastened by a silver ring. Gold thread was woven through his robes, and his slippers hung swinging from his toes as he lay back, studying the patterns the cedars made against the sky.

His sister was his twin, as long-limbed and golden-skinned, but more delicate, with darker eyes. And there was less of a hawkish cast to her face, for all that it was the mirror of his. In Rakhsar's face there was wit, humour, a flashing intelligence and curiosity. In Roshana's there was a gentleness entirely lacking in her sibling. And she did not have the hint of cruelty that dwelled in her brother's bright eyes.

'Cages,' Rakhsar said. 'Some are bigger than others, but in the end they all fulfil the same function. At least the bird can expect a long life, so long as he remembers how to sing. You and I, Roshana, our lives hinge on the whims of an old man. At any moment, the Honai could come for us. For me they *will* come, one day. I know that. I have known it since I was a child and saw the way our father looked upon my brother.'

Roshana said nothing. The truth could not be argued away.

'In the meantime we spin out our little lives here, like your bird, passing the time as pleasantly as we can, indulging in our petty little intrigues, hoping to catch his favour. Our father.' He raised a hand and grasped at the air. 'We might as well reach for the shadows in the sky. He has settled upon Kouros, my reliable elder brother. And even before Kouros is King, I will die, and you – if you are lucky – will be married to some functionary who is owed a favour.'

'Our father is a good man,' Roshana said quietly.

'Yes. He is that most dangerous of things, a good man who is doing what he sees as right. He indulged his own brother, and look what it cost him – Jutha gone, Artaka in endless rebellions, the monsters from across the sea marching towards the Middle Empire under the usurper's banner. Kouros will not make the same mistake. Father will not let him.'

Rakhsar sat up in a rush of movement, scanning the bushes around them. 'Did you hear that?'

Roshana sighed. 'There is no-one here but us, brother. Unless the birds can eavesdrop, we are safe.'

'Kouros has his spies too, you know. He has begun recruiting a new corps.'

'Where did you hear that?'

'From a spy of my own.' Rakhsar grinned.

'You are impossible today, Rakhsar. I will go in. It will be time for the dinner soon, and I should change. There are guests from the west.'

'Yes, but I doubt they'll have much of an appetite once father gets through with them.'

'Why? Rakhsar, what have you heard?

'What do you care? You have your nightingale to listen to.'

'Brother, I swear –'

Rakhsar stood up. He paced about the little manicured clearing as the shadows went back and forth across his face, the ancient trees above him creaking in the breeze.

'What have I heard? I hear *everything*, Roshana.

'I have heard that all is not well in the west. The enemy were given battle at the Haneikos river, and our troops were routed. The satrapies of Gansakr and Askanon are wide open to the invaders – all the land between the Haneikos and the Sardask is theirs now, right up to the city of Ashdod.'

Rakhsar paused, eyes gleaming, as bright and hard as shards of glass. 'There will have to be another levy – a real one this time. And if I know anything, I believe the Great King himself will lead it.'

'Our father, off to war? But he's an old man, Rakhsar.'

Rakhsar smiled sourly. 'He has my brother's broad shoulders to carry some of the load for him. In any case, the preparations have already begun. They're moving cattle west to Hamadan. It's my guess he'll take the Honai, too. And if they want to cross the Magron before the first snows, then the thing must be got under way very soon.'

Roshana shook her head in disbelief. 'How many years has it been?'

'Since Kunaksa? Thirty. A generation, since Ashurnan the Great won his empire and killed his brother. Now he must do it again.'

'And what of us?' Roshana's dark eyes widened. 'Are we simply to be left here?'

'That is my point, sister. The Great King leaves his capital. He takes with him his eldest son and heir. Do you really think he will leave me behind? He would be a fool to even consider it. No.' Rakhsar looked down at his slender fingers. His hands began to clench in and out of one another, as if he were washing them. It was as though he could not bid them to be still.

'No. This is my time. Kouros will have me killed before they leave for Hamadan, and our father will not interfere. That is the way it will be.'

A low chime carried through the air, a shimmering echo of noise that carried through the gardens like some tremor set off by the sunset.

'We are called,' Rakhsar said. 'Our beloved father bids us dine with him.'

'Do you really believe all this, brother?' Roshana asked. She offered Rakhsar her hand and he helped her up from the embroidered couch. He smiled down at her with real affection, but there was still that hard light shining in his eyes.

'You've lost one. Here, let me.' He knelt before his sister and placed her slim foot within the thin, scarlet leather of the slipper. Then he straightened, and took both her hands in his own.

'I am certain enough to act on it, and to risk death to avoid death,' he said in a low voice. 'For you, it is not the same. You have no stake in this – be married, have children, try to be happy. I will speak no more of these things to you – it is not your concern – but I wanted you to know, Roshana.'

'You're leaving,' she said. 'But how can you? Rakhsar, they have you watched night and day.'

'I have the thing in hand.' He bent and kissed her. 'I should not have told you, but I wanted to say goodbye. I had to let you know.'

'Take me with you –'

'Impossible. Do you know what it would mean? You have never left the city, Roshana. You do not know what the world is like.'

'Nor do you.'

Rakhsar's mouth curved in a scimitar sneer. 'I have a pretty good idea.'

Again, the low chime of the gong, carrying over the birdsong. They heard footsteps on the flags of the path, and turned as one. Into the clearing stepped a small girl, a dark *hufsa* in the livery of the household.

'Great ones,' she stammered, eyes downcast, 'I am sent to beg you to come to table.' She went to her knees and then bobbed up again.

'One of yours?' Rakhsar asked.

Roshana shook her head. 'She's one of Kouros's slaves, I think.'

Rakhsar strode over to the girl and kicked her in the ribs, sending her sprawling. 'Get you gone, and tell your master Prince Rakhsar comes when it suits him.'

'Yes, lord,' the girl gasped, and hobbled away, holding her side.

'She did you no harm,' Roshana said quietly.

'He sent a *hufsa* to fetch us, as though we were tenants in his house. While our father lives, Roshana, our blood is as high and royal as that of the mighty Kouros and the bitch-mother who whelped him.' He offered his arm. 'Shall we go, sister? Shall we smile and bow and eat and drink with our family?'

Roshana clicked up the latch on the nightingale's golden cage and swung open the door. Then she took her brother's arm.

'We'll make a grand entrance together.'

THE PALACE OF the Kings was so old as to make the count of decades and centuries into an irrelevance. The only structure in the world which predated it was said to be the Fane of Bel itself. The Great Kings of Asuria had made it their seat for as long as their kingships had existed; it was said, in fact, that the kitchen levels of the ziggurat had been the original palace, but had been relegated to humbler usage as the structure was reworked and added to by Asur's descendants. Some irreverent scholars maintained that the kings continually added to the palace ziggurat in order to overtop that of the High Priests, but if so, they had not succeeded. The twin hills of Ashur stared at each other across the teeming plain of the great city like two titans sprung from the same womb. The palace itself was as large as some cities – no-one had ever counted the rooms with any accuracy, but there were thousands – and enclosed a wide open space in which were planted the Imperial Gardens. These were as big as half a dozen farms, a landscape to themselves, with rivers and woods and pastures and herds of animals, flocks of birds, shoals of fishes. The Asurians believed that a beautiful garden partook of divinity. It was pleasing in the eyes of Bel, a reflection of heaven itself.

At this time of year, the Great King did not always dine in the echoing chambers of the palace, but as the whim took him, he would eat under the sky amid the trees his forbears had planted. On this evening, a silk canopy had been erected in the garden and plain wooden benches and trestles had been placed upon the grass, within sight of a glittering river whose waters were pumped up from the bowels of the ziggurat by a legion of blind slaves. Lanterns were hung by the hundred in the trees about the spot, and as the evening darkened it seemed that a host of golden flickering stars had been ensnared and set to shine throughout the woods.

The King himself sat apart on a black wooden throne, as was his wont, and the only other mark of his station was a diadem of black silk bound about his temples. A steady stream of fast-moving barefoot slaves bore the food to the tables, watched over by a tall, cadaverous Kefre who bore a silver-shod staff of ebony. The guests came one by one up to the black throne and went to their knees before the Great King before he bade them rise with a wave of his hand, and a smile for those he liked best.

Men had been known to pay massive fortunes for the chance to kneel thus, and catch the eye of the ruler of the world. His smile, or the absence of it, had blessed or blighted lives.

The diners were then ushered to their place at the tables by discreet pages, sons of the nobility who were brought to court to serve their king and act as surety for their families' loyalty. Informal as the outdoor setting might seem, there was a rigid hierarchy to the place-settings, and no amount of coin in the empire could move a diner any closer to the Great King's plate than the High Chamberlain decreed.

Back in the trees, unobtrusive but ever-present, the King's Honai leaned on their spears and watched the diners intently. Others stood closer-to with strung bows in their hands, whilst their commander, Dyarnes, stood behind the black throne in full armour, the clasp of a Royal Companion shining on his corded forearm. Asuria's Kings had met their end in many places, and the palace, even the tranquil gardens, had seen its fair share of treachery and bloodshed down through the centuries. It was the way the world worked, and no man who wore the diadem ever forgot it.

There were children in the trees also, laughing and chasing one another while the Honai watched on. They flashed in and out of the last light of the sun, as carefree as birds, while their elders lined up to do obeisance to the man who had fathered them. The children were all scions of Ashurnan, their mothers a host of concubines from every satrapy in the empire. They were all brothers and sisters, but did not know it.

KURUN WATCHED THEM from behind a tree, these golden, beautiful children, so much taller than him, so carefree. They baffled him. There was no purpose to the way they chased one another through the darkening gardens, flitting like fireflies about the lanterns. What were they at – what purpose did it serve?

He shrank into deeper shadow as a hulking Honai strode by, the lanternlight setting his armour aflame with reflections and smeared shadows. Kurun could see the shine of his eyes in the dark. It was the sign of the highest castes, like the golden skin and the hawk nose. He could not begin to imagine what all ten thousand of these creatures must look like arrayed for war – it defeated the imagination.

He began to shrink back the way he had come, fear rising up now to strangle curiosity. He was naked, having left his fine white chiton behind in the palace, his brown skin a better match for the twilit woodland. He had been told to stay by the kitchen platforms, but the haughtiness of the palace staff had been too much for him, and the beauty of the evening had enticed him outside.

'You must be as dumb as a stone, as still as a vase, when you are up there,' Fat Borr had told him, his face shining with earnestness. 'A slave in the world above has no feelings, no needs, no loves and no fears.'

And yet, Kurun was also a boy – one who would soon be a man – and there was in him a spirit which neither his life nor his intellect had yet tamed entirely. He had left his station, knowing it would be hours yet before they began to return the dishes and platters for the descent to the kitchens. He had walked the corridors of the palace as though he belonged to them. He was just one more striped chiton scurrying along the marble, and his anonymity had emboldened him further. The man's caution had given way to the boy's curiosity.

Until he had found himself under the open sky, and for the first time in his memory, had looked up at the stars.

They had dizzied him, smote him open-mouthed with their beauty, their myriads, swirling in half-guessed shapes and foaming breakers, as though splashed across the black vault of the night sky by the hand of God Himself.

And against them, the darker shadow of the great cedars and cypresses of the gardens. Kurun had never in his life before seen trees in such numbers, planted in grass, no order to them it seemed – they were not lined in avenues, or placed in pots. They were real, massive, fragrant with resin, alive with the wind. He touched them with something approaching reverence, running his hands down the ancient bark.

Kurun looked back. The King's feast went on

amid the trees like some magical pageant. There was music now, someone softly strumming an instrument Kurun knew nothing of, singing a song he had never heard. But the melody of it wrenched at his young heart. Tears rose in his eyes. This, then, was heaven – this was how the gods lived. And he could even see the far figure of the Great King himself, seated on his black throne with his white komis thrown low about his beard and smiling – smiling!

He would have so much to tell when he went back down to the kitchens. He would have such a story. It swelled up in his breast, and the tears rose higher in his eyes for the beauty of it all.

The blow caught him entirely by surprise.

He found himself blind, lying on the ground with grass in his mouth, the taste of blood. No true realisation of what had happened, just a vague impression of something large, a white explosion in his mind. His head was dragged up by the hair, and then released to crack down on the roots of a tree.

'Greasy little bastard. Better tell the captain. And Farnak, warn the others. He's just a slave, but you never know.'

'He has the mark. A nice little arse, too.'

'I'll save some for you. Now go.'

Kurun choked as a huge hand took him by the throat and lifted him up. He could see nothing through his tear-drowned eyes but the bright distant spangle of the distant lanterns in the trees. The music played on. He could hear children laughing.

Another blow, which broke open his lips against his teeth.

'Who are you and what is your purpose here?'

He blinked, eyes clearing at last, rational thought fighting through the bewilderment and rising terror in his heart. 'Nothing,' he croaked. 'I do nothing.' The question had been asked in good Kefren, the language of the court, but Kurun knew enough of it to reply in kind.

'A naked little *hufsan*, hiding in the trees. What are you, some kind of wood nymph?' The fingers on his throat loosened. He was released, to collapse, gasping, on the grass in the dark. Above him two violet lights blinked. He could smell leather, sweat, the metallic tang of bronze. One of the Honai.

'I'm from the kitchens,' he stammered. He clasped one hand about the tree root below him as though seeking strength from the scales of the gnarled wood. 'I meant no harm, master.'

'What in Mot's Blight is a kitchen slave doing here in the gardens? You need a better story, boy.' A hand ran over him, almost a caress. The fingers glided over his buttocks. The Honai chuckled. 'Not a single scar. You have the skin of a girl. Who are you here to fuck, *hufsan*? You tell me true, and you may yet leave here with those pretty little balls still attached.'

'I – no-one. There is no-one, may Bel hear me. I just – I just wanted to see the trees, the stars.'

A laugh. But then the Honai tensed, and straightened. Kurun looked up to see more massive shapes looming over him, more bright eyes shining in the night. There was a slap of flesh on bronze. 'My lord!'

'Easy, Banon. What is it that's so important you have me dragged from the King's side?'

'A spy, lord. I found him lurking in the trees. He claims to be from the kitchens. The other posts have been alerted.'

Perfume in the night, a taut, bracing smell of sandalwood.

'Stand up.'

Kurun did so, his hands instinctively clasped over his nakedness.

'If this boy is an assassin, then he's the prettiest I've yet seen. What's your name?'

'Kurun, master.'

'Who is your superior in the kitchens?'

Kurun hesitated. 'Auroc, master – but he knows nothing of this. I just –'

'Shut up. Banon, go down to the kitchens. I know of this Auroc. Bring him in. I will question him later.'

'The slave says he wanted to see trees and stars, my lord.'

There was a general rustle of amusement among the Honai. The one who smelled of sandalwood leaned close. Kurun could smell the wine on his breath. 'Trees, is it? How would you like to be nailed to one, little Kurun?'

Kurun said nothing. The enormity of it all was chilling his flesh, turning his tongue to wood.

'What shall I do with him, lord?'

'Take him to the cells – and mind he gets there in one piece, Banon. It's not your job to work on him. Prince Kouros will want to handle this. No need for the King to know.'

A hand fell on Kurun's shoulder, gripped the bone. 'As you wish, sir.'

Sandalwood leaned close again. The violet eyes stared into Kurun's face. 'I hope the sight of the stars was worth it, *hufsan*.'

Kurun was dragged away, limp as a child's doll in the grip of the Honai.

THREE
THE KING'S SONS

I HAVE BEEN lucky, he told himself. He looked out on the great cedars, which were as old as the very line of his family, and exhaled silently, the happiness nothing more than a passing brightness across his face. No more. A king must always think of who might be near, even when they were those he loved best in the world.

And those he loved best must never be aware of their position, for that would mean their lives were cast into the Game. The unending game, of who does what to whom in this world.

I am past sixty, an aged man. A monarch past his prime.

I am the most powerful person in this world.

And yet. He looked out across the gardens, past the assembled diners and the hordes of courtiers and attendants who flitted across the grass in the lamplight, beyond to where young voices could be heard under the deeper shadow of the woods.

Look at these children, playing beneath the stars. They are my sons and daughters, and I know them not. They are to be reared like blood stock, brought to maturity and then winnowed out, until I can find one worthy to hold all this in his hands. *His* hands.

Bel, Lord of sunshine and song and fruitfulness, look upon me now. Your brother, Mot, has brought a second great storm into my world, and I need you now. I need a way to look into the hearts of my enemies.

He stared out, impassive, at the night-time garden, the quiet river, the playing children who were his and yet not his. He strove to hoard the memory of it, to set this scene in amber, or imperishable crystal, and set it aside in some untwisted portion of his mind. He knew how to do this. He had practised it for many years. As long as he had been a king.

Give them time. Give me time. Lord of us all, lend me your patience.

'Majesty.' It was Dyarnes, faithful as a hound, ever beside him. His father Midarnes had died at Kunaksa, leading the Honai, and now the son stood in his place.

God-of-all, Ashurnan thought – has it really been thirty years since that day?

'Yes, Dyarnes.'

'There is an intruder in the gardens – my men have him. Will you give me leave to see to it?'

'Of course. You will miss the best of the wine, Dyarnes. I will have Malakeh keep you a cup.'

Dyarnes bowed deeply, then fastened his komis about his face and strode off.

Kouros paused with his cup halfway to his beard. 'Is something amiss, father?'

'Dyarnes has it. Enjoy your wine, Kouros. Smell the stars. Drink with your brother and let me see you be civil to one another.'

Kouros was one of those known across the empire as a Black Kefre. His hair was dark as a crow's back and he was heavily built, but he had the eyes of the high castes. His mother was not here tonight – she disliked dining out of doors – and he had inherited her colouring.

Beautiful Orsana, whom Ashurnan had taken as First Wife some thirty-five years before. She came from Bokosa, capital of the vast, rich satrapy of Arakosia. Back in the half-mythic past before the Great Wars, her ancestors had been kings, and Ashurnan's union with her had bound the proud Arakosans ever closer to the imperial family.

Ashurnan remembered the first few years of their marriage. It had been like coupling with a panther, and he could not help but smile at the memory.

His gaze travelled down the table. Rakhsar and Roshana, the twins borne by his second wife. They had *their* mother's looks, as fine and graceful as the thoroughbreds her country reared. Ashana had been a beautiful, willowy girl, a gentle soul. Ashurnan had married the spitfire Orsana out of political necessity and pure lust, but Ashana had taken his heart. A Niseian princess, she had seemed too good for this world, and so it had proved. She had given Ashurnan the twins, and then died soon after – of a fever. Or so it had been decided. Ashurnan had not gone back to his First Wife's bed since, for the rumours had tallied too closely with his own suspicions.

After that there had been minor wives, countless concubines, a garden of beautiful faces. But Orsana remained First Wife, his Queen, and she vetted them all. There would never be another Ashana, another woman to share his heart with. He had been lucky, that once.

The Great King raised his cup, and tilted it first to Kouros, his eldest son, and then to Rakhsar and Roshana, the twins whose mother he had loved. The three siblings returned his salute, and up and down the long tables the other guests let their conversations wither into the warm air, and watched.

He held their eyes one after the other. Kouros, dependable, thin-skinned, eternally suspicious and yet always on fire for some word of affection or commendation. Roshana, whose face seared something in Ashurnan's heart, so that it was sometimes hard to look upon her beauty for the memories it evoked.

And Rakhsar, mercurial, sardonic, the brightest light of the three, and the most dangerous. Ashurnan loved his younger son, but did not pretend to himself that he knew him at all. Rakhsar's flashing wit turned aside any attempt to know him. Roshana understood him, perhaps, but Ashurnan did not believe he ever would.

And there was the pity of it.

The Great King drained his cup, barely tasting the

wine. Beside him the Taster sipped, and then nodded, and the royal cupbearer refilled it from the jar.

The three royal siblings drank their own wine, Kouros and Roshana barely sipping theirs, Rakhsar emptying his cup with a flourish and a grin. He had about him the air of a condemned man who is intent on savouring every morsel of his life, whereas Kouros was like a priest wedded to duty and penitence.

Kouros, and Rakhsar, blood of my blood, flesh of my flesh. One will be King, and one must die. That is the way our world works.

An image lashed through his mind – his brother's face at Kunaksa as his own scimitar opened the throat below it. Ashurnan closed his eyes a second. Thirty years. He was an old man now, and in his dreams his dead brother's face was always the same. He could still smell the dust of that day, kicked up in vast clouds by the horses. He could hear the Macht death hymn as they advanced.

He had witnessed a dozen battles since then, but always, Kunaksa was foremost in his mind. It had been his first, and though the imperial records might say otherwise, he knew it had been a defeat.

And now they come again.

God, I am too old. I do not have the strength. I am no longer sure I even have the wit to choose the right men to fight for me any more.

The wine smote him – he had eaten almost nothing. The sour suspicion that his Queen was trying to poison him cut the appetite. That cat-eyed bitch. How much of a hold did she have over Kouros? Could he be his own man?

And Rakhsar – would the cruelty in him ever bloom into full, disastrous flower?

I must stay alive, he told himself. There is no time for this. I am Great King, and it is I who will take on this fight, as I did once before.

He raised the hand which had killed his brother and stared at it. The liver-spots on the golden skin, the blue-wormed veins thick about the knuckles. Then he looked down the table at Kouros again. Imagine the empire ruled by those knotted brows, that thick-boned forehead, and behind him his mother, whom the palace slaves lived in terror of. Not fear, or respect, but stark terror. She had once bade the Honai rape a pretty little Bokosan noblewoman to death, because the girl had refused her beloved son's advances.

Power is cruelty, in the last examination, Ashurnan thought. But for some the pain is an end in itself.

Kouros was an adequate leader of men, and he had a following in the army. The Arakosans provided the best cavalry in the empire, and they would follow him to the death, for his mother's sake. If Kouros were to be discarded, it would mean something akin to civil war, here in the heartland itself. There was no other option.

And yet, watching Kouros's powerful jaws champing his food, Ashurnan's heart sank. The empire, clamped in those dour jaws. At any other time, it would knuckle under the Black Kefre and his mother, go on as it always had; but this was not any other time.

Malakeh leaned close, leaning on his ebony staff of office. Gaunt as blackthorn, the old Vizier had run the clockwork of the court for a quarter of a century.

'Lord, the western messengers have been fed and are waiting.'

'Where are they?'

'On the Ivy Terrace. They have spoken to no-one.'

'Good. I will go to them, Malakeh, alone.'

'Lord –'

'Alone, Malakeh. We are not to be disturbed – no Honai. But tell Dyarnes.'

The Vizier bowed. Ashurnan almost thought he could hear the old man's spine creak. He rose, holding out a hand to keep the assembled diners in their seats. Even after all these years, he still felt a flash of impatience at the protocol of the court. He had pruned away as much of it as he dared, but a Great King needed some pomp and mystery about himself, even among those who knew him well.

Kouros stood up despite the gesture, setting down his cup. Ashurnan hesitated a moment, and then motioned his eldest son to follow. He did not have the strength or the patience to put Kouros in his place in front of the whole table.

Or did he? Ashurnan turned, and said to Malakeh, 'Have Prince Rakhsar join us.'

THE IVY TERRACE was on the northern edge of the gardens, half a pasang away under the starlit trees. Ashurnan's father, Anurman, had built it, as a place to sit and drink wine with his friends, his comrades-in-arms. Anurman had been a fighting king, a man who made and kept friends with an ease Ashurnan could only marvel at. He had drunk under the ivy there with Vorus, the Macht, and Proxis, the Juthan, both of whom had loved him like dogs, both of whom had betrayed his son. Proxis had taken Jutha out of the empire and now it was an independent kingdom. Vorus had let the Juthans leave at Irunshahr when the utter destruction of the Ten Thousand was teetering in the balance.

There were charcoal braziers lit on the terrace, and a few lamps. The three figures rose from their seats at the Great King's approach and went to their knees. Ashurnan studied their faces. All three were Kefren of high caste. Two, he did not recognise, but the third was a familiar face.

'Merach,' he said. 'It has been a while.'

The grey haired Kefre smiled and looked him in the eye. Merach had been his personal bodyguard. They had ridden side by side at Kunaksa. There were few people in the world Ashurnan trusted more, for Merach was utterly devoid of ambition. He was a soldier, simple and pure. But he was also an Archon of the western army.

'Despatches?'

Merach looked at the ground, opened his palm and gestured to a leather-topped scroll-bucket on the table.

'Enough to keep a man reading for a month, lord.'

Kouros was already breaking the seal on the bucket and rifling through the scrolls within, like a pig rooting for truffles. Rakhsar stood to one side, face in shadow.

'Suppose you tell me yourself, Merach,' the Great King said, though it was already written across the Kefre's face, which was as grey as his hair.

Merach looked up. There was weariness carved bone-deep in his features, and the grease of a hungry man's meal on his chin.

'The Haneikos River was a disaster, Lord. He came at us through the water with his line and we held him on the bank. We had good ground, as good a position as I've ever seen men hold. But his cavalry broke the left. He has five thousand armoured horsemen – he calls them his Companions, and they are both Kefren and Macht. Lord, he has Kefren of our own caste fighting for him!'

Kouros looked up from his scroll. 'Impossible! You are overwrought, Merach.'

'Lord, I saw them myself. They destroyed our flank –' Here Merach's voice sharpened. 'We had Arakosan cavalry stationed there, but he blew through them like a gale.'

Kouros threw the scroll at the kneeling Kefre. 'That's a lie!'

Merach went silent, bowing his head. It was Rakhsar who retrieved the scroll, rolling it up on its spindle. 'Brother, you might want to hear the fellow out before you begin throwing things at him,' he said with a smile.

'Go on,' Ashurnan said. He fumbled for a chair, and it was Rakhsar who slid one behind him.

'I bear the official despatches from satrap Darios himself – you can see his seal on the scrolls.'

'Why send you as his messenger?' Kouros demanded,

undaunted. 'You're an Archon of the western army, not some despatch-rider.'

'He hoped that my presence would give weight to what he had to tell,' Merach retorted.

'Mind your tone, general. I am a royal prince.'

Rakhsar poured himself some wine from the table, smelling it before sipping. 'Father, despite my brother's luminous presence, shall we let these men get up off their knees? The stones are hard on the bones.'

Ashurnan nodded. He looked at his younger son, and immediately Rakhsar gave him the winecup. 'I shall be your taster,' he said. 'It's not the best, but I've had worse.'

'General Merach shall speak now, without interruption,' Ashurnan said tiredly.

'And with some wine to loosen his throat,' Rakhsar said, handing the grey-haired Kefre another cup.

There was a quiet. The wind moved in the ivy, and there was the hoot of an owl off in the trees. Not another sound. They were in the midst of the greatest city in the world, but the ziggurat lifted them far above it, and the wind here was night-cool, as though they were in the foothills of the mountains. The scent of the honeysuckle which wound through the ivy came and went with the breeze, too sweet, too heavy for the charcoal-warmed dark.

Merach drained his cup. 'Our left was destroyed, and in the centre he had us pinned. He lost a lot of men there. The bodies piled up so thick in the water they changed the river's course, and the water ran red as a pomegranate crushed in your fist. His cavalry wheeled on our phalanx's rear, and after that the thing fell apart, and it became a hunt. They chased us for pasangs across the plains south of the Haneikos. We took fifty thousand spears up to the river. I doubt a fifth of that made it back to Gansakos. We lost our baggage, our stores, the paychests, even the remounts. He has light infantry who work with javelin and what they call a *drepana*, a curved, slashing sword. They run as fast and far as horses.'

Merach placed his empty cup on the table with a click.

'My lord, I am told you knew something of this defeat already – you have the meat, but Darios wanted me to bring you the raw bones. I have been two weeks on the road, killing three horses a day to stand before you. Darios bade me say that Gansakr is lost, and Askanon cannot hold. He is moving his quarters south to Ashdod, and if necessary will stand siege there.

'My lord, we need another army. We need your presence on the battlefield to inspire our people, as you did at Kunaksa. We need the Honai. Without such a grand levy, the outer empire cannot hold. This is no mere adventurer we face. This man comes to conquer.'

'We know the facts of these things, Merach,' Kouros growled. 'Every satrap west of the Magron has been forwarding rumours of your disgrace for weeks. Perhaps we do not need a grand levy – perhaps we only need generals with a little backbone.'

Merach lowered his gaze. His eyes were as bright as coins caught in the sun. He said nothing.

'Bravely said, brother,' Rakhsar drawled. 'It's quite a feat to insult a man who cannot answer back – you truly have the knack of it.'

'Go back to the women's quarters, Rakhsar. We talk of the real world here. If we want to hear harem gossip we will send for you.'

Rakhsar smiled, but only with his mouth. 'I doubt you need my help for that, Kouros. There's not a whisper comes out of there that your mother has not heard before anyone.'

Kouros drew himself up like an infuriated bear. 'You bastard spawned little shit! You do not speak of my mother – she is Queen of the empire – yours is nothing but forgotten bones.'

'Indeed – well, the Queen would know all about that, don't you think, brother? When you visit her, do you drink her wine, or do you bring your own?'

Startled, Merach had to step back as the two brothers lunged at one another, Kouros a black bulk, Rakhsar a rapier-lean shadow. They bore no weapons, but seemed about to fly at each other's throat nonetheless.

'Stand still!' Ashurnan shouted, his angry bellow clear as a cymbal in the night. His head swam, and it seemed that there were black flies circling in the light of the lamps.

The two princes froze, their eyes locked on one another, the hatred sizzling in the air between them.

Perhaps I should leave them to it, Ashurnan thought; get it over with here and now. But the part of him that had grown grey since Kunaksa, that had sat on a throne for four decades, was too disgusted.

'You are princes of the empire, sons of the Great King, not brawlers in some hut in the Magron. Bel's blood, do you think you can behave so in front of me? Is this how kings are made? I have seen traitors go to the spike who show more respect to the diadem than you. Get out of my sight – and do not speak a word to one another as you go. I will deal with you – both of you – later. Now go!'

Kouros glared at his father, and in that instant, Ashurnan saw the older man within him; the heavy jowls, the down-turned lines about the petulant mouth. Then he strode off, feet pounding into the ground as if each step set his seal upon it.

Rakhsar lingered a few seconds more. His face was one perpetual sneer – what would it take to wipe it off? Then he bowed to his father and sauntered away into the trees.

'Perhaps they will finish their argument out in the dark,' Merach said, and then coloured. 'Forgive me, lord.'

'That is not their style, either of them,' Ashurnan said. He waved a hand impatiently at Merach's two mute, horrified companions, who were standing forgotten on the edge of the light. 'Go – leave us.' Then he rubbed his eyes, trying to wipe away the black circling flies.

'More wine, Merach – pour it for us both.'

When they were drinking again, Ashurnan said; 'Kouros is a coward, for all his size. He has a good head, but he is thin-skinned as an ugly girl, and his mother's venom has curdled something in him. Rakhsar, he is all scheming and planning, but all to his own back. He thinks nothing of larger things. These, Merach, are my sons. The ones whose voices have broken, at any rate.'

'They are your sons: they are not King. Lord, there is yet time for one of your other children to grow into a man.'

Ashurnan tilted his head to one side and smiled crookedly. 'One reason I have always trusted you, old friend, is that you have all your life retained the simplicity of the soldier. And if truth were told, I kept you from this city so that it would remain that way. You know nothing of the workings of the Court and the Harem. These young boys who ran about under the trees this evening – they will all die before they become men.'

Merach bared his teeth a second in a spasm of anger. 'I should speak no more.'

'You may say what you like – it is why Darios sent you.'

Lord, forgive me.' He looked down into his cup. 'Is it the Queen?'

'Who else?' Ashurnan smiled again. 'A marvellous woman, Orsana. She would have made a fine ruler of this empire in her own right, but she must work through her son, who is an inferior instrument.

'She will tolerate no other. It is something I have become almost reconciled to, Merach. I have shielded Rakhsar this long because I thought there was promise in him, but I know now I cannot gainsay my wife. Kouros will succeed me, if this phoenix from the west leaves him anything to rule. And Orsana will control the empire at last. It may actually be for the best. She is a poisonous bitch, but she is as able as I am, and lacks my streak of absurd sentimentality.'

'I call it honour,' Merach said, and the anger was still smouldering in his eyes.

'Kings cannot afford a sense of honour, my friend.'

'Then they are not worthy of the name. Lord, this enemy of ours out in the west, this young man who calls himself Corvus; he –' Merach hesitated a second. 'He took in the wounded we left behind us in our flight, and he had his surgeons treat them as though they were his own. He has not ravaged the land as an invading army ought, and his men are under savage discipline.'

'Ah,' Ashurnan said. 'The Macht. They are something to see, in battle, are they not?'

'They are like some great machine. He has drilled them to perfection, foot and horse alike. They are clad all in scarlet, as their mercenaries once were at Kunaksa. This boy is something remarkable, my lord. In seven years he has taken almost two hundred feuding city-states and made of them a nation.'

'Indeed. I wonder what his plans for us are.' Ashurnan emptied his cup and tossed it out of the lamplight, the gesture a flicker of fury. When he turned back to his friend, his eyes glowed like those of a wolf caught in firelight.

'This empire will endure, Merach. It has stood for so many centuries that men have stopped counting them.

'It *is* civilization.

'The Macht are barbarians, a race which does not belong to this world, an aberration of nature. They will be defeated by me and mine as the founder of my line defeated them in the ancient days. The empire cannot fall. If it does, it will topple us all into a dark age the likes of which history has never seen before.

'I will take the field – the preparations have already begun. You may begin your journey back to Darios in the morning. Tell him the Great King is coming, and with him shall march the full army of the empire. He will see us at the end of this summer. Until then he must hold at Ashdod. He must hold the passes of the Korash Mountains for me, no matter what the cost.'

Merach nodded, eyes shining.

'And Merach–' Ashurnan rose to his feet, a majestic figure, golden-skinned, the diadem a black line across his forehead. 'I do not care how this invader behaves, or how gently he treats our people. The Macht must be allowed no quarter. We will take no prisoners and show them no mercy. You must make Darios understand this. We are fighting a different kind of war from those we have known before.' Ashurnan drew his lips back from his teeth as he spoke, like an animal snarling at its enemy.

'It is no longer enough to defeat them. The Macht must be exterminated.'

FOUR
BROKEN NIGHTINGALES

There was a comfort in the coolness of the stone. Kurun pressed himself into the corner of the cell farthest from the door, curled up like a woodlouse. The floor was sheened with condensation, for it was colder than the air. Kurun wiped his palm across it and tried to use the accumulated moisture to wash himself, to wipe the filth away, but the blood, and other matter, was a caking, slimed mess from his buttocks to his knees. He gave up, pressed his forehead to the kindly stone, and emptied his mind. There was nothing more to think of. If he lived or died it meant nothing now, to himself or to anyone else.

A rattle in the lock brought him upright in a spasm of terror all the same. His feet scrabbled on the floor as he tried to push himself farther into the corner of the cell. Now the stone was his enemy, unyielding, spurning his flesh.

The door swung open, lamplight blinding him. He held up a hand like a man staring into the sun.

'Can you walk?'

He nodded, crawled up the wall, his fingers hunting for gaps in the blocks. Then his legs left him, and he hit the floor with a slap.

'Bel's blood. Banon, you made this mess; go pick it up. We don't have all night – I'm expected back at the gardens.'

A bulk that blocked out the light. A familiar smell. Kurun came alive, punching and scratching like a frightened cat.

'Be still, you little bitch.' A massive fist clouted him on the side of the head, sending lights shooting through his mind, filling his ears with a high-pitched hiss. He was picked up and tucked under one arm by the tall Honai.

'Bring him – and make sure you clean out that cell after. This is not the undercity.'

'Yes, sir.'

Kurun was carried into torchlight, head down, like a rabbit brought home for the pot. He saw sandaled feet tramping, wisps of straw on stone. He retched, but there was nothing left to come up. He clenched his eyes shut, wondering what death would be like. It could not be worse than what they had done to him already.

'Strap him in, and then get back to your post. And Banon, clean yourself up, for pity's sake. He's slobbered all over you.'

'It was worth it, chief.'

Kurun was in some kind of chair. His wrists were buckled to the arms with leather straps. Then his legs were pulled apart. He tried to fight, but the pain was too much. He was strapped at the ankles and knees, his thighs held apart. He opened his swollen eyes.

A small, windowless room, much like the cell he had left. A tall, magnificently dressed Kefre watched him. He knew the face, but the smothering panic blotted out anything else. Sandalwood perhaps, the fragrance dim as a broken spark outside his heart's thunder.

There was a table by the far wall, and an old *hufsan* was busy at it, spitting on a stone. Then Kurun heard the steady rhythmic scrape of a knife being sharpened, the rasp of steel on stone which was intimate to him after all his years in the kitchens.

'Lord, no, please. Kill me if you want. But not that.' The tears fell from his eyes in silver ribbons.

The Honai said nothing. He seemed preoccupied. He was reading a scrap of parchment. He grunted.

'Your friend Auroc has disowned you, boy. Says you are quite the little troublemaker.'

'Auroc? No – Lord, no. I beg you.'

For the first time the Honai's bright, violet eyes met his own. 'You have spirit, slave. For a kitchen scullion to spy upon the Great King and his family! I hope you were well paid.'

'No-one paid me. I was stupid. I did not think.'

'Maybe.'

The door opened. In came a massive, black-haired Kefre with a heavy face. His eyes were dark with anger. At once, the Honai went to one knee, then straightened. Deference sat deep-planted on the Honai's countenance. And fear.

'My Lord Kouros. This is the boy.'

The dark Kefre loomed over Kurun, ignoring the greeting. 'Did you get anything out of him?'

'Nothing of use. He holds to his story.' A pause. 'My prince, I think it may be the truth.'

'I am not a spy!' Kurun screamed.

Kouros knelt until his face was level with Kurun's. He held out a hand. Without a word, the elderly *hufsan* in the corner came forward and set the knife within it. Kouros felt the edge, his gaze never leaving Kurun's face.

'Was it my brother?' he asked, softly. 'Was it Prince Rakhsar?'

Kurun's vision was broken into a spangled mosaic of tears. 'Lord, I am a kitchen slave,' he whispered hoarsely. 'I am nothing.'

The violet eyes studied him. The Kefren prince exuded anger, like perfume made rank by sweat. The hand which held the knife trembled slightly. There was a smell of burning in the room. The *hufsan* at the table had uncovered a clay firepot and was blowing the coals within into life.

At last Kouros seemed to relax somewhat. He breathed out.

'I believe you're right. The boy is telling the truth,' he said. 'I can see it in him.'

The Honai nodded. 'Youth makes for foolishness. What shall I do with him, my prince?'

Kurun was sobbing with relief, sagging in the leather bonds that imprisoned his limbs. 'Thank you,' he whispered. 'Thank you, lord.'

Then Kouros leaned close, a flash of movement startlingly swift in so bulky a form. He grasped at

Kurun's soft flesh, and the knife sawed a second, then slid cleanly through. A jet of blood, black and shining, spattered Kouros's face. Kurun shrieked.

At once the *hufsan* scuttled forward, holding a skewer of iron whose tip glowed yellow. He thrust it between Kurun's legs and worked the point back and forth, as though he were smearing plaster into a crevice. A sickening smoke rose. Kurun screamed and strained in the chair until the straps were bloody and the sinews in his neck stood out like wires.

Kouros studied his handiwork. The Honai handed him a linen towel and he wiped his face.

'He's a pretty one, all right. Just the sort Rakhsar would like.' Then he smiled, and set a hand on the Honai's breastplate. 'No – the lady Roshana. Have him sent to her. Let her know the whole way of it. She has a heart of corn, a soft spot for waifs and strays. This will let her know what I do to her brother's spies.'

'Even when they are not spies at all. A capital notion, sir,' Dyarnes said, face impassive.

The grin on Kouros's face sat uneasily. It did not seem to suit his features. 'A clean cut, Dyarnes?'

'Very clean, my Lord. I could not have done better.'

'The Great King's son must never shrink from using the knife when he deems it necessary. I never shall. Have him sent to my half-sister's apartments just as he is.'

'Yes lord. It shall be done tonight.'

The uneasy, un-right smile was still on Kouros's face as he left. Dyarnes stood looking down on Kurun a moment more.

'Give him something for the pain,' he said to the *hufsan* in the corner, his golden face twisted with disgust. And then he swept out of the room without a backward glance.

'So, you joined a Royal dinner without invitation,' the old *hufsan* chuckled. He bent and picked up the bloody piece of meat from the floor and waved it in front of Kurun's pain-glazed eyes. 'These are bigger than most, my young friend. Say goodbye to them now. Your life is starting over again tonight. You were very lucky.'

'Lucky.' Kurun slurred the word. He had bitten through his own tongue, and his mouth was full of blood.

The *hufsan* was a bent, brown creature in a dun robe the same colour as his skin, His eyes were bright as a bird's, and he had the long fingers of a musician, or a scholar.

'Rinse your mouth out.' A bowl was placed at Kurun's mouth. 'Good. Now spit – over your shoulder.'

The bloody liquid dribbled from Kurun's mouth. The old *hufsan* wiped it away with the cloth Kouros had discarded.

'You are no spy of Rakhsar. I could have told him that.' He took a mortar from the table and scooped out the contents with one hand. Then he knelt between Kurun's legs and began gently smearing it over the seared gash there. Kurun came to life again, struggled in the chair, moaned thickly.

'Hold still. If it's done right now, you'll still look pretty down there, and you may even have a cock that works. This was done to you later in life than usual, so you may keep something of your manhood about you. You'll never need to shave, though.'

He put the mortar away, wiped his hands, humming like a man content with his work, and produced a vial of amber-yellow liquid. He put it to Kurun's bloody mouth. 'Don't waste a drop. This is juice of the poppy, and you're lucky to get it. I think Dyarnes liked you. And the prince knew it, or he'd have gutted you for the fun of it. Believe me, I've seen it. But the black bastard still has some shame about him. He knows a needless killing would get back to his father. Dyarnes still serves two masters.

'There. Good boy. In a moment or two you'll feel the pain go, and all the worries of your little life. I'll unbuckle you then.' He stroked the boy's thick black hair.

'You are alive, and young, my friend. This shall pass, as all things do. It is not the end. Believe me, I know.'

'Who?' Kurun gargled.

'My name is Hiram. I'm from the Harem.' He giggled. 'Hiram of the Harem, that's me. They dragged me out of my bed to make sure you wouldn't bleed to death. Yours aren't the first balls I've picked up off the floor, believe me.'

'Kurun shook his head, stared at the door. 'Who –' he repeated.

'Ah, I see. Well, you have been mixing in elevated company this night, kitchen-boy. The tall Honai was Dyarnes, master of the King's Bodyguard. And the black-haired, grinning monster who sliced your manhood off was no less than prince Kouros himself, whom most think will one day sit in his father's chair and rule the empire. He thought you a minion of his brother's. Or perhaps he didn't. It hardly matters.' Hiram grinned, showing yellow teeth as uneven as the gaps in a broken fence.

Kurun sagged in the chair. His eyes dulled. 'Death,' he said, a long whisper that tapered into a sob.

Hiram stroked his hair again. 'Not death, little one. Not tonight. Kouros tried too hard to be cruel. Roshana will see that you are well treated. She has her mother in her. And this will not be the first time Kouros has left something broken at her door. I remember, when they were children, he once strangled her favourite nightingale and set it on her pillow.' Hiram's face grew grim, the fine-wrinkled skin tightening about his mouth.

Kurun was sleeping now, breathing deep, his head sunk on his chest. Hiram began to unbuckle him from the chair.

'From the kitchen to the Court. You are going up in the world, boy. One day you may even think the price was worth paying.' His face twisted, something like self-mockery flitting across it.

'One day.'

Across the ziggurats of the city the sunrise poured down, catching the golden plated Fane of Bel and setting it alight in a gleam of yellow flame. Those in the teeming streets below looked up at the sight and touched their foreheads in salute to the sun, to Bel the life-giver.

The world had been given another morning.

Along the Huruma the priests went in procession with their long-handled snuffers, putting out the street-torches and welcoming the dawn with ancient sonorous songs whose words they no longer understood, but whose melodies were woven into the very fabric of Ashur itself.

The traffic was already moving in long lines through every gate in the fabled walls, and in the irrigated fields beyond, farmers walked waist-deep in the last of the night's mist. The air about them was alive with the croaking of frogs and the white egrets rose like flocks of ghosts from the palm trees.

Even at this early hour, there was a promise of heat behind the moist cool of the air, and shimmers of insects rose out of the damp ground to hang in clouds overhead. Summer was growing, and the season was turning towards the white blinding days of heat and dust that marked the zenith of the year.

Summer was growing, and the snows in the mountains were retreating up into the peaks, widening the passes. The good grass was thickening underfoot and the soil was hardening. This was the beginning of true campaigning weather.

It was the time for the fighting of wars.

FIVE
FLIGHT OF PRINCES

THE LADY ORSANA rose well before dawn, even now that the mornings came earlier. She bathed in the mosaic pool with her maids all about her, and picked out what to wear from a procession of living models, who stood in front of the fragrant steaming water one by one. A fingertip lifted slightly, and Charys, the Queen's Eunuch, clapped his white hands to confirm the choice.

After she was dried, Orsana sat naked as a trio of artists who had been brought from all over the empire went to work on her face. They lengthened the lashes of her eyes with kohl, painted the lids malachite green, blushed her cheeks with Tanean vermilion and powdered her skin white with crushed chalk. She rose, and her clothing was draped around her as though on a statue. Her mane of heavy black hair was combed out until sparks crackled in it, then it was coiled simply down one collar-bone. In candle-light, the regime took twenty years off her age.

Lastly, the thin white-gold circlet that signified high royalty was placed carefully on her forehead. Slaves had lost their hands at this point for smearing her cosmetics.

A mirror of silvered glass was produced, and she studied herself in it. Her lips pursed ever so slightly. She lowered her eyelids, adopted the aloof, guarded pose which was her way of looking at the world, and raised one white, long-nailed hand to brush the attending slaves away.

Then Orsana strolled out of the dressing-suite, sipped some watered wine, and was ready to do battle with the day. She took up her accustomed position on a divan of midnight silk. Her maids arranged her robes artfully about her, and a bowl of fruit and a cup of wine were placed within easy reach. She sat, a silken spider, at the very centre of the harem, in a vast circular chamber which was dotted with fountains and hung with tapestries. Incense idled through the air in blue skeins, and petal-stuffed cushions were scattered everywhere on the tessellated floor. In this chamber, only the Queen had furniture to sit upon. Everyone else reclined on the cushions or stood. Beautiful young women kept station around the walls, giggling and gossiping behind pillars of Kandassian marble. These were the King's concubines, and he had not chosen one of them himself.

A long-haired eunuch with a hip-desk padded from behind the hangings and went to one knee.

He bowed his head, as pretty as any of the women around him. He lacked a finger on his left hand, his only imperfection.

Orsana nodded minutely at him. He opened the hip-desk bound to his body and produced a number of papers one by one.

'Lady, lord Merach of Gansakr presents his respects, and would be grateful if you would receive him ere he leaves for the west.'

Orsana smiled, raised a hand and swung it in dismissal.

'The Road-Stewards would like an audience today to discuss arrangements for the move to Hamadan.'

Orsana blinked. The white hand moved again.

'The caravans are in from both Kosan and Ishtar. The merchant lords Amur and Peshtos send their greetings and beg to attend you as soon as they have made a suitable selection for your approval.'

'They rode in ahead of their trains two days ago, to be with their mistresses,' Orsana said with a smile. 'That delay will cost them. Go on, Nurakz.'

'The Prince Kouros, your son, desires an audience at once. My lady, he waits at the door.'

'Is that all?'

'Yes, lady.'

'Send in my son, and then clear the chamber. And Nurakz, draw up a letter of credit on the House of Arkanesh, and have it ready here before noon.'

'Yes, lady. For how much?'

Orsana stared at him. Nurakz went white, bowed his head, and withdrew.

'Charys, you will stay, of course,' Orsana said as

the concubines within the chamber rose like a cloud of butterflies taking flight.

The tall eunuch bowed. He had a face like that of a totem fashioned out of white clay and left in the rain. Although he had the eyes of the high caste, his features were broad and strong as a soldier's. He was bald save for a topknot of hair dyed cornflower blue and gathered up with a silver ring. A scar ran like an errant worm down one side of his neck, and his pale, hairless hands looked strong enough to strangle a camel.

The doors of hollow bronze clanged wide, and Kouros strode into the room in a billow of linen that was as blue as his mother's robes. The doorkeepers hauled shut their charges behind him with rather more care.

'It is to be done, mother; he's going. Ashurnan will take the field. He leaves within the week.' Kouros began biting his nails.

Orsana did not seem surprised. She nodded wisely, but within she was genuinely startled.

'Merach,' she said.

'Yes. He talked to him all evening. I tried to have an ear on it, but failed. Rakhsar –'

'Rakhsar?'

'He knew no more than I. I made sure of it. He has made this decision on his own, mother.'

Orsana raised one eyebrow, plucked at her robe. Chalk dust fell from her face in minute avalanches.

'You must go with him, then. And our plans must be brought forward. That is all. This is no great disaster, Kouros.'

Her son was gnawing his thumbnail, stripping back the horn to bring blood. 'Darios assured me it would be of no moment, this – this *invasion*.'

'I do not think he lied. I think only he has been overtaken by events. Darios is a loyal agent.' Orsana stirred, moved up the divan and sipped at her wine. 'Son, you must remember that some happenings have no author – they simply happen. There is not always a conspiracy afoot.'

'Yes – yes, of course – don't preach, mother. I am not a fool. I know these things – I have ears and eyes everywhere.'

Everywhere I bade you plant them, she thought. She was torn between love and exasperation. The lot of all mothers.

'We have some warning, at least. How sure are you of Dyarnes?'

Kouros looked away, savaging another finger.

'It is hard to tempt a man who can go no higher. Commanding the Honai is the summit of his ambition.'

'Then you must threaten him with the loss of it,' Orsana said sharply, a hornet-sting emerging from the honeyed voice.

Kouros collapsed onto a tall cushion. 'I know, I know. Dyarnes must be handled more carefully. He is of the old nobility. If he thinks we compromise his honour, we will lose him utterly.'

Orsana smiled. 'Well put. We also know he despises Rakhsar –'

'I am not sure he does not despise me as well, Mother.'

'He is of the Asurian tribe. They despise everyone from beyond the Oskus, and always have. Play on his pride, and on his command. What about his second?'

Kouros brightened. 'Ah, Marok. He is ambitious, and he has enough of the Magron blood in him to make him insecure. A great horseman – no-one can ride a Niseian like him. And he loves women.'

'Then I do not need to draw the picture for you any further. A gift of two beauties, one four legged, one two-breasted. That will start the thing. A gift from the prince cannot be refused, and gives him a sense of debt.'

'I do not need some kind of tutorial, mother. I have known Marok and Dyarnes since I was a boy.'

'As they have known you. They must be certain that the boy is no more, that a king stands in his place.'

Kouros shifted uneasily in the depths of the cushion, plucking at his blue robe as though it had offended him.

'Then you must give me more money. My father thinks it is good for a prince to rub along on a pittance; it imbues character, he says.'

Orsana raised one eyebrow. 'Very well. I am having a draft drawn up today on the Arkanesh House. You shall have some of that. But do not make too big a splash with it, Kouros. You must not draw your father's attention.' Then she all but chuckled at the idea of Kouros splashing money around. Her son looked at her sourly.

'When have I ever –'

'Yes, yes – that virtue not even I ever had to instil in you. No-one could ever accuse my son of being a spendthrift.' She smiled at him with something approaching affection. 'I remember when you were a child. No-one could part you from your toys, even when they were worn ragged. You used to sit alone in the gardens and play with armies of toy soldiers, and give them all names.'

'You kept me from all others,' Kouros said, quietly. 'Even the slaves.'

'You were the eldest son, the heir,' she retorted. 'There was no-one else worthy for you to associate with. I never let any of them forget who you were – never.'

'I suppose you didn't.' Kouros's face slumped in a kind of sadness, but only for a moment. It clenched again almost instantly into its lines of habitual anger. He thrashed his way out of the cushion and kicked it across the smooth marble of the floor.

'When I am King, they will queue before my throne to befriend me,' he said. 'They will kneel, every one of them, and beg for my favour. Mother, I want Rakhsar to kneel before me ere he dies.'

'Don't be absurd, Kouros.'

His face spasmed, then he drew himself up. 'No – of course – you're right.' He turned away. 'I must go. Thank you – thank you, mother.'

'Have you no kiss for me?'

'Yes – yes, all right.' He leaned over her like a blue thundercloud and let his lips touch her chalk-hued cheek. She touched his face. 'You are not as other men, Kouros. You must be larger than that.'

'I know. I have always known.' He turned, one fist knotted in his robe, then halted. 'And Roshana. Must she also –'

'Roshana must share her brother's fate. You know this. Were she to marry some high noble, that man would be in a position to make a claim for the throne, however specious. We have been over this, Kouros.'

He nodded. 'Goodbye, mother.'

'Call on me this evening. We shall have more to discuss.'

His shoulders slumped. 'Yes, mother,' he said, and walked away looking somehow defeated, a shambling mountain.

IT WAS NOT far, as a raven might fly, from the Queen's seat at the heart of the harem to Roshana's apartments. Even on foot, a swift-striding man might cover the space in under an hour, if the Honai were to give him free passage. But it was a great distance in terms of palace politics. One might almost say it was insurmountable.

The twins who were the issue of Ashurnan's first love were generously housed in a tall, free-standing complex several stories high, whose balustrades were formed by the living limbs of gashran trees, native to the sheerest slopes of the eastern Magron. Here, they sprouted from gaps in the massive stone blocks of the structure, and they had been trained over centuries of wiring and pruning to make of their growth an adjunct to the architect's vision. The

Gashran was an interwoven complexity of stone and living timber, and had been given over to the lesser princes of Asur's line for time out of mind.

Not for nothing was it set apart from the rest of the palace. Honai patrolled its grounds night and day and questioned or escorted anyone who ventured close; a Great King must needs keep an eye on the doings of his offspring, both high and low. The Gashran was not a prison – it was beautiful, luxuriously appointed, a palace in itself – but it was a monitored place.

Rakhsar and Roshana had lived within the bark and stone of its bewildering arrangements for all of their lives.

Roshana stood now in her own chambers, looking down at the sleeping boy in the bed before her with her komis drawn up around her nose. Above it, her eyes were bright amaranthine lights.

'Will he live, Barzam?'

The tall Kefre bowed behind her. 'Yes, lady. He is young, and he has the strength of the undercity in him. I have seen many of his kind recover from far worse.'

'You will attend to him every day, Barzam.'

The Kefre spread his spatulate hands. 'Lady, with all due respect, is that really necessary? This is but a *hufsan* slave, a creature of the –'

'You will do as I ask, or I will find a physician who will.'

'Of course, lady. I am wholly at your command.'

'Thank you, Barzam. If you have any further instructions for the staff, you may leave them with the steward on your way out.'

Wordless, unseen, the tall Kefre bowed behind her and left noiselessly.

On the other side of the heavy door he was brought up short. Rakhsar grinned at him and clapped him on the arm like an old comrade. 'Barzam! She has you physicking her new pet, has she?'

'She seems determined that the creature should survive.'

'She was always like that. I've learned to let her have her way in these things. It's not often Roshana digs in her heels, but when she does, Bel himself could not move her.'

'It is always a pleasure doing the bidding of the lady Roshana,' Barzam said, somewhat stiffly.

Rakhsar took his hand and placed into it a small pouch of doeskin that clinked as it left his fingers.

'Your patience is much appreciated, Barzam. And your discretion, also. She means no disrespect.'

'Roshana could not offend me. I delivered her,' Barzam said, unbending a little.

'I know.' Rakhsar winked. 'I was there.'

HE COULD MOVE extremely quietly when he set his mind to it. He eased the door shut behind him and stood with Roshana's slim back within arm's reach. Cocking his head to one side, Rakhsar considered his moment.

'Do not creep about like that, Rakhsar,' Roshana said without turning around.

'I could have been an assassin.'

'Then he would have the same garish taste in perfume as you.'

He joined her before the bed. They touched hands.

'Sister, you pick a strange time to take in a stray. One might almost think Kouros planned it this way.'

'He does not have the forethought.'

'His mother does.'

'No – this is all his own work. He has not changed since we were children. Even then, he was happiest off alone torturing something.'

Rakhsar bent over the boy. 'He's a pretty one. I can see how he has stirred that soft heart of yours. What exactly –'

'He was raped and castrated. I think Dyarnes had a hand in it. It is why he left last night's dinner.'

'Noble Dyarnes, father's loyal shadow,' Rakhsar said dryly. He lifted the coverlet, peered below, and winced. 'When my time comes, I hope to God they take my head off first. Poor little bastard. Well, I suppose we can find some corner to tuck him into before we go.'

'We take him with us.'

'You jest, sister. This is not some nightingale you can carry in a box. What purpose would it serve?'

'I will not give Kouros the satisfaction.'

Rakhsar laughed. 'Were you of a less fastidious nature, you could have had Kouros eating rice from your hand from before his own balls dropped.'

'Do not be crude, Rakhsar. And I'd rather be dead than flirt with that murderous oaf.'

Rakhsar sighed. 'My sister, so brave, so honest, as straight as a spear-shaft, and as likely to bend.' Something like asperity crept into his voice. 'How lucky you are to have the conniving Rakhsar as a brother, to dirty his hands so that yours stay clean. We can not all afford your scruples, Roshana. The little catamite stays here.'

'You know better than to argue this with me, Rakhsar.'

They glared at one another. Finally Roshana touched her twin's shoulder. 'When are we to leave?'

'Tomorrow night. I have arranged for a party in the grounds. We will slip away during it, under the noses of the Honai. I have briefed some slaves to provide distraction.'

'And then?'

'And then, sister, we must brave the passages of the undercity. I have a useful Kefre in our pay, a kitchen-master. He was questioned by the Honai last night and I thought the jig was up, but it turns out it was only to do with some errant slave.' He frowned, looked at the boy in the bed. 'Bel's blood, I hope you are right about Kouros. If this is all connected, then it's over for us before it begins.' He turned to one side, deep in thought.

'If Orsana suspected, we would be dead already,' Roshana told him. 'The boy's coming here is a coincidence.'

Rakhsar stood up, as brisk and serious now as a soldier. 'When he wakes, I should like to talk to him. He's a creature of the undercity himself. Perhaps he will not be dead weight after all. You have your people warned?'

'Three. Maidek, Saryam and Ushau.'

Rakhsar nodded. 'I know them. Ushau for strength, Maidek for sense, and Saryam for companionship.'

'I could not have put it better myself. And you, brother?'

He smiled. 'I go alone.'

'Is there no-one –'

'That I can trust? I am the younger son, Roshana. If Bel himself took me into his embrace, I would check my pockets afterwards.'

'Perhaps that will change, when we are elsewhere.'

'Perhaps. We have the whole wide world to escape to, but there's barely a corner of it that does not know the imprint of the empire. Places to hide in may not be easy to come by.'

'And is that all you mean to do – hide?'

'I mean to survive, sister, by any means necessary. I am young yet. The world changes – the Macht are invading, the Jutha are in rebellion. Who knows what fractures and alarms and opportunities tomorrow may bring?'

Roshana hugged herself as though suddenly cold.

'I just wish it were done, and we were away.'

'One way or another, that part will be over soon enough.' Rakhsar looked down on the bed, at the face of the sleeping boy. 'In the end, I wonder if there is much we can do to influence our fate. They took this boy's manhood last night, all his hopes for posterity, and then shoved him from the wings onto the stage of history. I hope he profits by the exchange.'

It was the cooler air that woke Kurun. It blew on one side of his face, and he was moving against it, but his right cheek was resting against warm flesh.

And then the pain.

The groan mushroomed out of him, seeming to leave him not through his mouth but by every pore of his tattered body. He writhed.

Immediately a pair of arms clutched him close. He was gagged, but not bound. He tried to wriggle free, ignoring the pain that seemed to flood his frame from the waist down. The arms clamped him tight against a huge, muscled chest, broad as a door. He might as well have been a kitten in the coil of a python.

'Be still, you little fool,' a deep voice said. 'Mistress, he is awake.'

'Open your eyes.' A woman's voice.

He saw a blur of white in dark, and eyes above it, bright as shards of window-glass catching the moons.

'You are among friends, boy. My name is Roshana, and I will not let any more harm come to you. Nod if you understand.'

He recognised the perfect Kefren of the Court, smelled perfume tinting the night air, and nodded. Her fingers fumbled at the back of his head. They were cool, and the light of Anande the Patient glittered on her painted nails. The gag came off, leaving a sourness in his mouth.

'My name is Kurun,' he said doggedly, forcing down the pain, determined to make himself known. He would not die nameless.

'You must make no noise – do you understand me? Not a sound, if you wish to live. Be brave for me now, Kurun.' The cool fingers traced a line down his cheek for a moment, and then she had turned away.

Kurun raised his head slightly, and saw the jowled underside of a broad, hairless face, dark as walnut. 'What's happening?' he whispered.

The arms crushed him closer, and a dull grunt of agony left him.

'No noise,' the deep voice above him said. 'You make another sound, and I will break your neck.'

Kurun went limp, fighting the pain, the dark swirl of confusion. He could smell damp earth, and growing things. They were in the gardens, padding quickly and silently from shadow to deeper shadow, while above them, pale Anande shone down in a sky spattered full of stars. He blinked his eyes clear and tried to focus.

They halted, and there was a tense, frozen time of waiting. They were in among the trees, crouched like assassins. In addition to the ebony giant who held him and the komis-wearing lady, Kurun identified a *hufsa* girl, plainly clad as if for journeying, and a thin Kefre with a face as bonily angular as that of a mantis. Both bore packs too large for their frames.

Then another joined them. A masked Kefre who bore a naked scimitar. He dropped his komis to reveal a long, fine-boned face. He kissed the lady through her own veil. 'It's done, sister.'

She was looking at the sword, and the fine black line along the blade. 'He took the money?'

'He refused it. I offered him Bokosan steel instead.'

'Rakhsar!'

'Do you think this a game, Roshana? The way is clear, now. My contact waits by the kitchen platform. We must hurry.'

'You have blood on your clothes.'

'It doesn't signify, not at night.' The jewel bright eyes surveyed them all with the dispassion of a snake overlooking a nest of mice. 'I see you brought him.'

'I said I would.'

Kurun dropped his gaze as the Kefre stared at him. 'Ushau, do not let him make so much as a squeak.'

'Those are mistress's orders,' the deep voice rumbled above Kurun's head.

'Good. Now follow me, all of you, as quick and quiet as you can.'

They dashed across a space open and bright under the moonlight, and before them the buildings of the palace reared up like some sheer-sided mountain, decked here and there with yellow-burning flammifers. Kurun fought down a roll of agony that brought his gorge rising. He shut his eyes, pressed his forehead against the hot chest of the giant who bore him.

'Stand here. Stay clear of the walls,' Rakhsar snapped. 'Saryam, mind your cloak – if it catches in the pulleys you'll jam us in the shaft.'

They were standing on one of the platforms connecting the palace to the kitchens below. Rakhsar tugged on the communication rope, and at once there was a jerk. The thick wood trembled under their feet, and they began to descend.

Into darkness. Rakhsar up-ended the illuminating torch in its sconce and the last of its sparks winked out as they bounced off his bloody sword. The air popped in Kurun's ears; they were descending very fast. Then there was a dull boom, and the platform was still, staggering them with its sudden halt.

'My prince,' a familiar voice said.

'Auroc – nicely done. Now point us right for the undercity.'

Kurun stared open-mouthed in shock, and found shock staring back at him. Auroc's face was bruised and swollen, but wholly familiar; the first familiar thing he had seen since leaving the kitchens.

'I'm sorry,' he said to the kitchen-master, the words a sob, gargled out of the giant's grip.

'I thought they killed you,' Auroc said, disbelieving.

'They damn near did,' Rakhsar said. 'Auroc, lead on. We are short on time.'

Auroc dragged his gaze from Kurun's tearstained face. 'Yes, of course. Follow me, my prince. I will take you to the Silima. From there, you follow the road all the way down.'

There was a time that followed when Kurun's head bobbed on Ushau's chest and his tears came hot and free. But the thought that had occurred to him could not be pushed aside.

The Silima? It did not seem right. It was akin to a burglar leaving a house through the front door. The Silima was the main thoroughfare of the undercity, and it was guarded night and day.

'Auroc,' he said thickly. 'Master, the Silima cannot be taken. We cannot travel it and stay hidden. There are better ways.'

'Be quiet,' Auroc said quickly. He was sweating. And to Rakhsar, 'Lord, the Silima is the quickest way out of the ziggurat. You will be on the streets within the hour.'

Kurun felt fear as cold as water down his back. 'Master, I do not think –'

Auroc struck him across the face.

Kurun swallowed that pain along with the rest. He had to point out the mistake. Auroc was wrong. He wanted to save him from his error. At last he said to Rakhsar, 'Lord, this is not right. My master is guiding you awry.'

Rakhsar brought up the keen point of the scimitar and levelled it easily at Auroc's throat. 'Is that so?' He studied the kitchen-master for a long, brittle moment.

'Kouros questioned you, didn't he?'

'Lord, I was interrogated due to a misunderstanding – this whelp here left his post and spied on the King in the gardens. I was held responsible. That's all, I swear it!'

'Even I have heard of the Silima,' Roshana said. She dropped her komis and stepped closer to Auroc. 'And if I have heard of it, then it is no secret.'

'It is the fastest way down to the streets,' Auroc persisted. He wiped his brow. 'It is a busy thoroughfare, yes, but all the easier to lose yourselves in.'

'Auroc,' Kurun whispered. He was weeping. 'I meant no harm to you.' His voice rose. 'Masters, I know a better way.'

'Shut your mouth –' Auroc raged, and cocked his fist.

'You will not strike him again,' Roshana told the kitchen-master evenly. She turned to Kurun. Those beautiful eyes were hard as sunlight on snow. 'Are you sure of this?'

'Lady, you can kill me if I am wrong. But I know that you cannot leave the ziggurat by the Silima – there are guards at every junction. Folk of your caste are never seen there – you cannot go unnoticed, not all the way to the bottom. Auroc is sending you wrong.'

'Is that it, my friend?' Rakhsar asked softly. The scimitar-point never wavered. 'Did Kouros dig the truth out of you?'

'My – my prince,' Auroc stammered, 'I am your faithful servant.'

'I bought you – that is as far as your faith goes. Now tell me, Auroc, what have you told Kouros of our excursion?'

Auroc looked as lost as a landed fish. No words came. Rakhsar nodded grimly. 'You see, Roshana, why I trust no-one? As long as loyalty can be bought by the deepest purse, Kouros will always outbid us.'

Auroc finally collected himself. He glared down upon Kurun, in despair and sudden fury. 'You stupid little fool. I was trying to help you. You would have risen under me, Kurun. We would have served under the sun together. Now you have killed us both.'

'Not him. Me,' Rakhsar said, and he thrust the scimitar into the kitchen-master's throat.

The tall Kefre stood there, eyes wide, hands flapping like wounded birds. His knees began to bend but the sword-blade held him upright. Blood gurgled out of his neck, the rent in his flesh widening around the steel of the scimitar. Then he sank, still upright, and slowly slid off the blade to collapse like a boneless heap of rags on the ground. Under him, the black pool opened out like the quickened blossoming of a flower.

Rakhsar stepped back from it to save his shoes. He wiped clean his blade on the kitchen-master's robe, then turned to Kurun with a face like an ivory mask. 'You had better be right, boy, or I will make an end of you less neat than this.'

Kurun's tongue seemed frozen to the roof of his mouth. He squirmed, but the giant Ushau held him fast. Roshana was still looking at him, something desperate in her face now.

'Kurun,' she said gently. 'Now you must tell us where to go.'

THEY TROD THE narrow corridors of the slave-city, mazing their way through the intestines of the ziggurat. They drew stares wherever they went; it was impossible to disguise the high-born nature of Rakhsar and Roshana. It was in their eyes, in their clothes, in the very way they walked. Resourceful though the twins might be, they had no real experience of life below the summit, and took it as no more than their due when the lesser inhabitants of the undercity drew back to let them pass, staring open-mouthed.

Kurun was in the lead, still clasped in the arms of the ebony giant. He muttered directions to Ushau, picked a convoluted path towards the less inhabited regions of the undercity. In doing so, he steered close to the cliff of his knowledge of the place, taking the company down little-used tunnels and passageways. As they descended, so they began to hear through the very stone the rhythmic thump of the waterwheels far below, upon which thousands toiled to water the gardens of the Great King. The sound was like the ceaseless beat of some enormous heart.

Here, the denizens of the dark ways were even more wary than those above, darting into shadows and side-alleys as the company passed. Rakhsar had drawn his sword again, and his eyes gleamed with a light of their own. His sister took his free hand, and the twins proceeded thus while the two other servants brought up the rear, bent under travel-bags, and as wide-eyed as owls in the hot deepening darkness.

'Here,' Kurun said at last. He squeezed shut his eyes a second, fighting a wash of nausea. He felt wetness on the backs of his thighs, and dared not speculate on it.

They were in a wider space, an arched passageway so low that Ushau's head scraped the ceiling. Beyond there was more light, torches burning, a heat slightly less heavy, and the sense of moving air. There was noise also, the rattle of iron wheel-rims on stone, the braying of mules, and the clink of masonry. Many voices rose and fell, not the sea-rush of an aimless crowd, but the purposeful give and take of people at work.

'This is the stone-cutters' valley,' Kurun said. 'We are at the level of the streets now. If we go through here, there is a gateway which is always open in daylight, and then we are outside.'

'It must be near dawn by now,' Rakhsar said, wiping his face.

'They will sound the chime when the sun rises,' Kurun told him tiredly. 'That's when the shift changes. That would be the best time to try for the outside.'

He was fading away. The torchlight seemed to be circling a loom of widening shadow. His face was gripped by strong fingers, and shaken.

'Stay with us, boy. When we stand under the sun, you can sleep all you want.'

'He is bleeding, master,' Ushau said.

'Set him down.' Roshana's voice, quick and sharp.

Kurun was laid down on the stone. They opened his legs and peeled the soaked chiton from his thighs. He cried out, but the scream was smothered by Ushau's huge palm, and the other held him down while Rakhsar and Roshana examined him. Rakhsar's upper lip peeled back from his teeth. 'Bel in his heaven, what a mess.'

'Maidek,' Roshana said, 'Can you do something?'

The skull-lean Kefre knelt beside them. He looked Kurun's injuries over with some interest, like a man at a market-stall.

'They closed the wound with fire, mistress, but missed part of it. I would bind the boy's legs together for now. He will need to be sewn up, but I cannot do that here. I need –'

A brass clang rattled through the air, as though some titan had dropped a metal pot out of the sky. Rakhsar stood up. 'Your butchery can wait, Maidek,' he said. 'That'll be the chime the boy spoke of. Ushau, clamp him tight.'

The light grew, grey and cool across the massive chamber ahead. It revealed gangs of *hufsan*, who were now straightening from their labour upon orderly rows of squared stone, heaps of rubble. A swarm of talk rose. Suddenly the place seemed crowded, as more apron-clad *hufsan* trooped in from outside, and from stairways and ramps leading down from the dark bulk of the ziggurat above. The tall gateway loomed beyond, brightening moment by moment. There was an inrush of cooler air that brought the dust of the stoneworkers with it to grit their teeth, and something else. The mingled stinks of the world beyond, the promiscuous perfume of the city itself.

'The boy was right,' Roshana said. 'That is the light of the dawn.'

'Up. Move,' Rakhsar snapped. 'Follow me.'

He had sheathed his sword, but kept his hand on the hilt as they trailed through the work-gangs, gathering rock-dust, the sweat and toil of the slave-city pressing in on them with the milling crowds of workers. The fresh, cool air of the city beyond drew them on, filling their lungs. Rakhsar uttered a strangled laugh as they stepped out of the ziggurat, into the morning cacophony that was Ashur, and looked around themselves like an island of idle fools in a sea of busy people.

'I smell grilled frog,' Rakhsar said to his sister, grinning. The sweat lay like pearl beads on his forehead. 'What say you we treat ourselves to one, and then find a place to lay our heads for a while?'

He strode off, and the rest trailed after him like

the tail of a kite. Ushau looked down on Kurun and tapped a knuckle against the boy's chest.

'You are a good little fellow,' he said. Then he held Kurun close, and followed his master, and they were lost in the coursing torrent of faces, bodies, flapping feet and waving hands that was the Imperial City, while behind them the ziggurats were lit up, level by level, by the burgeoning light of the dawn.

SIX
FRIENDS IN ODD PLACES

ASHURNAN FELT THE palanquin move under him, with the stately pace of the elephant that bore it. He drew back the fine weave of the curtains to look up the road ahead, and once again his fist clenched involuntarily as he took in the line of wagons, pack-animals, cavalry and marching men that stretched to the bright, dust-hazed horizon.

Dust in his beard. Dust in his shoes. Dust in the very food he ate. Asuria itself was impregnating every part of him; his own country, the heart of empire, the place his ancestors had walked and ruled for years beyond count.

His father Anurman, whom some named *the Great*, had deigned to speak to him of the empire once. One did not *rule* it, any more than a mariner dictated every movement of a ship at sea. One steered it. And sometimes, it took patience to get it back on course when the waves were in your teeth.

I am older now than my father was when he died, Ashurnan thought. I have ruled longer than he did. I have fought fewer wars, but those in which I have taken part have been greater than any he ever saw. Does that make me a better king than my father, or a lesser?

Once again, his thoughts travelled back down the dusty pasangs of the Royal Road, to his capital.

Where are you now, Rakhsar? In some highland castle, fomenting rebellion? Or down in the marshes, peering into some peasant's fire? No – that is not your style.

Again, his fist clenched and unclenched.

I should have given him a command, taken him with me. He has an energy Kouros lacks, and courage.

But that was his heart talking. He had been as generous with his own brother, and Kunaksa had been the result.

It has always been Kouros, he thought. I cannot stand against both the Macht and Orsana. I have not the strength.

But he found himself smiling, despite the gloom of his ruminations. It had been a long time since he had been part of an army on the march. There was no denying that it brought back good memories as well as bad, a tincture of youth.

One war at a time, he thought.

AT LONG LAST, the Great King himself had set forth from Ashur on campaign, with the first contingent of the Imperial Levy, and the bulk of the Household. This was but a tithe of the force that would eventually form up on the far side of the Magron Mountains, but still it choked every road leading west for dozens of pasangs. Ten thousand Honai, five thousand Arakosan cavalry who had crossed the Oskus only the week before. Twenty thousand of the local levy, small farmers called up to the banners of the King, the year's second harvest thickening in the fields behind them, their wives and sons left to gather it in as best they might.

And that was just the beginning. To the rear of these fighting men marched another army. Teamsters, smiths, leatherworkers, carpenters, herdsmen, slaves by the thousand, and an amorphous gaggle of wives and children who could not bear to be parted from their menfolk. These were nearly as numerous as the clanking columns who bore spear and shield, and every night since leaving Ashur they had straggled into camp hours after the vanguard of the army, spent and dust-painted, but ready to attend to the needs of those who had been called upon to bear arms, to fight the Great King's war for them.

And that still did not include the Great King's own entourage. In his youth, Ashurnan had been stubborn, proud and fit enough to travel almost as lightly as one of his junior generals; a half dozen mule-carts carried everything he needed to live in comfort in the field. But he was old now, and his sense of what befitted a king's campaigning had changed. Two hundred wagons carried his personal tents, his furniture, his carpets, his stores of food and drink, his favourite concubines (Orsana had picked them for him, and he had not argued the matter).

His Household was an army in itself, moving ahead of the rest of the troops to escape the tower of dust they kicked up (for this was not real campaigning, not yet; the Macht were still thousands of pasangs away), and he had his scouts and stewards out on the roads ahead to make sure there was a suitable campsite each night. In the past, Great Kings had stayed with local nobles on their travels, but Ashurnan had learned early in his reign that to put up the King and his fellow travellers for even one night could beggar the richest satrap in the empire.

And besides, when those same nobles came to offer him obeisance in his vast, multi-coloured, towering tent, its gilded poles as thick as the masts of a mighty ship, one could see that the effect was worth the effort.

The Great King on the move was like some force out of nature, as impressive as the grandest storm, and these petty princes and Archons and local lords were to be the officers in his levies. On their loyalty, or respect, or fear would turn the fate of the battle to come. Let them look upon the grandeur that was Ashurnan, and tremble. It would stiffen their resolve when the Macht came marching towards them in full panoply of war.

The grandeur that was Ashurnan. The Great King sipped from his cup, cold water sprinkled with the juice of limes, crackling with ice from the straw-insulated chests further down the column. Most of the folk in this great host had never seen ice; they were creatures of the lowlands, and their lives had been spent in the shimmering, irrigated fields of the Heart of Empire. But now when they raised their heads and looked beyond the dust, they could glimpse snow on the rim of the world, the white peaks of the mighty Magron, and in their foothills the King's summer capital, Hamadan, where for centuries the Asurian Kings had gone to escape the stifling heat of the low country. Hamadan was the fortress-key to the Asurian Gates, the only path an army could take through the Magron to the Middle Empire beyond. And it was there, in the land of the Rivers, that Ashurnan felt the matter would be decided.

He did not believe Darios would be able to hold the line of the Korash; his army had been blown to chaff. No, the thing would happen in ancient Pleninash, somewhere on the Imperial Road between Kaik and Irunshahr.

Somewhere on the same line of march that the Ten Thousand had taken, a generation before.

That same bloodied highway was going to see another bloodletting, but this one would be greater even than Kunaksa. Ashurnan could feel it in his thinning bones, and he felt no relish at the prospect. He still remembered vividly being woken from sleep after the first day at Kunaksa, when he had thought the thing won, only to be told that the Macht, leaderless, alone, betrayed, were nonetheless attacking, and putting to flight the best the Empire could throw at them. He remembered those sombre men in bronze and scarlet advancing remorselessly over their own dead, marching in cadence, singing as they came. And a chill ran up his backbone at the memory.

KOUROS REINED IN his horse with a jerk, the animal jittery under him, catching his mood. He rode a Niseian, as did many Kefren with money or high blood, but he disliked the beast. Coal-black and fiery tempered, like all its kind, it had been bred for the hunt, for war; two activities Kouros knew little of. He carried a whip, which few Kefren horsemen did, the high-born of the empire having been brought up with horses since childhood. There was a semi-mythical bond between the high-caste Kefren of Asuria and the Niseians. Legend had it that the tall black horses were a gift to the world from Bel himself, and their sire was the west wind.

Darker myths even said that the big horses' forbears had been brought east by the Macht in their youth, but this was not a tale that found much favour among the Niseian breeders.

Kouros did not name his horses, nor did he ride for pleasure. The animals were a necessary accessory to him, nothing more, and nothing could make his eyes glaze over faster than a group of petty lords discussing studs and bloodlines. They were animals, that was all. Kouros's world was to do with people. Horses were nothing more than transport.

He sat upon his horse now, biting his thumbnail, looking down on the dust-shrouded Imperial Road leading north-west to Hamadan. To the south and east more dust-clouds rose, like tawny stormclouds anchored to the earth. More columns of marching troops. They were converging from all over Asuria, and more were behind them. His spies told him that the Arakosan main body was still a week to the east, eight thousand heavy cavalry bright as kingfishers in the blue-enamelled armour of their people. His mother's people.

His people.

His mother never let him forget his Arakosan blood. She came from a line of kings as ancient as that of Asuria, and considered herself as royal as any scion of Asur. Minosh, satrap of Arakosia, was her cousin, and they had been close as children, the palace in Bokosa housing a more easy-going regime than that of Ashur. Minosh was a satrap of the Great King, a loyal servant. But he was also a great ruler in his own right. Minosh had to be wooed, if Kouros's claim to the throne were to be set in stone.

Especially now, with Rakhsar on the loose.

Kouros bared his teeth in anger, thinking on it, and when the horse began to dance and snap under him he seized the reins and yanked back hard. He used a hard wolf-bit on his horses, which was essentially a bronze blade laid against the tongue. It was not unusual for him to turn his mount over to the grooms with blood dripping from the animal's mouth.

Rakhsar, free and alive. He thought he had stopped every bolthole, covered every contingency.

His mother had flown into a rage at the news. It

had meant she must stay in Ashur through the heat of the summer, to watch over the city for Rakhsar's mischief.

She had stripped one of her slaves at random and whipped the girl's flesh from her white back in front of him. He had not so much as dared to wipe the blood from his face, but stood there dumb and motionless while the screaming slave died under her blows. Orsana had stood afterwards with her black hair skeined over her face, eyes socketed in blood, the hem of her robe soaking it up from the puddle mosaic of the floor.

How can you be King? She had shrieked, and Kouros had felt terror he had not known since childhood. She had whipped the slave, but the blows had been meant for him.

After that it had been a relief to leave the city, to join his father's army and eat dust day after day, to ache with the constant riding, to sweat like a serf in the daily swordplay his weapons-master insist he practice.

But still, his thoughts were constant – where was Rakhsar? And Roshana.

He had loved Roshana once. She had been kind to him when as children they had occasionally been allowed to play together. Those moments had been like miracles to him.

But her love for her brother curdled his feelings for her, for between Rakhsar and Kouros there had been nothing but black, unalloyed hatred from the first. It was as if they had the instincts of wild dogs, sensing a rival in the pack. It was unreasoning from the beginning, and then as they grew older there had been too many more reasons to ever begin to question it.

But he had wept, in private, over Roshana, for she was one of a handful of people who had shown him kindness without hope of gain, for no other reason than pure decency.

It was why he hungered now to catch and degrade her, to force himself on her in front of her twin, to wipe that knowing sneer off Rakhsar's face one last time, and then expunge it from the world forever.

Tears rose in his eyes as he pitied himself, remembering the utter loneliness of his childhood. There had been one other in those days, a single other who had shared his world for a time. But his mother had disapproved. Orsana's disapproval meant mutilation, death, exile. No-one was allowed to come close to her son, who would one day be ruler of the world.

His mother loved him, but that love frightened him, for it was entangled in expectation and ambition and bloody, unyielding determination. She loved him, but if he could not be King, then he did not like to think what that love could do.

There were times when he wished she was... gone.

And he thought of what it would be like to be King, to do as he pleased, and the thought settled his mind, calmed him. He even patted the rancid, foam-flecked neck of his horse as though he cared.

'Barka,' he said.

From the huddle of riders a respectful distance behind him, one trotted forward. A Kefre, but low-born, with dark eyes and long hair dyed red as an apple and bound in an oiled queue. He had a sword scabbarded each side of his saddle's pommel and wore a plain leather corselet studded with bronze. A scar tugged down one corner of his mouth, so it looked like he was leering, but his eyes held no humour.

This was Kouros's weapons-master; an Arakosan, brought to Ashur fifteen years before by Orsana to teach her son how to be a man. He was also the only person who had ever beaten the young prince, for mistreating a horse. Kouros had gone to his mother at once, and the Arakosan had never laid a hand on him since, but Kouros still remembered the beating. He knew Barka despised him, but he also knew the Arakosan would die for him without thought, because of who his mother was.

'My prince?'

'Do we know yet where the imperial tent will be sited tonight?'

'Yes, lord. The scouts have plotted a site some twenty pasangs ahead, on the outskirts of Kinamish.'

'And my household?'

Barka pointed below, to where the Imperial road was a long snake of dust, a golden caterpillar inching across the land with black ants crawling within it.

'Our gear is with the Great King's caravan, as always, lord.'

Kouros was aching for a bath, some wine, something softer than a saddle to take his bulk. He frowned. The entire army and everyone in it travelled at the pace of the slowest ox-cart in the Great King's baggage train. And no tent could be pitched before the King's. It would be many hours yet.

Kouros wiped his face, his palm coming away gritty with dust. Kinamish was a small town with some of the amenities of civilization. It was unnoticeable, unimportant. It was perfect.

A well-mounted man could be there in an hour, if he pushed his horse. The timings had worked well.

'Let us ride ahead, and make sure the people of Kinamish are ready to receive my father,' Kouros said lightly.

Barka looked at him. He had an unsettlingly direct gaze that was wholly free of deference. Since Orsana had spoken to him, all those years ago, he had never again ventured to correct the young prince, but Kouros always knew when Barka disapproved of him. He would have rid himself of the scarred Kefre long before, except that he knew – somehow – that Barka could be trusted utterly. The weapons-master might not think much of his prince, but he would never betray him. It was the closest thing to loyalty Kouros had ever experienced. Almost.

'Very well,' Barka said. 'The escort also, my lord?'

'No.' No, that might attract attention. Kouros snarled inside at the thought of being patiently taken to task by Dyarnes or another of his father's veterans. They feared him – all of them – but they still had the casual confidence of old campaigners. And there were things they did not need to know.

'You and I, Barka – we'll go alone.'

'As you wish, lord.'

* * *

THEY PUSHED THE horses hard. Kouros's riding was graceless but effective; he made the animal do what he wanted, and there was never any emotional connection between horse and rider. He had seen his father commiserate with hardened soldiers on the death of a favourite horse, and had been utterly baffled by the sight. These were grown men with blood on their hands, who would have a thieving slave crucified without a moment's thought, and they wept over a dead animal.

The big Niseians pounded along willingly enough, for they had been travelling at a crawl all morning. Barka sat his as though stuck to it, moving with the rise and fall of the animal, the reins an irrelevance, held lightly in one hand. He talked to his horse in a low voice now and again, crooned to it like it was a child he wanted to reassure.

Baffling.

The last pasangs of the Heart of Empire rolled along under them, the land rising to meet the Magron mountains, which were a huge cloud now on the western horizon, dun-coloured and tipped with white, forests a darker stubble at their knees.

There was no irrigation system in this part of the world, for the moist easterlies struck the mountains and shed their water freely in tumbled thunderheads every spring and winter. The land was a less violent green than the manicured fields of the Oskus valley, and much of it was given over to pasture. They herded cattle here, and goats to clear up after them.

The people were the shorter, darker, upland *hufsan* who made up the bulk of the empire's populations.

Herd boys stopped to stare at the two superbly mounted Kefren who galloped past them, and Barka, with a boyishness quite unlike him, waved at those they passed with a white grin splitting his leathered face.

He is happy, Kouros realised. He is genuinely happy to be galloping along, slathered in sweat, miles from the capital, with only the ground to sleep on and the prospect of some half-seared campfire meat to eat tonight.

To ride a horse, to use a bow, to tell the truth. Those were the ancient tenets of life for the Kefren, still given lip service even in the opulent luxury of Ashur's palaces. Kouros's mother never tired of telling him that in Arakosia the nobles still trained their sons how to shoot from the saddle, that a Kefre's word was counted a contract as good as any scribe's scrawl.

But Orsana had been in the Harem these thirty years and more. What did she know?

Kouros had been at intrigues since he was a child, recognising his elevated status and working on it, utilising slaves and tutors and bodyguards and their dependence on his favour. No bows or horses, there, and not much of the truth, either. Leverage was what counted; the ability to hold a person's dismissal or disgrace over their head.

He smiled a curious half-smirk as he rode along.

Nobles had given him their wives for a night to buy his favour, and the more unwilling the woman, the sweeter it had tasted. He loved to be there to give the husband back his wife the next morning, to see the eyes of them both. That moment was better than the sex itself.

'Kinamish,' Barka said, pointing, ruining his sordid little daydream.

'I am not blind,' he snapped.

'Lord, we should slow our pace, rest the horses.'

'We're nearly there, Barka. They can rest all they like when we reach the town.'

'As you wish, my lord.' Barka's high spirits withered. He was again the grim-faced guardian.

THEY DISMOUNTED IN a tawny square of mud-brick buildings. Kinamish was not important enough to need a wall, and this far into the Heart of Empire it would not have occurred to the inhabitants to build one. Asuria had not known the footfall of war for generations, and only the greatest of her cities still maintained defences, more out of tradition than anything else.

There was a tavern, with a vine-shaded loggia. Leaving Barka with the steaming horses, Kouros sat himself there. He dropped his komis from his face and slapped the dust from his clothes with his riding-gauntlets. Slowly, as the local drinkers, farmers and ne'er-do-wells watched, the colours emerged from his garments. Kingfisher blue, imperial purple, and the silver embroidered horse heads of the royal house. The loggia cleared around him, and he smiled again, clicking his fingers for service.

'Wine, and cold water,' he said without looking up.

'At once, my lord.'

He did not seem surprised when he was joined at his table by another traveller, who sat down beside him without ceremony and reached for the communal olive-bowl, wetting his fingers on the oil and then applying it to sunburnt patches on his nose. With the same hand the newcomer dropped the folds of his own komis, and sighed. He was a broad-faced Kefre with a cropped head and eyes as bright as cornflowers. His skin and his clothes were all the colour of the dust that puffed in pale zephyrs around the little square. When the water arrived he drank straight from the jug, and, wiping his mouth, he left on his face a smear of clean skin the colour of new wood.

'Straight from the well, none better. My thanks to your honour.'

Kouros sipped his wine, grimaced, then swallowed half the cup. 'Tell me you have news, Kuthra.'

'I have. Maybe not the type you'd like to hear, but useful nonetheless.' The dusty Kefre stared at Kouros expectantly, and with a sliver of mockery folded into his smile. 'You've put on weight, brother.'

'The hazards of palace living.'

'Ah, of course. It's been so long I had forgotten. How long has it been, Kouros, since I shared the heights with you?'

Kouros shifted in his chair, though his gaze never left the other's face, and there was a strange glimmer in his eyes. 'I am here for information, not to reminisce.'

'Indulge me. We see each other so rarely, these days.'

Kouros reached into his blue robes and brought forth a doeskin purse, a beautifully made thing which looked to have been chosen with some care. As it settled on the table it clinked heavily. Kuthra did not once look at it, but continued to study Kouros's face.

At last, Kouros said, 'It is seventeen years.'

'Seventeen years! How fast they have flown. Do you remember how we used to meet in the darkest corners of the gardens to lie under the trees and talk of all the great things we would do when we were grown? You would be King and I would be at your side. I would look out for you, and keep the jackals from your back. I wanted nothing more.'

Quietly, Kouros said, 'Neither did I.'

Deliberately, Kuthra raised his right arm and set it on the table. The folds of his travelling gear fell back to reveal a stump at the wrist, an old wound long seamed shut in a swirl of flesh.

'Such a pity your mother did not agree.'

The two men looked at one another. Finally they both leaned close in the same second and embraced, burying their faces in each other's shoulders.

Kouros took Kuthra's face in his hands. There were tears in his eyes. They brimmed, and spilled over onto his cheeks. 'It was the price for your life.'

'I know. She should not have made you watch, though. She knew you would blame yourself for it, when it was her doing alone.' Kuthra wiped the tears from Kouros's face with his only hand.

'She has mellowed since then.' They both began to laugh. Kuthra thumped the table with his stump.

'More wine here! Are you all asleep? Landlord, step quick now!'

'Don't draw attention to us,' Kouros hissed urgently. 'This is risky enough as it is.'

'We sit face to face once every four or five years, if we are lucky. The rest of the time it is letters and notes and whispers in the dark. Let me drink with my brother Kouros – let us raise our cups together for a little while at least, like normal folk.'

'If Orsana knew –'

'Fuck Orsana. She will not live forever.' Kuthra leaned in and set his hand on Kouros's. 'Brother, one day you will be King, and on that day and every other after you will have me by your side, and I will always keep the jackals from your back.'

'You shall be a prince again, Kuthra.'

'Once a prince, always a prince,' Kuthra grinned.

The wine arrived. It was a dry, bitter vintage from the foothills of the Magron, but it quenched the thirst.

'Let us speak of princes, since we're here,' Kuthra said casually. At once, Kouros's face changed. Some of the old rancour settled into it, dragging it down.

'You have located them?'

'I have located them three times, brother, but on each occasion I have been like the slow fox, snapping at the tail feathers and missing the meat. They left Ashur on foot, which was clever of them, and then bought nags from a dealer in Goronuz, twenty pasangs up-river of the city. After that they disappeared for a while. I have our people watching the Asurian Gates like vultures at a hanging, but the Gates are not the only way over the mountains. There are many lesser routes that a small party might manage.'

'Kuthra, are you telling me –'

'I picked up their trail again west of Hamadan. They showed sense enough to avoid the city and went straight up into the highlands. I know they swapped horses for mules, and they may even be on foot again by now. But they have disappeared, brother. We have no agents that far into the Magron.'

'Bel's blood. You're telling me we've lost them.'

'Only for now. They cannot stay up in the mountains forever, and we have as many eyes in the Middle Empire as we have here. When they descend again they will be easily traced, for they will be wanting horses again, no doubt. That is if they make it through the mountains. Rakhsar and Roshana are creatures of the city; they may not find the heights to their taste. They could become truly lost, or die in an avalanche or a snowdrift, or fall prey to the Qaf.'

Kouros shook his head. 'Rakhsar will survive. He always does. Three times over the years my mother has tried to have him killed, and each time he has lived, through his absurd luck as much as anything else. Kuthra, you must get back on his trail. My father has not stood in our way until now, but if Rakhsar were to suddenly appear in front of the Imperial tent and beg to accompany him on campaign, the old fool might weaken. He doesn't like me; he knows I am the only sane choice as heir, but he has this damnable attachment to the memory of that Niseian bitch he tried to supplant my mother with. He grows sentimental in old age. There's no telling how he might let things go, not any more.'

Kuthra nodded, face hard. 'Brother, you need not concern yourself. Unless Rakhsar can grow wings, I will have him, in the end.'

'If anyone can, it will be you.'

'You know that your mother has people out on the same errand. A horde of them, sniffing around every bolt-hole in the empire.'

'You must get there first. I want Rakhsar and Roshana brought in front of me, alive.'

Kuthra raised an eyebrow. 'Both of them, or just Roshana?'

Kouros's face darkened, blood filling it. 'Just do as I ask.'

'They must both die, brother. It has gone too far for that. There was a time when perhaps you could have spared the girl, but that time is gone. It is simply a question of whose hand they perish at. You must not make it personal.'

'I make everything personal,' Kouros said, bitterly. 'It is the way I am.'

'As you wish.'

'Don't look at me like that – you remind me of Barka – dutiful and disapproving.'

'You need to grow a thicker skin, Kouros.'

'I have only the one I was born in.'

'And Orsana has been flaying it off you strip by strip, since you could walk.' Kuthra held up his stump. 'She has marked me less than you. I count myself lucky to have escaped the Court so cheaply.'

'You were lucky your mother was nothing more than a slave.'

'We are all slaves, Kouros. Even your father is trammelled and confined by his station. Do you think him a happy man?'

'Are you happy, Kuthra?' Kouros's voice was hoarse and earnest.

'I am. I have no ambitions, and I know those whom I love and those I hate. My life is simple –'

'You're a spy – you slink across the empire like a cat at midnight. How simple can it be to live with all your secrets, to kidnap and slaughter strangers at another's bidding?'

Kuthra shrugged. 'Perhaps I lack a certain curiosity. I have my orders, and I fulfil them. I get paid, and I spend the money. Then I get more orders. Thus the wheel of my life turns.'

'I wish I could take my horse and ride away with you, right here and now, Kuthra. We could cross the mountains together, leave all this behind.'

'And do what?' Kuthra tapped the back of his elder brother's hand. 'You were born to be what you are – I do not know if being King will make you happy, Kouros, but I do know that not being King would crack your soul. It is the way you have been made.'

They drank the last of the wine, the resin-scented vintage oiling their throats, loosening up their minds. Kuthra sat up straight suddenly. Barka had reappeared at the side of the loggia.

'Lord, the horses are rubbed down, and fed and watered. May I have your permission to eat?'

Kouros nodded. Barka bowed slightly. His gaze flicked to Kuthra and a half-knowing light came into his eye. Then he walked away.

'My brother's keeper,' Kuthra said.

'He serves my mother.'

'I know Barka, Kouros, or his type at least. The Arakosans, they say, are Asurians before the coming of the cities. Folk who retain the memory of a simpler time.'

'The horse, the bow, the truth – I have heard all this at length from my mother since my ears could hear.'

'There is truth to it. You can trust Barka, so long as you do not ask him to dishonour himself. That is what the Arakosans are like. Faithful as dogs, and as vicious. You wrong one, though, and you have an enemy for life.' Kuthra nudged his brother with a smile. 'There is more Arakosan in you than you know.'

Kouros rubbed his forehead. 'When I talk to you, Kuthra, I feel that there is another man buried in me who raises his head and sees some chink of light ahead in the darkness. I was that man once, or could have been. It is he who says these things to you now; and the Kouros they all hate, my mother's son, he is gone.

'But it is only for a little while. One day there will be no light left, and the darkness will be all.'

'Not so long as I live.'

'I have done cruel things. Sometimes I feel that I am a poison-filled jar, full to the brim and ready to spill over.'

'You're a better man than you give yourself credit for, or you would not feel this way. We have all done terrible things, Kouros – our lives have called it out of us.'

'There was a boy, back in the city, a kitchen-slave who took it upon himself to spy on a dinner my father gave in the gardens.'

'Some lackey of Rakhsar's?'

'I thought so, at first. But I knew, when I questioned him, that he was telling me the truth. That he had been there out of sheer curiosity, the stupidity of his youth. And I gelded him anyway, with my own hands, and sent him to Roshana.'

Kuthra leaned back from the table and chuckled. 'Now, that is something your mother would do.'

'I know.' Kouros looked up, and his eyes were haunted. 'I did it because I had it in my power, and I was angry, and I wanted to hurt something. That same evening, when my father met with the couriers from the west, he had Rakhsar join us, affronting me before the whole table.'

'At least you let the boy live.'

'I was ashamed, afterwards. Kuthra, can a king feel shame, if there is no-one to tell him he does wrong?'

'I will be there, brother. I promise, I will tell you.'

Kouros knuckled his eyes like a tired child. 'I hope so.' He stood up. 'It is time I was back with the column. The Heir cannot disappear for too long without comment.'

'I understand.'

But Kouros took Kuthra's stump-wrist in his grasp as the other rose in his turn.

'They think I am a monster, Kuthra. The spoilt, twisted product of my mother's ambition. Perhaps they are right. But I will tell you something they do not know.' He paused, lowered his voice almost as if afraid.

'My brother, Rakhsar; so charming, so quick with his wit and his smile...

'He is worse, far worse than I.'

PART TWO

DREAMS OF FIRE

SEVEN
A KUFR IDEA

AHEAD, THE MOUNTAINS rose in a long serried parade clear across the sky. As the sun settled into the lowlands of the west, so the saffron light coloured the peaks and slopes, tinting the snowfields and filling the valleys with shadows black as ink.

Leading up to the mountains, climbing steadily from the wide river-plain below, a series of bristling snakes inched their way eastwards as though nosing for a crevice to sleep in. Now and then as they moved they caught the sunset in a flickering line of light.

They were columns of marching men, each pasangs long. They filled every road leading east, and trudged uphill in their patient thousands with the last of the sunlight bright as flame on their bronze armour, winking on the spearheads.

On their flanks columns of horsemen rode, red-cloaked like the infantry, their helms hanging from their saddles and lances resting on the shoulders of the riders. Knots of unarmoured cavalry swarmed over the rising hills further to the east of their fellows, their ranks as formless as a summer cloud of gnats.

This was the satrapy of Askanon, the wide floodplain of the Sardask and Haneikos rivers. Some of the most ancient cities of the Kufr stood here; Eskis, Kumir, and mighty Ashdod. They perched on their tells of earth and stone like castles of sand on a beach, whilst around them rivulets and rivers of armed men coursed across the earth.

The armies of the Macht were on the march again. To their rear, thick bars of black toiling smoke rose up the sky, lit bright and bloody by the sunset. To their front, the Korash Mountains stood marking the borders of the Middle Empire as they had from time immemorial.

The city of Ashdod had stood for perhaps five thousand years. It rose up like a tiered cake out of the plain, the brick and timber walls which encircled it as dark and warm in hue as an earthenware bowl. Within those walls the population numbered many tens of thousands, perhaps more.

And now it was burning.

'They rely too much on mud and straw for their defences,' Fornyx grunted. 'They should have gone to the mountains for stone and made their walls of that.'

'If they had,' Rictus said, 'We'd be sitting outside them still. The Kufr don't think like us, Fornyx. They haven't had our history, where every city is at the throat of every other, where every man has his spear. They're a peaceable folk, by and large.'

'Much good it may do them.'

They listened. As the evening darkened, so the fires in the city grew brighter, until they began to define its silhouette against the darkening plain. They could be heard, a distant roar, sometimes the deeper rumble as some building collapsed, its timbers burnt through.

'Druze reckons we'll collar maybe twenty thousand Kufr tonight,' Fornyx said, his tone lowered. 'That's twenty thousand more shoulders to the wheel. It worries me, Rictus, this reliance on Kufr sweat. Can't we just do the damn thing by ourselves? I don't like being followed by a train of slaves.'

'Parmenios needs labour, and there aren't enough of us to go around,' Rictus said with a grim smile. 'And we're not even in the Middle Empire yet. All we've seen and done so far, Fornyx, is the warm-up act before the real players take to the stage.'

'You think he'll come? The Great King?'

'He will.' Rictus gestured to the distant hell of the burning city. 'Corvus has made sure of that now.'

'Is that why he did it? And him so delicate about civilians and all. I wondered if the little bastard hadn't just had a tantrum.'

'I don't think there's anything he wouldn't shrink from, brother, if he thought it necessary.'

'I just wish he wasn't so damned cold-blooded about it, is all. He just gave the order, no quarter, and there we were hip-deep in gore, whilst up to now we've been treading on tip-toe through this country, and it as ripe and rich as a willing woman.'

'Darios defied him, after being offered good terms,

This had to happen. What's the matter, Fornyx, are you getting squeamish in your old age?'

'Maybe I am. And maybe you're not so high and mighty about killing as you once were.'

Rictus stared at him. 'What do you mean?'

'I mean he has you in his spell, like half the army. If he told you to advance on the gates of hell, you'd start planning the route.'

'That's horseshit and you know it.'

Fornyx shrugged, and tugged his worn scarlet cloak tighter about his shoulders. In the failing light, his narrow, pointed face seemed vulpine, especially when the distant flames caught his eyes.

The two men stood leaning on their spears atop a low tell midway between the burning city behind them and the head of the marching columns farther east. Further down the slope a body of spearmen, several centons strong, stood with their shields resting against their knees in the age-old posture of the waiting soldier. They, too, were cloaked in scarlet, and one among their number held a banner, somewhat ragged, and hard to make out with the fading of its colours. It might have carried the image of a canine head.

'Two days to the mountains, at this pace,' Fornyx said in a lighter tone. 'You've been through the Korash, of course.'

'I have.' It was in the Korash Mountains that the remnants of the Ten Thousand had finally fallen apart. They had split into competing factions, and then the winter had swooped in on them, and with the snow had come the Qaf.

It was in the Korash that Rictus of Isca had been voted leader of the Ten Thousand, except that there had been nowhere near ten thousand left of them at that point.

Rictus raised his head and looked at the high land to the east, that rampart of stone and snow, and something like a shiver went down his spine, the chill wind of his memories.

It would be different this time – he knew that. They were not a hunted band of starving men, but a mighty army, well-supplied and, above all, united.

And they would stay united.

'Corvus has been giving us orders for long enough now that you should know what he's about,' he said to Fornyx. 'It does no good questioning his intentions.'

I don't piss and moan in front of the men – you know that,' the other retorted. 'Only to a select friend or two, those who have known me for somewhat longer than Corvus has.' He walked away, descending the slope, using his spear as a staff.

Rictus almost called him back, but thought better of it. Fornyx would never do more than tolerate Corvus, and he could never think of the strange, brilliant youth who led them as his king. He was here because Rictus was here, and perhaps because he knew no other life.

There had been a time, back after Machran, when it might have been different. Andunnon was thriving; the quiet valley where Rictus had once made a home was risen from its ashes. Philemos lived there now, married to Rictus's beautiful daughter Rian, and there were children in the house by the river. His grandchildren.

But every time Rictus had tried to settle there, to forswear the scarlet, the image of his own wife had swamped the joy in the place. Poor, wretched Aise, the only woman Rictus had ever loved, whose life had ended in torment and suicide.

Because of him.

I have too many ghosts, he thought. Even Fornyx does not truly understand that.

He remembered his own father, as fine a man as he had ever known, slaughtered after the fall of Isca. Another home in flames around him.

For Rictus, the hearth of a good home brought back too many evil pictures to his mind. Whereas in the camp of an army he felt at ease, and when his soldiers died it was something expected, even fitting. And he knew that in this thing, he and Corvus were the same. The King of the Macht preferred a tent in the open to the halls of a palace, and he was never happier than when surrounded by comrades in arms, all of them bound to a single purpose – that dream of fire which had launched him on his extraordinary career.

It was this which drove him, as much as any lust for conquest. He was afraid of what life would be at the end of the final campaign.

That is the frightening thing, Rictus thought – to get to the end of it all, and find it meant nothing – any of it.

Better to keep marching.

For the older men in the army the very concept of a king was still strange, a Kufr idea. It helped that

Corvus had no sense of ceremony about him, and had acquired no airs or graces since his crowning in Machran all those years ago, in the wake of the great siege. He was as like to be found sharing rough wine with a bunch of conscripts in the evenings as he was to be in the royal tent.

But he was their king – that much he had earned – and Rictus, thinking on it, found himself almost surprised at the sense of protectiveness he felt towards the young man who had conquered them all.

I never had a son, and I will never have one, now. But if I could have had one like Corvus, I would have been content.

That night, they trooped into Corvus's great tent, stinking of smoke and blood, their feet blackened with soot and their faces smeared with it. The long trestle table was cleared of maps and pointers and inkwells and the paraphernalia of military planning, and the high officers of the army sat in their sweat-sodden scarlet chitons and passed jugs of wine up and down, drinking from them in turn like brothers at a wedding.

His Marshals, Corvus called them, and he had formalised the rank within the army. Each of these men commanded many thousands, and all of them had shed blood together. Each was as powerful as a king unto himself.

They were all Macht save one, all veterans of many battles, and yet most of them were young, though Corvus was still the youngest of them all.

Rictus sat with Fornyx on one side and the Kufr Ardashir on the other. Save for Valerian, who was now second of the Dogsheads, these were perhaps his closest friends, if one did not count the King himself. Fornyx had fought at Rictus's shoulder for going on twenty-five years, and Ardashir had saved his life at the siege of Machran.

Further along the table was dark Druze of the Igranians, who never seemed to lack a smile or a cup – usually with dice in it, not wine. He was fuller-faced than he had once been, but he could still run down a horse. It was his men who had been first into Ashdod after the walls were breached. The ensuing slaughter did not seem to have dimmed his humour.

One-eyed Demetrius, almost as old as Rictus, led the conscript spears, and was a harsh, unsmiling man who was one of the finest trainers of men Rictus had ever known. He could take a snivelling boy and make a soldier of him, in a process he had refined over the years into a model of efficiency and brutality. He was lame now, though, the legacy of a wound he had taken at the Haneikos River. He had stood in the water there and held the line while the river ran red around his knees.

Teresian sat beside him, an unlikely other half. He was a tall strawhead that a stranger might have said was Rictus's close kin, so similar did they seem. He commanded the Shieldbearers, those spearmen who had volunteered for the army and were in the ranks for life, because they found that the life suited them.

In a previous era they would have been mercenaries, but since the world had changed they were now part of the standing army that Corvus kept in being at all times. Before his coming, a city might have maintained a professional cadre of a centon or two to train its citizens. Since the Macht had acquired a king and become a nation, that had all changed. The Shieldbearers were kept ten thousand strong at all times. Even Rictus did not know if, in this, Corvus had been inspired by the original Ten Thousand, or by the Honai of the Great King.

The last of the Marshals was a small, round-shouldered but heavily muscled man with a bald head. He did not seem like a soldier, and in fact at one time he had been Corvus's chief scribe. This was Parmenios. He had a genius for building and engineering projects, and was even more ingenious at engineering their destruction. He was master of the siege train, which since Machran had become a permanent part of the army's establishment.

His sprawling kingdom embraced oxen, mules and slaves by the thousand, wagons, teamsters, metal-workers, tanners, rope-makers and angular machines of war, all built to his own designs, dismantled, and reassembled every time the army came across a walled city which insisted on shutting its gates in the face of the Macht. It was his rams, catapults and siege towers which had brought down the walls of Ashdod, and which were even now being taken down and repacked within their heavy long-bedded waggons for the advance into the mountains.

That completed the list of Corvus's high command. These men who sat at the long table sharing the wine led an army which dwarfed the one Corvus had used to unite the Macht, and more soldiers were pouring over the narrow straits between Idrios and Sinon every day.

There were no more wars in the Harukush. Corvus had left behind a garrison at Machran under Kassander, who had once been polemarch of that city's army. The cities still trained new classes of fighting men as they always had, but these now tramped east for a stint in the overseas army instead of remaining at home, where the temptation to foment mischief might prove too much. So it was that Corvus harnessed the energies of his people, and gave them outlet in an exotic, faraway campaign.

Fornyx, unwilling to grant Corvus credit for anything, had once told Rictus that they had created a great beast which had to keep on the move to survive, eating up the world as it went.

And even to himself, Rictus had to admit that there was some justice in that.

THE WINE RAN to their heads somewhat, for it had been a long day. Lower down the ranks, this would have produced laughter, ribaldry, meaningless boastful exchanges and fistfights, but here in Corvus's tent these men who led so many and had seen so much simply grew more thoughtful, spoke in quiet voices among themselves, and stared at the smoothworn wood of the table.

'Where in hell is he?' Fornyx asked.

'Where else?' Ardashir smiled, his long golden face

hollow-painted with smoke. 'He's out checking on the men one last time.'

'Or the horses,' Rictus added. Corvus liked to walk the horselines at the end of the day. He loved the animals as much as he loved his troops, and seemed to find in their company some kind of peace.

'He has half my men pushing up into the foothills. They'll be camping in the heather tonight,' Druze said. 'It's like Phobos is at his heels.'

'There are fifty thousand Kufr swarming the countryside like ants who've lost their hole,' Demetrius rumbled. 'We cannot advance while the city is still burning – it's chaos down there.'

Teresian yawned. 'Well, the men are happy. It was a rich city, and good pickings.'

'Only for those who got there first,' Fornyx told him. 'Your greedy bastards swiped the lot, Teresian, and the fires took the rest.'

'Fortune favours the light fingered,' Teresian said with a smile, and finding his jug almost empty, he poured the last red drops upon the tabletop. 'For Phobos. This was one of his days.'

'For Phobos,' Rictus repeated, and up and down the table they all, save Ardashir, repeated the phrase, faces suddenly sombre. The god of fear had been abroad today indeed. They had all seen the Kufr women who had thrown themselves from the walls rather than be captured.

The sentries at the tent entrance clapped their spearheads against their shields and stood straight. A lithe, boyish figure stood with the darkness behind him, the light of the lamps within the tent vanishing as it struck the black cuirass he wore. He touched one of the sentries on the shoulder, called him by name, nodded at the other as though they were old friends, and then strode into the tent.

At once, the assembled Marshals rose to their feet. The young man in the black armour stood still, and looked them up and down. He was lean as a snake, pale-skinned, with strange violet-coloured eyes that seemed almost to possess a light of their own. A silver circlet sat on his black hair, which shone with the lustre of a raven's wing. He looked underfed, tired, and there was an old scar at the corner of one eye.

'All hale and sound,' he said. 'Even you, Druze. You went over that wall so fast this morning I thought you must have had a bet on it.' Druze grinned.

'Rictus.' The newcomer tugged at the neck of his cuirass. 'Give me a hand, will you?'

Rictus helped him unfasten the wings of the cuirass and raise them, and then undid the black arrow-shaped clasp under the left arm. The cuirass came open and he lifted it, then set it upon its stand at the back of the tent.

Corvus stretched, and looked his Marshals up and down again. He seemed weary, and his strange eyes were sunk in orbits of purple flesh. But his high voice filled the tent.

'Well, don't tell me you've drunk all the wine, you dogs – Ardashir, go get the pages to bring in some more, for the love of God. And food, too – we're all famished.' Then he called after the tall

Kufr. 'No; water and towels. We'll wash first. We're not barbarians – not all of us, at any rate. Seat yourselves, brothers. It's been a long day, and it's not over yet, but we've seen off the worst of it.'

THE TENT CAME to life. More lamps were lit, the pages ran hither and thither, braziers were kindled and sticks of meat set to grill upon them. The Marshals washed and were brought clean linen and oil. Then the table was laid. Cups of glass appeared, platters of bread and fruit and a wheel of hard army cheese. More wine, the fresh green drink of the outer empire.

Corvus sat at the head of the table and it seemed that his presence among them had lifted some constraint. The tent filled with talk, and toasts were proposed, to the men, to the horses, to the wine itself. They did not speak of killing or burning or the sack of cities, but revelled in the fact that they were alive another day, with all their limbs and senses, and Antimone's wings were beating elsewhere.

How many years since Machran – six, seven? Rictus and Fornyx had been new to this table then, feeling their way through a certain amount of hostility and resentment, slightly bewildered by the strange-eyed boy at the head of it and his vast dreams. Now Rictus knew the men around the table as well as he had known anyone in his life. There was still friction there, even conflict from time to time, but they were all harnessed to the one chariot, and the charioteer handled them with consummate skill.

Fornyx was telling one of his inexhaustible filthy stories. Most they had all heard before, but every time there was a fresh embellishment which would set the company in a roar. Rictus peered up and down the table, studying his fellow marshals; and caught Corvus doing the same.

The King never truly rested. Even now, he was looking them over as a rider will examine his horse after a race. He was distracted only once, when a page came over and whispered in his ear. He smiled, said something inaudible back to the page, and touched him on the arm. The boy left the tent, aglow with the King's momentary attention.

Rictus had led men most of his life. He knew he was a fine commander, a born leader. But Corvus possessed a quality that soared above such prosaic gifts. He could inspire. He made men want to please him, to be like him. It was a marvel to watch, and even now Rictus felt privileged to be able to see it close-to.

Corvus caught his eye and smiled crookedly. After ostentatiously downing his first glass of wine at a gulp, he had shifted to water as was his wont, and he barely picked at his food. But he joined in the belly laughter as Fornyx came to the scabrous climax of his story, and thumped the table with as much vigour as the rest.

AT LAST, THE tide went out, the meal was done and the table cleared. Back came the maps and the pointers and the inkwells, and the sound sank again.

They could hear the shimmer of the cicadas outside, and the night-time noises of the camp around them. Thousands of men were bedding down in the dark about hundreds of campfires, and the hulk of Ashdod was sunk now to a sullen red glow in the distance. But despite the food and the fine wine and the new linen and the laughter, many in Corvus's tent could still taste smoke in their mouths.

The King rose, picked up an ivory pointer and let it range over a map of the country on both sides of the Korash Mountains. The men at the table became silent, watching.

The pointer traced the route from Sinon, where the army had crossed from the Harukush, to the Haneikos River, where they had destroyed the army of the satrap Darios, east across Gansakr to Ashdod, which now lay in ruin behind them, and so to the foothills of the mountains, and the pass of Irunshahr, where once the Ten Thousand had walked.

'Brothers,' Corvus said quietly, 'Here we stand. Two day's march from the high country, some two hundred pasangs from Irunshahr on the far side of the mountains. We have crossed the sea, established our base of operations at Sinon, and beaten back the first riposte from the enemy.' He paused.

'I do not expect any more organised resistance on the part of the empire for some time. We will be in the Land of the Rivers before the Great King can gather his forces.' He tapped the tip of the pointer lightly upon the inked vellum. 'That is where the decisive battle will take place – if we are fortunate.

'Common rumour has it that Ashurnan has already begun marching west to meet us, with the Honai and the imperial troops. This is the main effort of the enemy. What has gone before has been mere skirmishing.'

There were some murmurs at this, and Corvus smiled.

'We faced some fifty thousand men at the Haneikos River, the greatest army all of us save Rictus has ever seen. But I tell you, brothers, that when the Great King himself takes to the field, we will be fighting many times that. This Kufr has fought the Macht before – he saw what they could do, at Kunaksa, and again at Irunshahr. There are some things even old men do not forget.'

A rustle of amusement as Fornyx patted Rictus on the back solicitously.

'The battle of the Haneikos, and the sack of Ashdod, have shown him that we are not mere raiders, nor are we here to annex a few outlying provinces of his empire. He knows, now, that we mean to take all of it from him.'

'Are you so sure of that?' Fornyx asked.

'I have made sure of it. I sent him a letter.'

Exclamations up and down the table. Druze laughed aloud, incredulous.

'I have captured Darios, satrap of this province, alive. He survived both the Haneikos and the taking of Ashdod. I would hazard he is a resourceful man. So I have sent him east bearing a message for his master.'

Corvus tossed the ivory pointer onto the map with a flourish.

'I told Ashurnan that I have come for his crown, his cities, his palaces and all he possesses, and I will be satisfied with nothing less than all of it.'

'Phobos!' Fornyx cried. 'You don't do things by half, do you?'

'He will take us seriously now,' Corvus said, an odd gaiety creeping into his face.

'But it will slow him down, too,' Rictus mused. He stared closely at Corvus. 'You're betting he'll take longer now to complete his levies, to gather as many troops as he can; and that we'll be well beyond the mountains before he can intercept us.'

Corvus nodded. 'I do not mean to be hemmed in by rocks and stones when the thing happens. I want open country for the cavalry.'

'They say the Great King has cavalry too,' Ardashir said, with a raised eyebrow. 'The Arakosans are not to be taken lightly.'

'They damn near destroyed the Ten Thousand at Irunshahr,' Rictus said quietly.

'They are no match for the Companions. And besides, brothers, we will not be alone in this thing.'

At this, Corvus held up one long finger, then turned without explanation and left the tent.

The Marshals looked at one another. The silence was such that they could hear the spent charcoal shifting in the braziers.

'Can this be done?' Teresian asked at last.

'The whole empire – he wants the whole thing,' Fornyx said, shaking his head.

'It's what he has always wanted,' Ardashir told them. 'We knew it from the beginning, or should have.'

'It can be done,' bald Parmenios spoke up for the first time. 'He has me on it, evening up the odds.'

'Can you invent us fifty thousand new spearmen?' Demetrius growled. 'Because that's what it'll take. We don't have the force to do this, not here, not even with the reinforcements coming in. And that's to say nothing of the garrisons we'll have to leave behind on the way. The boy's a genius, but he's lifting his throat to the knife with this.'

'It can't be done,' Fornyx agreed. 'Rictus; you have his ear more than any of us. You must speak to him.'

Rictus's face did not change. He stared at the map on the tabletop, at the names thereon, where a generation before he had bled and killed and watched his friends die. At last he said, 'Let's hear him out.'

Corvus chose that moment to re-enter the tent. He was not alone. Beside him walked a strange, squat figure with oddly dark skin whose eyes had the same yellow gleam as a wolf's.

'Brothers,' he said. 'Let me introduce someone. This is Marcan, and he has come a long way to see us.' He raised a hand and a page came forward with a glass and jug. The boy spilled the wine as he poured it, and retreated again in some confusion. The newcomer flicked the liquid from his fingers, raised the glass to the astonished marshals and drained it, but tipped the last few drops out onto the floor of the tent.

'For Mot, lest he thirst,' he said in a deep, hard voice like the creak of timbers in a tunnel.

'He is Juthan,' Ardashir said, wide-eyed.

'I am Marcan of Junnan, of the free kingdom of Jutha,' the stranger declared. 'I give you greetings.'

The Juthan's skin was a deep grey, and he came up only to Corvus's shoulder, but was broad as the barrel of a horse. His hands were massive, shovel-like, and he had large, flat features. But there was humour in the yellow eyes, as he stood there and took in their open-mouthed stares.

'Marcan is an emissary of King Proxanon of Jutha,' Corvus said breezily. 'The Juthans have been at war with the empire since the time of the Ten Thousand. Now it has occurred to both Proxanon and myself that we could be of use to each other. Brothers, shift up and let us find a seat for our new ally.'

Seated, the Juthan was as tall as any one of them, so massive was his torso. It was as though some crag from the mountainside had been chiselled off and set in their midst.

'What does this mean?' Demetrius asked, his one eye blinking. He was kneading the half-healed wound in his thigh without realising it, bringing fresh blood to the dressing. Druze tapped his arm and he stopped.

'It means that we are not alone in opposing the Great King,' Corvus said. He set a hand on the Juthan's shoulder. It looked as small as a child's resting there.

'Proxanon offers us five full legions in support of our endeavours. That is fifty thousand spears, Demetrius, and the Juthan are hardy fighters, by every account I've ever heard.'

'They're not Macht,' Demetrius muttered.

The Juthan turned his head and looked at the one-eyed veteran. 'No, we are not Macht. But the Great King has been trying to destroy us for thirty years, and has failed. We must be doing something right.'

His Machtic was heavily accented, but almost perfect. Rictus found himself wondering where he had learned it.

Teresian spoke up. 'Corvus, my king, I am with you in this thing, to the death. But if we are to do it, then let us do it alone. War without allies is a simpler thing. And if these Juthan once betrayed the Great King, who is to say that they will not one day do the same to us?'

Marcan's yellow eyes flashed. He made as if to get up, but Corvus pressed on the Juthan's shoulder. He remained in his seat.

'The Juthan fight for their freedom,' he said plainly. 'And that is something the Great King has never been willing to give them – not after three decades of rebellion. What would they have to gain?'

'Times change,' Fornyx spoke up. 'No offence to our grey-skinned friend here, but what if Ashurnan changes his mind and decides to recognise his people's kingdom in return for their fucking us up the ass?'

'I wouldn't fuck you if yours was the last ass in the world,' the Juthan growled, and the table lit up with laughter. Druze thumped the wood.

'Well said! But Fornyx makes a good point. Do we have any guarantees beyond the word of this fellow's king, whom none of us have ever met?'

'We have conditions,' the Juthan said. He looked up at Corvus and the King nodded.

'We will fight only in the Land of the Rivers. We cannot leave our own borders undefended by following you clear over the Magron. And we claim the city of Tal Byrna, which currently belongs to the Tanis satrapy. It guards the approaches over the Abekai River, the underbelly of Jutha. With it in our possession, our country would be made secure.'

'We would do well to remember,' Corvus said, 'that while the Great King has not been able to subdue the Juthan, neither have they been able to win the war for their freedom. Our coming into the empire is their best bet to finish it, and obtain their independence once and for all.'

'And we also have something to take on trust,' the Juthan added. 'Who is to say that, the army of the Great King defeated, you will not take it into your heads to add Jutha to your possessions? It was once one of the richest and most productive satrapies of the empire.

'Your king has given his word that will not happen, and I believe him. You must believe our king's word also. The Juthan will fight by your side in the Middle Empire until the Great King is driven out. After that, you are on your own again.'

'Plainly spoken,' Rictus said, and all eyes turned to him. 'Let me speak plainly also. I admire your people. I saw them at Kunaksa – they have no lack of courage. But if you do betray the Macht, you must know what kind of enemy we are, and what kind of man leads us. It would not end well for your people. This is not a threat. I state it as mere fact.'

For the first time the Juthan dropped his eyes. 'I hear you,' he said. 'Your name is known in my country.'

Corvus and Rictus looked at one another across the table, and Rictus nodded minutely. Corvus patted Marcan's huge shoulder.

'I believe it is settled. You may go back to Proxanon, my friend, and tell him we welcome his help, and we embrace his people as brothers in our great enterprise.'

Marcan smiled strangely, shaking his head. 'I will send back the rest of my embassy, but I stay here with you.' He looked at Demetrius, whose one eye was still glowering.

'The King thought there might be a problem of trust between us at first, so I am to remain here to assuage your suspicions, as a hostage.'

'What's a single Juthan to him, more or less?' Demetrius snapped.

'This Juthan means more to him than most. King Proxanon is my father.'

EIGHT
MEMORIES IN THE STONE

Beneath their feet, the land changed, becoming stonier, a mangy pelt of grass giving way to upland heather, stretches of black mere, oozing peat bogs, and stone. More and more grey rock strewn across the earth and pushing up through it, the bones of the world uncovered, tawny with lichen, warm to the touch under the sun of early summer.

They left three morai, almost three thousand men, in and around the ruins of Ashdod, under orders to mop up any enemy remnants that might still be hiding out in the surrounding villages; and Parmenios dropped off part of his immense waggon train and a mora of his engineers to begin the work of reconstruction. Ashdod was to be rebuilt as the capital of the new Macht province, and this time her walls were to be reared up not in mud brick, but quarried stone. Five thousand of the newly enslaved citizens of the city would provide the labour for the undertaking. The rest of the army was moving on.

Into the mountains.

The Korash were not the Harukush, and the pass that ran through them from Ashdod to Irunshahr was wide enough for an army to take in normal marching order. Perhaps forty thousand fighting men followed the meandering gash through the peaks, their way cleared by the tireless Parmenios and his work gangs, both slave and free. Druze's Igranians went ahead to reconnoitre the route, and on the flanks of the marching columns Ardashir's Companion Cavalry picked their way, the Kefren riders caching their lances with the baggage train, and stringing their great recurved compound bows instead.

It was summer, but there was still snow in blinding fields across the pass, some of it knee deep. And as the year warmed, so the ice higher up the slopes melted, and the men below had to keep their eyes open for sudden avalanches.

But they were Macht, most of whom had been weaned in the shadow of the Harukush. They were not starving, pursued and hauling waggonloads of wounded, as the Ten Thousand had been, fleeing in the opposite direction thirty years before.

Rictus knew this. And he kept to himself the spasm of helpless memory which had struck him as they entered the mountains.

They had been less than a week on the High Road, and were making good time, when it began to snow. It was no winter blizzard, but a fine-skeined drizzle of grainy snowflakes that dotted the men and melted, and greyed out the way ahead.

The world was blank, nothing more than the stones underfoot and the steam of the straining men in front. Voices were lowered, as if some primitive instinct had kicked in, and even the progress of the tens of thousands of men and beasts who trailed through the mountain pass for pasangs became subdued as the snow fell on the sounds and muffled everything.

But Rictus, wiping his eyes as they watered, thought he saw something out in the snow.

He rode a horse from time to time now, an animal as quiet and biddable as the livery-master could find, and he kicked it into an unwilling trot, doubling the column, looking for Corvus.

The King was never in the same place for long. Though his baggage and his personal bodyguards might keep rigidly to their allotted positions on the march, he travelled up and down throughout the day, on foot and on his big black Niseian, dismounting to talk to the men and their officers, galloping upslope to check on Ardashir and his flanking cavalry, or forging ahead to meet with Druze.

A conscript with blistered feet, finding the going hard, might look up to find the King marching beside him, asking after his health, wanting to know his name and where he hailed from. A few minutes' talk, and then the King would be off again, but the footsore soldier would bask in the glory of his moment, envied by his comrades, forgetting his weariness, and willing now to charge mountains for the strange young man who led them.

Thus Rictus found Corvus. He was marching along with a file of Demetrius's newest recruits, the ones who had been sent east to fill in the gaps after the Haneikos battle. These youngsters had a thin time of it, for they were green as grass and the only men in the army who had not yet been blooded in a great fight. But Corvus was strolling alongside them now, as earnest in talk as if they were his oldest veterans. He told them one of Fornyx's dirty stories, which set up a roar for yards up and down the files. He did not tell it as well as Fornyx, and Rictus was not even sure he found it amusing himself, but he told it well, with the skill of a natural mimic.

The boy could have been an actor, if all else had failed, Rictus thought.

Corvus looked up at the snowbitten red cloak on the horse, raised a hand. 'It's my old warhorse,' he cried, 'on his old warhorse. Phobos, Rictus, can't you let us find you something better to ride than that nag?'

'She suits me well enough. Corvus, a word, if I might.'

Corvus mounted, raised a hand to the farewells of the grinning spearmen who a half hour before had been glum as owls, and he and Rictus trotted upslope, into the falling snow.

'I may have seen something. We're well into the mountains now, and this is the place for them.'

'Qaf?'

Rictus nodded. Corvus brightened. 'What a wonder that would be – like seeing a myth made flesh.'

'I'd rather we saw none of them,' Rictus said. 'Besides, they may not attempt anything against so great a host.'

'The officers are forewarned, which is more than you were,' Corvus said, gripping the older man's arm a moment. 'Rictus, don't worry!'

'A hazard of advancing years; one begins to worry about everything.'

THEY WENT INTO camp that night as usual, the men in concentric rings with their feet to the flames of the campfires – campfires which were appreciably smaller than they had been at the outset of the march, for the only wood they could burn now was that which they had brought with them in the waggons.

The horselines were heavily guarded, and on the King's orders the sentries were doubled. Such precautions would normally have elicited some groaning from the veterans, but they, too had glimpsed unsettling sights in the quietly falling snow throughout the day, and they turned to with a will.

Corvus himself did not seem to sleep these days at all, and he did not spend the night in his tent, but walked the camp ceaselessly all through the dark hours, checking with the guards, running the orderly officers ragged.

Finally, he joined Rictus and Fornyx at the Dogheads' lines, and the three of them walked out beyond the camp and its firelight, driven by some impulse they could not define. They stood in the dark, listening.

But the night was silent. Even what wind could be heard was far off, up in the peaks above their heads, keening like a new widow. The snow fell steadily in the darkness, the flakes fattening, blanking out the world and hiding the stars utterly.

'A night like this,' Corvus said in a low voice, 'feels like a moment before the making of the world. Not a light, not a sound. Nothing but the cold dark and the stone. It is as though we were at the beginning of all things.'

'Or the end,' Fornyx said, with a gravity quite unlike him. 'Antimone is close tonight, brothers – can you not feel it? I swear I can hear the beat of her black wings when I close my eyes.'

Something moved, out in the dark, a rattle of stone. They went very still, save that Rictus and Fornyx lowered their spears in slow, graceful arcs until the aichmes pointed outward. Corvus did not twitch a muscle. He was rapt, as if listening to a song.

And then they saw it. Taller than a man, with two lights blue as sapphire for eyes. It was paler than the mottled stones behind it, and were it not for the eyes it might have been nothing more than a squared-off crag itself. It was watching them, not five spear-lengths away. Rictus found his own heart high in his throat, thumping hard and fast; with his mouth open he could hear the blood going through it, a sound like the panting of a dog.

And then it was gone. The lights went out as it turned and unhurriedly picked its way upslope, not dislodging so much as a pebble now, in its passing. Fornyx advanced as though in a trance, spear still levelled, but Corvus held him back.

'Let it be. It did not come to fight. Not this time.'

IN THE MORNING it seemed more than half like a dream to Rictus. He woke to find Valerian trying to blow life into the grey coals of last night's fire, his scarred lips pursed like the neck of a drawstring bag as he blew red life into the ash. When a flame had licked up, Rictus threw aside his cloak and the fine covering of snow which had stiffened it, and sat hunkered and shivering, aching, feeling as old as he ever had in his life.

'What's the matter with your tent?' Valerian asked, passing him the wineskin. 'Was there a mouse?' He grinned, the lopsided ruin of his face making the gesture singularly sweet.

'The old need less sleep than you think,' Rictus said, tossing the skin back to him.

'There were things in the dark last night. Men all along the column saw them. It's the talk of the camp.'

'The camp always has something to yap about,' Rictus said, stifling a groan as he rose to his feet and his limbs straightened.

But he felt better, for some reason. The sense of

dread that had been with him ever since the army had entered the mountains was gone. It was as though an old nightmare had been explained away.

THERE WERE NO more sightings in the night. The army continued on its way unmolested for several more days, until one morning there was a shout up at the van of the column, and word was sent down that Rictus was to go forward at once.

He pushed the patient mare hard, her unshod hoofs crunching in the frostbitten ground, and one of Druze's Igranians met him near the head of the army, panting, his drepana resting on one shoulder. He pointed eastwards, to where a knot of horsemen and infantry were gathered together over a mound of scree.

'Corvus wants you, chief. Seems they've found something.'

The King was standing peering at something he held in his hands. Druze was beside him, and tall Ardashir, who felt the cold more than most, being a Kufr, and was almost unrecognisable in his layered furs.

'What is it?' Rictus asked, dismounting stiffly.

Corvus did not speak, but handed him a rusted shard of iron, heavy to the touch, half as long as a man's forearm.

It was an aichme, an iron spearhead of Macht design.

And looking at the oval-shaped mound of rubble and stone, Rictus suddenly realised.

This was a burial mound.

His fists tightened a moment on the spearhead. So powerful was the memory that he saw other men standing there with him: young Phinero, and bald Whistler, who had been members of Phiron's Hounds, the light infantry of the Ten Thousand. Other faces jockeyed for position also. So little had the surroundings changed in thirty years that for an insane second Rictus thought he was about to see Jason himself come striding up the slope to join them.

He dropped the aichme as though it burned.

'What happened here?' Druze asked, dark face puzzled. 'Who did you fight?'

'The things in the night,' Corvus answered him. 'Didn't you ever read the story, Druze? The Qaf attacked them here, after the Ten Thousand split up. Rictus was voted warleader, but a fool called Aristos took a disaffected few hundred and split off from the main body. The Qaf slaughtered them, but they made it to the coast too.'

Rictus caught the King's eye. Aristos had survived, long enough to kill Corvus's father, on the very shores of the sea they had marched so far to reach, almost within sight of home.

'We're wasting daylight, my king,' he said, as harsh as an old crow. 'We must get moving.'

He mounted his horse, wincing at the click of pain in his knees. Corvus continued to watch him.

'Wherever we travel, Rictus, death walks before us. We all go into the dark together.'

'With the Curse of God on our backs,' Rictus whispered. Then he tugged hard on the reins and turned the long-suffering mare away, setting her face towards the east. Towards yet more memories.

EIGHTEEN DAYS AFTER entering the Korash Mountains, runners from Druze came sprinting back down the column, hallooing as they came. The slow-trudging infantry and even slower baggage train ground on for hours before they could see with their own eyes what had so excited those at the forefront of the army.

Green country, opening out before them like some dream of summer.

The mountains withdrew, sinking into the rich warm earth of Pleninash, the Land of the Rivers. From the commanding heights of the foothills a man might see hundreds of pasangs across the plains below, the sun glinting on the gleam of water everywhere, a warmth in the air unknown even in the Kufr lands west of the mountains. There was no breeze from the sea here to leaven the rising heat of the season. There would never be snow, nor even a hard frost in this green country.

For the first time, the men in the army felt that they had truly entered a foreign land, where even the taste of the air in the mouth was strange, and the earth smelled of something else. Some of the Macht, small-farmers in a previous life, bent and grasped the soil of this new place in handfuls, as though it were somehow different from that they had known before.

And as the army spread out to the east, the single vast column splitting up into half a dozen smaller ones, so men hurriedly doffed the furs and blankets they had worn on the slow march through the high country hitherto. There was a warmth in the air here, though they were still in the uplands, and there was heather underfoot. They could sense the heat of the approaching summer, and wondered at the flat verdant world before them, already shimmering in the heat and alive with a chorus of insects.

Thus did the host of King Corvus of the Macht enter the Middle Empire, in the forty-first year of the reign of the Great King Ashurnan.

NINE
DANCE OF ARMIES

THEY LINED UP around the walls of Irunshahr in full battle array, deliberately taking their time. The reasons for this were manifold. Firstly, it had been three weeks or more since a single man in the army had done any drill, and the raggedness of their formations as they took up position around the upland fortress threw Corvus into a white-lipped fury.

He never raised his voice when he was angry – only when it suited him to appear so. But when he spoke quietly, and his eyes flashed and the blood had left his already pale face, then his officers knew that he was in earnest.

So the men trudged into position meekly, shouted at by centurions whose faces were as scarlet as their cloaks, cursed for useless idle sons of whores. But it was the sight of their young king, sitting silent on his black horse and watching them without a single word of disapprobation, that truly unnerved them. They began to step more lively after that, to leave behind the 'mountain shuffle,' to straighten their backs and hold their spears tight against their bodies, so that, as one centurion put it, the weapons did not wave around like a thicket of limp pricks.

But the protracted deployment of the army suited Corvus's purposes for two more reasons. Firstly, because the walls of Irunshahr, tall, grey and forbidding, were now lined with thousands of the fortress-city's inhabitants, and the spectacle of tens of thousands of Macht on the ridges below would do wonders for their attitude.

And lastly, Parmenios had set up shop on a convenient hill not two pasangs from the city gate, and was busy assembling some of his infernal machines to impress the defenders further with the hopelessness of their plight.

Corvus meant to take Irunshahr, one way or another, for it was the gateway to the west, and it guarded their lines of communication with the Macht homeland. Those lines were long and frayed enough without leaving the city intact and untaken to worry them finer still.

Once Parmenios had finished his arcane work, his machines were hauled and pushed by a small army of Kufr slaves up to the back of the Macht lines. His own skilled engineers then went to work with a will, and many was the conscript spearmen who looked to his rear in some consternation as he stood in file, wondering what the angular timber and iron machines behind him were about to do.

The smell of burning pitch carried over the breeze, drifting across the ranks of the army. The warhorses of the Companions caught the familiar reek and began to prance and sweat in their formation, while the Kefren riders soothed them in their own language.

The Companions were up front, where the Niseians and their riders could be clearly seen. They had donned their best battle armour, cuirasses of leather and layered linen studded with bronze scales and worked with lapis lazuli and black enamel. Their horsehair crests moved idly in the warm air. They were a magnificent sight, clad in their red cloaks despite the warmth of the day, and with their lances holstered in stirrup-cups, every shaft carrying a newly tied pennon.

'Ardashir's lot have dressed for the occasion,' Fornyx said to Rictus as they stood together a few paces in front of the Dogsheads. 'Wonder what their Kufr will make of our Kufr.'

The thought had occurred to every Macht in the army. The Companions had won the day at the Haneikos, but had been kept aside at the sack of Ashdod. They loved Corvus to a man, and Rictus was fully convinced they would follow him anywhere, but Fornyx spoke his thoughts for him when he said; 'Ever wonder what they would do if Corvus were not here to lead them?'

What would any of us do? Rictus wondered silently. And he put the thought away, as something unlucky.

There was a swooping noise, then a sharp *crack* as one of the catapults at the back of the line was loosed. The long arm of the contraption swept through half a circle, and launched into the air a globe of fire which soared high across the blue sky. It cleared the walls of the city with ease and disappeared into the buildings on the hill behind. A strange noise, like a wail, passed over the people on the walls. And then Corvus rode forward with a green branch in his hand, accompanied only by Ardashir.

'I want to hear this,' Rictus said, and began to march towards the walls also. Fornyx joined them, and they were a fearsome looking pair, both clad in Antimone's Gift, both red-cloaked, wearing the close helm with its transverse crest which transformed a man's face into a fearsome anonymous mask, both bearing their shields with the raven sigil painted upon them.

They stopped when they could hear Ardashir's voice shout loud and clear up to the figures on the walls. He was speaking in Kefren, of which Fornyx knew nothing and Rictus only a few words, and the two men looked at one another and laughed at their own simplicity.

There was an exchange. Corvus began to speak, in Kefren as perfect as Ardashir's, and Rictus thought he could almost feel the army behind him shiver at the sight of their king speaking Kufr like a native.

'One day that chicken will come home to roost,' Fornyx muttered, frowning.

The exchange went on for some minutes, and it was punctuated by the agonised screeching of leather and wood being wound tight on spoked pulleys, as Parmenios's crews began to methodically cock back and load the dozens of catapults reared up in a long line behind the fighting men. The smell of burning tar grew, and in the ranks of the Companions the big Niseians neighed and stamped and blew through their noses, impatient to be let loose, to be allowed to carry out what they had been bred and trained to do.

Then there was a different sound, a heavy rumble. Almost, Rictus thought he could feel it as a vibration in the very ground beneath his feet.

The gates of Irunshahr, massive cliffs of green bronze, began to grind open.

As they did, the men of the army clashed their spears against their brazen shields and let out a deep-throated cheer.

'The little bugger has done it again,' Fornyx said. He doffed his helm, wiped his sweat-gleamed hair back from his forehead and shook his head ruefully.

'He didn't sleep for a week after Ashdod,' Rictus said. 'He won't let that kind of thing happen again if he can help it.' And he was profoundly glad in his own heart. A battle in the open was one thing, where men squared off against their enemies in open war; but the taking of a city was a nightmare he had experienced too many times. His home city, Isca, had died in front of his own eyes, and at the fall of Machran he had seen the worst that men could do to one another. And to the innocents that got in the way.

Fornyx clapped him on the arm. 'Who knows? We may sleep under a roof tonight, Rictus, with a cup of real wine in our hands instead of that army piss. Things are looking up!'

There was indeed a roof for them that night, and as grand a one as could be imagined. There were perhaps fifty thousand people in Irunshahr, but they were outnumbered by those who now camped outside the walls. All day the carts and waggons and pack animals had gone back and forth between the fortress city and the tented town below it. Irunshahr was feeding Corvus's army with what remained in the city granaries at the end of spring, and it was a startling amount.

In an excess of relief, perhaps, at the unexpectedly civilised behaviour of the Macht troops, the governor of Irunshahr, Gosht, had bade his people raid their larders to placate the invaders. The Macht had not eaten so well since they had left the shores of the sea. Despite the time of year, Irunshahr's hinterland had already seen one harvest gathered in, and if Bel were kind would see another before the summer was out. Such was the richness of the Middle Empire, and the Macht, used to the hardscrabble farming of their own country, marvelled at it.

The city was not part of any satrapy, but because of its strategic importance had been allotted a governor instead, and stood independent of the lowland provinces. From its gates the Imperial road ran all the way to the Magron Mountains in the far east, and from there through to Ashur itself, capital of the world.

The reason for the city's sudden capitulation became clear as the Macht moved in to survey the place and establish a garrison. There were no more trained soldiers within the entire circuit of the walls than in the average town back home. Perhaps a centon of Gosht's personal guard remained. The rest had been commandeered by Darios and taken west. They had died at the Haneikos and at Ashdod. Thus, for Irunshahr, surrender had been the only sensible option, for the levy of the Great King had by all accounts and rumours not yet crossed the Magron, and was still weeks away.

That night, the marshals of the army dined in the great hall of the governor, and somewhat to their astonishment, Gosht himself was invited by Corvus to attend. He sat at the King's right hand, in the place of honour, an elderly Kefre with almost translucent, golden skin, and a long, pointed beard dyed deep red.

It was a stilted meal. Corvus and Ardashir tried to make conversation in the kindliest way with the old Kefre, but he replied in monosyllables and merely stared up and down the long table at the assembled Macht generals and their strange king, in a mixture of bafflement and fear. When his eye alighted upon Marcan, the Juthan, a light of real hatred crept into it. Finally he excused himself and rose, the King rising with him, as solicitous as if Gosht had been an elderly uncle. The old Kefre recoiled from Corvus's touch instinctively, as a man will pull his hand back from a flame, and was seen out of the vast, echoing hall by two of his attendants, round-eyed *hufsan* almost as bewildered as he.

'You may be pushing courtesy too far,' Ardashir said to Corvus. 'You scared the old fellow half to death – I think he expected to be poisoned, or stabbed to death where he sat.'

Corvus was buried in thought, tossing an empty wine cup hand to hand and catching it with that quicksilver grace unique to him. 'We shall have to leave a sizeable garrison here,' he said absently, and tossed the cup to Druze, who whipped it out of the air and commenced to fill it.

There were no pages attending the diners tonight; Corvus had given them all leave to roam the city as they might. Only a few *hufsan* slaves had attended the meal, and they had been dismissed when the governor left. The marshals could lean back in their high-backed chairs and stare at the ornate ceiling, finger the silver knives and plates thoughtfully, and generally gape their fill at the way in which a governor of the empire lived. Their chairs were upholstered in silk, which it seemed a crime to sit upon, and the carpet beneath them was circular, as brightly beautiful as a sunrise. All about the walls hung tapestries of the same calibre, and wonderfully made weapons too beautiful to ever take to war.

'Ashdod was a pigsty compared to this,' Teresian said, too taken aback even for avarice.

'Don't get over excited,' Fornyx told him. 'We've checked the treasury; Darios stripped it bare before he went west. What was left, we captured at the Haneikos in his paychests.'

'I dare say there's more secreted here and there,' Teresian said, smirking.

The King slammed his cup down on the table, startling them. 'This city is mine now, and everything in it. Anyone who steals within these walls steals from me, and will be dealt with accordingly.' In a softer tone, he said, 'Besides, you're rich enough Teresian. What are you doing, saving up to be King?'

There was laughter up and down the table, though it had an uneasy edge.

'As I said,' he went on in a quieter tone, 'This city will require a real garrison. It guards the road any reinforcements will have to take from the Harukush. And the mountain pass will have to be patrolled.'

'With Irunshahr in your hands, you also guard the northern flank of Jutha,' Marcan spoke up, his bass deep enough to tremble the cups. The men at the table looked at him. He did not speak much, but he was often there, at the corner of things. Corvus did not seem to mind that the Juthan sometimes joined them at table, even when they were discussing strategy. Rictus had tried to bring up the subject with Corvus, but the King had just laughed.

'My father's legions will be on the march by now. It is good that you have a secure base here in Pleninash. The news will travel fast.'

'I look forward to the day when your people and mine fight together, Marcan,' Corvus said, with that genuine smile which charmed so many. It was impossible to see if the yellow-eyed Juthan was seduced by it. One might as well have smiled at a stone.

'Who do we leave here?' Fornyx asked.

'I'll think of someone – not you, Fornyx – we all know you love the Kufr too much.'

'Best make sure you can trust the beggar, whoever he is. The man who commands this city has his foot on our neck.'

'I will think of someone,' Corvus repeated, an edge in his voice. Fornyx was one of the few people he had never charmed.

'Rictus, I want you to ride out with Ardashir in the morning. He's taking a mounted patrol east along the Imperial Road, to get a feel for the route and look out for the enemy.'

'Me? I can barely sit a horse,' Rictus said, surprised.

'You sit it better than you think,' Corvus told him. 'And I do not expect you to have to charge into battle, brother. I want someone with Ardashir who has seen this country before.'

'But he's Kefren – what does he need me for?'

Ardashir smiled. 'Rictus, I may be Kefren, but this is my first foray east of the Korash. I know as much about the Land Between the Rivers as does Fornyx, or any of the rest of us.'

'My knowledge is thirty years old.'

'The empire does not change much from year to year.' This was Marcan. 'I can sit a mule, Corvus. May I join them? I know something of this country also.'

The King looked at the blank grey face of the yellow-eyed Juthan, his hostage.

'A capital idea,' he said at last, and raised his glass. He ignored the looks the Macht marshals darted up and down the table.

* * *

A HAZE ROSE over the land south of Irunshahr, a fug of woodsmoke, excrement, rising sweat, cooking smells, and snoring men. The miasma of an army. It was as familiar to Rictus as the smell of bread to a baker.

The patrol set off early, picking their way through the tented city beyond the walls with the sun rising in their faces, a squat disc of red smeared with cloud, whose rise could be tracked with the eye if one stood still for a few minutes to watch. The Juthan stared at it with his livid eyes as his mule followed the tall rump of the Niseian in front.

Rictus rode beside him, as they were equally uncomfortable on horseback. But if the tall Kefren on their mighty horses were amused by the sight of the odd pair, they did not show it. Rictus was something of a legend in the army, and it was well known that the King considered him his second in command. Also, he was a cursebearer, and anyone who bore one of the black cuirasses inspired a certain amount of awe in the ranks.

Marcan had dropped his reins and let the mule pick its way according to its own good sense. He raised his arms to the rising sun, closed his eyes, and said something in a hard, clicking language Rictus had never heard before.

'The Kefren worship Bel, the sun, the renewer,' he said to Rictus's curious look. 'But the Juthan revere Mot. The Kefren would have us believe he is the god of blight and sickness and disease. But there can be no life, unless death has gone before. We worship Mot as the power which brings the one true end to all of existence. That is the final truth – we all die. We cannot say who or what will be born. Therefore Mot is the centre of life itself. All that goes before death is chaos.'

'We worship Antimone, goddess of pity and death,' Rictus said. 'She does not protect us, but she takes us to her when we die, and brings us to God, and intercedes for us.'

'The Juthan and the Macht are more similar than you think,' Marcan said. 'My grandfather's best friend was a Macht general, Vorus, who in this very place let our people go free from a slavery they had known for untold centuries. We venerate his name. For that reason, as well as all the others, we will fight with you. It is a debt worth repaying.'

Turning, Rictus found the Juthan watching him.

'I know who you are,' Marcan said. 'Your name is also known to my people.'

'Your people have long memories,' Rictus grunted.

'As long as the stone, we say. We were a nation of slaves, and slaves forget little.'

Rictus had meant to make some quip about the fifty thousand spearmen, but something in the dignified mien of the Juthan stopped him. To the average Macht, the Juthan and the Kefren were all Kufr, all inferior foreigners, barbarians. He had never realised quite how unalike they were. Not just physically, but in the very stuff of their thoughts.

The sun rose, the heat grew. The patrol continued down the Imperial Road as though they were ordinary citizens of the empire about their business, and indeed, save for Rictus, they did not look out of place.

Once they were twenty pasangs from Irunshahr, the abandoned, bereft look of the countryside was ameliorated by their first sight of the inhabitants. They began to see *hufsan* farmers guiding buffalo through waterlogged fields. Others were knee deep in the brown water, planting seedlings one by one. On higher ground there was wheat and barley, tall and green but with the gold already coming into it. And there were orchards of pomegranates, apples, oranges and scented lemons, each as large as Rictus's fist.

It was an abundance, a seething, thriving, growing world. The irrigation channels were surrounded by wild irises and alive with frogs, and white egrets pattered through the lowland like flags planted in the green-tipped mud. And everywhere the sliding rattle of cicadas, crickets, the belching of toads, and the darting iridescent brilliance of dragonflies.

'They have waystations on the Imperial Road,' Rictus called forward to Ardashir, 'and each has a garrison.'

'We are fifty,' the Kefre said, turning in the saddle and setting his knee on his horse's rump. 'It will not even be sport, Rictus.'

Soon after, one of the waystations appeared out of the stubborn mist creeping along the irrigation embankments. It was a massive square tower of fired brick which rose out of the sodden fields beside the road and was surrounded by smaller blockhouses.

There were fenced-in paddocks on all sides, and in them every manner of beast which had ever been trained to bear a burden.

The road itself was clogged by many carts, some little more than two-wheeled barrows, others grander, with gaily painted canopies of linen and leather. And there were several tall-sided waggons hitched to camels that looked more bored than any creature had a right to be.

In the midst of this scrum of vehicles and beasts, a crowd of Kufr, both Kefren and *hufsan*, were standing arguing, gesticulating and jumping up and down in fury. Perhaps a dozen armed guards were blocking the road with wide-bladed halberds, and their officer was waving a scimitar that glittered white in the sun, and shouting himself hoarse at the crowd.

Ardashir turned back to Rictus again, and he was laughing. 'Perhaps we can be of help, eh, Rictus?'

Rictus muttered. He had no spear, only a drepana, and he felt unsafe and ill at ease on the horse. Beside him, Marcan reached back of his saddle and with a hissing sound drew forth a long white knife, as wide as a child's wrist. 'You miss your spear,' he said to Rictus. 'For me it is the weapon of my people I would have here, the *akson*. It is not fitting for a man to fight with a knife.'

'Or on a damned horse,' Rictus muttered. The cavalcade of Kefren riders on the massive Niseians surged past them. 'Lances!' Ardashir called out in his clear voice, and they cantered forward in twos with the long weapons pointing at the ground. The sun set their magnificently caparisoned armour alight; they looked almost too glorious to be warlike, but the crowd bickering in the roadway ahead did not seem to have any notion of the threat. Nor did the officer who was haranguing them.

Rictus slid off his horse and at once felt better, though his view was reduced. Marcan stood beside him; the squat Juthan came barely to his breastbone.

'He's telling them to clear the roadway,' Marcan said, scratching one cheek with the point of the knife. 'This is a strange way to fight a war.'

'I have sometimes thought the Kefren do not take war seriously enough,' Rictus admitted.

But then there was a scream. Rictus saw the white flash of a blade, and somehow the Kefren officer was down, and Ardashir's troopers were barrelling forward with lances levelled. The crowd in the road exploded across the fields, and there was blood in the dust, the clang of steel on steel. Rictus's mare whinnied in alarm and he soothed the beast by slapping it hard on the head with the flat of his sword.

Then it was over. Rictus and Marcan walked down the road like men arriving late at a funeral. There was not much to see, but for a litter of bodies skewed across the stone-slabbed road, and a host of abandoned vehicles, from one of which came the sound of a crying baby.

Ardashir was on foot, his horse standing unconcernedly beside him. The other troopers had dismounted, exchanged their lances for bows, and were fanning out through the little knot of buildings while a few of their number did duty as horse-holders. Ardashir rose from one of the bodies grim-faced.

'Damn fool. He had no need to start that. I would have disarmed them and let them go – what's a dozen more soldiers to us now?'

Rictus looked down on the dead Kefre. He was young, and though Rictus had never fully admitted this to himself, he thought that, like all high-caste Kefren, he could have been Ardashir's brother. The features of the race seemed all so alike. To a Macht, at least.

'He was armed, he had his blade drawn. It was honourable enough,' he said, gruffly. Better than being trampled to death in the middle of a phalanx, at any rate.

'Chief.' One of Ardashir's men had emerged from the waystation tower. 'There are a lot of documents in here, but not much else. What shall we do, fire the place?'

Ardashir's eyes cleared. 'Bring the papers, round up the horses and cattle, and then torch it. There's nothing to discover here. If the Great King's army is in the Middle Empire, then it's nowhere near us. These were just *hufsan* customs officials, checking over a caravan which was still heading west.'

He turned to Rictus. 'Customs officials. Bel's blood, Rictus; do they even know what's going on in this country?'

'They know,' Marcan broke in sombrely. 'The wheels take a time to set turning, that's all. Once the empire sets things in motion, it comes down on you with the weight of a mountain. You have not yet felt that power, but it will come upon you, as sure as the rising of the moons.' He gestured at the endless shimmering plains to the east.

'This wide country will drink a river of blood, your people's and mine, before the thing is done. Do not be impatient for that time to begin.'

TEN
LEARNING ASURIAN

RAKHSAR KNELT IN the noisome water of the ditch and breathed softly through his mouth, ignoring the mosquitoes whining about his face. Up ahead the road was clear, and the only light was that of a single torch left guttering in a sconce on the waystation wall, with moths as big as sparrows fluttering around it.

He looked up. Firghe, moon of patience, was setting, and the pale glow of Anande had begun to rise in the north-east. All across the sky between the two moons the stars blazed in a welter of spangled lights. He felt he had been staring at stars, at the moons, at the black night sky, for a long time. He could barely think of walking upright and unafraid under the sun.

I am still here, he thought. I have made it this far, and I am my father's son.

He brought the pommel of the scimitar to his swollen lips and sucked gently on it. He was very thirsty, for they had lain up all day, and the insects of the Bekai River valley had sucked them dry. The stinking water of the ditches had not yet tempted him, unlike Roshana.

He turned, his eyes a gleam of violet light in the dark, and beckoned to the deeper shadow of the overgrown ditch. Tall irises rose on both sides, creating a space almost as good as a tunnel, but he had grown to hate their fragrance with a passion. If ever he sat on a throne, his palace would not have an iris within ten pasangs of it.

The boy splashed to his side first, his dark skin a perfect camouflage in the night, the same colour as sun-paled mud.

'You know what to do,' Rakhsar said, and Kurun nodded. He climbed out of the ditch and padded across the road, a dark shape against the dust. Then he ran noiselessly up to the waystation, a passing shadow, no more.

Roshana was beside him now, breathing heavily, her face darkened with smeared filth. He touched her cheek gently, and felt the swollen stipple of bites ringing her eyes. Behind her the looming hulk of Ushau rose up in the ditch like some child's monster.

'Make sure she does not stumble,' Rakhsar said in a sharp hiss to the giant *hufsan*, and Ushau nodded.

The shadow reappeared at the side of the nearest blockhouse, and waved.

'Time to go,' Rakhsar said in a whisper, and he laboured out of the ditch. He was barefoot, for the muck had sucked the footwear off all of them days ago, and as he stood upon the roadway the familiar agony of his blisters began to throb again.

Slippers! He thought. And I once considered myself wise in the world. We knew nothing.

Roshana was hauled out of the ditch by Ushau, protesting feebly. She could barely take her own weight, and at an impatient gesture from Rakhsar the big *hufsan* scooped her up in his arms as he had Kurun in the early days of their flight. The three of them hobbled and hopped across the road, Rakhsar spitting with pain and anger, the scimitar a carmine gleam in the last light of the red moon.

A horse ruckled softly down its nose in the shadow behind the blockhouse. Kurun was already lifting a halter from a peg on the wall. They heard laughter within, and there was the yellow gleam of a lamp under the ill-fitting wooden door.

The door opened, and the light was like a white, silent explosion in the night, so accustomed had Rakhsar's eyes become to the dark.

'Two horses!' he hissed to Kurun, and then he moved in with a strange, light-hearted happiness, the scimitar held two-handed, the blade resting on his right shoulder.

A dark silhouette in the doorway, and the beginnings of a shout, felt as much as heard. Rakhsar swung the sword with all the pent-up fury of the day, and the beautifully chased blade took the figure in the doorway at the collarbone.

The blade went through flesh and bone as it had been crafted to do, and the superlative steel continued the arc, through the ribs and lights, until it was free again. The shape in the doorway fell in two cleanly sliced pieces. Something akin to laughter gurgled in Rakhsar's throat. He recovered, as the best weapons-masters in the empire had taught him to do, and when the second *hufsan* came charging out of the lamplight he skewered him as cleanly as a frog on a grillspike.

Again, recover. The doorway was blocked with bodies, or parts of them, and even the dust could not swallow up the slick ropes of clotting gore sliding out of the bodies like shit from a dysenteric sphincter.

'Rakhsar!' it was Roshana's voice, hoarse and low.

He stepped backwards. The night was ruined with shouting now, and the red moon had set. Anande, that the Macht named Phobos, moon of fear, had risen, and Rakhsar stood in the cold rising light under the stars, and laughed.

The horses were stamping and panicking at the smell of blood. Ushau sat on one, as incongruous as a dog on a chair, with Roshana in his arms. Kurun clung to the back of the other, fists knotted in its mane. The animal half-reared under him, but he hung on with the tenacity of the undercity.

There were other *hufsan* in the doorway now, standing in horror, their feet swathed in the mire of their comrades' gore. They saw Rakhsar standing before them with the black-slimed scimitar, his eyes blazing like those of a wolf caught in torchlight, and that wide grin splitting his face.

'Come out to me, if you dare!' he cried, and the

happiness and the laughter fluttered in his breast until he felt he could barely breathe, and barely needed to.

The figures retreated inside, back to the lamplight and the sanity within. Rakhsar leapt the fence, and in another bound he was up behind Kurun, and he felt the horse gather itself under him, aware that there was a thing on its back now which could master it and would brook no rebellion.

Still laughing, Rakhsar kicked the animal's ribs, and it took off into an instant canter, while behind him its fellow lumbered along gamely, Ushau thumping it mightily on the shoulder with one great fist, Roshana a limp figure in front of him, her white face hooded by a mat of black filthy hair.

THEY GALLOPED LIKE fiends along the Imperial road in a pale cloud of moonlit dust, and once they had left the waystation behind the night was dark and tranquil again, except for the exertions of the beasts that bore them. Rakhsar had always been a good horseman, but Kurun was bouncing upon the withers of the animal like a sack, and Rakhsar heard him cry out in pain, his fists clenched in his groin.

'Throw up a leg – I'll hold you,' he said to the boy, and Kurun writhed until he was sat on the horse sideways, and only Rakhsar's arm kept him from sliding off feet first. Rakhsar kissed the boy on his salty, dust-caked neck, and gripped the barrel of his mount between his knees until the animal grunted. He looked back, and saw Ushau still belabouring his own horse, to some effect, for it was killing itself to keep up with them. Rakhsar reined back into a canter.

'The next stop is Arimya,' he said into Kurun's ear. 'I have an estate there I've never seen, and I have need of a bath and a bed.'

'Yes, lord,' Kurun said.

'As do you, my stinking little friend.'

THEY LEFT THE road and cast off across the fields and paths to the north of it shortly before dawn. It was while they stood stock still in a thicket of tamarisk, holding their horse's noses, that they saw the pursuit storm past. A dozen *hufsan* soldiers on the hardy scrub ponies the lower ranks rode, trotting up the wide stone road and shouting to one another, spears in their fists and apprehension written all over their faces.

They passed, and the travellers drew a breath.

'We have Mot's luck with us,' Rakhsar said.

'Don't say such things,' his sister snapped.

'We have become creatures of the night, Roshana, who live by guile and murder. We are Mot's children. Bel has turned his face from us.'

Roshana did not speak, but clambered awkwardly away into the bushes with a moan and squatted there. They heard the liquid gush out of her. A few weeks ago Rakhsar would have been scandalised. Now he merely gathered up some dry leaves and grass and joined his sister in the depths of the thicket.

She lay on her side, her skirts pulled up, white legs

drawn up to her stomach like those of an unborn baby. Rakhsar looked her over, and grimaced.

'Kurun!'

The boy came scuttling over at once.

'Master?'

'Clean my sister.'

He hesitated, and then with infinite tenderness he set to wiping Roshana free of the liquid filth that smeared her buttocks, her thighs, her private places.

'How long since you ate?' Rakhsar asked his twin, his face close to hers.

'No food – I cannot stomach it, even the thought.'

'We are a long way from the garden and the nightingales, Roshana. You must keep life in you.'

'I want clean water. I am so thirsty.'

'We'll find some tonight.' They had not realised just how different the world beyond the palace was. Not just in the obvious things, but in the very food they ate and the water they craved. The peasant farmers of Pleninash drank a liquid that was as opaque as soup, called it water, and seemed to thrive on it, as did Kurun and Ushau. Rakhsar could just tolerate it, but it had devastated Roshana.

'We will sleep in comfort tonight,' Rakhsar said fiercely. 'I promise you that.'

Beside him, Kurun finished his task, and pulled Roshana's garments down over her legs. Hesitantly, he patted the Kefren princess's thigh.

'Take your paws off my sister,' Rakhsar snapped.

'Forgive me, lord.'

'Do not forget your station, Kurun. I value you, but you are still only a slave.'

The boy hung his head. 'Yes, master.'

'Good.' Rakhsar touched Kurun under the chin, raising his head. 'Now help me get her to the horses.'

OFF THE ROAD the countryside was a patchwork of dyked fields in which rice rose green and thick from the water. There were raised causeways of red earth which the travellers took in single file, and each led to a junction of fruit trees – which they knew now to leave alone, for they were not yet ripe, though even the sight of the hanging peaches and pears set their soured mouths watering.

At the centre of each cluster of fields and clumped orchards would be a mud-brick hut with the earth packed into a yard around it, sometimes a rough wooden fence hemming in a few chickens, or a brace of hogs. They had avoided these little steadings up until now, but Rakhsar did not know how many more nights in the open Roshana could survive.

This night would be different.

A *hufsa* woman saw them as she went to the well with a leather bucket. She stopped in her tracks, and a naked toddler came running after her and set its fists in her skirts and began to wail.

'Talk to her,' Rakhsar told Kurun. 'Tell her we want food, clean water set to boil, and a place to sleep. I will pay her husband.' His hand settled on the hilt of the scimitar, and he made sure the woman saw it.

It was interminable, this reasoning with people.

Rakhsar was not accustomed to it. All his life he had stated what he wanted and it had been instantly to hand. He could barely get by in the common Asurian that the *hufsan* spoke, and this far into the backwaters of the empire, the people knew no Kefren.

And yet this, too, is my own country.

It had been easier crossing the Magron, for there were more places to hide in the high country, and the water was good, the highland folk a sturdy, hospitable breed who were used to seeing high-caste Kefren come and go. Their travels in the mountains had accorded more with Rakhsar's notions of what a heroic escape should be. At least at first.

They had lost Maidek and Maryam to an avalanche, and the horses too. Ushau had dug the rest of them out of the suffocating layered snow one by one, and the rest of their passage had been on foot. They had become thieves in the night, stealing and poaching to eat, afraid of every shadow, barely able to light a fire in the dark to keep the blood in their veins from freezing. Like dogs, they had huddled together, all differences in caste and station forgotten in the struggle to survive.

But it had hardened them. Kurun had healed with the astonishing speed of the young, and Ushau was well-nigh indestructible. Rakhsar had adjusted also, something long buried in him rising to the challenge. Even savouring it, as an angry man will savour his own fury.

But Roshana had shrunk before their eyes, a bird unaccustomed to life outside the cage.

And now it had begun to tease Rakhsar's thoughts in the darkest spaces of the night.

What if she dies?

And even; *she slows us down*. Better to leave her, somewhere safe.

But if they did, Ushau would stay with her, no question. Perhaps the boy, too. Rakhsar had no illusions about his own ability to generate loyalty.

And so they had limped along, down into the warm wet plains of the Middle Empire at last, into a floundering march of muck and insects and noisome water. No-one asked Rakhsar where they were going, and there were times he no longer knew himself. He knew only that they must continue west, ahead of Kouros's agents. They could not stop moving. They had come too far to be caught now.

But he knew also that there were not many more pasangs left in them.

THE INTERIOR OF the mud house was smoke-blackened, the earth floor packed hard as marble. The woman of the house was baking flatbreads on a stone griddle above the fire, turning them with the easy flick of long practice. The child clung to her leg, and when urine dribbled unheeded down its own, a little pi-dog came fawning out of a corner and licked it clean, before retreating apologetically again.

Roshana lay on a mud-built platform, covered in a thick mat of woven reeds. Aside from two stools made from the hewn cylinders of a palm trunk, this was the house's only furniture. The woman had a large shallow pot of poor iron which she took down from its place on the wall as if it were a king's crown, and setting it on the coals she dashed oil into it from a gourd and then tossed in some greens and corn. This she poked at for a few seconds, then tilted up the pot and emptied the shining contents onto two flatbreads. They were rolled up, torn in two, and offered round.

No-one spoke. It seemed to Rakhsar he had never in his life tasted anything so fine. Kurun smiled up at the woman from where he squatted on the floor, and she smiled back, warming to his beauty and his youth. Ushau thanked her gravely in Asurian, prayed briefly over the morsel, and then ate it in two bites, closing his eyes as he chewed.

Roshana could not eat. She lay on the woven reeds shivering, though it was sweating-hot in the house. The woman bent over her, touched her white forehead, sniffed, and then before Rakhsar could stop her, she had lifted up his sister's robes and was peering below, frowning.

Rakhsar leapt up. 'Don't touch her!'

The woman cowered, and the child began to cry. In the corner the little pi-dog bared his teeth and snarled.

'Master, she means no harm,' Kurun said. The boy rose and held out his hands like a priest blessing them both.

'My sister is not to be gawked at by some swamp-caste bitch *hufsa*.'

The woman spoke, lifting her child into her arms, gesturing to Roshana and then to Rakhsar.

'She wants us to leave.'

Rakhsar reached inside his sash-purse, which was now as thin as the sash itself. He found two copper obols and held them out. 'Give these to her. Tell her my sister must sleep here tonight. We cannot leave.'

The woman took the money, and her eyes grew shrewd. She spoke again.

'She says she can help the lady Roshana.'

'Well, let's see if she can, Kurun. But I shall watch over her, and if she does us wrong, I shall have Ushau break her neck. And her brat's, too.'

THE WOMAN WAS alone. As they sat there through the night, she told Kurun that her husband had been sent for by the Great King to fight in his army, and had gone east some weeks before.

She talked almost continually as she worked, and little by little the sense of the words began to order itself to Rakhsar. Asurian and High Kefren had once been the same language, but the high castes that dwelt in the ziggurats had drawn apart from the *hufsan* who made up the bulk of the empire, and over centuries of privilege their speech patterns had changed. Since the Great King spoke this evolving language, so did every courtier, high ranking officer and civil servant of the empire. It had become the language of the rulers.

All high caste Kefren still knew Asurian, for they mixed with the lower orders on a daily basis; but for Rakhsar and Roshana it had been different. They had never known the need to learn Asurian. What little they possessed was a half-remembered relic crooned over them by their wet-nurses.

I was never allowed to learn it, Rakhsar realised. Right from the beginning, it had been decided that there was no need.

Try as he might, he could not blame his father for this. He sensed the hand of Orsana.

A prince who cannot speak to his people. How ingenious of her – and such a simple thing to accomplish in the rarefied world of the palace, where even the slaves knew the high tongue.

But after all these weeks on the road listening to Ushau and Kurun, and now to this woman, Rakhsar's inquisitive brain began to decipher the meanings of the half-familiar, half-alien words. He sat on one of the palm-trunk stools and watched, and listened, and for once in his life began to appreciate that one could gain without demand.

The *hufsa* woman stripped Roshana and washed her with warm water, then rubbed her down with palm oil scented with lavender and thyme, an incongruous fragrance in the smoky confines of the hovel. Ushau and Kurun went outside for this, but Rakhsar watched, and even went so far as to help the woman rinse out Roshana's hair. Clumps of mud were so fastened in it that the woman despaired of the brush, and Rakhsar offered her his own knife to make the cut.

She took the pearl-handled blade gingerly, as though afraid to touch it, but once her dark fist covered the ornate hilt it became just another knife to her, and she began to cut away Roshana's heavy black mane of hair, which had doubled in weight from its cargo of mud. When she had finished Roshana was left with a scalp as shorn as Kurun's, and looked more like a boy than he did, the strong bones of her face accentuated by the weeks of lean living.

She opened her eyes; she had not spoken a word or uttered a protest through the whole operation, though she had whimpered some when the *hufsa* sawed a little too vigorously.

'I am glad to be rid of it,' she said, quietly.

'You are more beautiful than ever,' her brother told her, and meant it.

The *hufsa* was more sure of herself now. While her child and the little dog lay sleeping in a warm tangle on the floor, she heated water to boiling and then began twitching off handfuls of herbs from the drying bundles on the walls. These went in the water, and the smell of them in the steam that rose was wondrously refreshing, like some breath from a cooler world.

Finally, she sat by Roshana and took the girl's head on her knee, then made her drink the hot herb-infused brew sip by sip.

By the time she was done it was far past the middle of the night. The woman pulled a handwoven blanket over Roshana and stroked her black, spiky scalp.

'It will grow back,' she said in Asurian.

And Rakhsar understood her.

Then she curled up on the floor beside her child, without further ceremony, and went at once to sleep.

Rakhsar stayed awake, watching the woman, her child, the twitching dog, and his own sister, now hardly recognisable but sleeping soundly on the peasant mat, in a smoke-blackened house made of mud.

And he knew something akin to peace, for the first time in his cosseted and quarrelsome and watchful life.

ELEVEN
A CUP OF WINE

FROM IRUNSHAHR THE army uncoiled and began to march east. The raven banner snapped in the wind on the topmost tower of the fortress, and they were cheered to the echo by the three thousand Macht left behind to hold Corvus's latest acquisition. At their head was Valerian, the Dogshead with the ruined face who had once loved Rictus's daughter.

His appointment was a promotion, but he had not taken it well. All his adult life, Valerian had marched with Rictus and Fornyx and the Dogsheads. He was one of the originals, an almost extinct breed. But now he was to live in a palace with three whole morai to command and a city to administer, and it seemed almost like a punishment. Because he was going to miss out on the great fight to come, a battle to ring down the ages as Kunaksa had.

On Corvus's orders, Rictus had persuaded him

to take the command. There had been a time when he would have liked nothing better than to see his daughter marry the scarred young man with the gentle spirit, who had seemed already a son to him. But that was all in the past now. Rian was swimming strong within the tide of her own life, and Valerian was a good enough man not to resent it. He was also utterly trustworthy. Even Rictus had not been able to come up with a more fitting occupant for the post. If it came to it, Valerian would die on the walls of Irunshahr rather than open the gates to anyone save Rictus and his king.

But it was something of a blow, nonetheless, to march away once more with the ranks of those he trusted that little bit thinner. And the Dogsheads felt it too. Kesero, the big, bluff whorechaser who had been the banner-bearer these ten years, was moved up to second-in command under Fornyx.

Rictus's status within the army was increasingly nebulous, but it was generally recognised that if Corvus were ever brought low, it would be Rictus's task to take command. Even Demetrius did not dispute that. But it did leave Rictus sometimes feeling a little bereft. Fornyx commanded the Dogsheads just as well as Rictus ever had, which was hardly surprising, since Rictus had moulded and trained up the younger man from an early age. And Rictus found himself as much a quartermaster-general and military sounding-board to Corvus as anything else.

The role of wise counsellor was beginning to grate on him. He might find it difficult to crack his limbs into movement some cold mornings, but he still had a good fight or two left in him. He could still stand in the front rank if he had to.

Down the Imperial Road the infantry marched, ten abreast, while the cavalry and Druze's Igranians went ahead and spied out the lie of the land, and noted those regions which were rich in foodstuffs and livestock. As the infantry marched east, so herds of cattle and goats were hustled west, to join the moving larder in the midst of the baggage train. And Corvus sent small mounted parties out to the south, also, to watch for any word of King Proxanon and his five legions.

Two weeks, they travelled like this, living off the land like a tide of locusts, but such were the riches of Pleninash that they did not leave starvation in their wake, and Corvus kept the men on a tight leash. Only once did he have to rear up the gibbet and gather the army in to witness punishment. Three men, conscripts, had left the line of march to raid a farm and force themselves on a *hufsa* woman they found there. Their centurion hunted them down, and Corvus hanged them without hesitation or pity, and left their bodies dangling for the crows while the whole army was marched past. This was the same affable young man who went up and down the column every day inquiring after their welfare, who told them dirty stories around the campfires at night. His face as the men died on the gibbet was marked by many; a grim white mask that seemed somehow not human at all.

There was no more straggling after that, and there were no more unanswered names at the morning roll calls.

If there was a thing missing, which rattled with every member of the army, high and low, it was the absence of the enemy. Along the Imperial Road, which led them like a ribbon tied to the beating heart of the empire, the troops took the surrender of two more large cities. Anaris and Edom, thriving metropolises built on high tells in the Kufr way, and visible for scores of pasangs across the flat plains. They both surrendered as Irunshahr had, opening their gates without a fight and soon after opening their granaries and their treasuries also.

There was satisfaction at these gains, and the men appreciated the fact that they never had an empty belly after the day's march, but the sense of epic adventure that had taken them across the Korash was missing. Centurions reported mutterings around the communal centoi as the men cooked their evening meals. They would march forever, and take city after city – but to what end? They were paid what they always had been, and no-one was becoming rich despite the staggering wealth on display in every city they passed. There had to be more to the expedition than this. At the moment, their pockets were no fuller than they would have been serving in the Harukush, and since the Haneikos there had been barely a battle worth the name.

* * *

'THEY'RE BORED,' RICTUS told the other marshals one evening, stamping into the King's tent and shaking the rain from his cloak. It had come on dark and thick and wet this past few days, though still stiflingly hot, and the bronze was greening with verdigris; mould was attacking every strap of leather, and the very fabric of their clothes was beginning to rot on their backs.

'They're eating like pigs, and they haven't had to bleed in a battle-line these two months and more,' Demetrius retorted. 'Don't the stupid fucks know when they're well off?'

'They can be fickle as girls, soldiers, especially veterans,' Fornyx said. He was nursing a cup of wine and staring into an unnecessary brazier, keeping an eye on the skewered frogs that sizzled above the coals. He sighed and finished his drink, tipping out the last of it onto the floor of the tent. 'For Haukos, to give us patience.'

'No word from the east?' Rictus asked. He held out his hand, and Teresian gave him a brimming cup.

'Not so much as a fart,' the strawhead grunted. He'll still be in the Magron. I've heard how the Great King travels. He brings his harem, they say. How many wagonloads of girls do you suppose he's hauling over the mountains?'

'I've a mind to go and help him haul,' Fornyx said, with feeling. 'I've cobwebs in my crotch, it's been so long.'

'I know what you mean,' dark Druze spoke up from the corner. 'I tell you, brothers, there are a few fellows among the latest conscripts who are beginning to look good to me.'

They laughed at that, and were still laughing when the King entered the tent, his black hair plastered flat by the rain and his face more than ever like a mask of immutable bone. He was muddied to the waist, and clods of clay dropped off his bare legs as he stood motionless a moment, his gaze taking them all in with one flat sweep.

A page came forward to take his cloak, and he smiled mechanically at the boy, but his eyes were far away.

'Make yourselves at home,' he said mildly, but there was something in his tone that made them all take to their feet.

'Parmenios and I have been wrestling waggons out of the mud down the road a way,' he said, still in the same mild tone. 'It seems to me my teamsters are growing careless.'

Rictus handed the King his own wine, and Corvus raised the cup, and downed the contents at a gulp. Then he tossed the cup away.

'We are becoming comfortable. We march, we pluck a city from the world like a man takes a fig from a tree.' He strode forward, squeezed water out of his hair, refused the linen towel offered by another of the pages, and stood over the long table that was set up in the tent at the end of every day's march. Inked on the long map across it was the progress of the army.

There was something different about the King this evening. A crackling, damped-down energy which could be sensed by them all, as a dog smells approaching thunder.

'Do you remember how hard they fought at the Haneikos, brothers? How you, Rictus, and Fornyx and Teresian, went at it shield to shield in the river, and dammed the water with the bodies?'

He turned away from the table. His eyes were shining, and a strange smile bent his mouth.

'It was glorious, was it not?'

He thumped his fist on the table, so hard the timber jumped.

'I said to you once, Rictus, that if it were not for the glory of it I would not be here at all. I meant it.'

'I know you did,' Rictus said quietly.

'If I was content with coin and power and a crown I could have stayed in Machran. I did not enter the empire to become rich, brothers. I came to earn a name, to make a story.'

He pointed at Rictus. 'This man is a legend. He led home the Ten Thousand, or what was left of them, brought them to the shores of the sea and so found his way into all the books of history that will ever be written.

'Before Rictus commanded the Ten Thousand, they were led by another man, named Jason of Pherai. Do any of you here, save Rictus, know his name?'

Blank looks. The smell of burning frog.

'Of course not. He died in a tavern brawl in Sinon. Yet it was he who took on the leadership of the Macht after their generals were killed at Kunaksa, he who brought them back west as far as the Korash.

'He was my father.'

Almost a decade, they had known this young man, and to none save Rictus and Fornyx had he ever said as much. The marshals stared at their king in astonishment.

'I knew no man better –' Rictus began.

'He is forgotten! Do you see how easily it happens, brothers? How quick we fall through the cracks in history, our names lost, our deeds as good as dust?'

Again, that strange smile, something unearthly about it.

'That will not happen to us, to me or to you. I will not allow it.'

The table was thumped again. 'Marcan's people have sent us word. The Great King is over the mountains. His muster is complete. As we stand here, he is crossing the Bekai River at Carchanis, some four hundred pasangs away.'

A cloud of exclamations. The marshals crowded up to the map-table. Wine-cups were cast aside. Fornyx swept his burning frogs from the brazier with a wave of his hand and stood rubbing his beard, his eyes as wide as a deer's.

'Those waggon-loads of girls make better time than we thought,' he said.

'Any word on numbers?' Demetrius asked.

'We can assume there will be a lot of them,' Corvus said with a human grin. Mercurial as ever, he seemed to have warmed to their reactions in a moment.

Only Rictus and Ardashir stood back from the table, watching the King, silent.

'Brothers, this changes everything. The Great King is not on the Imperial Road. He has struck north, following the line of the Bekai and gathering the last of his levies as he goes. Carchanis will be his base of operations, and the river will guard his left flank and rear. He has only to wait for us in line of battle and the thing will begin.'

'If he's come this far, he won't leave the river in his rear – he's not stupid enough for that.' This was Demetrius, head tilted to one side to bring his eye to bear on the map. 'He'll come out, Corvus. He'll march west, to give his cavalry room to shake out.'

'I believe he will,' the King said.

'Four hundred pasangs – that's fifteen days' march, less if the two armies are converging,' Fornyx mused. He was biting his beard.

'We can expect to see his skirmishers any day now,' Druze said, and his dark face was split by a wide white grin.

'This is news the army must hear,' Corvus said briskly. 'Brothers, there is no time to lose. Our stroll through the empire is about to become more earnest. I want you all to go to your commands and break word of this around the centoi.'

'They'll piss themselves when they hear this,' Teresian said, and he cackled.

'At dawn I want you all back here. We shall have a council of war before the tent is struck. After that we must pick up the pace, and the columns must be tightened up. Druze is right; if the main host of the enemy is at Carchanis, then he will have sent a screen of light troops ahead to look for us. It must be destroyed. Ardashir, you must warn the Companions. Druze, your Igranians will work with them. That is all. Now, get out of here and get into that rain. There is a lot to do before morning.'

The marshals trooped out, talking amongst themselves. Ardashir turned to Rictus and said in a low voice. 'He has forgotten something.'

'No, he hasn't,' Rictus replied.

The tall Kefre looked profoundly troubled.

'I mean to say it, Ardashir,' Rictus said.

Ardashir touched his arm, as if for reassurance, and then left in the wake of the others.

Corvus bent over the map table like a man lost in a book. He righted a wine-cup, and smeared the red dribble it had leaked across the vellum.

'All pages are to leave,' he said in a clear voice, and the two boys at the door, who had listened agog to all that had passed, ducked out of the tent.

The rain was a thunder on the leather canopy above their heads. Corvus did not turn around.

'You did not leave with the others, Rictus.'

'I have no command. Fornyx runs the Dogsheads now. I am merely –'

'A mascot?' Corvus turned, and smiled to take the sting out of the word.

'I am your advisor; I am –'

'Sometimes I feel you are Antimone's shadow, always looking over my shoulder.'

'You did not tell them everything, did you Corvus?'

The King poured himself some wine, filled a second cup and left it standing on the table. Rictus did not touch it.

'I told them what they wanted to hear, what the army needed to hear. And it was the truth.'

'But not all of it.'

'Damn it Rictus, men have shrewish wives easier to put up with than you!'

'And fathers.'

'You are not my father.'

'But I did know him. He was my best friend, and a better man than I. He is not forgotten, and nor will you be.'

'My thanks for the reassurance. Now say what you mean to say.'

'Do not let your hunger for glory take these men to needless deaths, Corvus. There was no mention made just now of King Proxanon and the Juthan legions. Why is that?'

Corvus leaned both hands on the table and stared at the stained vellum upon it, the lines and names, the inked-in mountains and rivers. A whole world, a vastness of ambition, contained upon a tabletop.

'I thought it would be Fornyx who noticed first.'

'Sometimes you can make even him believe. But I know you better than any of them, Corvus, save Ardashir.'

'Do you? I suppose that is so. You are the only one I ever feel I have to explain myself to, Rictus.'

He sighed, as if resigned, but Rictus did not think that was what he felt.

'The Great King received word of our agreement with Proxanon. He has detached an army to attack Jutha. The legions cannot join us in time. They are already committed to battle somewhere west of the city of Hadith, three weeks away.'

'Where is Marcan?'

'I sent him south, to rejoin his people, and to tell his father of my plans. He may yet be able to tie in with us.'

Rictus breathed out softly. 'And what are the Great King's numbers, Corvus? Do not tell me you don't know.'

'He detached a sizeable force to attack Proxanon, but the Jutha still reckon the main body at some two hundred thousand spears.'

Now Rictus approached the table, took the wine-cup, and gulped half the contents down, baring his teeth at the sharp taste.

'Even with the recent reinforcements, we can only put some thirty-five thousand into the line.'

'Thirty six,' Corvus corrected him.

'And you mean to seek battle.'

'I do.'

Rictus glared at the younger man. He rapped his knuckle against the black cuirass that Corvus wore, the twin of his own. 'This does not make you immortal, Corvus.'

The King smiled tightly. 'It helps.'

'We cannot do this. We must wait for Proxanon to come up. We need those extra spears. Antimone's blood, Corvus, they will double our numbers!'

'We will not wait. There is no guarantee that Proxanon will prevail in the field. We may find ourselves with a victorious imperial army in our rear as well as the horde of the Great King to our front. Better to move now, and move fast. Numbers do not count for as much as surprise. And I'm hoping to give the Great King a very nasty surprise indeed,

Rictus. I will announce it in the morning – we will move by forced marches from now on.'

He was elevated, exalted even. Two spots of colour burned on that terrible pale face.

'If we beat the Great King's army on our own – on our own, Rictus – then we will have broken his hold on the empire. It will fall apart. And what is more, it will be a Macht army which has prevailed, without allies, without help from the Kufr or anyone else.'

Exasperated, Rictus exploded. 'For God's sake, Corvus – you're half Kufr yourself!'

The winecup came up in a blur, smashing against Rictus's cheekbone, staggering him. Wine sprayed in the air, soaked his cloak, and ran in rivulets dark as blood down his black cuirass.

He straightened, blinking the stinging liquid out of his eyes. Twenty years earlier, even ten years, he would have launched himself at Corvus for that, king or no. But now he simply stood there with his head ringing, and a great sadness crowding his mind.

Corvus raised both hands to his mouth like a woman. 'Rictus – Rictus, my brother, I am so sorry!'

Rictus turned away.

'I've had harder blows from whores,' he said. And then he stumbled out into the rain-lashed night, blind with the wine and the hot, growing light of his own anger.

TWELVE
MOT'S BLIGHT

KOUROS STOOD LIKE a piece of statuary with the sweat sliding in worms down the small of his back. The armour he wore had been made for him a few years before, and had once fitted him like an ornate second skin, but he had lost weight in the last few weeks, and now there were angles in his bones that were not so well padded as they had been. And he had forgotten how heavy the helmet was.

But he stood motionless beside his father's throne, for he was part of a larger tableau here today, and all of it was on display for the baying myriads of the army, who had been assembled to witness something rare: the execution of a high-caste noble. It was not often they were able to see someone so elevated pay for a mistake, and though the assembled crowds were as silent as the Great King's presence demanded, still there was that whispering susurration, a surreptitious chatter. No-one could silence an army completely, for in their thousands the soldiers were invulnerable, anonymous.

But there was a hush of sorts, nonetheless, as Dyarnes strode forth upon the dais in armour so bright it pained the eye to look upon, and called for silence in a voice almost as brazen.

'Bring him forth,' he cried.

Darios had been fettered with silver chains, as befitted his station, and he walked across the dais in a himation of blinding white linen, his hair loose, face impassive.

The Great King sat silent and motionless on the throne as the traitor approached. His komis was drawn up around his face and only his eyes were visible, as hard to read as frosted glass.

Darios stood and surveyed the crowd with contempt. Then he collected himself, turned, and went on his knees before the Great King. Ashurnan gave away no flicker of interest.

The executioner stepped forward, a massive *hufsan* from the Magron, bearing a scimitar as long as a man's leg. He stood waiting.

Dyarnes spoke up again. He had a fine, ringing voice when he cared to exercise it, and he looked as tall and indomitable as some bronze-clad god in the shining sunlight.

'The traitor Darios, having betrayed our army at the River Haneikos, surrendered the city of Ashdod, and then deserted his own troops, is likewise charged with entering into communications with the enemy.

His fate is death, by decree of the Great King. Your eyes shall witness it, so that you may know what it is to betray your lord.'

'I have something to say,' Darios spoke up.

Dyarnes looked quickly at the Great King. Upon the arm of the throne one hand moved slightly, a sideways flick of negation.

'The prisoner will not speak,' Dyarnes said, and his voice was thick and raw. 'Executioner.'

The scimitar caught a flash of fire from the sun as it arced through the air, and Darios's head left his body in a clean-shorn instant. Kouros watched with close fascination, and was certain the eyes blinked in surprise before the head thumped to the timber of the dais.

The assembled soldiers roared their approval. The execution of their own rendered them dumb, but to see a high caste Kefre lose his head was as good an afternoon's entertainment as many had known in all their lives. They cheered even as the Great King rose from his throne.

Ashurnan stepped forward, studied the medals and ribands of blood that lay scattered across the dais as though he could make an augury of them, and then turned without a word, the cheers still shaking the air, and disappeared into the hangings behind the throne, and the towering tent beyond.

The executioner raised the head into the air by its topknot, and now the eyes were dead as glass.

'Behold!' he cried in common Asurian, 'The fate of all traitors!'

'Set it on a spike at the gates to the royal enclosure,'

Kouros said, studying Darios's features, as fascinated as a boy pinning butterflies.

'My prince –' Dyarnes and Darios had been friends. For a second the commander of the Honai had raw grief carved across his face.

'Those are the Great King's orders.' Kouros set a hand on the other man's arm for a second, judging the gesture necessary.

'Yes, my prince.' Dyarnes retrieved the grisly relic from the executioner, and then walked off the dais with his friend's head cradled in his arm, the blood from the severed veins and windpipe still streaming fast, darkening the bright shine of his armour.

ONE SEGMENT OF the Great King's tent had been lifted up to catch the breeze and let in the bright summer sun, Bel's blessing on the world. Ashurnan stood at this gap now in a simple robe of blue silk, the diadem a black band across his forehead. Above him, the immense structure creaked and swayed in the wind like a ship at sea. It was so large that living trees were accommodated within, with lanterns hung all along their branches, and in one corner there was a stream of clean water whose banks had been walled off for two pasangs beyond the tent so no other mortal might pollute it.

This was campaigning in style. Now that they were down from the mountains, and the worst of the march was over, with intelligence pouring in from the west and south; now the Great King could unbuckle a little, and enjoy the comforts his two hundred personal waggons had hauled all the way from Ashur.

Now the details and suspicions which had dogged him for all those weary pasangs could be dealt with.

Kouros doffed his helmet with a barely suppressed sigh of relief and joined his father.

The royal enclosure was partitioned off from the rest of the immense camp by a stockade and ditch, which the Honai patrolled in their hundreds. Within that wooden wall were the stables, the harem, the cook-tents, and herds of the Great King's own personal animals, to be slaughtered at his word alone. The round hill with its palisade was the ziggurat, replicated here in the Middle Empire on a smaller scale, but with a hierarchy as rigid as in its stone-built original.

Beyond the stockade, the camp of the army rolled out like a sea to every horizon. At night when the campfires were lit, they rivalled the stars above, and the glow of them could be seen in the sky from fifteen pasangs away. The men camped according to geography, so that within the immense encampment were many different districts, and distinct rivalries.

The Arakosans kept themselves apart, and as cavalry they took the best ground with easy access to pasture beyond. The *hufsan* of Asuria huddled together in narrow lines as though replicating the slums and alleyways of Ashur. And the small farmers and craftsmen of Pleninash slept in sprawling formless crowds, for they had only just come in, many of them, and they were still being regimented by their officers. For them, the coming of the Great King had been a cataclysm to overturn their world.

It could almost have been an entire people on the move, a dispossessed city staining the face of Kuf with its masses, and sucking dry the fertile farmland for many pasangs around. Despite the hundreds of provision-bearing waggons that lumbered into the great camp every day, the army could not remain in one place for long, or there would be no more food to gather in. Even Pleninash had its limits, when encumbered with a horde such as this.

'You know why I had Darios killed,' Ashurnan said to his eldest son, not turning around.

'He failed. He let the Macht over the Korash and –'

'He was your mother's creature. He had been for a long time.' Ashurnan turned now, and the light behind him made of his face a black shadow with azure coins for eyes.

'This is not the palace now, Kouros. We do not intrigue for trifles here. This is war. Soon you will be on a battlefield facing the Macht for the first time. There is no more time for conspiracy.'

He glided forward. Kouros had to steel himself not to retreat before his father, so strange and fey did the older Kefre seem in that moment. It was as though he were half in another world.

'You will be King, Kouros. Be satisfied with that. It may happen tomorrow, or it may happen in ten years, but you will wear the diadem. There is no-one left to challenge you. Why can you not be content with that?'

Ashurnan's tone was genuine, but there was anger

simmering in it too. Kouros fought down a stammer as he replied.

'I serve you, father. I know now I am not yet ready to sit on the throne – these last weeks have taught me that much. It is just that Rakhsar –'

'Rakhsar is dead, or lost. He is gone, and Roshana with him.' There was no mistaking the grief in the old man's voice now. He walked away. A gold-leafed table sat upon a brilliantly woven carpet, and around it the green grass of Pleninash spread out, shorn as fine as the carpet-weaver's work, yellowing now without the sun. Ashurnan poured himself wine, raising a hand to halt the advance of the old chamberlain, Malakeh, who stood with a pair of household slaves not ten paces away, his staff of office balanced on a stone so he could still make it ring when he chose.

'Drink.'

Kouros did so, watching his father over the rim of the cup, sweating.

'Now I will drink,' Ashurnan said, with an odd smile. Kouros passed him the cup. The Great King sipped the wine, but did not seem to enjoy it.

'Your mother's reach is long, Kouros. I do not think you know just how long. Darios was once my friend, and she turned him.'

'He was still your friend –' Kouros said earnestly.

'One cannot serve two masters. You might want to tell Dyarnes that, also.'

The sweat turned cold on Kouros's back. 'Dyarnes?'

'He and Darios rose through the ranks of the Honai together. Their wives are cousins. But you will have known that.'

He had not. It was a little something Orsana had chosen not to share with him.

'A king must be his own man, Kouros. And if there is something my forty years on the throne have taught me, it is that he needs his friends also. I do not have a talent that way – and nor do you. Your grandfather did. He never feared an assassin in his life, and he did not scruple to drink wine no-one else had yet tasted. Because he had friends he trusted about him.'

'Kings can trust no-one – you told me that once.'

'I did not. I believe those are your mother's words. There is wisdom in them, though. But your mother has not known life above the snowline like I have. She has ladies in the harem and at the court who would spill their last breath for her. For myself, if I need a friend, I buy one. You will be like me, Kouros. The throne will not make you happy.'

Kouros was shocked. His broad, heavy face worked in genuine perplexity. His father had never before spoken to him thus.

'If I could go back to the early years, before Kunaksa, then I would know what it was like to trust others. I trusted my brother – I loved him, for all that he was a self-centred, unlovable fellow. He brought the Macht into our world, and you know the result. We are still paying the price for that today. A brother's betrayal. My forbearance.'

Ashurnan turned away, set the chased crystal of the wine-glass on the gold table.

'I killed him with my own hand, Kouros. And there is not a day in my life since I have not seen his face as my sword took the life out of it.'

'It was the right thing to do,' Kouros grunted. He had a bewildering urge to set his hand on the Great King's shoulder, as though Ashurnan were a normal father, and he a normal son.

'Of course it was. But it has never left me. We grew up together, you see, as real brothers do. It is why, when I had sons of my own, I swore to keep them as separate as I could.'

He turned back again. He was smiling.

'Do you remember – can you remember – how you and Rakhsar used to play together, and look after little Roshana, all of you naked and filthy in the gardens like three little *hufsan* brats? I carried all three of you in from under the trees one day, just like that, and sat on the throne with you all in my arms, and blessed God and the women who had borne you. I thought myself as lucky as any man in the world.'

'I was too young. I do not remember,' Kouros said, looking down. He did not want to remember.

'I resolved to go back on my own decision, to raise you all together as a family should be raised. Perhaps I was a fool. I probably was. In any case, your mother kept me to my word. She was first wife, and Ashana was a gentle soul who bowed to her commands.'

'My mother is a great woman,' Kouros growled.

'Yes, she is. She brought me ten thousand Arakosan cavalry. One does not gainsay a woman with a dowry like that.'

'You insulted her with that other one. You would have supplanted her. You humiliated her!'

'I was in love,' the King said quietly. 'Have you ever been in love, Kouros?'

Kouros bent his head, blinking, his jaw working as though he had a lump of gristle between his teeth. It was a question no-one had ever asked him before, but he knew the answer instantly.

'No,' he said, the word choked out of him.

His father watched the workings of his face, his own dark with sadness.

'Son, you lie.'

Kouros turned away, eyes burning, the rage rising in him, the black desire to choke the life and light out of something, someone, anything.

'Do not turn your back on me.' The snap of command.

Ashurnan's eyes flashed.

'You will not understand this truth until it is too late, but you will hear it now. Kouros, if you hunt down your brother and sister – if you kill them – then I promise you that you will never know a moment of true peace for the rest of your life. Even throned in glory over all the empire, that remorse will eat at you, and you will grow old and empty with the gnawing of it. Listen to one who knows.'

'One cannot be a king, and do what one wants – you did tell me that,' Kouros snarled.

'What eats at you will one day put a canker into your reign. You are young, Kouros. You do not have to be the man your mother wants.'

'I am my own man!'

'We are none of us our own man. We only try to do what is right and honourable, and in time that honour becomes part of us. Once it is lost, it is gone forever. Hear me in this, son.'

Kouros faced his father, the blackness rising in him, that familiar sweetness. It would be so easy to bring up the iron brim of his helmet and swing it at the old man's head. He knew he had the strength in him for that one blow, and one blow was all it would take.

But instead he strangled the impulse, as he daily murdered so many others. He leaned close and kissed his father on the cheek.

'Do you think I have it in me to be a good man?' he asked, child-like, unable to hold in the question.

'You are a better man than Rakhsar.'

And that was all he was given.

He bowed deeply, his heavy face impassive, and left the Great King's tent without ceremony. The Honai straightened as he passed them. Beyond them, the immense encampment hummed and steamed and smoked to the far horizon. He felt that the blackness in his soul could have eaten it all and asked for more.

Mot's Blight is in me, he thought. It must be done. My mother is right. The old man is too soft for the days ahead.

He called his guards to him, and then stalked off to his own complex of tents, where he would find something suitable to defile.

My Dearest Son,

I write in some haste and with my own hand and I will add no polish to my words, but know they come to you with all your mother's love. If the seal upon this letter is broken, you must hold the messenger to account. If it is not, and it has reached you before the two moons rise on the month of Granash, then you may reward him.

Kouros looked at the sweating, filthy, horse-smelling *hufsan* courier who had brought this letter, along with a bucket of others as a blind.

'What is your name?'

The *hufsan* was light-boned as a girl, and he looked as though he had not slept in days. His brown skin had a greyish tint.

'Jervas of Hamadan, my prince.'

'You have done well. Eleven days from Ashur to Carchanis – it must be something of a record.'

'Thank you, my prince. I killed nineteen horses –'

'You stopped at Ab Mirza, as we had arranged?'

'Yes, lord. The second letter is hidden in the rim of the scroll bucket. The seal is intact, I swear it.'

'Excellent. Now leave me, Jervas of Hamadan. My chamberlain will see to your needs. Remain close at hand. There will be a return journey soon.'

The *hufsan* sagged a little. 'Thank you, my prince.' He withdrew, taking the acrid stink of horse-sweat with him.

Kouros began to read again, but was distracted. 'Anarish!'

The chamberlain tucked aside the tent flap and bowed.

'Get that girl out of here. Her snivelling is making my head hurt.'

The naked, weeping girl was led away, red, bloody stripes livid upon her skin. Kouros's face closed, as it always did when he was deciphering his mother's code. He knew it off by heart, but still had to mouth the words aloud as he rearranged them, and occasionally he had to count upon his fingers down the alphabet.

Rumour outruns horses, they say, and I am certain as I write that Darios has failed to hold the passes of the Korash. If that is so, your father will take the opportunity to remove him. He has had his suspicions about Darios for many months now.

That leaves our position weakened. You must make sure of Dyarnes if you can, and if not, then Marok, his second in command. I know Marok's wife, or one of them, and he is well pleased with his gifts. But you must not approach him directly. It is enough to hold him in play.

I shall hold the capital. It has turned out well. The nonentity, Borsanes, whom your father left in command, has acceded to all my wishes. We now have Arakosans we can trust within the walls, and more are on their way to Hamadan as we speak.

Not a word of the war – the real war. Orsana lived in a bubble that was rarely pricked by events beyond her own private horizon.

Rakhsar must be found. As long as he is at large, there is a danger – you know this. I have agents out all over Pleninash, but as yet there is no firm word of him. He has estates near Arimya, and I have sent some people there also, though I doubt he would be so foolish as to visit the place. You must sound out the senior officers of the levies. Rakhsar may be in touch with some of them. In any case, he will be active and on the move – it is not in him to sit still, nor to choose discretion over a gaudy gesture. Trust our Arakosans – they are your people and will not betray any son of mine. Use them to help you track your brother down.

Our Arakosans. They were hers and hers alone. Kouros did not deceive himself otherwise. She had agents watching him as surely as she had them out looking for his brother.

He put the letter aside. It hurt his head to decode it, to have his mother's voice in his ears from a thousand pasangs away.

She charges me high rent for the nine months she bore me, he thought with bitter humour.

The second letter he found after a few minutes scrabbling around the interior rim of the despatch-bucket. Under the leather lining it lay, still sealed with cheap tavern wax, the intaglio design the same as that he wore on his signet ring. He smiled as he looked upon it, and then peered out the flap of the tent's private chamber.

'Anarish, no-one enters until I say otherwise.'

The chamberlain did not so much as blink. 'As you wish, lord.'

No code here, and a handwriting as florid and graceless as Orsana's was minute and spiderish.

Brother!

Give you joy, I am still alive and still able to put it in a tavern girl when I have a mind to. I write from a town named Orimya, west of Carchanis. From what I hear you are encamped on the western bank of the Bekai River, two or three day's ride to the east. I rejoice to find you so close, but am alarmed to find myself square in the path of such a juggernaut as the Great King's army. I trust that when the inevitable collision occurs you will not do anything so absurd as fight. There are common soldiers enough for that.

I approach my news the long way round – my apologies. I have tracked our quarry down at last. There is an estate north of here near the city of Arimya which our friend appears to own, though he will never have seen it. I set people to watch the place weeks ago, just in care, and these associates tell me he is there now. It appears he has lost all sense. Or perhaps he merely tired of life below the ziggurat. In any case, I will be in position within two days, and soon your worries will have a stopper on them. You may even wish to join me yourself – the house is but two hard day's ride from the encampment of the army. In any case, I will remain at the place to await further instructions once the principals are secured. I know you wish to see them yourself before any final decisions are made.

Wish me Mot's luck, brother. I feel him drawing early upon the world this year. They say he shadows the advance of the Macht, and his darkness is upon their faces.

A last point. The courier who bears this note is a worthy fellow, who had to cast over half of eastern Pleninash to track me down. I have sounded him out, and my nose tells me his affections are worth winning. He is a born horseman, with discretion and good sense. Such qualities should be recognised. You should use him to send me your reply. His former employer has no further claim on his loyalties, by the way.

K

There it was. Rakhsar had been run to ground at last.

Kouros sprang to his feet and began pacing up and down the tent feverishly. There was not space enough for his joy; he swept out of the place, startling the chamberlain, drawing surprised jolts from the guards.

The darkness outside, barely a darkness at all. The world fairly blazed with light. Both moons were up and Firghe was almost full. Between them the stars swept in a gleaming horse-tail of diamond. And below, the campfires of the army stretched for as far as the eye could see, as great as a city, a crop of lights sown upon the sleeping earth and now in full flower.

I am the better man, Kouros thought. He told me so, and it is true. And Rakhsar will know it too before he dies. And Roshana –

Roshana will feel me in her flesh. She will know my strength. I will bring her pleasure in the pain. I will own her. I will collar her. She will kneel naked at my feet and beg for my touch before I am done with her.

'Anarish!' he roared, all aglow, the breath filling his lungs like wine. 'Send the courier to me. And have the horses saddled and packed for a journey. Dismiss the night's guards and send me the morning shift. Be quick, Anarish!'

The black light within his soul was in full flower, cackling and dancing with glee.

THIRTEEN
THE GARDEN IN THE NIGHT

THEY HAD FOUND the house shut up, neglected but not quite derelict. The gardens were overgrown with a kind of shabby loveliness: rose-bushes run wild, vines covering an outdoor terrace and making of it a shaded bower. The orchard was heavy with unpicked fruit, and more lay at the feet of the trees, worm-eaten apples and pears and pomegranates, like the mouldering skulls of a forgotten battlefield.

But there was water in the well, and the key which Rakhsar carried fitted the lock, though it would not turn. Finally it was Ushau's brute strength that smashed open the door, and as they trooped inside, swallows swooped past their heads, screaming madly, and there were wands and bars of light stabbing down through the holed roof, making brilliant sunlit shapes all about their feet.

Just inside the door was a beautiful mosaic-covered fountain, dry as sand. Behind it, two staircases led up to the outflung wings of the house, the steps littered with leaves, as gapped and broken as a beggar's mouth.

'Nice to see they kept the place in good order,' Rakhsar said, strolling past the fountain, his hand on his sword-hilt.

'They thought we would never see it,' Roshana told him. 'We were never supposed to come here.'

'Perhaps we shouldn't have – I wanted to have a look, though. It is the only thing I own, outside the ziggurat.'

'It's beautiful,' Kurun said, stepping light-footed across the broken tesserae, whirling round like a dancer, smiling. 'It is like a secret place. And the gardens!'

Roshana smiled. She put her arm about the boy and stroked the nape of his neck. 'Perhaps we could stay a while.'

'Ushau, take the left. I will take the right,' Rakhsar said. 'We'd best examine the lie of the place. Roshana, when you are done fondling our little eunuch, I want you to find some way to strike a light. There should be cellars, and I would kill someone for a cup of wine.'

They scattered through the house, exploring like children. The place had been abandoned and left to the elements, and the quick-growing vegetation of the fertile plains had all but smothered it. Creepers edged in at every window, dislodging the shutters with tendrils as thick as a woman's wrist, and some of the mosaic floors were all but hidden by a growth of weeds and thorns, stands of giant mushrooms in damp corners. Geckos watched them warily from the walls, and the swallows continued to dart about their heads in protest, dropping balls of mud and flitting within inches of destruction as they carved aerobatic loops around balustrades and broken arches.

At the back of the house they found the kitchens, and they were massively built and in better repair. There was a fireplace wide enough to roast a brace of pigs, rusted fire-irons which could still be swung above the flames, and copper pots gone green but still with a bottom to them. They found knives, skewers, and earthenware jars with the seals intact, and opened them one by one, finding good oil, vinegar, and – marvel of all – honey, congealed hard as plaster, but still sweet and good.

Kurun kindled a fire in the broad kitchen hearth while Roshana hauled water out of the well and filled a trough outside for the horses. The water was clear, iron-tasting, and she had only to brush the skimming insects off it to drink her fill.

At the back of the house the kitchen garden was surrounded by a high wall – broken now, but within it were tomato plants, peppers of every hue, massive onions and wild garlic, and a riot of herbs. Roshana and Kurun gathered whatever caught their eye, brought it indoors in the folds of her cloak, and set to scrubbing some of the copper pots by the crackling smokeless fire. Kurun began sharpening one of the long iron knives on a whetstone, paused to stare blindly at the blade for a long moment in a spasm of unwanted memory, and then grimly carried on.

Rakhsar and Ushau entered the kitchen bearing dry lamps, which they filled from the jars and set to burning. With the lamplight and the firelight, and the water boiling, it was as homely a place as they had known in months.

The dark drew in, and secret creaking and rustling and skittering could be heard through the house, above the squeak of the hunting bats outside. When they had all eaten, the twins threw their bedrolls on the stone before the fire and sat upon them, Roshana sewing a rent in her robe, Rakhsar sharpening his scimitar with long screeching sweeps of the whetstone. Ushau went outside, to look upon the horses and keep an eye out, though it seemed barely credible that anyone would ever chance upon such a forgotten place who was not searching for it.

Kurun sat in a corner, nodding with tiredness, forgotten for the moment. The kitchen and its warmth reminded him of happier times, back in Ashur before the world had gone mad.

But he did not want to go back. He sat at the edge of the firelight and watched Rakhsar and Roshana, and found himself filled with simple wonder, at the things he had seen and the widening of the world he knew. He had crossed the Magron Mountains, been buried in snow, seen people die sudden and violent deaths. He had watched the sun rise over the endless plains of the Middle Empire.

And he had known these two, this royal pair. He had been caressed by the Great King's daughter.

He would not have missed any of it. Not even for the thing which had been taken away from him.

'ARE WE SAFE here?' Roshana asked her brother. In the firelight, her eyes were huge and dark and her face white.

'For a while, perhaps. We will stay a few days, no more.' Rakhsar continued to sweep the whetstone down the sword blade.

'Surely they will give up on us, leave us alone. Brother, perhaps they think us already dead.'

'Roshana, you know as well as I that Kouros and Orsana will not be satisfied until they stand over our corpses. Just because we do not have soldiers thundering after us on horses does not mean we have not been watched, and followed.'

'Have you seen anything?'

'I don't know.' Rakhsar laid down the sword on his thigh and squeezed shut his eyes, bright lights in dark hollows. 'Sometimes I see a spy behind every bush, and sometimes, like tonight, I cannot conceive of ever being tracked and found again. But this place is probably known to our enemies. They will look for us here eventually.'

'What are we to do, Rakhsar, keep running west until we meet the Macht, or reach the sea? It has to end.'

'I am thinking on it.'

'Rakhsar –'

'I said I am thinking on it!'

They sat in silence after that. Roshana picked out

the wayward stitches she had been sewing without seeing, and began again. The whetstone began its thin glide along the blade of the scimitar once more. In the corner, Kurun watched, head nodding. In his hand he had the sharpened knife with which he had prepared their supper. The blade grew warm against his flesh. He slept.

BEFORE DAWN KURUN was up and awake. He bent, blew life into the fire, added some sprigs of dry creeper to it to bring up the flame, and set a pot of water upon the coals.

Roshana and Rakhsar lay in one another's arms, still asleep. The privations they had both undergone in the last weeks and Roshana's shorn hair made them look more than ever like reflections of each other. Kurun knelt beside them, and touched Roshana's cheek. His brown fingers traced the soft line of her earlobe. She murmured, and Kurun straightened.

Ushau sat upright by the wall, watching.

'Do not mistake your place, young fellow,' the giant *hufsan* said softly.

'I mean no disrespect.'

'I know. But remember what you are, and what blood flows through them. We are not in the ziggurat now, but they are still far beyond us.'

'They would be dead if it were not for us.'

'That is of no account. One day, if they are spared, they will live in a palace again, lords of the world, and we will be forgotten.'

'They will not forget us – how could they?'

Ushau smiled, and leaned his head back against the wall. 'Go look on the horses.'

Outside, the birds were singing in invisible crowds from every bush and tree. Not even in the Gardens of the Great King had Kurun ever heard so many together. The sun was rising fast; it seemed to slide up the sky with unseemly haste in this part of the world, so that the moment of the dawn, that daily miracle, was barely to be experienced before it was over.

The horses were head-hung and silent, though they turned to Kurun as he approached, knowing his smell. He had brought them an apple each, and they ate them with relish, but seemed barely awake.

The sunlight rose over the broken walls of the garden, flooding the back of the house, warming the world. Tendrils of mist which had been coiling along the ground withered at its touch, and Kurun stood feeling the light and life of Bel the Renewer soak into him. It seemed to him in that moment he had found for himself a corner of a better world, and he knew that in such a place he could be happy, even if he were only a slave.

FOUR DAYS PASSED in peace and silence. The disparate foursome lost the aches and pain that constant travel had ground into them, and began to feel rested, clean, almost normal. The headlong urgency of the past weeks faded, and in the warm air of the lowland summer, the snows of the Magron became but a dream. Their lives in the ziggurat seemed more distant still, a memory to puzzle over.

In a chest in the upstairs of the house they found clothes, put away with bunches of lavender and columbine so as to deter the insects. They were, it seemed, plain garments, suited to a prosperous lower-caste household. Roshana set to adjusting them with her wayward needle skills, and Rakhsar took Kurun farther afield, to look over the estate which had been bought in his name at his birth.

Poplars, cypress and plane trees had been planted in lines fanning out from the house, but over the years the lines had become irregular and entangled with saplings and all manner of secondary growth. The borders of the estate were impossible to define, though Rakhsar and Kurun stumbled across a deep, overgrown ditch with water running at the bottom of it which seemed a boundary of some sort.

They raised partridge, pheasant, and – once – a magnificent heron out of the wetter ground as they beat the bounds of the little kingdom. There was no sign of people anywhere, and the city of Arimya was a mere bump of shadow on the hazy horizon.

But there was something almost indefinable which intruded on the peace. Kurun could not put a word to it until Rakhsar lifted his head and sniffed the air like a hound.

'Woodsmoke,' he said, frowning.

They looked back at the house, and saw the black bar of smoke rising from the kitchen-chimney, like a marker set in the sky. Rakhsar swore, and began to run.

They pelted into the kitchen as though they had wolves on their tail, and saw Roshana by the fire, feeding it with mossy branches she had picked up in the garden. A thick smoke rose from it, to be sucked into the mantle above.

Rakhsar said not a word, but shoved his sister aside, grabbed a fire-iron, and began raking the burning wood out of the hearth. He stamped upon it and beat it with the iron until the kitchen was filled with smuts and sparks and they were choking on it.

'Where is Ushau?'

Roshana was bewildered. 'I sent him for more wood.'

'Get out of my way, you stupid bitch.' Rakhsar grabbed at a pot of water, which was full of peeled onions, and threw it on the last of the coals. A billow of steam went up. He stood, panting. Roshana cowered against Kurun.

'What is wrong – what did I do?'

'We cannot have smoke. Are you stupid? How many times have I told you; if you must have a fire in the day, the wood must be powder-dry. You've just signalled our presence here for pasangs all around.'

'I'm sorry. I didn't think –'

'It was not burning long, master,' Kurun said.

'Long enough.' Rakhsar stood, looking into the ruined fire, still breathing heavily. 'We have been here too long. We are forgetting our fate.'

Roshana began to sob silently, and Kurun put his arm about her shoulders.

'Stop crying, sister. It will not do anyone any good.'

'Do we have to leave? Can't we stay here?' she wept.

Rakhsar lifted his head, incredulous. He spun round, pushed Kurun out of the way and took his sister by the upper arms. He shook her like a terrier worrying a rat.

'Is that what you thought – that somehow we could set up home here? My dear sister, I credited you with more wit – even this boy knew better.'

'I'm tired of running,' Roshana said brokenly.

'Are you tired of living?' He released her. To Kurun, he snapped, 'Get her out of here, and then clean this mess up.'

'Yes, master,' Kurun murmured.

'And keep your little paws off her, boy. You may have no balls, but I see what's in your eyes. Now get out.'

THEY WERE AFRAID again. For a short time they had dared to believe the worst might be over, but they all recognised the truth of Rakhsar's words. That afternoon they began methodically to pack up food and bedding and anything else they could glean from the house which would speed their onward journey. The hearth remained cold and black, and the weather took a turn for the worse in the early evening, a long slew of thunderclouds edging east over the world, and then congregating on the wide plains west of the Bekai River.

Rakhsar did not let them light so much as a single clay lamp, so agitated had he become. He stood and stared out at the silver sheets of the rain, the patient horses standing under it with the bags already packed upon their rumps, and whatever peace they had all known in the last few days entirely gone. The house seemed dank and cold in the rain, streams of water pouring through the threadbare roof and puddling on the floors. It was as though it knew they were leaving, and was turning its face from them.

It was the middle hours of the night before the rain stopped, and Rakhsar herded them out into the dripping garden. Roshana was lifted up onto one of the horses by Ushau, and then the little company went in single file around the drenched, dark building, the overgrown trees and bushes snatching at them with wet fingers. They were soaked before they had gone fifty paces, but finally they were at the front of the house, and here the rest clambered on the horses, Ushau behind Roshana on her horse, Rakhsar and Kurun on the other. It was dark as pitch, with not a star showing; but in the clouds to the west there was a faint red glow as Firghe, moon of wrath, rose far above the swollen thunderheads.

They did not look back. The path ahead was a slightly paler bar between black overhanging trees, a tunnel of growth that smelled of dank earth and wild garlic in the dark. The rain had subdued all sounds of life save the frogs, which were burping to each other in the ditches, a mindless chorus.

They disappeared into the tunnel, the horses clopping along through fetlock-deep puddles, and the water streaming down on them from the trees above – everywhere, the sound of gurgling water, the whole night awash.

Rakhsar reined in and set his hand on his sword-hilt, stiffening like a downwind deer.

'Kurun,' he whispered, his lips close to the boy's ear. 'Listen.'

It was the merest tangle of distant noise, but it rang out, clear of the dripping water and the frogs and the breathing of their own animals. There was a click of metal on metal, like a spoon clattering against the bottom of a pot. Or a spearhead on armour.

And all at once a horse neighed, high and clear in the night, the sound as startling as a horn-blast.

Rakhsar's own horse, a mare, began to reply, and he punched it between the ears. It threw its head up but was silent, knowing better than to argue the point.

Roshana's mount crowded up against them, the animals abreast in the narrow lane. 'What is it?' she demanded in a low hiss. For a second she sounded just like her brother.

'Trouble. Back away, Roshana – back to the house. We cannot leave this way.'

They turned the horses round. The darkness pressed close on them now, and everything was soaked and awkward, twigs poking their faces, leaves slapping them derisively. Firghe broke through the clouds for a few moments, and his red light streamed down on them, bloodying the puddles.

There were men standing in the lane behind them.

Roshana cried out, a dark wail. Rakhsar drew his scimitar.

'Do not try it, Rakhsar,' a voice said, in good Kefren. 'I have my people all around you. There is nowhere to run.'

Feet splashing in the water, the flicker of movement. The wind had begun to pick up, and the limbs of the trees moved in mockery of their fear, mimicking the shapes of the hunters.

'I'm not running,' Rakhsar said clearly. He shoved Kurun off the horse with his rein-hand and raised the red-gleaming sword in the other. Then, with a wordless cry, he kicked his mount in the ribs, and the beast whinnied and leapt almost from its haunches into a canter, straight down the lane.

Kurun toppled into the ditch at the foot of the trees. There was reassurance in the undergrowth about him. He felt almost invisible. He drew his knife and lay wide-eyed.

Then Roshana screamed, and he clambered to his feet with a snarl.

They were coming up the other end of the lane also; shadows pelting on foot, weapons raised red in the moonlight. Ushau was off the horse and charging them, an immense shape wielding the gleam of a kitchen hatchet. Roshana's horse bolted, galloping after Rakhsar with her clinging to its neck. Kurun stood alone in the lane. He saw Ushau scatter the figures to their rear like tailor's dolls. There was the clang of iron on iron.

'Forgive me,' Kurun muttered, and he began to sprint after Roshana and her brother.

'Hold your ground!' someone shouted in Asurian. 'That's no warhorse. Stand fast!'

It seemed that Rakhsar was going to ride down

the figures in his way, the wicked scimitar point questing for their faces, but at the last moment the horse balked and twisted, lost its footing in the muck underfoot, and fell heavily in a spray of water. Then it was all flailing hooves, teeth and mane as it struggled to its feet again.

Rakhsar rose with it, his eyes shining red as they caught the moon. He slashed the animal's flank and it screamed in pain and kicked away from him, bowling over the men before it and sending them flying.

Rakhsar held onto its tail and was pulled with it. The scimitar licked out and one of the men sank to his knees, hands pressed to the streaming slash in his throat. He toppled onto his face and lay gurgling and drowning in the bloody lane.

Roshana's horse came galloping through a moment later. Someone struck out at its forelegs; it cartwheeled with a scream and she went hurtling through the air, splashed to the ground and rolled like a ball of rags. When she raised herself groggily to her hands and knees, one of the attackers kicked her in the head and she went down again.

Kurun sprinted up beside this man – a stocky *hufsan* in a leather cuirass – and stabbed up, beneath the waist of the armour, feeling the blade go deep, deep, until his very fingers were in the wound.

He pulled the knife out with a grunt, and then stabbed again, and again. He punched the knife into the man's flesh in a silent frenzy, and as the *hufsan* sank to his knees, he shifted his grip on the blade, and stabbed down into the side of the man's neck. The *hufsan* collapsed like a puppet with slashed strings, ripping the knife out of Kurun's nerveless fingers.

He ran to Roshana, but was kicked aside. A curved blade licked out and took him in the ribs, the blow not a sharp thing, but like a solid punch. He clasped his side, gaping like a landed fish, and went down with his head resting at Roshana's feet, his face half-buried in water. It was raining again, and he could feel the drops strike his cheek, but from his breastbone down, there was no sensation at all. It was as if his legs had suddenly disappeared.

A foot flipped him over; a shadow looked him in the face, and then ran on. There was a chaos of shouting. Roshana was dragged limply away. But he could still hear swordplay, the clack and ring of steel.

'Kill them, master,' he whispered. 'Save her.'

Then his eyes rolled back in his head, and he no longer felt anything, and the red moon made a bone-carved mask of his bloodless face.

THE HORSEMEN CHOKED the lane, a stamping cavalcade of them. Kouros cursed and swore and lashed out with his riding crop as he strove to get to the forefront of the crowd. He had brought too many, and had not thought about deploying them, merely told his guards to charge hell-for-leather towards the house in which Kuthra had finally cornered his half-brother. A dead horse in the lane had brought down two of the lead riders, and the rest was chaos.

Some of them were bearing lit torches, and the fitful yellow light almost made the thing worse.

The Niseian under him remembered its training. It shouldered the other horses aside, biting and kicking with the fury of its rider. A wild leap, and it was over the bodies on the ground – a surprising number of them – and then Kouros was galloping alone up the track. He cast aside the whip and drew his sword.

Another horse. The Niseian crashed into it deliberately, the big warhorse knocking the smaller animal clear off its feet. But the shock shook Kouros in the saddle. He dropped his sword, gripped the pommel of his saddle with both hands, and struggled to stay on the wild warhorse's back. The reins now loose, the Niseian lifted its head and screamed out a challenge to the blank darkness of the house looming under the moon. There were more bundles underfoot, and it danced over them; like all horses, it was unwilling to step on a body.

Kouros roundly consigned the animal to Mot's shadow, and leapt off. It sprang away. Now he saw that the girth had slipped and it was trying to kick the saddle free. The iron-shod hooves went by his head so close he felt the wind. He dropped to the ground, scrabbling for his sword, a little incredulous that his moment of triumph should have taken such a turn. He came upon a warm body lying in the rainwater, a boy's face that seemed familiar. He could not find his sword, and splashed through the puddles while the rain grew colder on his back. At last he found a hilt to hand. A long kitchen knife, bloody to the handle – it would do; it would have to do.

He stood up. 'Kuthra!' Where were his men? He looked back down the track leading from the house, that tree-dark tunnel, and saw shapes milling there, shattered torchlight, a meaningless melee. What were they at?

No matter. They would be with him by and by.

'Kuthra!'

He ran forward, wiping the rain out of his eyes, puffing. Bushes and undergrowth everywhere, a veritable jungle out of which the dark bulk of the house rose like some lightless monolith, and behind it the red moon glowed in a speeding welter of broken cloud.

'Here, brother,' a voice said. And there was a dark shape sitting at the wall of the house, like a man taking his ease. Kouros sprinted to it, cursing the heavy cuirass he wore and his water-filled boots that sloshed at every step.

Panting, he knelt, and saw Kuthra's pain-racked face, a smile guttering across it like the last flicker of a spent lamp.

'Almost on time, Kouros. But not quite.'

'Where are you hurt?' Kouros felt a thrill of shock and grief blast through him.

'He gutted me. A good swordsman, our brother. I did not know that.'

'Where is he?' Kouros was weeping soundlessly. He tried to clasp Kuthra's hand but could not pry the other's fingers from the great wound in his belly. The very leather of Kuthra's cuirass had been slashed through, and there were nameless shining things bulging between his straining fingers.

'Oh Kuthra, my brother.' He wept like a child. 'I will take you out of here. My father's surgeons –'

'I am a dead man, Kouros. Rakhsar has done for me in fair fight. Do not trouble yourself.'

Kouros leaned until his forehead and Kuthra's were touching. He kissed the dying man on the cheek. There was nothing else in the world but that face he loved. The one person in creation he trusted.

'Kill him for me,' Kuthra whispered, blood on his teeth. 'I should have lived. I wanted to see you King.'

'I need you, Kuthra.'

'You must find someone else to trust, brother. Your mother's people are here also. That was the problem – we brought too many to this party.'

'Roshana?'

'Here somewhere – she may be dead. I made a mess of things, right at the last. Forgive me, Kouros.'

'I love you, my brother. There is nothing to forgive.'

Kuthra smiled. 'You are a better man than you know. Be a good king. Remember me, Kouros.' He struggled, as though he had one last thing to say.

'*Kouros –*'

But there were no more words. Kuthra sighed, and his face took on a look of mild surprise, as though things were not quite what he had thought. His head tilted to one side and came to rest against his brother's face, so that Kouros's tears were on both their cheeks. The straining hands relaxed.

Kouros took one hand in his own, the blood gluing their palms together.

'Goodnight my dear brother,' he whispered, and

bent his head. He knelt there beside the body in the soft rain, and above them both the Moon of Wrath beamed full and bright in the cloud-streaked sky.

IT WAS BARKA who found him, and knelt beside him in the rain. He took one look at Kuthra's waxen face, and set a hand on Kouros's shoulder.

'My prince.'

'Get your hand off me.'

'There is work to be done, Kouros.'

'Find Rakhsar. I want him alive, Barka. The man who takes his life will lose his own.'

'We have found the lady Roshana.'

At last, Kouros raised his head. Barka recoiled from the look on his face.

'She lives?'

'She lives.'

Kouros rose to his feet. He looked down at Kuthra's body.

'Give me your cloak.'

Wordlessly, Barka handed it over. Kouros took it and laid it over his dead brother's body.

'He will come back with us, Barka. We will bring him back and give him a funeral worthy of a prince. What was denied him in life shall be given him in death, I swear it.'

He raised his head. His eyes shone with a vulpine light.

'Now, take me to my sister.'

* * *

THEY HAD FANNED out and were beating the bushes in line as though flushing out a boar for the spears of the hunters. Torches had been lit here and there along the rank, and by these they kept their intervals and advanced through the forgotten fields and choked thickets of the estate. There were dozens of them: Kuthra's men, Orsana's men, and Kouros's personal guards.

Rakhsar hunkered in the bottom of the overhung ditch with the water running fast round his knees. He had caught his breath after the chaotic fighting up at the house, and reckoned now that he was near the edge of the estate. But beyond it the country was more open, bare as a table in the moonlight. Anande was rising sluggishly now, diluting the light of the red moon and turning the rain into a gem-like shimmer in the air, more a mist than anything else. Dawn could not be far off; he had not much time to waver over his options.

If he could steal a horse, it might yet be enough. He was a better horseman than his clown of a brother, or any of the men he had brought with him. With a good Niseian between his knees, Rakhsar would leave them eating his dust.

But Roshana.

He did not know if his sister was dead or alive, free or captured. Ushau and Kurun were gone, that he knew, but he could not leave without knowing about her. He could not do it.

And so the decision was easily made, in the end.

He hauled himself out of the ditch, stood under the shadow of the juniper and gorse, smelling the blossoms, smiling slightly. The line of beaters was some half-pasang away. And behind them he thought he caught more movement amid the scattered trees on the horizon. Cavalry.

At least Kouros deemed us worthy of a small army, though half a dozen fellows who knew their job might have done better.

He looked down at the black blade of his scimitar. A present from his father, the Great King. It had turned out to be the most useful gift he had ever received.

And all those hours of training had not gone for naught after all.

Kouros, just let me once get close, and I will share our father's gift with you.

He took off at a loping run for the house. The men in the distance saw him at once, and a cry went up, as hounds will sound at the sight of the fox. The blooms of the torchlight began to cluster in pursuit. Rakhsar grinned, and broke into a flat sprint.

On the horizon, the distant cavalry checked at the sight of the running torches in the fields, and changed course towards the house also, like moths summoned by the light.

FOURTEEN
THE HORSEMEN IN THE DAWN

DAWN WAS COMING, a pink brimming light in the eastern sky that lit up nothing as yet but which had brought all the thickets and trees into an explosion of birdsong. A summer morning heralding a hot unclouded day to come. The longest days of the year were here.

The night had been long enough. Rakhsar grunted as one of Kouros's stragglers popped up in his path, almost as startled as he. The scimitar licked out and did its work – he gave almost no thought to the motion – and the *hufsan* gave a sharp cry, like a man who has stubbed his toe, and then slid to the ground; not dead, but useless now, scrabbling in an agonised world of his own. Rakhsar ran on. There was not a gleam of metal left to see on the scimitar's blade; it was congealed black to the hilt.

The walls of the house were almost the same shade as the sunrise, the colour in them shallowing as the light grew. No-one else stepped in Rakhsar's path, and he slowed, gathering the breath in his lungs. His arms and legs were trembling with fatigue and the reaction to the night's violence.

Dead horses, an open space with many men standing in it, others bent over wounds. One was on his hands and knees drinking from a puddle like a dog.

Roshana also was on her knees, naked, a stripe of blood down one side of her face. He arms were bound behind her back, and there was a leather collar at her throat. Kouros stood holding the leash. He tugged on it sharply as Rakhsar approached, the armed men making a lane for his brother. Roshana's head was tugged upwards. Her eyes were beyond tears. She stared at Rakhsar a moment, and then lowered her face again, turning away and squirming as if she could hide her nakedness.

A black heartbeat began to thump in Rakhsar's head. For a moment he was almost dizzied by his own hatred. He blinked, tried to produce his trademark sneer, but found he could not. His face was as raw as an open wound as he faced Kouros and his sister, and around him the men made a circle, and hefted their weapons in their hands thoughtfully, eyeing the black-bladed scimitar as though it were a thing animate in itself.

'She had such lovely hair,' Kouros said. 'It is such a shame to see her cropped like a convict.

But it will suit her well for what I have in store.' He tugged on the leash again. Roshana choked, but said nothing, not lifting her head. She was kneeling in a puddle and her thighs were so pale they were almost blue. She began to shiver.

'You and I have a lot to bury here, Kouros,' Rakhsar said evenly. 'You have prevailed, and I will die. You will be King and I will not even be a footnote in history. But I ask you now to show mercy. Not to me – to Roshana. She has never once done you harm. She does not deserve this.'

Kouros considered. He did not look like a man on the threshold of triumph. He had been weeping, and there was a lost look in his eyes despite the savage snarl that seemed fixed on his mouth.

'Barka. Bring forward your burden.'

The weaponsmaster was carrying a body on his shoulder, wrapped in a travelling cloak. He set it on the ground and Kouros knelt and pulled back the folds to show a broad, bloodless face somewhat like his own, though with more *hufsan* blood in it. Roshana tried to move away from the corpse, but he caught her by her slim arm and tugged her closer. Rakhsar advanced convulsively, and immediately all about him the ring of soldiers tightened, and the swords lifted, like the heads of hounds catching a new scent. Rakhsar froze.

'Behold my brother,' Kouros said brokenly. He pulled back the cloak further to reveal the stump of one arm.

'My mother took his hand, to mark him. And

you killed him, Rakhsar.' He stroked the dead face. 'He would have walked through hell for me, had I asked him.'

Then Kouros stood up. 'Drop your sword.'

Rakhsar stood fast. 'You think I will go down as easily as that?'

'Drop your sword, or we will open your sister's pretty legs and I will have my men rape her one after the other in front of you.' The lost look had gone – even the hatred. Kouros's eyes were cold as slate, no emotion left in them.

'Kouros –'

In the distance, growing louder, the sound of hoofbeats began to rumble in the air, growing closer. A great many horses.

'I think father is looking for us,' Kouros said. And again, 'Drop your sword.'

Rakhsar looked at the ring of men surrounding him, and then at his sister. Her face was white, with black holes for eyes.

'Give me your word you will not harm her.'

'I give you nothing. Drop your sword.'

Another trembling second. Kouros gestured impatiently with one hand, not looking behind him, and a clot of his men converged on Roshana. They threw her to her back on the wet ground. Two grabbed her ankles. She screamed, and thrashed in their grip. 'Rakhsar – fight them – fight them!' she shrieked.

Rakhsar dropped the sword.

Kouros smiled slightly, and raised his hand, and the men paused. Roshana went still in their grasp.

It was as though they were manhandling some sculptor's white-marble masterwork.

'Take his arms,' Kouros said, and his men closed in on Rakhsar, two on each side. They pinioned him. Kouros drew close, pulling from his belt a cheap kitchen-knife.

'Not so good as the blade our father gave you, but iron is iron, Rakhsar.'

'What a king you'll make, Kouros,' Rakhsar drawled; a last, defiant sneer.

Kouros drew close, set one hand on his brother's shoulder, and looked into his eyes.

'This is for my true brother,' he whispered. 'As I promised him.'

And then he plunged the knife into Rakhsar's belly.

He twisted it, hearing Roshana scream behind him. Rakhsar's feet left him. He writhed, teeth clenched on the pain. He made barely a sound.

'Drop him,' Kouros said to the men, and Rakhsar was released to collapse into the mud at their feet. Now he did groan, a thin sliver of blood trickling out of his mouth.

Kouros studied his struggles for a moment, and looked at the blood on the knife as if wondering how it had got there. Finally Barka spoke up.

'My prince, what of the lady?'

Kouros turned. There were horses cantering up the lane. His father's men had come too late.

He went to Kuthra's body, and covered up the dead man's face again.

'The men will do as they please with the lady.

When they are done, she is to be killed. I do not ever want to see her again, alive or dead.'

'No!' Roshana screamed.

The sunrise was over the house now, and the birdsong had grown into a deafening chorus. The horsemen slowed to a trot, and filed into the open space before the house. They were mounted on Niseians, in full armour, and they bore lances. More were streaming across the fields. They were all Kefren, and they wore red cloaks. More and more kept coming, a steaming cavalcade of horseflesh and gleaming bronze and iron.

Two of them reined in before Kouros, and the smaller of the two doffed his crested helm. He had the features of a *hufsan*, but finer, and with the pale colouring of the high castes. He looked the scene in the yard over, and his gaze paused on Roshana, held naked in the grip of four soldiers. Something in his face changed, as though the bones had grown more pronounced.

'What's going on here?' he asked quietly in Kefren.

'My lord,' Barka said. He ran forwards. 'Kouros!'

'Who is your Archon, and who sent you?' Kouros asked. 'Speak quickly, man.'

'Release that woman,' the slightly built horseman said. And though the words were spoken softly, something in the tone of the voice seemed to crawl cold into the spine of every man standing there.

'Do you know who I am?' Kouros asked, his own voice rising. 'Do you have any idea?'

The man ignored him. 'First rank, lances, second rank, bows!'

There was a clatter as the horsemen raised their lances out of the stirrup-sockets. Others were unslinging compound bows from their saddles and nocking arrows to the strings. The men in the yard, a loose ring around the bodies, shrank in on each other and faced out, somewhat bewildered.

'How dare you!' Kouros cried.

But Barka had strode in front of him, covering him with his own body.

'Who are you?' he asked the lead horseman.

The youth leaned forward in the saddle, his bright eyes burning.

'I am called Corvus, and I am King of the Macht.'

A moment of stunned silence. They stood looking up at him in utter incomprehension. Corvus smiled slightly, a widening of his tight mouth, no more.

'And who are you?'

Barka launched himself at Corvus with a roar, sword cocked back in his hand.

Two broadheads struck him before he had moved six feet, staggering him. He dropped his sword, turned to Kouros.

'Flee!' he cried. A third arrow took him in the throat, bowling him over, and he fell on his back, gripping the shaft with one hand as though holding it in place.

Chaos broke out. The cavalry leapt forward, the Niseians half-rearing as their riders kicked them into motion. The iron-tipped lances jabbed out and the armoured bulk of the horses knocked men off their feet and trampled them when they went down.

Kouros turned and ran.

A lance speared him through the shoulder, piercing his corselet and his flesh in one thrust. He barely registered it. He leapt over Kuthra's body, fell on his side in the mud, got up again and kept running. A wall of black horses met him.

He rolled beneath their hooves, scrabbled along the ground like a wounded beetle, and was beneath them. He looked up to see the belly of one of the great beasts above his face, and hurled himself through its back legs. It sensed him, and kicked out hard, the iron-shod hoof catching him in the side, breaking his ribs. He breathed in pure agony, the pain flooding through his body with the very working of his lungs.

But he got up at a crouch and kept running, saw a shadowed, overhung ditch ahead and dived into it head first.

He splashed into the water, the pain from his shoulder now beginning to rise, his arm numb and useless. He crawled along the ditch on his belly, choking, sputtering, half-drowning. The morning was raucous with the sounds of fighting, men and horses screaming, the clash of metal. This cannot be, he was thinking.

It was all that would lodge in his head. *This cannot be*. The utter astonishment of it all kept him going, took his mind off the pain. But his body was weakening fast. He tucked the bloody knife in his waist-sash. It was his only weapon and he was damned if he would lose it.

After a hundred paces, he climbed out of the ditch and floundered into the shade of a tamarisk thicket. Thorns tore at his face, and he had to shut his eyes as they sliced his eyelids. But he kept going, a high whine rising in his throat, like that of a mistreated dog. He did not know in which direction he was fleeing, but he did not pause or stop to think; the instinct in him was too strong for that. He kept going, fighting the agony, knowing only that he had to get away, away from the men on horses and the thing which led them.

THE YARD WAS a used-up battlefield, the puddled mud now lathered with blood and studded with corpses. Corvus dismounted and sheathed his sword.

'Ardashir,' he called. 'Bring them in. We don't know what else is in the area. I want pickets thrown out a pasang on all sides.'

The tall Kefre nodded and set off at a trot, calling for his men. There were horn-calls, like the huntsman recalling his hounds.

Corvus knelt in the mud over a high-caste Kefre who was still living, clutching at a wound in his belly. He was sharp-featured and handsome, but his lips were blue. His breath came in short, agonised gasps.

'You are Corvus,' he said, looking up at the pale

face. And he made a noise that might have been a laugh.

'I am Corvus.'

'Save my sister. She is an innocent.'

One hand left the gaping belly-wound and grasped Corvus's arm. 'Save Roshana.'

'The girl is safe,' Corvus reassured him. 'Let me look at you, friend.'

The fist went back into the wound. 'I am already dead. My name was Rakhsar, and I was a prince of the empire. My brother Kouros –'

He shuddered, his body clenching up. And then the breath came out of him in a long, slow sigh, and he lowered his head, the fine features sinking into the mud, the earth of Pleninash filling his dead eyes.

Corvus straightened, frowning.

Ardashir trotted back and dismounted. 'This is a mess, whatever it was.'

'Is the woman all right?'

'She's been mauled a little, but she'll live. I wonder what happened here?'

'Police the field, Ardashir. I want information. Anyone who still lives, we bring with us.'

A trooper came galloping up to them and hauled in his horse in a flash of spray.

'My king – riders approaching from the east, at least a full mora of them. Heavy cavalry – they have blue-enamelled armour and they ride Niseians like us.'

'Arakosan cavalry,' Corvus said. 'The main body must be closer than we thought. Well, that's good to know.' He looked down at the dead Kefre at his feet. 'Bring this man along also, Ardashir. Dead or alive, he interests me.'

Ardashir called for help from a rank of horsemen standing nearby. The body was lifted out of the mud and slung on the back of a horse like a sack.

On the back of another horse, a Kefren girl with a close-cropped head watched, and let the tears cut white lines down the filth caking her beautiful face.

FIFTEEN
MANY ENEMIES

KURUN OPENED HIS eyes.

To utter strangeness. He did not know where he was. He was lying on his back, and above his head there was a darkness that moved and creaked and bulged. It was like being in a womb with the wind beating upon it.

Lamp-light. The steadying glow of a wick flickering in a clay saucer. That, at least, was familiar.

And pain. It was not urgent, but a mere background singing. He seemed to remember that it had once been much worse.

He turned his head, and saw Roshana at his side. She was in a willow-woven chair, and her head was resting on his bed, by his arm. He lifted his hand and touched her hair, a velvet spikiness which was pure pleasure to run his fingers through.

I am alive.

He could not add up any rational series of events to bring himself to this moment, but in this moment, he did not care. It was enough that he and Roshana were alive and he could brush her hair with his fingers. It was more than enough.

She opened her eyes. No other part of her moved, and she suffered him to stroke her hair as they stared at one another.

I love you, he thought. He smiled.

She took his hand in her own and their fingers entwined, his brown and strong and calloused, hers slim and blue-veined and soft.

'Rakhsar is dead,' she said softly. And the moment soured. The memories began to assemble in their ghastly ranks, and it came back to him.

'Ushau?'

'Dead. We are all that is left, Kurun.'

Her eyes were bloodshot and he saw now that her temple was bruised, a purple stain that rose into her hairline. Instinctively, he tried to rise, but the shocking burst of pain in his side left him open-mouthed. Sweat broke out on his body. He clenched her hand in his until he thought he could feel the slender bones creak.

There was a flare of light that dazzled Kurun. When he opened his eyes again, they were no longer alone. Two others stood over the bed. One was Kefren – or at least he seemed Kefren. There was a strange cast to his features that could not be easily slotted into any of the types which Kurun had known since a child in the ziggurat. He was slight and lean, but there was something in his eyes that belied his size; an authority remarkable in one so young.

The other was huge, a hulking, broad-shouldered fellow with grey hair and a scarred face. He was old, but looked as though he could fell a horse with one blow. He was not Kefren, nor *hufsan*.

'Macht,' Kurun whispered. 'You are Macht.' His blood ran cold and he flinched in the bed.

Roshana cupped his face. 'Don't be afraid, Kurun. They saved us. Their surgeon stitched your wound.'

'Where is this place?' Kurun demanded. He lapsed into low Asurian, such was his terror.

The smaller man replied in good Kefren, the language of the court. 'You are in the encampment of the army of King Corvus of the Macht.' He smiled, and the severe set of his bones seemed to soften. 'You are my guests here. You have no reason to be afraid.'

The big Macht said something in a guttural language Kurun could not understand and the small Kefre cocked his head like a bird to listen, then looked down on Kurun once more. He shook his head.

'The surgeon says you must keep to your bed for three more days, Kurun, and he has had his knife in so many folk that we must respect his knowledge. Roshana here will wait on you – she has insisted.' The young Kefre smiled again, looking at Roshana as she crouched by the bed. He had good eyes. When he was younger he must have been beautiful, as pretty as a girl. But there was little of that left in the lean face now.

As he stared upon Roshana, the eyes were still those of a boy.

'I will look in on you both again later,' he said. 'There are men outside the tent who will attend to everything you need – you have only to ask.'

'Are they Kefren?' Roshana asked him, looking up like a cornered deer.

'Yes. They are Kefren of my Companions. You may trust them with your lives, as I have.'

He left the tent. The Macht followed him, but paused at the flap and looked them both over. He wore a red chiton and on his feet were heavy studded sandals pale with dust. He, too, let his eyes linger on Roshana, but not in the same way the other had. It was as though the sight of her face pained him. Then he was gone.

THEY WERE ONLY one day and a night in the tent when a group of Macht threw back the flaps and began dismantling it around their ears. Roshana had created a komis out of an old blanket and she threw it across her face and shouted questions at them, which made them shrug and grin, the more brazen winking at her as she hovered protectively over Kurun's bed. The leather panels of the structure were untied and rolled away with startling speed, and then the ash poles which supported them were lifted out of their post-holes and disappeared also.

Kurun levered himself upright in the bed, ignoring the pain, astonished by what the dismantling of the tent revealed.

They were surrounded by a sea of men.

As far as the eye could see, whole hillsides were covered with moving figures, horses, mules, carts and waggons. Everywhere, tawny-coloured tents similar to their own were coming down, like mushrooms collapsing in on themselves. And thousands upon thousands of Macht were coming and going, loading vehicles, saddling horses, forming up in regimented lines. It was mid-morning, and their activities began to raise the dust out of the ground so that the whole immense scene was fading out minute by minute before their eyes.

Then Kurun's bed was raised high in the air by four brawny Macht – in full armour, save for their helms. A tall Kefre stood by barking instructions in their harsh tongue.

'What are you doing? What's happening?' Roshana demanded, with a hint of the palace princess.

The Kefre pointed with one hand. 'We are on the move, lady. You and the boy have been assigned a waggon. I suggest you get into it.'

'But we were told –'

'The army is on the march, my girl, and we've no time to argue. Now go get in the waggon or I'll have to snap you up and toss you in it myself.' He smiled to soften his words.

'I demand to see your officer. I demand to see the King!'

'The King's busy, lady. Don't you know there's a war on?'

The waggon was well-sprung, and drawn by four mules. Two Macht sat up front, one with a spear, one with a whip, and they chattered incessantly to one another, drank from a wineskin with the hair still on, and spat over the mules' rumps. The dust thickened like a fog, and within that fog was a bedlam of noise. The trundle of iron-rimmed wheels, the braying of mules and neighing of horses, men shouting at one another, the crack of whips. And above all else, a growing rhythm, a cadenced thunder so vast it was felt in the flesh rather than heard by the ears.

Tens of thousands of marching feet, tramping over the earth of the Middle Empire by rank and file, in massed centons and morai.

The Macht army was on the move.

For the rest of the day, the waggon lurched along interminably. The mules were allowed to halt briefly to water, from leather buckets passed hand to hand down the line, and then they were off again, chivvied along by unseen voices in the dust, men swearing, coughing, an acrid reek as they relieved themselves on the march, and the rising stink of their sweat, which even the dust could not choke out. Summer was blooming into full, brassy flower across the lowlands of Pleninash, and the lush green country was being beaten into a swath of dust by the army's passage. The heat rose under the canvas canopy of the waggon until it hung like thirst in their throats. They drank all their water by early afternoon of that day, and one of the teamsters had to run off down the column for more, uttering unmistakeable profanities in his own tongue as he did so.

Kurun sat propped up against Roshana in the bed, the frame clicking on the wooden floor of the waggon as they lurched along. He was naked save for the yellow dressing that was bound around his ribs, but was no longer self conscious before her, and their sweat mingled through the linen shift that the Macht had given her to wear, her dark nipples poking the threadbare material. Such things no longer seemed important; all the senses were stunned and then dulled by the immense exodus which had swallowed them.

THEY SLEPT AT last, clinging to each other, juggled in the narrow bed like dice in a box. So used to the motion of the waggon did they become that it was only when it halted that they woke, the world blue-dark all around them and a coolness descending upon it with the oncoming dusk. There were many voices outside, and the light of a fire soaking through the canvas canopy.

Their bodies were soaked in sweat and covered in dust. Kurun's wound throbbed and ached, but it seemed less profound than it had. He could move, stiffly, slowly. Roshana helped him slip on a wool chiton, and they descended from the waggon with the care of the very old.

Eyes around the fire watched them, and someone tossed them a bulging skin. It was water, not the rancid-smelling wine the Macht drank, and they shared it swallow for swallow, Kurun drinking until he felt his stitches would burst.

A space was made for them by the fire, and they squatted there amid conversations they could not understand, staring into the flames and then at each other. They held hands, needing the touch of the familiar.

One of the men rummaged in a huge leather bag, produced two wooden bowls, and tossed them over, along with two flattened sticks that might conceivably have been seen as spoons. Then he said something and pointed to a larger fire some distance away in the gathering darkness. He made an eating motion.

'They're cooking,' Roshana said. 'I can smell it. He's telling us to go and eat.'

'I'm not hungry,' Kurun lied. He did not feel he could stagger as far as the cooking fire.

'Then I will go.' She collected the bowls with a click and stood up while the Macht around the fire watched. She hesitated a moment under all those hard, inquisitive eyes, and then strode off.

There was a vast cauldron, so large she could have sat in it with a lid over her head. Within was a steaming mess that smelled more appetising than it looked. The Macht were gathered around it in rows as though the cauldron were the stage of an amphitheatre. A man stirred its contents. He shone with sweat, was shaven-headed and scarred, and when he smiled Roshana saw that his teeth were ornamented with silver wire.

She stood, as out of place as a lamb in a wolf's den, and held out the two bowls she had been given.

Silence fell around the cauldron. The silver-toothed man grinned at her, and slopped whatever-it-was into the bowls. He held them out to her, and as she reached for them he drew back again, making a face. A splatter of laughter about the fire.

Some of them stood up. They were behind her. Roshana stood rooted to the spot. She felt a hand touch her buttock and squeeze it. Another slid up her bare thigh. She shuddered, cried out.

And was pushed aside. A huge figure entered the firelight and one of the men behind her was taken by the nape of his neck and tossed aside like an errant puppy. The newcomer swung his arm and the Roshana heard the impact of bone on bone. Another one of her tormentors went down clutching his face. The silver-toothed cook quickly handed Roshana the bowls. She spilled half their contents, her hands were shaking so badly.

It was the old Macht, the tall one who had been in the tent. His eyes glittered like grey shards of glass. He snapped out orders that sounded like curses, and the crowd about the cauldron began to break up at once, men getting to their feet with an alacrity that spoke of fear. Then he set a hand on Roshana's shoulder and guided her away.

They rejoined Kurun at the waggon. The old Macht reached down easily and seized one of the teamsters by the throat, drawing him to his feet. He held him as though he meant to choke him, and the fellow sputtered out excuses and apologies, the meaning clear in any language. The big Macht dropped him as a terrier will discard a dead rat. He nodded to Roshana and Kurun, and then stalked away into the darkness.

They sat with the bowls in their laps, the food almost forgotten.

'Who is that?' Kurun asked.

It was the teamster who replied. Rubbing his throat ruefully he jerked a thumb.

'Rictus,' he said with a croak.

THE CAMP NEVER went quiet that night. It was so hot in the waggon that Kurun and Roshana lay on the beaten grass beneath the vehicle, a single blanket between them. They did not sleep for a long time, but listened and watched like latecomers to a show at the theatre, trying to make sense of it all. They could hear columns of men marching in the night, and cavalry. The stars were dimmed by the myriads of campfires. The night was bristling with movement.

'There are so many,' Kurun whispered. 'I did not know there were so many. And Kefren fighting with them, too.'

'The Great King has more, a hundred times more,' Roshana told him.

'They are not like these. The Macht frighten me, even more than the Honai did.'

'That is because they are strange, Kurun. The Macht are not of this world. They are Mot's curse upon it, sent to punish us.'

'But they saved us.'

'They are animals, all of them.' Roshana bent her head and began to sob silently, and when Kurun set his hand on her shoulder she shook it off.

'I should have stayed. I made Rakhsar take me with him. I should have stayed. He would have escaped then, Kurun. He could have been away, and free, but now he is dead. My brother is dead.'

Finally she let Kurun take her in his arms, and he held her, rocking her like a child, until the tears dried and she slept. He lay holding her for hours, feeling the blood seep out along the line of his stitches, but bearing the pain, enduring it as he had endured so many other things in his short life.

And he realised it was possible, whatever the philosophers said, to feel despair and hope in the same breath.

THE GREAT CAMP seethed, unquiet as an opened grave. Thousand-strong formations of infantry were moving out of the firelit lines to the open country beyond, where more men waited with banners in the dark, to show them where to stand and plant their spears. The Macht army was deploying in darkness, so that they would greet the dawn light with their ranks fully formed, like some army of myth sprung out of the earth itself.

Pasangs to the east, there was a glow in the sky that eclipsed that of their own camp. Ten thousand fires were burning bright, strewn in a vast carpet across the sleeping earth.

The army of the Great King.

PART THREE

GIFTS OF THE KUFR

SIXTEEN
THE FIRELIT PLAIN

In Corvus's tent, the Marshals stood before the map-table in an armoured line, helms in the crooks of their arms. They were a grim-faced set of men, and they stared at the map and at the varicoloured wooden blocks upon it as though they might read some augury of the future therein.

'He is encamped some twenty pasangs away, a normal marching camp,' Corvus said. 'He knows we are somewhere in the region. But I am betting that he has no idea just how close. Druze and Ardashir have destroyed every patrol they have encountered and the main body is moving out as I speak. Brothers, we have not yet been found out.'

'You'd better be right,' Fornyx said. 'In the morning he's going to come marching across that plain and see us standing in front of him, and we'll have to either shit or get off the pot.'

'He'll attack – he has to,' Corvus said. 'He will be in line of march. He should see us about mid-morning, while half his army is still coming up the road behind him. He will form up what he can at a safe distance – and that is when we will hit him. Parmenios's machines will strike his ranks at a distance he does not think possible, and so he will elect to close with us as fast as he can. He will commit his troops as they come up, and we will deal with them piecemeal.'

'I'm glad you're so familiar with the Great King's intentions,' Fornyx said. He looked thoughtful, but did not press the point.

'And there is no word from the Juthan?' Demetrius asked.

'Not for a week now. They are coming up as fast as they can, but they will not make it in time. Brothers, this time tomorrow, it will all be over, for good or ill.'

'For good or ill,' Rictus repeated.

'The dispositions have been made,' Corvus said briskly. 'Tonight the men sleep on their arms, those that can. The line is forming five pasangs east of the camp. There's a wide plain there, no ditches or orchards or vineyards. It's as flat as a theatre stage. The local people call it *gaugamesh*, barren ground. Rictus, I want the water-carriers out at daybreak, going up and down the line. Tomorrow will be hot, and the men will be standing to arms for some time before the thing begins in earnest.'

Rictus nodded, and exchanged a glance with

Fornyx. The Dogsheads were going into battle without him. He had important duties behind the lines. He commanded the reserves, which was something; five thousand green spearmen who had not yet seen battle. But for the most part, his concerns for the morrow were logistical. And he hated it.

Does Corvus no longer trust me? He wondered, and dismissed the thought almost as quickly as it had arrived. The truth might even be the opposite.

'Brothers,' Corvus said quietly, 'I know that we have come a long way together, from the Harukush to this place. But we are only a few days march from the Bekai River. Beyond that, the Magron, and beyond that, a world none of us has ever seen before. They say that there are more people in the city of Ashur alone than in the whole of the Harukush, and that the wealth of the Middle Empire is nothing compared to the riches of the imperial heartlands. Asuria is the richest place in the world. If we defeat these people tomorrow, I tell you it is all ours for the taking. The morning after tomorrow we will all be as good as kings.' He smiled. 'Even you, Fornyx.

'One day to fight through, as we have never fought before – a day of glory which they will talk about for the rest of all time. That is tomorrow. Brothers, tell me honestly, right now; would any of you – any single one of you – wish to be anywhere else but here right now?'

There was no answer needed to that. His words had written it across all their faces.

He has done it again, Rictus thought. This is how he makes men die for him. He paints pictures of glory they all want to be part of.

But Rictus needed no more glory. He had seen enough of that in his life; enough to turn the stomach. When the others left the tent, he remained behind, as he often did.

'What are you going to do, Rictus – talk me out of it?' Corvus asked him.

'No point in that. You're set on doing it this way, and you are my king. I will support you, Corvus.'

'Tepid words, brother. I never thought I would see the day when Fornyx was happier with my plans than you.'

'Perhaps I am getting old.' Rictus shrugged. 'Phobos, I *am* old. You were right to take me out of the front line.'

'You nearly died at the Haneikos, Rictus,' the younger man said softly. 'I cannot let that happen. Of them all, I trust you most.'

'And Ardashir.'

'And Ardashir. But we grew up together.'

'Listen to me, Corvus. There is no longer any profit in denying your heritage. Do you think that the five thousand Kufr of the Companions would follow you so loyally if you were all Macht?'

'Rictus –'

'Hear me out, without wasting any wine this time. If I cannot speak my mind to you, then I should roll up my pack and march home.

'Fight the battles as you always have, by all means. But use your mixed blood to win the peace afterwards. If you portrayed yourself more as a... as a –'

'A Kufr?'

'As a Kefre, among his own people, then you will find this empire you're making easier to rule when the bloodletting is done.'

Corvus glared at the older man. 'I've been playing the Macht for long enough, is that it, Rictus? Now that we're here in the empire, I can revert to my true self – a Kufr. How do you think the army would take that?'

'You are both Macht and Kufr. The two bloods that are in you made you what you are. Without either, we would not be here now, and the thousands of men forming up to the east of this tent would never have thought to march so far. They follow Corvus, their king.' Rictus smiled now. 'And if he is a strange-looking little wight with something of the east about him, then what is that? Men need a hint of difference in the leaders they follow.'

'Not too much difference. A King of the Macht with Kufr blood – I do not think they are ready for that yet, Rictus.'

'Many suspect it already. We are surrounded by the Kufr, Corvus, and the men see now what is in you. They see that the people of the empire are your people also.'

'You are becoming something of a philosopher in your old age.'

'You take the spear out of a man's hand, and he must fall back on something. Words, usually. Or wine.'

Corvus drew close. 'I will think on your words, brother. Do not think I will not. Ardashir has already said similar things, though he cannot be as direct as you. No-one can.'

Corvus turned away again, and laughed, a free, unforced laugh – the first Rictus had heard from him in a long time.

'Look at us, discussing the disposal of an empire that is not yet ours. There are two hundred thousand Kufr asleep on the plain east of here who have come to dispute that little fact with us, Rictus. We could both of us be dead by tomorrow night.'

'I could choke on a plum stone tonight, or take a fit while having a shit. Men must make provision for a future, even when they are not so sure they will live to see it.'

Corvus turned away at this. Over his shoulder he said, 'Do you know the full story of the skirmish at the farm Ardashir and I became caught up in some days ago?'

'I know you brought back some wounded waifs and strays, and a body we burned with more ceremony than it warranted.'

'The girl is beautiful, is she not?'

'The boy, too, though the surgeon tells me he is a eunuch. Last night I had to slap sense into a few of our people who were about to have some fun with them.'

Corvus glared again. It was his battlefield look. The eyes went wide until there were whites all around the iris, and his voice lowered an octave. Rictus did not believe it was a conscious thing, but it was like watching something possess him, and it never failed to unnerve anyone who saw it.

'Who were they? Name them to me.'

'I will not. They were fools, and I slapped them down. There was no harm done. We are not going to start hanging men on the eve of battle, Corvus, no matter who they were pawing.'

'You do not know who she is, Rictus. The girl, I have discovered, is a daughter of the Great King himself, a royal princess.'

Rictus snorted. 'What?'

'It's true. I have had some of the story from her, some from the Kufr wounded we brought back to camp in the wake of the fight. Her name is Roshana. Her brother Rakhsar died on the field, killed by his elder brother, the heir to the throne.'

'You mean to tell me –'

'They were all there together, the elder pursuing his younger siblings – or half-siblings. I had the Great King's eldest son on the point of my lance. I could have killed him, Rictus, but I was distracted.'

'The girl.'

'The girl' – Corvus shrugged – 'and the small matter of a thousand enemy cavalry. But yes; her face is enough to distract any man. It is the stuff of tall tales, is it not?'

'Phobos! And the heir to it all got away, you say.'

'Possibly. It was the strangest thing. Only Ardashir and I, and now you, know the whole truth of it.'

'This girl, also, is the strangest thing...' Rictus tailed off.

'You're not as incisive as you think, brother. I have

been thinking over some of your ideas for a long time now. It seems to me we have been given a sign, a gift if you like.

'If all goes well – if this time tomorrow we are alive and whole and victorious, then I intend to make this royal princess, Roshana, my wife.'

RICTUS WALKED OUT of the camp that night, clad in the Curse of God and carrying a drepana, but with the rest of his panoply left with the baggage. He strode out under the stars, leaving behind the milling assemblies of the army and the startled sentries, and trudged up to a low knoll some two pasangs from the camp lines, where a trio of lonely olive trees huddled. There was stone in the grass at his feet, and he realised the mound was something man-made and ancient, its history buried under more history, millennia of stories laid down in layers, forgotten now. Perhaps it had been a tomb, perhaps a place to speak and be heard. Now it was simply somewhere he could sit and look out in the night at the turning darkness of the world.

There was a stifled curse in the dark, the click of hobnails on stone, and then a wineskin was tossed out of the gloom and struck him on the chest.

'You're getting to be an eccentric old bastard, you know that?'

Fornyx's voice.

'And you're blind as a mole, if you stub your toes in starlight as bright as this.'

Fornyx sat down beside him in the dry grass. He wore full armour save for his helm, and swore at the clasps as he undid them. Then he tossed his black cuirass to one side as if it were a thing of little account, and pulled the cork from the skin.

They shared the wine, a swallow each, back and forth as if it were some wordless game.

'I wish Valerian was here,' Fornyx said.

'Lord of Irunshahr. The boy made it a long way. I wish him well.'

'May he find himself a bow-legged woman who bears him many sons,' Fornyx said solemnly. He took another snort, and wiped his mouth.

'The men will miss you out there tomorrow,' he said, quietly.

'I'll be out there. I'll just be behind instead of in front.'

'Kesero is useless. Fifteen years in the scarlet and he hasn't the sense of a goose.'

'But you tell him to stand somewhere, and he will stay there. That's why he was banner-bearer all those years.'

'Too stupid to retreat,' Fornyx agreed.

'Keep him in the centre; he'll do well there. And watch your left. Don't come unattached from Demetrius's flank. Many of the latest draft are green as grass. If they see a gap, they'll go to pieces.' Rictus paused. Fornyx was looking at him, smiling into his beard.

'There's an old saying about grandmothers and eggs, Rictus. Let me see if I can remember how it goes...'

'Fuck off, you shortarsed little shit. Give me the wine.'

They drank. Rictus unbuckled his own cuirass and hauled it off. He laid the black plates of it on his knee and wiped a palm across them.

'You ever notice, Fornyx, how even the dust will barely stick to a black cuirass?'

'I know. Water, too. Once Corvus becomes king of the world he should get old Parmenios to take a look into the things, see if we can't hammer out a few more.'

'I don't think we ever will. Whoever made them, their art is lost for good.'

'I could never wear a bronze cuirass again. The weight! I've heard old men say that there's a forgotten place in the deep Harukush where they mined the stuff that makes the Curse of God, but that it was lost in some disaster. Fire, flood and earthquake – the usual tales.'

Rictus set Antimone's Gift aside.

'What won you over?'

Fornyx paused with the neck of the wineskin on his lips. 'Eh?'

'Corvus. How did he do it? There was a time not so long ago when you were the most awkward bugger at the table, but now he has you convinced. Did his genius dazzle you at last, Fornyx?'

'Genius? Genius, my arse.' Fornyx drank deep. The wine ran black from the corner of his mouth.

'He said he would take Machran, and he did. He said he would be King, and he was. Now he says he will be Great King, and I want to be there to see that day, Rictus. He has us all now, caught in the fire of his dreams. We can no more turn away than the moth can leave the flame. For some it is power, riches – the chance to be something approaching a king. For others like me, well –' he grinned. 'I just want to see how it turns out.'

'You don't argue with him any more, or question his strategy.'

'No. Because he has proved himself. And also, we all have you to do that for us. He will take it from you, Rictus, and if it were one of the other marshals, I believe he would get that look on his face – you know the look – and blood would flow. But you, he still listens to.'

'I can't be the conscience of an entire army, Fornyx.'

'You're doing all right so far. And he knows it – that's why he has taken you out of the front line. He needs you, Rictus, and we all know it. If there was no man around rash enough to speak the truth to his face, what would he become?'

'Perhaps that's the reason the ancient Macht got rid of kings,' Rictus said wryly.

'Well we're stuck with one now, may Antimone watch over him. We'll need that little bastard and his hare-brained plans tomorrow, to help even up the odds.'

They drank some more. The skin was half-empty, but the wine had not gone to their heads. The stars were a little brighter, perhaps, but that was all.

'Did you see the girl he brought back to camp?'

'The little Kufr with the shaven head? Half the army is talking about her. A little beauty, they say.'

'She reminds me of Aise.'

Fornyx was shocked into silence for a moment. Rictus's wife had been dead these seven years, and he rarely spoke her name.

'When she was young. She had the same pale face, that fine-boned strength to her. The black hair. Do you remember, Fornyx?'

'I remember,' his friend said heavily.

'I've been thinking on her lately. The early years when we were all together: you, me, Aise and poor Eunion. Building that house stone by stone at the river. The pictures are in my mind tonight, as clear as if it were yesterday, and not a quarter of a century ago.'

'Rictus –'

'I don't want to remember, Fornyx. Not those things. I don't want those memories in my mind, the knowledge of what happened after…' His voice thickened.

'Tomorrow, when the thing begins, I will be where I belong; standing beside you in the front rank.'

'Rictus –'

'Hold your tongue and drink, Fornyx. You think I would let a little shit like you take my Dogsheads into battle? The last battle, if Corvus is right. You say you would not miss it for the world. Well, neither would I.'

Rictus smiled. He was drunk at last. He felt it come upon his mind like a blessing.

'My wife is a long time dead, brother. I know that. But her face has been in my head ever since Machran; it is clearer to me than the faces of my grandchildren, than that of any man I ever killed.

But in the *othismos*; in that black dream of Phobos where there is nothing but blood and sweat and death – in that heart of battle – it is then that I feel free, and unafraid. Only then. It is the only place I know where the memories cannot follow.'

He squeezed the last of the wine down his throat while Fornyx watched.

'In the morning, little brother, I shall be by your side where I belong.'

SEVENTEEN
GAUGAMESH

THERE HAD BEEN reports of dust clouds to the west, and scouts had been sent out to investigate, but none had returned. For three days now, the Great King had been ordering parties of cavalry into the west to find his enemy, and in all that time none of them had come back, save one.

But the Macht were out there somewhere, as Kouros could testify.

He rode in the swaying palanquin with his father, the motion of the elephant easier on his wounded shoulder and knitting ribs. He bore the pain better than he once would have, and he found the Great King looking at him now and again in a kind of reappraisal. The feverish paranoia of earlier days had gone. Rakhsar was dead, and for the first time in his life, Kouros felt at ease. There was no-one else now. The intrigues were over at last.

They were far back in the endless column, which was itself one of several unending snakes of men and animals trickling their way across the flat, fecund country west of the Bekai River. The city of Carchanish, sixty pasangs behind them, had been transformed into an enormous supply dump. Foodstuffs, waggons, fresh horses, armour and weapons were flooding into a vast stockaded second city which had been constructed on the east bank of the river. This was their base of operations. If they did not contact the enemy some time in the next few days, that base would have to be brought forward, with all the labour that entailed. And this was one of the reasons why the progress of a large army was so agonisingly slow.

I never knew that the waging of war could prove so tedious, Kouros thought.

Rakhsar's face, as the blade went into his belly. That sneer gone at last. Kouros dwelled on the image, warming himself at it like a man at a fire.

His father was watching his face, as if he knew what his eldest son was thinking. Kouros shifted on the padded cushion, his ribs flaring into pain. He could not meet his father's eyes, even now.

Horses galloping past. They stamped to a halt, and there was shouting, an unthinkable breach of protocol so close to the King's person.

'What are they at?' Ashurnan muttered, disturbed from a reverie.

'My lord – my lord!' A familiar voice.

Both Kouros and Ashurnan lifted aside the gauze curtains of the palanquin and looked down. It was

Dyarnes, helm off and komis thrown down around his chin.

'What is this, Dyarnes?' Ashurnan demanded.

'Forgive me, my king, but we have sighted the enemy – they are directly to our front and already in line of battle.'

'What?' Ashurnan sputtered. He looked up at the sun in some bewilderment. It was early morning, and the column had barely gotten under way. The men at the rear had not even begun marching out of last night's camp yet.

'How close are they?'

'We must form the line at once, lord. With your permission, I deem it imperative that we bring in the other columns and deploy for battle.'

'Are they advancing?'

'Not yet. They're just standing there.'

'How many?' this was Kouros, hissing with pain as he leaned over the rail of the palanquin. The elephant tossed his head under them and the whole construction rose up and down like a boat on a wave.

'They are not many, my prince – not a fifth of what we have brought.'

Then why stand and wait for us? Kouros wondered.

'Bring in the columns – deploy the troops,' Ashurnan snapped. 'We must attack as quickly as possible, before they can get away. Move up your leading elements, Dyarnes, and send a courier to the rear. The men behind us will have to run. We must crush them, Dyarnes – do you hear me? They must not escape. And bring me my chariot.'

* * *

So THIS WAS what happened when the enemy was tracked down at last.

Chaos.

Kouros could not remain on the Great King's elephant without the Great King, nor was he fit to ride a horse, so he joined his father in the royal chariot. This was an immense affair drawn by four black Niseians and crewed by a driver and two bodyguards, Honai chosen by the Great King himself. A parasol overhung it to keep the sun off their heads, and there were holsters of javelins in front of either wheel.

The vehicle was beautifully sprung, ornamented with enough precious stones and chased silver to buy a city, and it had loops of red Bokosan leather to steady oneself by. The floor, also, was red leather, criss-crossed straps embroidered with golden wire. And rearing above it, the purple imperial banner was suspended from a cross-piece of varnished oak. It had been built to catch the eye, to provide a focal point on the battlefield, and to reassure the assembled thousands that their lord was in their midst, watching them.

It thundered up the roadway now, scattering everything in its path, preceded and followed by a hundred picked cavalry from all over the empire, though most wore the blue-enamelled armour of Arakosia. The Great King himself took the whip, and flicked it over the rumps of the straining Niseians with a smile in his beard.

Kouros studied his father discreetly. For days the old man had been withdrawn and uncommunicative. He had not been told that Rakhsar and Roshana were dead, but he seemed to know nonetheless. He had watched Kouros with that odd new look, and bade him join him on the back of the elephant, an honour not bestowed lightly.

Could it be respect? The Arakosans had gone out to look for Kouros and brought him back more dead than alive. Ashurnan had expressed no concern, asked no questions. But he had treated Kouros differently ever since.

And for once, Kouros had enjoyed writing a letter to his mother.

THE COLUMN HAD fractured all around them, and companies of infantry were spreading out across the plain on all sides, some running, all being screamed at by officers both mounted and afoot. There seemed to be little order involved, but the milling mobs were at least all moving the right way. Every one of them had their faces turned to the west, and the sun was behind them. Even the simplest peasant conscript could be told to keep the sun on his back. The army was disordered, chaotic and confused, but it was advancing in the right direction; a flood of men pouring across the earth in the rising dust.

Let the King of the Macht try and halt this tide, Kouros thought. And he gripped the hilt of the cheap iron kitchen knife in his sash. He had kept it as a kind of talisman. His brother's blood was still black upon it.

The green country around them was leached away. The land rose slightly, becoming a plateau many pasangs wide standing somewhat above the fertile plain. The ground was stonier here, crossed by the dry ruin of ancient watercourses, and the dust was choking, kicked up by men and animals to tower in the sky. This was empty country, a pocket of scrub savannah which was as ancient as the tells of the green river valleys. Too arid for crops, or even to support a herd of goats, these raised pockets of desert were known as *gaugamesh* in the Asurian tongue: a place blighted by the god Mot, where no man might grow things.

This is where we fight? Kouros wondered. He squeezed the waterskin that hung in the chariot, and thought of the tens of thousands all around him, and the dry country which they were traversing.

By tonight, if they find a river they will drink it dry.

There were Honai in a line up ahead, the occasional flash of sun-caught metal through the dust. The chariot came to a halt amid a cloud of cavalry and one by one the imperial couriers filed in behind it, young men of the lesser nobility whose fathers had paid a fortune so that their sons might gallop across battlefields carrying the Great King's orders. Alongside them clustered a knot of scribes and other attendants, who were dressed as though they were still in the palace. Their finery was utterly incongruous in that sere landscape.

Ashurnan stood gripping the rail of his chariot

and peering into the dust. A hundred paces in front of the wheels, the ten thousand spearmen of the Honai were forming up with a speed and precision that belied the chaos of the rest of the field. Eight ranks deep, their line stretched some pasang and a half, though both ends were invisible. But it was reassuring to see those tall warriors standing stolidly in front of them. This was to be the centre of the army, the very heart. Everyone else would take their dressing from the Great King's chariot, and would link up with that formidable phalanx.

'This will be a knife fight,' the Great King said to Dyarnes, who was standing by the chariot with his helm in the crook of one arm. 'It will be won or lost at close quarters. But we must use our archers at the start, once the dust settles somewhat. When the general advance is signalled they will be firing blind, and after that we must throw in our people at the enemy and overwhelm them. There will be no fancy manoeuvring today, not in this place. The dust hides everything. And double the couriers, Dyarnes. A lot of them will become lost today. I want two riders bearing each message.'

'Yes, lord. At what point do you wish the advance sounded?'

'As I said, wait until the dust settles. The men must be able to see the enemy in order to close with him. As soon as the Macht line is visible, I want you to start with the outer formations – we should outflank on both sides. But hold back the Arakosans, Dyarnes. They are to be kept for the killing blow.'

'Yes, my lord.'

* * *

THE SUN BROKE through the dust now and again, providing vignettes of war; masses of ranked troops trudging west, shuffling into position. A forest of spears all catching the light in the same moment, like a flashing gleam of teeth. And all around, the sodden thunder of marching feet, an echo that trembled the very flesh of the earth.

Kouros drank water from the skin, his mouth dry and sour. Thanks to his injuries, he was not wearing armour, though the bronze helm on his head had already caught the heat of the sun and felt as though it were a hot vice bearing down on the bone of his skull. The Great King wore merely a black diadem, and bright blue silk robes that concealed a breastplate underneath. He bore a plain steel scimitar which could have belonged to any man on the field, and which had seen much use. Kouros abruptly found himself wondering if it were the same sword with which Ashurnan had killed his own brother, thirty years before. He touched the knife in his own sash.

We are alike in that, at least, he thought, and licked his dry lips again.

The dust began to sink in the centre of the army, as the men found their places and stood with their shields at the shoulder, leaning on their spears. Kouros could hear them talking to one another. Asurian of half a dozen different dialects, some so strange as to barely constitute the same language. Good Kefren in the ranks of the Honai up front.

A column of leather-armed skirmishers went past with armfuls of javelins and the crescent-shaped shields of their calling, short-legged *hufsan* from the mountains who seemed as cheerful as men walking to a wedding.

The whole world is here, he thought. He remembered the slight, pale youth on the black horse who had called himself Corvus. There was Kefren blood in him – he had never suspected that.

What kind of man is he, to think he can fight the whole world?

Blue sky again, and the sun was high in it. It must be midday at least.

'There they are,' Ashurnan murmured. He reached out one hand and set it briefly on Kouros's arm. 'There they are.' The golden glow of his face had gone. He looked sick and old and tired.

'They're so close!' Kouros exclaimed.

A swift-footed man could have run between the armies in minutes. Kouros was able to make out the red chitons of the enemy spearmen, the bronze-faced shields painted with some pattern he had never seen before, a bird of some kind. They stood as immobile as a wall, all across the plain, their length punctuated by hanging banners.

'I will break that line today.' Ashurnan said quietly. He motioned to the scribe with his hip-desk who stood behind the chariot.

'An order for Dyarnes. He is –'

A swooping sound, as though some monstrous hawk had stooped for the kill. Instinctively, they all looked up. To their front, something exploded into the front ranks of the Honai and there were shouts of pain.

'What is it? What is happening?' Kouros demanded, hugging his ribs as though afraid they would fly apart.

A file of the Honai had been hurled into ruin, men lying dead, others dropping their shields and spears to assist the wounded.

Kouros looked up again, baffled, and saw a shower of what looked like arrows arcing up from behind the Macht line. But they were not arrows. Each was longer than a man. They came down in a black, monstrous hail.

And struck the ranks of the Great King's bodyguard.

The shafts were as thick as a man's arm, the heads cast in black, barbed iron. They punched through shields and breastplates as though the bronze were paper, and skewered two and three and four men at a time, knocking down whole files like wooden skittles bowled over by a child's ball.

Ashurnan's face was transformed by outrage. Dozens of these great bolts were now hurtling down out of the unclouded sky.

'Message to Dyarnes!' he shouted above the growing cacophony. 'Advance – advance at once with all the infantry!'

An explosion of dirt and stone, and the Niseians yoked to the chariot reared in fear as one of the massive bolts slammed into the ground at their feet. This was not warfare as they understood it. They began to dance and bite and neigh.

The ranks of the Honai were buckling and reforming, the files knocked apart only to be brought together again. They were the best soldiers in the empire, and would not retreat or break, but they could not hit back either. They could only die helplessly under the obscene barrage.

Ashurnan's bodyguard, an armoured Honai who towered over his lord, thrust both Kouros and the Great King behind him.

'Move us out of here,' he barked to the driver. 'This is no place for the King.'

The chariot wheeled round, the four horses pulling with a will, the driver lashing their backs with the long whip. They cantered away from the Honai phalanx, and the Arakosans followed them. Up and down the immense line the word went out that the Great King was retreating, that he was wounded, that he was dead. But the rumours were quashed by the sudden order to advance.

Like a great stone starting to roll downhill, the vast army of the empire began to move forward, a juggernaut bent on vengeance.

RICTUS WAS THIRSTY. There was still water in the skin at his back, but he was saving it for later. He knew that as soon as the fighting began he would forget his thirst. If he survived, he would be desperate for that water afterwards. If he did not, someone else would drink it.

Cheers and whistles went up through the ranks as the first of Parmenios's machines sent their deadly missiles soaring off towards the dust-choked line of the massing enemy. They gave way to a kind of awed silence as the ballista bolts struck home. The Macht spearmen watched as the Honai were battered by that relentless aerial assault. They saw shields tossed high in the air, men cartwheeling, impaled on the heavy bolts like frogs on a skewer.

Beside Rictus, Fornyx gave a low whistle. 'That is no way for brave men to die,' he said.

'They can die any way they like – there are more than enough left over for us all,' Rictus rasped.

'What are those troops? They're just reforming like nothing has happened.'

'Those are the Honai,' Rictus said. 'The Bodyguard. They're the best he's got.'

Fornyx smiled. 'Just as well Corvus has us facing them, then.'

There were three thousand Dogsheads in battle-line opposite the Great King, and they were the centre of Corvus's line as the Honai were the centre of the enemy's. Rictus had fought the Honai at Kunaksa. It had been one of the hardest fights of his life, and he had been young then.

But I know more now.

'Something's stirring,' Fornyx said, and there was a rustle of talk through the ranks. Men eased their shields off their shoulders so that their arms took the full weight of the bronze-faced oak. They moved their spears from side to side to loosen the sauroters in the hard ground. A few files across from Rictus someone was pissing where he stood, and the acrid reek of it carried down the ranks, along with the inevitable catcalls and jeers.

'How does that bastard have enough water in him to piss it out?' Fornyx asked. 'I'm dry as an old crone's cunny. I don't even have spit.'

The dust flagged up the enemy movement, drawing all their eyes. It was almost imperceptible at first, until the formations began to loosen up and draw apart.

'He's coming on willingly enough,' Rictus said. 'Corvus was right about that, at least. I'll bet half his men are still on the road behind, or running up into position.'

'Fuck,' Fornyx said with feeling. 'I'd be running if I had Parmenios's pins raining down on me.'

'Ready arms!' Rictus cried, and up and down the line the centurions took up the cry. The Dogsheads closed up, each man's shield protecting the spear-arm of the fellow to his left. The phalanx clenched itself like a fist.

'Stand fast and wait for my word!' Rictus shouted. 'File-closers, take the count!'

Starting out on the left, the men began to count down their numbers starting from the front man in the file. The numbers were called out like some repetitive ancient ritual, and it almost seemed like one to Rictus, who had heard it so many times on so many far-flung battlefields.

'Arrows!' Someone shouted. ''Ware arrows!'

'Shields up!' Fornyx bellowed.

They came down in a black rain, Kufr broadheads lancing out of the sky. The Dogsheads lifted the heavy shields and leaned into them, like men sheltering from a storm. The arrow-cloud smote the bronze with an unholy metallic racket, like hammers in a tinsmith's shop. But even over that noise, Rictus could still hear the distinctive meaty slap as some of them found flesh.

Men were going down, cursing and groaning. It felt as though someone was poking the face of Rictus's shield with a stick. An arrow came down close enough to his toes to throw dust upon them. Another passed through the transverse horsehair of his helm-crest. He shared a look with Fornyx. The younger man was grinning into his black beard. An arrow skittered off the wing of his armour and bounced away into the faces of the men behind.

'I thought it looked like rain,' Fornyx said, and down the line the comment spread, and men managed to laugh at it as their comrades fell about them.

The volleys passed. To the front, the dust had hidden everything again, but out of that dust came the sullen roar of the enemy advance.

'Wounded to the rear!' Rictus cried. 'Close up – close up, lads. We're about to earn our pay!'

They burst out of the dust thirty paces ahead, a boiling mass of wild-eyed men bearing crescent shields and short spears, no order to their ranks, but stark momentum in their sheer numbers.

'Spears!' the order went up, and the aichmes were levelled at the oncoming tide. The phalanx tightened over the bodies of its own dead and wounded. Rictus ducked his face behind the rim of his shield, gritted his teeth, and dug his right heel into the hard ground.

'See you in hell, brother,' Fornyx said, teeth bared and set like those of a dog.

'See you in hell,' Rictus repeated.

And then the enemy wave slammed into them.

'THE DOGSHEADS ARE engaged,' Parmenios said to Corvus, wiping his hand across his gleaming bald scalp. 'He moved some of his levies across the front of the Honai, but the move disorganised them some. They should not prove to be a problem for Rictus.'

'He's saving his best,' Ardashir said, and patted the neck of his restless horse.

'But he is throwing everything else in as fast as he can,' Corvus said. 'Good. That is as it should be. Parmenios, you're sure he had his heavy horse out on our right?'

'I'm sure. There's a dried up river-bed out on our left – he doesn't want his cavalry to break their necks in it. All but a tithe of his horse is facing the Companions. But Corvus –'

'Speak up. It's quite a noise they're making down there.'

'He has a hundred thousand men coming up the roads from the east. Once they're in position, they'll swamp us.'

'One thing at a time. Repoint your machines, Parmenios. I want you to start bombarding his cavalry. It doesn't have to be a heavy fire – just enough to stir them up.'

'At once.' Parmenios wheeled his mule, kicking it savagely, and trotted away to the rear, where hundreds of his engineers were working upon the great ballistae. They had piled rocks under the front timbers of the machines to elevate their fire, and a steady train of fast-moving carts were galloping up from the baggage train with fresh missiles to feed them.

A courier cantered up, his face a mask of dust. He had to spit and wipe his mouth before he could speak.

'My king, Marshal Teresian sent me to say he is heavily engaged out on the left. He is holding, but the enemy is trying to outflank him.'

'Go to Druze. Tell him to peel off a mora to help Teresian. What's your name?'

'Deiros, my king.'

'Deiros, you must tell Marshal Teresian to hold the line of the riverbed. He cannot retreat from that position. Is that clear?'

'Yes, my king.'

'My name is Corvus, lad. Now get going.'

The youngster sped off, eyes alight as though he had been somehow honoured. Ardashir chuckled.

'You call them *lad*, now?'

'I feel old enough to be their father, some of them.'

'When do you want me to move?'

Corvus grinned, and instantly years fell off him. 'When I join you, Ardashir. You think I'd let the Companions go into battle without me?'

Ardashir gathered his reins. 'Brother, remember one thing; if you go down, we all go down.'

'Where is your faith, Ardashir? If old Rictus can fight in the front rank, then so can I.'

'You knew?'

'I always know.'

FOR PASANGS ACROSS the plateau of Gaugamesh there now extended a brute mass of struggling men. The slender line of the Macht had received a succession of hammer-blows as the imperial forces came up, formation after formation, and launched themselves at it. Had they coordinated their attacks, then Corvus's line would have broken, chopped apart by sheer numbers. But the levies of the empire pitched into the battle as soon as they came off the line of march, and one by one their attacks were blunted by the stubborn professionalism of the Macht spearmen.

Out on the left, they were fighting along the banks of the dry riverbed, Teresian's morai thrusting down into the crowded ranks of the Kufr struggling up the crumbling, sunbaked sides of the bank. On that flank some enterprising Kufr commander had thrown a fresh levy out to the north, seeking to outflank the position, but just as it seemed they were on the verge of success, Druze and a thousand of his Igranians pitched into them, swinging their drepanas to terrible effect and shrieking the high war cry of their own hills. The levy was broken, and hurled backwards.

These were small farmers and tradesmen of the Middle Empire. They had been marching for weeks, learning the ways of an army, sure of their own numbers and the authority of the high-caste Kefren officers who led them. But they had not reckoned on the utter bloody confusion of battle. They had never before seen what the sweep of a drepana could do to a man's body when wielded by an enemy who had been fighting for years, and was well-versed in the chaotic savagery of war. They saw their friends and neighbours slashed to quivering meat around them, and streamed away in disorder.

Druze met Teresian to the rear of the line. Six thousand Macht were standing fast here, and the riverbed at their feet was filling with bodies so that the Kufr were climbing over their own mounded dead to come at the spears. The dust shrouded everything, and the roar of the battle was unlike anything that even the veterans had experienced before.

Druze drew close so he could be heard, his dark head next to Teresian's straw-bright one.

'I secured your left for now, but they'll try again,' he shouted. 'There are too many – they're going to pour round that flank soon. I'll leave you my mora, but I have to get back to Corvus. He needs me in the centre.'

'I need more of your men, Druze,' Teresian told the Igranian. 'That, or cavalry. There's nothing behind me – they cave in my flank and the whole line will fold.'

'Refuse your left, but stay anchored to the riverbed.'

Teresian nodded grimly. 'Tell Corvus if he has any tricks left to pull, we had best see them soon.'

Druze took his forearm in the warrior's grip. 'Hot work, brother.'

'Fucking thirsty too. We need water; my men are chinstrapped.'

'I'll see what I can do. Would you like me to wash your face and put you to bed, or do you want to play for a while?'

'Fuck you, you black-eyed Igranian cocksucker.'

They grinned at each other, and Druze ran off, back to the centre of the Macht lines.

IN THE CENTRE the blows were falling fast and hard. The first attack had been beaten off in minutes, but had been followed almost instantly by a second, and a third. It seemed that there was an endless procession of enemy formations streaming forward to slam into the ranks of the Dogsheads. The Macht stood their ground and fought each one to a standstill, until they had to retreat several paces just to get clear of the corpse-choked ground. Then they stood fast again, and watched another line of screaming Kufr come charging out of the dust.

This was not phalanx fighting – it was not the *othismos* as the Macht understood it. The Kufr ran up to the line of shields and hacked at them with axes and short swords, while the wicked aichmes of the spearmen jabbed out in short, economical thrusts to cripple and slay them. The leather corselets of the levy infantry were little protection against a Macht spearhead, and many of the enemy did not wear helmets either. They ran up to the line and battered upon it, and died. Some got lucky, and caught tired or already wounded men and saw their blades strike home, but most died to no result, except to make the men in the shield line more tired, to break off a few more spearheads. To bring down a few here and there and make a gap which was closed moments later.

Extravagant it might have been, but it was slowly becoming effective. The Dogsheads were being worried to death, worn down in increments. And each and every one of them was aware that the Great King's Honai were still out there opposite them, waiting in the anonymity of the dust.

'He may be attacking everywhere, but he's going to make a real play for it here,' Rictus told Fornyx. They stood panting, spitting white and leaning on their spears. There was a momentary lull in the fighting, but they could hear the cries of the Kefren officers in the ochre cloud to their front and knew it would not last long.

'Then I wish he'd fucking get on with it,' Fornyx said. 'I could do with a lie down.'

'He'll send in the Honai when he's ready, and try to break clear through. He does that, and he has a free path to the baggage behind.'

Fornyx looked Rictus in the eye. 'We're doing just fine. Do you really think his Honai can break us, Rictus – us?'

'They are ten thousand, Fornyx, and they fight like we do, shield to shield. We've been at it all morning while they've been leaning on their spears. Just because Parmenios managed to skewer a few of them doesn't mean they're not ready to pitch in. No – they'll be right in our lap soon. We have to be ready for that.'

'Corvus should be told.'

'You can be sure he knows. The boy's not stupid – he placed us here for a reason.'

'He put us here to die, it seems to me.'

'He put us here to stand, and die. To give him time to work his magic elsewhere. That's why he wanted me out of the line for this one.'

'Little bastard,' Fornyx said. 'I might have known. Remember Machran, Rictus? He did the same damned thing.'

'Because we're the best he has.'

'Chief, here they come again,' the man beside Rictus cried.

'Stand to!' Rictus shouted, the words cracking in his dry throat. 'Shields up, level spears –'

And so it began again.

THE AFTERNOON DREW on. All along the battlefront, the troops of the Great King were being steadily sent in to the meat-grinder. As well as attacking constantly on every front, the imperial forces were still coming in from the east in an unending stream, shaking out into line of battle, and then going forward. Sometimes those advancing were shaken and disordered by the fleeing remnants of the men who had been up at the spears before them, but they went in anyway. In this respect the dust was a blessing for the Kefren officers. Their men were walking into the battle blind, unable to see the true extent of the carnage ahead. Not until they began stepping on their own heaped dead did they realise what lay before them, and by then it was too late.

The smell of blood rose in the air, the stink of sweat, urine and ordure. The fighting took men and squeezed everything out of them, along with their lives. Already the flies were black about the bodies, and men in the midst of combat would find the carrion insects buzzing about their mouths and eyes as they fought, one more torment in a world of them.

Kouros flapped his good hand in front of his face as though it would rid him of the smell. He had perfume on his komis, and tugged the fine material tight about his mouth, trying to breathe. Trying not to breathe. It was not as he had expected.

He had been in battle before now, but his previous experiences had been nothing compared to this. He had taken part in ragged running fights with bands of runaway slaves, road-bandits and misguided rebels, but those skirmishes had been more akin to hunting than to warfare proper. He had never in his life before seen men stand and fight as the Macht were fighting now, destroying legions of levies, piling the ground black with bodies, and then dressing their lines, ready for more.

'What are they?' he asked aloud. 'What kind of things can they be, to stand like that?'

It was his father who answered him. 'At Kunaksa, we slew their leaders and took their baggage. We had them surrounded and outnumbered five, six to one.

But still they attacked, and routed my entire army. They were thirsty, exhausted, half dead on their feet – I can still see it now – and they kept coming down that hill. They beat us that day because they thought they were already dead men. Only the Macht fights like that. Like a cornered animal, bereft of reason. That is why they are so dangerous.'

Kouros stared. The dust came and went in rolling clouds. He caught glimpses of the fighting lines to their front, a vast river of murder. He could not imagine what it must be like, up there at the spearheads. It must be very like hell itself.

'My lord, we have word from the Arakosans out on the left.' This was Marok, Dyarnes' second-in-command. A tall, dark Kefre, like a lean version of Kouros, he was the one who loved women and horses, and who had more of both thanks to the generosity of the King's heir. He glanced at Kouros and nodded his head in a half bow of acknowledgement.

'The Macht have begun loosing off their great arrows again, into the ranks of the cavalry. The Arakosans are taking casualties. Their Archon, Lorka, asks your permission to advance.'

Ashurnan raised a hand, and Marok went silent and bowed deeply. The Great King was looking west intently, trying to pierce the curtain of dust.

At last it opened a moment. Another attack had been beaten off; there were hundreds of figures streaming in panic from the Macht line. But that line was not as tidy as it had been. It bulged and bent here and there, and there were gaps in it now as the enemy hauled away his wounded and brought men out of the rear to fill the gaps at the front. The red-clad ranks did not seem as thick as before.

Ashurnan looked at the sky. He was sure of it now. The sun was still high, but it was westering. Soon he would have it in his eyes.

'Couriers,' he snapped. At once, half a dozen mounted Kefren were at the back of the chariot, their mounts stamping and snorting under them.

'Go to Lorka and the Arakosans. Tell him he is to advance at once. He must assault the Macht right wing and then swing behind them. I will send follow-up levies behind him.'

Two couriers wheeled their horses round and burst into a canter. They took off as if racing each other.

'Marok,' the Great King said. 'Go to Dyarnes. Tell him he is to take in the Honai. I want him to assault the centre and break it. He will be supported with everything I can send up. I want him to split the enemy and keep going, right to the baggage if he can. Is that understood?'

Marok blinked. Some of the colour left his face. He bowed. 'Yes, Great King.'

'And Marok, tell Dyarnes not to jeopardise himself. He is to remain behind the main assault.' The Great King smiled. 'You, Marok, will lead the attack in person.'

Marok looked quickly at Kouros, then back at the King. He bowed. 'You honour me, lord.'

'Break the Macht line, Marok. Show me your loyalty.'

Marok turned away and walked slowly back to the Honai lines, tugging on his helmet as he did so.

'A good man,' Ashurnan said. 'Ambitious.' He looked at Kouros and smiled a scimitar smile.

'A favourite of your mother's, I believe.'

Two massive bodies of troops now began to grind into motion. On the left the Arakosan cavalry broke into a trot, eight thousand heavy horsemen in several columns. Their ranks were ragged and disordered, for Parmenios's missiles were still plunging out of the air, and few could miss such a packed target. There were scores of horses lying on the ground, kicking the last of their lives away, and the Arakosans were seized by rage at the screams of the beautiful Niseians. When the order to advance was given they surged forward with a will, a massive tide of flesh, bone, bronze and iron. For fully two pasangs they covered the earth, and before the dust of their own advance covered them they seemed from afar to resemble a tumbled avalanche of lapis lazuli stones, so bright was their blue armour. The buried thunder of their advance carried clear across the battlefield, like the anger of some earthbound god.

The Honai heard it as they took up their spears and began to advance, to the sound of horn-calls and long flutes. Ten thousand tall Kefren in polished bronze. Their armour also caught the sun, and it seemed that a host of blazing statues had come to life and were advancing across the field. The levies moving forward on their flanks gave a great cheer, and it was taken up all along the imperial lines, until a hundred thousand voices were shouting together in a moment of pure exultation. The mood of the entire battlefield shifted. The weary Macht lifted their heads in a moment of cold doubt, and the fresh levies who were still coming in from the east heard that sound and stepped forward with a will, sure that they had just heard the sound of victory rolling towards them out of the dust.

'GIVE US A DRINK, will you, Rictus? I've a tongue like a block of wood.'

Rictus leaned his forehead against his spear. He tried to spit, but nothing came out.

'I sent it back with Kesero after he was wounded. There's none left.'

'Damn it. I'll die thirsty.'

'So will we all, brother.'

'Look at them. Someone in this country can teach drill.'

They stared at the advancing ranks of the Honai, marching in perfect time to the flutes, a shrill, unearthly noise.

The Dogsheads stood surrounded by mounds of dead, the enemy's and their own. They had thinned out the line to keep connected to Demetrius's conscripts on their right and Teresian's veterans on their left. They stood four deep now, half their regular formation. Behind them, the wounded were lying in a carpet of broken, writhing humanity, painted black with flies. The carts could not load them up fast enough to take them back to the baggage train.

Behind the wounded were a few hundred of

Parmenios's engineers, manning ballistae and looking distinctly nervous. Behind that there was nothing but empty plain all the way back to the waggon-park holding all the army's supplies, some two pasangs to the rear.

'We're a bit thin on the ground,' Rictus said mildly. He had never felt so tired in his life before. A few nicks and scratches were all that the fury of the battle had so far inflicted upon his flesh, but he was bone weary.

I am too old, he thought. Corvus was right.

And yet, when he lifted his head and looked at the Honai advancing towards him, marching to the sound of flutes, something in him leapt.

I am as much made for this as is the head of a spear.

A sense almost of happiness.

'I don't think much of their music,' he said aloud. And then, louder, 'What say you we make some music of our own, brothers?'

Half a dozen of them took him up on it at once, and began the slow, mournful chant of the Paean, the death-hymn of the Macht. It went down the line like smoke on the wind, and rose higher, fighting down the shrill pipe of the approaching flutes.

Thousands took it up, not only the Dogsheads, but the morai to left and right in the line. It rolled out of the Macht army like the murmur of a storm, and grew. The men straightened at their spears, lifted their heads from behind their shields and sang, until the singing was the loudest thing on that enormous tortured plain, and the sound of it carried clear across that deadly space, even to the ears of the Great King himself.

'Close shields! Level spears!' the orders rang out, but the singing went on, drowning out the Kufr flutes and horns.

The Honai gave a great collective snarl, and quickened their pace.

The Macht were still singing when the Great King's warriors smashed into their line.

EIGHTEEN
DEATH HYMN

DRUZE STOOD PANTING and lathered in dust before Corvus, Ardashir and Demetrius. He took a swallow from a proffered waterskin and rinsed his mouth. When he spat the water out it was brown.

'He's doing it – he's committed the Honai at last. They charged into the Dogsheads like the end of the world. Corvus, he is about to cut us in two.'

Corvus nodded. He did not look in the least surprised.

'How are the Dogsheads faring?'

'They've lost near half their number, but you know what they are. They'll not retreat, not with Rictus there to hold them.'

A flash of something like anger passed over Corvus's face. 'That damn fool,' he said, exasperated. 'He'll end up dying there.'

'You should have told him,' Ardashir said.

'That I was sacrificing his men – again? I needed the Dogsheads to hold for a long time – that's why I put them there. I had to get the Honai moving. But I did not mean them to stand to the last.'

'There will be none of them left if we don't start things in motion,' Druze said. 'The Honai can fight – they fight like us, and they're the biggest bastards I've ever seen.'

Corvus nodded as though some internal argument had been decided.

'Very well. Druze, get you back to your command. Hold them in readiness. But they are not to move before my order – understood? This is all about the timing.'

'Corvus,' Druze said, looking up at the pale man on the tall horse. 'They're dying fast, Rictus's people.'

'Wait for my command, brother,' Corvus said crisply. Druze stared at him a moment more, then nodded, and took off into the dust-shrouded chaos of the battlefield at a flat sprint, his drepana bouncing on his back.

'Demetrius?'

The one-eyed veteran stepped forward.

'Now is the time. The Arakosans are on their way. Your boys are about to earn their pay. You know what to do.'

'I know what to do,' Demetrius said heavily.

'Whatever happens, they must not break. If they do, the Arakosans will chop them to pieces. They must stand together. Green as they are, they must be able to understand that.'

'If I cannot make six morai of spears stand and fight on a battlefield, then you can have my other eye,' Demetrius snapped. 'But it won't be just the cavalry – he's sending other troops out on the right as well.'

'By the time they arrive, the thing will be over, one way or another.'

Demetrius nodded. 'It had better be,' he said grimly.

Corvus leaned in the saddle until his face was close to the frowning veteran. 'Have faith, brother.'

Demetrius pursed his lips, and uttered something like a laugh. Then he stumped off to where his command waited in formation behind the Companions. Six thousand inexperienced spearmen, the only reserve Corvus had on the field.

'Time for me to go,' Corvus said to Ardashir, donning his helmet with the horsehair plume. 'Don't get caught by the Arakosans, Ardashir, but make them charge home. If it means you must –'

'I know what it means,' Ardashir interrupted him. 'I will sacrifice the mora if it comes to that – we will all do as we are bidden today, my friend.'

'I wish Rictus had done as he was damn well told. He should have been commanding the reserve, not Demetrius.'

'Rictus would have been in the thick of the fight wherever you put him. That is his nature.'

Corvus nodded, the crest bobbing on his helm. 'See you in hell, brother.'

'See you in hell.'

* * *

RICTUS WAS ON his knees, his shield held over his head while he scrabbled in the bloody mire for a weapon to fight with. His spear was shattered, his drepana was broken, and were it not for the Curse of God, he would already have been dead several times over.

He found a short sword, old fashioned, the type his father would have carried, and levered it out of the sucking muck while all around him the fight went on, and he was buffeted by the men struggling around him. The dust had turned to mud under them, thickened by their blood, and other, nameless things. Rictus was plastered brown with it, his armour's cold gleam obscured.

He was on his feet again. He could feel the old wounds all over his body complaining, but ignored that winter-pain and gripped the slimy hilt of the sword in his fist while the heavy shield dragged at his left shoulder.

He was no longer in the front rank, but the front rank was fast becoming a mere concept. They were nothing more than a line of struggling men, sometimes two ranks deep, sometimes three. Like seaweed being moved ever farther up the beach by successive waves.

It had been a shock, when the Honai had crashed into them, for the Dogsheads had not yet fought Kufr like these. To begin with, the Great King's bodyguards were all picked for size; they towered over the Macht by a head and more. And they wore heavy armour; solid plate bronze polished bright, with heavy round shields like those of the Macht themselves.

But more than any of these things, they were willing to stand and die.

Rictus had lost contact with Fornyx in the press, and did not know if his friend was dead or alive. He had seen men knocked unconscious by the first clash, and then speared as they were held upright between the two pushing lines. The Macht had held doggedly, for despite their lesser size, they were stronger than the slender Kefren, and though the Honai were the best trained of any troops in the Great King's army, they had not seen the years of hard service that the Dogsheads had.

So they died fast – at first. Rictus himself had speared some senior officer through the eye-slot of his helm in the first moments, and had thus shattered his spear. The drepana had buckled against a brazen breastplate soon after. It was meant for cutting, not thrusting, and it had snapped like a biscuit. After that he had retreated into his own men, his feet balancing on corpses and the awful nameless sludge bulging through his sandals.

He backed clear out of the line for a moment, breathing hard. Looking up, he could see nothing of the sky; they fought in a tent of dust which hid everything more than twenty paces away. But he could hear the sound of battle beyond his sight, the all-encompassing roar of it from which individual screams sometimes rose in a high pitch of agony. The sound reminded him of Kunaksa, it was so intense, so utterly huge. He had known nothing like it in the last thirty years, not even at Machran.

He looked behind him. Parmenios's engineers had loaded their ballistae and were standing with their swords to hand. If – when – the Honai broke the line, they would not delay the Great King's elite for more than a few minutes.

Rictus tugged a man out of the line. The fellow was wide-eyed, with the rigour of the *othismos* still upon him, brown foam flecking the corners of his mouth. Rictus had to shake him, hard.

'Who are you – your name, man!'

The spearman had to think about how to respond. 'Serenos of Pontis.'

'Serenos, drop your shield and your spear. I want you to go south, to our right, and find one of the marshals or the King himself – you understand? Tell them that the centre is about to break. We need reinforcements – anything we can get – we need them now. Listen to me – do you understand?'

The man nodded dumbly.

'Good lad – now, go, and be quick, for Phobos's sake.'

Stark relief on the man's face as he ran off. For a second, Rictus envied him. There was a part of him that also wanted nothing more than to be able to disappear into the dust and wait for the noise to go away. All men felt that in battle. There was only one cure for it.

He bent, picked up the man's discarded spear, hefted it a moment thoughtfully, and then limped back into the fighting.

By some miracle he found himself close to Fornyx. He pushed forward into the front rank to replace a falling man, and immediately took a spearhead in the shoulder. It jolted him backwards a step but skewed off his armour, carving a track through the mud embossing his cuirass. He growled like an animal, the sound lost in that raging tumult, and shortened his grip on the spear. Past the mid-point he stabbed with it, the first thrust striking a shield, the second gauged more carefully, taking the glaring Honai at the neck and severing the bulging vessels there. It was like up-ending a bottle of wine. The Honai glared and raged a moment more, then gripped his neck, astonished, and sank down into the mud. Rictus plunged the sauroter onto the nape of the Kufr's neck, and saw the sputtering square hole it made as he yanked the weapon out again. Then it was forgotten, as the gap was filled, and another impossibly tall golden-skinned monster with blazing eyes was trying to kill him.

The Macht were pushed back. They exacted a terrible toll on the Honai as they retreated, for in their eagerness the Great King's elite were pressing forward heedless of losses, and their formation began to open a little. When that happened, the aichmes of the close-knit Macht would stab out with the swiftness of a kingfisher's strike. It was death for one of the Honai even to lower his shield to shout to a comrade.

But the Dogsheads had been fighting for hours now, and they were stepping on their own wounded as they fell back. The Honai dispatched the fallen without pity as they passed over. They outnumbered the Macht to their front some four to one and no amount of skill or valour could hope to hold out much longer against those odds.

'Break on the left!' a single shout, almost lost in the roar. But Rictus felt the thing shift around him. On both sides the Macht were falling back, not as part of a line, but in knots and fragments of still fighting men.

'Stay together!' he bellowed. 'Face your front, you bastards!'

The line was gone, engulfed like a broken dyke. Now the Honai were pouring through, chopping it up still further. The Dogsheads were an elite even among veterans; they knew that to turn and run meant instant death. So they fell back with their face to the enemy. They died with their shields still on their arms even when surrounded and stabbed to carrion by half a dozen of the enemy at a time. Their bodies piled up in mounds of bronze and scarlet.

Some centons hung together, what was left of them, and a tattered grouping gathered under the banner and faced out in all directions, fighting back to back now. Fornyx was the banner-bearer. He had lost his helm, and one eye was gone, nothing left but a torn hole, but he stood holding up the oak staff from which hung their ragged flag; the same one which had flown at Kunaksa, thirty years before.

Rictus joined him, and around the pair of cursebearers other broken remnants of the

Dogsheads coalesced, until there were several score brought to bay in a rough oval, a crowded mass of grim, exhausted men with the light of death in their eyes. There was no quarter given or asked, nor any thought of surrender.

Rictus dropped his shield and, taking Fornyx's free arm, he set it over his own shoulders and took some of the younger man's weight. Fornyx grinned, his teeth black with blood and dust.

'Where have you been, you strawhead bitch? Back of the line having a sit-down, I'll bet.' He tilted his head until it rested briefly against Rictus's helm.

'I knew things were in good hands,' Rictus told him. He pulled off his helm, and even the hot air seemed cool to him after the confining bronze. He kissed Fornyx on his bloody cheek.

'Antimone found us at last, brother.'

'Aye. She's been looking for us this long time.'

'We will go into her darkness together, Fornyx.'

But Fornyx did not respond. His weight grew as his legs buckled. His one eye was still open and that black grin was carved on his mouth. Rictus lowered him to the bloody churned earth at their feet. Only then did he see the blood trickling in a black bar from a gash in Fornyx's thigh. The blood was pooled about his feet; he had stood there a long time.

Rictus closed the staring eye, and then took the banner from his friend's hand.

Lord, in thy glory and thy goodness, send worthy men to kill me.

He set a hand on Fornyx's head, the kind of touch a father might bestow on his sleeping child. Then he straightened, the world livid, dazzling in his eyes, and in a low voice he began to sing the Paean once more.

It went unheard. The island of Macht was engulfed, the Honai crashing over it in their hundreds. They clambered over bodies still breathing and stabbed downwards at the dying men without looking to see where their spearheads went. Their faces were set towards the west, and the open space beyond the mounded corpses which was the rear of the Macht army. Unstoppable now, they surged on, hundreds, thousands of the tall Kefren cheering as they advanced at an eager trot.

They had broken the Macht line, and Corvus's army was now split in two.

NINETEEN
THE STANDARD OF THE KING

'Time to go,' Ardashir said calmly. He was looking at the oncoming torrent of Arakosan cavalry, which was approaching at a gallop, thousands of horsemen on beautiful Niseians, a glorious and terrible sight. He leaned in the saddle and set a hand on his banner-bearer's arm.

'Shoron, signal retire.'

The Kefren trooper, clad in scarlet like all of Corvus's army, tilted the banner horizontal three times. At once, Ardashir felt the movement of the ranks behind him. 'Quickly, brothers!' he cried. 'We don't want to be in the middle of this one!'

Almost a thousand Companion cavalry began filing out to the open flank in trotting lines, the warhorses bucking nervously under them. Ardashir let the mora file past and raised his hand in salute to the spearmen standing ready behind them, hidden from the enemy up until now. Demetrius raised his own fist in response and barked an order which was repeated all down the line by his centurions. The morai levelled their spears. Six thousand men, six ranks deep, one and a half pasangs long.

Ardashir broke into a canter, almost the last to leave the front of the phalanx. The Arakosans were perhaps two hundred paces away, a mass of horseflesh at full charge, the very earth quivering under their feet like a tapped drum. Nothing would stop them now; it was too late for them to pull up.

At the sudden sight of the spearline some tried to rein in, and went down, bowled over and crushed by the hordes coming up behind them. The outer companies tried to wheel left, but Ardashir's troopers were already curving round in a great arc to meet them and hammer in that flank. They were held on their course by their own momentum.

The horses balked at the sight of the steady line of spearmen; at the last moment they refused the contact. But the hundreds behind them could not see what was happening to the front rank; they piled into their fellows with a fearful crash. Ardashir saw one massive Niseian hurled end over end through the air, its rider a rag doll flung headlong into the crush.

It was a kind of carnage he had never witnessed before. Hundreds of horses went down, the Macht spearing them without pity, disembowelling the magnificent animals or jabbing out their eyes. Riders were lifted out of the saddle by the thickets of spears impaling them. Here and there the sheer weight of the animals broke in the Macht line, but the spearmen swarmed over the still-kicking beasts and fought while standing upon their beating flesh.

The Arakosans had charged into a wall of spears and armoured men, head-on and unprepared, and their own numbers were piling them upon the wreckage of the leading ranks. It was like watching a man's face being smashed repeatedly into a stone.

Demetrius's green spearmen stood their ground, and the Arakosans milled in front of them, horses rearing to bite and kick, their riders slashing with their tulwars and scimitars and light lances. But they were striking down upon a line of shields and bronze, whereas the aichmes of the spearmen were stabbing upwards into the soft flesh of the horses. When the big animals fell they entangled others, crushed their riders, lay thrashing and screaming in a mire of their own entrails.

'Get your horn, Shoron. Sound the charge,' Ardashir shouted over that holocaust. He felt sickened, but would not shirk his role in the slaughter.

Shoron lifted his horn from the saddle-pommel and blew the clear hunting call of the western empire, which the Companions had used since before the siege of Machran. Ardashir's mora smashed into the outer flanks of the Arakosans once again, Niseians fighting one another, Kefren killing Kefren, the red at war with the blue.

The Macht started to sing as the horn-notes died away. With their death hymn in their throats they began to advance, Demetrius out in front and waving them on. He stood atop a dead horse and pointed his spear eastwards like some warlike prophet.

The Arakosans were fighting their own horses now. They had been brought to a standstill and a ridge of their dead lay for over a pasang in front of Demetrius's morai, while they had now been assailed in the flank by a thousand of the Companions. They were brave men, superb horse-soldiers, but they had never encountered a Macht phalanx before, and no matter how intent they were on attacking, their mounts would not charge that unbroken battlement of bronze and iron.

They broke.

First in one and twos, then clotted groups, many clinging two to a horse. They streamed away from the advancing Macht, and Ardashir's Companions harried them in pursuit, breaking up any companies which halted and tried to reform. In minutes, they were in full retreat, their officers trying to stem the rout, beating their own men with their swords. That massive sea of horsemen began to pour back the way it had come, with the Macht phalanx advancing inexorably in its wake, and as the Arakosans fled, they slammed into the formations of levy infantry which the Great King had sent in behind them to follow up their assault. A boiling mass of cavalry and infantry was brewed up there in the towering, choking maelstrom, and the whole imperial left flank was thrown into utter confusion. Out of the dust to the west, the sound of the Paean rose out of six thousand voices, and confusion gave way to stark terror. The Arakosans gave up any attempt to rally and began to flee in earnest, galloping through the oncoming infantry which had been meant to reinforce their victory.

Demetrius's men came upon that vast mob of enemy soldiers, and the Macht went to work with their spears, while Ardashir's cavalry hung on the flank like a hound tearing at the legs of a maddened bull.

ALMOST TWO PASANGS away, in the broken centre of Corvus's army, the Honai were still in full, jubilant cry. Their formations had lost all order in their delight at having annihilated the much-vaunted Dogsheads. They considered the battle won; now they had only to secure the enemy baggage train and the Macht army would have the legs cut out from under it.

Dyarnes was near the rear of his men, still climbing over the clotted dead where the fighting had been thickest, and he paused to grab the shoulder of a fleet youngster with wild eyes.

'You – get you back to the Great King and tell him we are through the enemy line, and are advancing on his baggage.'

'The Great King?' the young Kefre sputtered.

'Tell his people, you fool – they're back at the Royal Chariot. Tell them I need further orders. We have this thing won, if I can but wheel some of my troops round to strike the enemy in the rear. The thing is won – you hear me?'

The Honai was grinning now, an open-mouthed grin like that of a cheerful dog.

'Drop your shield and run.'

The young Kefre took off, tossing away his helm as he sprinted into the dust. Dyarnes chuckled. He was alone save for a cluster of aides. One leaned close and shouted in his ear.

'Shall we recall the men, lord? Or halt them, at least?'

'Not yet. Let them have their triumph, Arnosh. I want them well clear of the line before I begin to turn them around.'

'It's won sir. We did what the legends said we could not – we broke the Macht.'

Dyarnes bent amid the corpses. They lay so thick he had to stand upon dead flesh.

'They did not break,' he muttered, staring at a white, snarling face. 'They did not run. They stood and died.'

Some new note in the tumult to the west, where he could still see the tail end of the victorious Honai companies. A breath of wind, a lift in the air, and suddenly it was as though a new stage had been unveiled in a close-packed theatre. His view opened out; he found himself staring at a moving crowd of thousands of his own Kefren, the King's Bodyguard in its moment of hard-won victory. He began to smile at the sight.

But then something else tugged his gaze south, to where the Arakosans were engaged in a sepia thundercloud, fighting their own battle. A wave of relief swept over him as he recognised the sight of cavalry spilling north across the plain, thousands of them. The Arakosans had done their work quickly; they must already have broken through the Macht right wing.

But there was no blue in that massive, arrow-shaped body of horsemen. They were clad in red, the colour of the Macht.

Despite the furnace-heat of the day, Dyarnes felt a nerveless chill steal along his spine.

'Oh, Bel deliver us,' he gasped. 'No – no, no!'

The Companions of King Corvus, four thousand strong, shook out into line of battle, and at the sound of a bright, tugging horn-call, taken up all along their galloping line, they brought down their lances and charged full-tilt into the scattered, disorganised mass of the Honai.

And that was not all. At the same moment, there came from the south a boiling mass of Macht infantry – not spearmen, but lightly armoured swordfighters, bearing wickedly curved blades of iron. They paused fifty paces from the Honai, then threw a shower of javelins. And then they pitched into the Kefren with a roar, the sword-blades catching fire from the westering sun as they arced through the air.

Dyarnes sank to his knees, aghast. The wind changed; the dust-cloud rose again, rolling across the plain to blot out the panorama he had glimpsed. He looked down at his hands, still clean despite the carnage surrounding him. A Macht face, bloodless and stiff, stared up at him in surly triumph.

As quick as that, like a cup slipping through one's

fingers. For a few minutes, he had seen victory with his own eyes.

'The King,' he croaked. 'The King must be warned.'

He looked up at a new note in the thunder of battle. Horses. They were coming closer.

He stood up and drew his scimitar.

And a hundred heavy cavalry exploded out of the dust before him.

THEY HAD BROUGHT fresh water in skins to the chariot, and wine for those who wanted it. Kouros took a cup, stood on the leather-strapped floor of the vehicle, and rinsed the dust out of his mouth.

The noise around him; that roaring cataclysm. He had almost become accustomed to it. Hard to believe so many men could make such a din for so long.

The sun was a white ball, in a sky the colour of tanned leather. It had crossed the meridian. If it were shining they would have had it in their eyes. How many hours had he been standing here, with his father's upright form beside him? Four – five? All those months of preparation, the gathering of the army, the logistical nightmare, the endless marching columns. All for these few hours in a lightless sky and a blinding storm of dust. How did one even know what was happening?

He wondered where Roshana was – whether the Macht had killed her, or merely taken her as a slave. For a few moments he dwelled with lubricious pleasure on the thought of her beauty in chains, serving the bestial needs of those animals. The thought cheered him. He drank more wine. His aching ribs took solace in the vintage and he grew more at ease, wondering when it would all be declared over. He craved a bath above all other things. The grit was grating in his very scalp.

There were shadows coming out of the dust, running forms, very like the broken crowds of the levies that had been sent up against the Macht line earlier in attack after attack. They ran past with mouths agape, fighting for breath, eyes like marbles in their heads.

They were Honai.

The wine curdled in Kouros's mouth. His father was leaning on the front rail of the chariot, saying nothing. The old man tugged down the folds of his komis as though that would help him see through the storm of dust, the running shadows.

Crowds of the bronze-clad warriors were looming up now, many painted with blood, their bright armour dull and scored. They had thrown away their shields to aid their flight; the age-old badge of the broken soldier.

The Honai. It could not be possible.

The Great King himself railed at them, shouting like a junior officer, to no avail. His cavalry escort halted them for a time. They staggered into the chests of the big Niseians, and many collapsed there, sobbing for breath. To run in full armour, in this heat, this dust; it was a killing exertion. But they were staggering on, pushing their way between the ranks of the horsemen, cursing the Arakosans and punching at the heads of the horses blocking their paths.

Finally the chariot bodyguard leapt down from the vehicle and seized one of his comrades by the wing of his cuirass. He swung him off his feet and shouted furiously into the Kefre's face.

'What has happened?'

The Honai took a moment to come back to himself; the panic was flooding his eyes.

'Cavalry. They hit us with thousands of horsemen, and other infantry. We were strung out. We thought it was over.'

'Have you seen Dyarnes?'

The Honai shook his head dumbly.

'Bel's blood,' the bodyguard said. He released the fellow and after a second the Honai got up, tottered in a confused circle, and then took off, staggering.

'My lord, we should go,' the bodyguard said to Ashurnan. 'If the Honai are broken, then we are exposed here.'

The Great King shook his head. 'I must know what has happened.' He turned to his couriers, who sat on their trembling, sweating horses like men eager to begin a race.

'Go forward. Find Dyarnes, or at least find out what has happened.' And to another one; 'Go to Lorka and the Arakosans. Find out what has occurred on the left.'

Kouros tossed aside his cup. 'Father!'

They were like ghosts. They charged out of the murk like shapes made of shadow and dust, and all at once the dust was swept away by the veering wind, and the sun burst bright upon them, setting alight the bright lance-heads, the swords, the gleam in their eyes.

Kefren on Niseians, a line of them. They might have been imperial cavalry, except that their garments were dyed red as holly-berries and their armour was strangely shaped. At their head rode a pale-faced youth, his eyes blazing under a horsehair crest, his very face shining, as though he had been just that moment incarnated from some terrible dream. His armour was black, as lightless as if it were made of a hole scooped from the very fabric of the world. There was a banner with the device of a raven upon it, sable on white, flying above his head. He raised his sword and cried out wordlessly. And Kouros felt a thrill of terror scale his flesh as he recognised the face.

'It's him!' he cried, and he leapt from the chariot even as the driver whipped the horses.

The cavalry charged into them like a foaming wall. Ashurnan drew his sword and laid about him like a young man while his bodyguard held up a shield to protect him. The chariot snagged, jerked, the Niseians that drew it fighting breast to breast with the horses of the newcomers. The driver had his whip-hand slashed from his wrist, and then his head was taken from his shoulders and he toppled in a fountain of blood.

The Arakosan escort had surged forward, and now the imperial cavalry were battling it out at a standstill all around the royal chariot, the horses biting and kicking, their riders hacking at one another and stabbing with short lances. The battle was here, now, right upon them. Kouros rolled along the ground while his barely knitting ribs grated in his chest and burst his mind wide open with the agony of it. But the fear that flooded him also kept him going.

The couriers were battling at the rear of the chariot, but they were unarmoured and young, inexperienced. The Kefren who fought them seemed transported; they battled like demons, and there were more and more of their fellows streaming in from the west, a veritable army of enemy cavalry which seemed to have somehow sprung up out of the dust.

Kouros stood up. He saw the Great King's standard tilt and then fall as the chariot was overturned. The horses still harnessed to it panicked and tried to bolt, dragging the vehicle along. His father was still inside it, hanging on with one hand and lashing out with the scimitar.

A horse knocked him down, its hoof striking him in the temple. Kouros barely felt it, but for a few minutes as he struggled to his knees in the midst of the melee, he found himself recording everything he saw with a strange, remote detachment. He saw Ashurnan speared through the chest by an enemy trooper and fall from the overturned chariot to be hidden behind the trampling feet of the horses. He saw the Arakosan escort fighting to the last for possession of the standard, men losing hands and arms to keep hold of it. But the blue-armoured Arakosans were now a mere struggling handful.

He saw the enemy cavalry, horsemen who were Kefren, yet somehow Macht, flood in a tide past the wrecked chariot. There was no-one left to oppose them, no-one left to kill.

He saw Corvus, the pale youth with the terrible eyes, dismount, and lay his cloak over the trampled corpse that had once been Ashurnan, Great King of the Asurian empire, ruler of the world.

And with that, the strange remoteness left him. Kouros staggered to his feet, the Macht cavalry galloping past him in squadrons to spread ruin through the rest of the army. They took with them the standard of Asuria, which had flown on victorious battlefields for years beyond count. It was a trophy now, stained with the blood of the men who had tried to preserve it.

He caught a horse with his good arm, and hung onto the reins like a man down to his last straw as it danced and reared around him. Somehow, he pulled himself into the saddle, wholly ignored. He did not wear armour, he bore no weapon that the enemy could see, and he was plainly injured. They left him alone; he was just one more fleeing Kufr in the dust and the destruction of the Asurian army.

The King is dead, he thought muzzily as he kicked the horse into motion and set the sun at his back. Long live the King.

He joined the mob of men and animals running eastwards, some in flight, some in pursuit.

He did not know where he was going. He knew only that he had to get away from that pale faced youth, the boy who had killed his father.

TWENTY
FUNERAL PYRES

As the evening came, tawny with spent dust on the wind, bright with the first of the moons, so the camp began to fill up again.

Roshana and Kurun sat outside their tent with their feet to a campfire that a chastened Macht had built for them, and watched as the waggon-park on the plain below the tented city came to life with torch and firelight. At first they could see clearly the slow procession of the waggons as they trickled in below, but later, when night fell, they could only hear them. They followed the progress of the convoys by the shrieks of those that were in them: the wounded of the Macht army.

'So many,' Roshana said. She was gripping her komis close to her mouth in one white-knuckled little fist. 'How can there be so many? They must have been defeated, Kurun. They are screaming in their thousands.'

'If they lost, then what of us?' Kurun asked.

'If they won, what of us?'

'I do not want the Macht to win, mistress.'

'Nor do I. But I hope Kouros was in the battle. I hope he died. I hope Corvus killed him.'

Kurun looked at the slight, crop-headed girl with the blazing eyes, and then he looked back down at the waggon-park and the field hospitals with a sigh. 'It is too big for me. I only know that I want to live. And I want you to live. There is nothing else.'

Roshana took his hand. 'There is still vengeance.'

'It is not for a slave to seek. He merely endures.'

'Not you – you are no slave. Not to me.'

Kurun said nothing. He knew better than to speak.

They could not sleep that night for the screaming; neither of them had ever heard anything like it. They sat wrapped in a single blanket and occasionally Kurun would scour the surroundings for scraps of wood to keep the fire going. But it was burnt down to a glowing nub by the time the solitary figure walked towards them up the slope from the waggons below. By that hour, many thousands of men had already returned to the camp, not just wounded, but infantry marching in cadence, in silence, shrouded by the ochre dust. And lines of limping horses too lame to bear a rider.

The shadow came into the last red light of their fire and they saw that it was a Kefre, a tall man of some breeding. He was covered in dust and dried blood and he moved with the slow careful steps of the very old and the very tired.

'My name is Ardashir,' he said to Roshana and Kurun, and the fire lit up a friendly smile in his haggard face. 'May I join you?'

He sat down without answer, though it was closer to a fall. Elbows on knees, he stared at the sullen coals and his eyes blinked slowly as though sleep was a precipice and he was on the very edge.

But he collected himself. 'The King sent me to see how you were faring, and to ask if there was anything you need. He apologises for not coming in person, but he... he had things to attend to that will not wait.' Here Ardashir licked his dry lips and pointed out across the plain to the east. There were lights out there in the black desert, moving torches, an impression of great activity.

'I am to bring you to a ceremony.' The words staggered from his tongue. Kurun offered the Kefre a waterskin and he smiled, and squeezed one swallow after another into his mouth until the liquid was brimming over and running down his neck. It carved tracks in the dust coating his skin.

'Ah, my thanks. I was beginning to wilt.'

'Who won the battle?' Roshana asked him in a low tone.

'We did, lady. The army of the Great King has been shattered and is in rout along every eastern road for forty pasangs.'

Roshana's mouth opened. But Ardashir had not finished.

'The Great King is dead. He died fighting, like a brave man. I am to bring you to his funeral with the coming of the dawn. My condolences, lady.

King Corvus would not have had it so. He would have taken your father alive had he been able, and treated him with honour. As it is, we have built a pyre worthy of him. It is lit at dawn. That is why I am here.'

He turned his head to look at Roshana. 'You were not close to your father.'

'He had many children. He barely knew most of them.' The shock of the news was cold upon them both. Kurun tucked his face into his knees and began to weep, not knowing why. For the death of a world he had known, perhaps. Nothing could be brought back now, any more than his own body could be made whole again.

'What of the crown prince?' Roshana asked. 'What of Kouros?'

Ardashir frowned. 'We captured no nobles. They are either dead or fled. Lady, on the plain of Gaugamesh east of here the bodies lie like a carpet for pasangs. Many thousands died today; we have barely begun to count them, let alone know who they were. This Kouros may be alive, he may be dead. There will be no way of knowing.'

Roshana nodded. She bent her forehead into Kurun's shoulder. Her own tears came now, silent. She, too, was weeping for she knew not what. For a father who had barely ever spoken to her? Or for the loss of that world which Kurun wept for also. For the brother who had disappeared with it.

Ardashir hauled himself to his feet. He rubbed his hand over his face, grimacing as the palm came away black. 'It is time, lady,' he said with the gentleness peculiar to him. 'We must leave now. There is a cart waiting to take you.'

Roshana looked up at him, like some beautiful lost beggar-child. 'I will come. I'm ready.'

THE PYRE WAS some thirty feet high, made of broken waggons, shattered spears and wizened trees felled from the scrub-scattered plain. The Great King's chariot had been hauled to the top of it, and his body was laid out upon its shattered frame, braced on a wooden bier. He had been wrapped in the red cloaks of the Macht infantry, and above his head the royal standard of Asuria flew, tattered and bloodstained, but catching the wind so that the rags spread like the pinions of a dark bird.

As the dawn light touched the standard, so Corvus stepped forward, bearing a lit torch which glared bright in the morning-dark.

The pyre caught quickly, the flames streaming along the base and reaching up as the wind fanned them. Soon the whole pyre was alight and roaring, and the sunrise lit it brighter still, and cast long shadows across the plain.

Many thousands had gathered there to see the pyre of a Great King. They stood filthy, grimed and bloody, but in perfect ranks and complete silence as the tall pyre began to collapse in on itself, the chariot at its top sinking into the embers below with a fantail of sparks, the Asurian standard itself catching light at the end and streaming away in one last bright flammifer.

Other mounds were then lit. All around the King's pyre they stood in gruesome piles, stacked high with anything flammable that could be found on or near the battlefield. Even sheaves of arrows had been stacked about the corpses of the Macht.

They were kindled one by one, and the Great King's pyre had the company of half a dozen others as large, but containing hundreds of bodies. The black smoke rose as the dawn light waxed and the red tint left the eastern sky. The soldiers trooped back to their camp, and behind them the pyres burned down to ash which the west wind took and blew across the earth in a grey mist, towards the peaks of the Magron Mountains.

FOR THREE DAYS, the Macht policed the great battlefield, searching for those that still lived, collecting the dead and burning them in yet more pyres, collecting a mountain of armour and weapons and other equipment which had been abandoned on the field. But only a tithe of them remained there to do this. Most of the army was already on the march eastwards again, the Companions in the forefront, harrying the survivors of the battle and travelling east among panic-stricken mobs of levy-soldiers who wanted nothing more, now, than to get back to their farms and their homes and their families. These were ignored; they were no longer any threat to the advance.

The prize in this race was the city of Carchanis, the great citadel that guarded the crossings of the Bekai

River and which had been used by the Great King as his base of operations. The lead troops of the Macht came within sight of the city four days after the battle, and at once sent word to its governor to surrender, or face assault and siege with no quarter given.

It was a bluff. The army was not yet in any condition to assault or besiege so much as a hamlet. Parmenios's siege equipment was still back at the waggon-park, and the men and animals of Corvus's army had been pushed to the limits of their endurance.

But the bluff worked. Governor Beshan of Carchanis opened his western gates to the invaders and surrendered the city, having first opened the eastern gates to allow the remnants of the Arakosans under Lorka to continue their flight.

Word was sent back to the tented camps around Gaugamesh. The battlefield was to be abandoned, and the entire army was to move up on Carchanish, where the Great King had stockpiled enough supplies to feed it for months. Corvus himself rewarded Beshan for his surrender by allowing him to remain as Governor of the city, but he also appointed a military advisor to help the Kefren administration cope with the change in pace. And to keep an eye on things.

The breakneck pursuit was called off for a few days to allow the bulk of the army to regroup and rest. Around the ancient walls of Carchanis the tented city of the Macht sprang up once more, like a plague of dun mushrooms. But it was not as large as it had been before Gaugamesh.

* * *

In his long life, Rictus had known many injuries, and he had learned how to deal with pain. But it seemed to him that the journey in the waggon-bed from Gaugamesh to Carchanis produced the greatest agonies he had ever known. And he did not know why.

His wounds were many, varied and uninteresting. None of them in themselves were even close to fatal, but the combination of them all had brought him as close to Antimone's Veil as he had ever been in his life.

He travelled in a well-sprung caravan which had been looted from the baggage train of the imperial army. It was superbly made, drawn by four quiet horses used to the traces, and it had a wooden roof painted blue and traced with silver filigree; a line of horses galloping endlessly round and around, their manes flying, their tails curling and tossing. Rictus lay on the rope-hung cot within the cart, sweating sour memories into the linen sheets, and watched those horses go round and around, waiting for death.

He was attended to by an old Kefren physician named Buri, who had been found in the wreckage of the Great King's army, and who had chosen to help the wounded of his conquerors. He was too old for flight or bitterness or ambition, and Corvus had found him to be an able man. He had set him the task of keeping Rictus alive.

He was aided in this task by Kurun, the *hufsan*

slave-boy, who, it seemed, had taken it upon himself to help the old man heal the Macht marshal. And because the youngster was often in the caravan with Rictus, the crop-headed Kefren princess, Roshana, was there also as often as not.

Buri did not know who Roshana was, and she did not tell him, but he did ask Kurun why the boy wanted to see the Macht veteran live.

'He helped us once,' was all Kurun would say, with a shrug of his narrow shoulders. And then he would be out the back door of the caravan, leaping off it as they plodded along in search of firewood or water or fresh linen. He had become an able thief, and the three Kufr in the caravan ate well. Rictus would eat nothing. He would only drink water, as much as any man could hold. It was as if he were trying to flush the dust of Gaugamesh out of his throat.

So it was that when they reached Carchanis, it was deemed a natural thing that apartments be found in the high citadel to accommodate them all close at hand to each other. By that point Rictus was able to sit up, though his raw-boned face had lost its colour and the flesh had fallen from his bones, so that his head seemed too big for his body. Buri's administrations kept his wounds clean and knitting, and fought off the dank fierceness of a fever; the same that was carrying off hundreds of the other Macht wounded. All the same, Rictus was gone for several days after their arrival in Carchanis, lost in some twilit world where Antimone watched over him and folded him in her black wings. Kurun watched over him day and night, pouring water down his throat and wiping the sweat from his body. And Roshana sat in a corner with her komis over her face and carried water from the fountained courtyard as though she were the servant and old Buri her master.

It was the sound of marching feet and the call of bronze horns which finally roused Rictus from his stupor. The city was full of the sound of an army, but the horns were deep and strange. They did not belong to the Macht, or to the empire. He opened his red-crusted eyes to find Kurun looking down on him, his young face hollow-eyed but cheerful. In Kefren, the *hufsan* said, 'Buri, the Macht awakes.'

'Help me up,' Rictus told him, knowing the face but not connecting it to any memory as yet. The boy seemed to understand him, but even in his gaunt state Rictus was too heavy to shift. Finally Roshana propped herself under his other shoulder and they helped him out of the bed. He stood naked between them, his body covered with purple wounds and linen dressings, and limped over to the high window.

Into the hot sunlight, the heat of it like a blast of memory. Rictus closed his eyes a moment against the glare, and when he could finally see again he found himself looking down on the serried clay-tile rooftops of a great city, as great as Machran or larger. The buildings of it swooped down with dizzying steepness to walls of pale stone far below, and beyond, a great river, brown as the back of a thrush, crossed by a massive bridge of ancient stonework. Beyond that, the green country of the

Middle Empire opened out into a shimmering haze of heat and dust, and beyond that lay the dark blue guess of the Magron Mountains at the edge of sight.

But that was not what caught Rictus's eyes. It was the dark worms of marching men slowly inching across the green country, blackening the pale roadways to the city with their numbers and their strange banners, the beat of their feet to be heard as a distant blood-quickening drum even up here in the heights of the citadel.

'Who are they?' he asked. Again, the boy Kurun understood him, though he spoke in Machtic.

'They Juthan. Juthan army here. Juthan King here today,' he said, the words ill-formed in his mouth but perfectly understandable.

'Where is this?'

'This Carchanis. Big city. Big river. Enough now.'

They tried to move Rictus away from the tall balconied window, but Rictus was as immobile as a standing stone, staring as though he had just seen the world for the first time.

'Carchanis,' he said. 'The Bekai River.'

And then, in a whisper, 'Fornyx, my brother.' He stood there with the two young Kufr under his arms, old Buri beginning to fuss and fret around him, and the tears came dripping from his eyes and trailed down a gaunt face as hard as stone.

THERE WAS A banquet that night, to welcome the King of Jutha into the city. Proxanon himself had led his grey-skinned legions clear across the Middle Empire, fighting several battles along the way, but he had missed the great conflagration of Gaugamesh. The long hall which was the centrepiece of the governor's palace was packed tight and bright with Macht and Juthan, and the city was flooded with them. The evening had been set aside for celebrations, the first Corvus's army had known since the battle. In the wake of their victory there had been too much to do, too many wounded to take care of, too many details to be rounded off, for there to be any real sense of their triumph. But now that they were ensconced in a rich, civilised city with plentiful provisions to hand and the prospect of some rest to come, the Macht king had declared a holiday. The city was decked out as though for a festival and hundreds of wine-barrels had been roused out of the palace cellars and set rolling in the streets. The smell of roasting meat hung over all, entire herds and flocks of animals slaughtered for a night of largesse, of excess. The men had earned it. They needed it.

The inhabitants of Carchanis, unmolested until now, drew inside their houses and locked the doors and shuttered the windows, while in the streets the wine ran in the gutters and the teeming soldiers grew steadily more raucous.

Rictus heard them as he lay by the tall window. He had insisted they move the bed there so he could feel the wind on his face and watch the torchlight in the streets below. A cup of wine sat in his hand, untasted, and a platter fit to feed a family had been sent up from the banqueting tables, still untouched. He sat and looked out at the warm, fire-studded night while Kurun squatted on the floor beside him, with his elbows on his knees, and plied him with endless halting questions in broken Machtic. The boy had a mind like a magpie, forgetting nothing, endlessly curious, and he was picking up the foreign tongue with all the speed of youth, intelligence and stubbornness that was in him. Rictus responded to his sallies with monosyllables, but he liked having the boy there beside him. Like some bright flame of life still burning bright beside the spent lamp of his own spirit.

The noise of revelry grew louder as the door to the chambers was opened, then shut out again. Rictus knew the footsteps that approached. He did not turn round. He could smell the wine, and some Kufr perfume. Kurun rose easily to his feet and bowed.

'Where is the princess Roshana?' Corvus's voice.

'The girl went to bed, though how she'll sleep with this racket I don't know,' Rictus said. He turned to look upon his king, now the most powerful man in the world.

Corvus had vine-leaves laced in his hair, and his eyes had been drawn out dark with stibium so that his white face was more of a mask than ever. The wine was heavy on his breath and he had a jar of it dangling from one hand. He smiled, sat down on the edge of Rictus's bed with a heaviness quite unlike him. He was drunk, Rictus realised. For the first time in all the years he had known Corvus, the boy was drunk.

Not a boy, though. Despite the painted face and the vine leaves, this was no callow youth who sat beside Rictus now, and the smile on his face was as painted as his eyes.

'How is my old warhorse – I meant to look in on you earlier – how is my friend Rictus? Old Rictus, old man. Never dead yet. How is he? Have some wine, brother –' He lifted the jar, slopping the red liquid on the bed.

'I have some,' Rictus said, raising his untasted cup.

'As well you should, Rictus. We should all have wine tonight, as much as we can hold. It washes away the dust. Boy! Drink with me!'

Kurun looked at Rictus quickly, and then gulped from the proffered jar as Corvus held it for him.

'That's the stuff, boy. Phobos, but you're a pretty one. Near as pretty as your mistress. I must look in on her. I'll be quiet. I want to see her –'

He raised himself from the bed, but Rictus took him by the wrist. 'Let her sleep, Corvus. Not everyone wants to drink tonight.'

'No – no – of course not.' He seemed to sober somewhat. His face changed. Rictus had never known any other man with such mobile features. For a second Corvus seemed on the verge of weeping, but then he seemed to collect himself. He poured a stream of wine to spatter redly on the floor.

'For absent friends,' he said thickly.

And now Rictus drank deep from his own wine, suddenly needing the warmth of it in his own gullet. His throat had narrowed. He tossed the dregs onto the stone as Corvus had.

'I did not mean them all to die,' Corvus said quietly. His words were slurred, but the thuggish gaiety had left him. He was himself again.

'I did not plan it that way – why would I? They stood beside you, Rictus, to the end. If you had not been there, they would have broken, and they would have survived. The Dogsheads.'

'They would have stood with Fornyx as they did with me.'

Corvus shook his head. 'A man will give his life for a legend. You should have done what I asked, and commanded the reserves. You disobeyed me.'

'I did, and you let me do it. Do you know why, Corvus?'

The King looked at him, hovering somewhere between anger and compassion.

'Because you knew why I did it. This was one party I could not miss. The greatest of battles. The start of a legend, perhaps. You would have done the same yourself. That is why you allowed me to take my place with my men. It appealed to the romantic in you.'

Corvus smiled tightly. 'As you say, I would have done the same myself.' He bowed his head.

Rictus stared into his wine, listening to the sound of the night-time city being painted bright and garish by the celebrations below.

'Did any survive?' he asked, a question he had not dared frame since his senses had come back to him.

'Forty-six,' Corvus said. He straightened and drank again. 'Forty-six out of close on three thousand. There's a legend for you. How the Dogsheads died at Gaugamesh. How that story of theirs ended there, right in front of the eyes of the Great King.'

'There are worse ways to die,' Rictus said, in a low rasp.

'It was a glorious way to die. I hope when my end comes it shall make such a story.'

'How did we come through, overall?'

Corvus was blinking hard. He rubbed his toe in the puddled wine on the floor.

'We lost something over six thousand men, dead or too maimed to ever fight again.'

'That's quite a butcher's bill.'

Corvus smiled a little. 'It was quite a fight, brother. An empire fell that day.'

'You really think that's the end of the fighting?'

Corvus shook his head. 'There will be plenty more fighting. But we will never face another general levy. I've invited all the governors of the lowland cities here. I intend to confirm them in their posts if they will swear me allegiance. Things will go on much as they did before. The Juthan have pacified southern Pleninash in their march to join us. Proxanon is a good man – you'd like him. Never smiles, but can set the table in a roar all the same. Drinks like a man who has just discovered his own mouth.

'His son will bring five thousand of his people across the Magron with us, as part of the army. It will help make up our losses. Plus, we have reinforcements arriving from the Harukush within the month – I received a letter today, from your friend Valerian at Irunshahr. More green spears headed east. They're already over the Korash Mountains. By the time we leave for Asuria, the army will be bigger than ever.'

But it will not be the same army, Rictus thought. Not for me. The Dogsheads are gone, finished. That part of my life is finally over.

Corvus seemed almost to pick up some current of his thought. He did that often with people; he seemed to be able to read them in some uncanny way. Now he said, 'Do not leave me, Rictus.'

'What?'

'Fornyx is dead, the Dogsheads are gone, the battle is won. I can see it in your eyes. I saw it in you every time I visited you in that blue-roofed cart they hauled you east in. You wanted to die. That's why I got in Buri, and set Kurun to watch over you. And lovely Roshana. I set them to keeping you alive, but death is still in your eyes.'

'Perhaps these eyes have seen enough.'

'They have not seen Ashur, the ziggurats of the Great King, the heart of empire. Stay with me, Rictus, I beg you.'

Startled, Rictus looked the younger man square in the face. 'What can I do for you, Corvus, that a dozen other men could not? You don't need my name any more – your own is greater now, greater by far. You have become a legend yourself.'

'Legends need their friends,' the younger man said. He hung his head.

Kurun was looking back and forth between Rictus and Corvus with such fierce concentration that Rictus almost had to smile.

'A man like you will never lack friends.'

Corvus stood up. Something harder crept back into his face. 'Perhaps you are right. Perhaps that is what it truly means to be a king. I would have liked to talk to Ashurnan about it. I would have spared him, had he lived. At least he died like a man should, sword in hand, facing hopeless odds.'

'It was we who faced the hopeless odds at Gaugamesh,' Rictus retorted. 'It is we who prevailed against them. Do not forget the men who died to bring you here.'

'I never forget them,' Corvus said simply. 'Any of them. I mourn them as you do, Rictus. But I will not give up on life because they are gone. A whole world awaits us – we have but to begin walking and it will open under our feet. To realise that – it is what it means to live.'

He turned, still unsteady, but sombre now.

'Would you be happy in the Harukush now, brother, in that little upland farm? Even before I knew you, you never really lived there – it was just somewhere to rest between campaigns. For men such as you and me, there is only the next turn in the road to look forward to.'

He looked back and smiled, boyish again. 'Stay here a while, and see how it suits you. Within the month, I shall be taking the army east once more, across the Magron Mountains and into Asuria itself. Follow me if you like. I shall leave the princess Roshana in your care; I don't think the girl cares much for armies.'

He lifted the wine jar in a final toast as he left,

and raised his voice to a shout.

'I will see you in Ashur, Rictus. I shall make kings out of us all ere the end!'

TWENTY-ONE
THE GIFT

It was just past midsummer when the Macht army left Carchanis for what most assumed would be the final stage of the expedition.

By that time, eight thousand replacements had arrived from the west, large-eyed boys in their fathers' armour who had been on the road from Sinon for the better part of two months. To begin with, they were folded into Demetrius's command, whilst he transferred several morai of his conscripts – veterans now – to Teresian. Thus was the Macht spearline brought back up to strength.

There were other changes also. Marcan, son of Proxanon, the Juthan king, now led five thousand of his own people as an integral part of the army, and the Juthan prince was named a marshal, part of the regular high command. The move caused surprisingly little upset within the ranks of the

Macht, though the Juthan camped separately from the rest of the infantry and there was as yet little mixing between the two races.

King Proxanon led the rest of his army back the way they had come, having signed a formal treaty of alliance with the Macht. He had finally secured his kingdom, which had been at war with the empire almost continually over the last thirty years.

The other cities of the Middle Empire varied in their response to Gaugamesh. Many sent representatives to Corvus at Carchanis, pledging allegiance. These were sent back to their homes with lavish gifts, and each was accompanied by a half-mora of Macht spearmen under a veteran centurion.

Some did not respond at all, and a few sent letters of open defiance. In the end, Corvus had to leave some six thousand men behind in Carchanish under Demetrius, an independent all-arms command which the one-eyed marshal was tasked with using to bring all of the rest of the Middle Empire to heel. He accepted readily, since in effect Corvus was making him de facto ruler of a vast swathe of the Asurian Empire.

The night after the appointment the old soldier finally married his camp-wife, a sour-faced little woman who had been following him from battlefield to battlefield for a quarter of a century. She bloomed overnight into a well-dressed lady and took to riding in a sedan chair borne by four brawny *hufsan* slaves. There were those who said that Demetrius would have been better off if he had stayed with the army.

That army was similar in size to the one which Corvus had brought over the Machtic Sea the year before, but there were many changes within it. The Dogsheads were gone, but Corvus now rewarded those who had excelled themselves on the field of battle by presenting them with silver-faced shields. In truth, they were made of highly polished steel, but the name stuck, and these men, many of them cursebearers, formed an elite within the infantry. They were commanded by a young centurion named Arsenios, who was a lion in the battle-line but whose principal prowess was in the field of wine-drinking. Most nights during the army's stay in Carchanis, he would throw a drinking party at which the guest of honour was invariably the King.

Day by day, something built up around Corvus which had not been there before. Inevitably, there were more demands on his time than there had been even in Machran, and the bald-headed stocky little engineer, Parmenios, performed many of the duties of a chamberlain for him, which was no great leap since he had been the King's chief scribe before his genius for invention had come to the fore. This meant that there was an extra layer to get through before a solitary soldier with a grievance could see his king in person. In the past, any member of the army might call upon the King's tent at any time, sure that, given a moment, Corvus would always get around to seeing him. But not any more. There were too many people clamouring for an audience with the conqueror of Gaugamesh. The soldiers were referred back to their officers, and they watched as an unending procession of Kufr dignitaries from all over the western empire were conducted into the King's presence without delay.

Part of this was city living, part of it was sheer administrative necessity, and part of it was down to changes in Corvus himself. He was less patient than he had been, more autocratic. Where once he would have won round his officers with at least the appearance of debate, now he simply issued orders, or better yet, had Parmenios's secretaries write them down and then sent his pages out to deliver them. It was as though the nature of his achievements had finally begun to sink home.

The army itself was only part of his concerns. His rule now lay over many thousands of pasangs of a foreign world, and he was ruler of places he had not yet seen. Cities he had never visited were erecting statues of him in an effort to curry favour, and his lenient treatment of those who surrendered to him willingly meant that not a day went by without an embassy from some obscure imperial province wishing to secure its place in the new order of things.

'It's a relief to be going at last,' Ardashir said. He stood over Rictus, as stately as a sunlit stork. 'This time in the city has brought it all home to him. He's at his best when on the move, nothing but that damned tent over his head.'

Rictus smiled. 'He can't be on the move forever, Ardashir. One day he will sit down and realise he can go no further. On that day, I will be glad to be elsewhere.'

'On that day he will need you more than he ever has before.'

'No. My time is past. I'm too broken and old now to ever stand in a spearline again. I am no further use to him.'

'My, you're a stiff necked bastard – as bad as he is.'

'Keep an eye on him for me.'

'Will you be coming east, Rictus, or will you stay here? You know that wherever you stay, Corvus will set you up like a king.'

'I've no desire to be one. I am not Demetrius – I don't have a wife whispering ambitious noises in my ear.'

'Then you will come east – good – that relieves my mind.'

'I didn't say that,' Rictus snapped. And then, 'Yes, I suppose so. I'm to bring Roshana to him anyway, once Ashur falls.'

'Does she know what her fate is to be?'

'I don't speak Kufr – I haven't asked. It would not surprise me, though. She's not stupid.'

'If it happens, then Ashurnan's grandson may one day be Great King. The more things change –'

'The more they stay the same.' Rictus smiled up at the tall Kefre. 'You be careful, Ardashir. You and Druze are the only people left with the army he still listens to.'

'I'll be careful – it's in my nature. I leave the heroic gestures to you Macht. The Kefren are a more pragmatic people.'

'I have learned that. I am glad that I have one to call a friend.'

Ardashir bent and embraced Rictus in his chair. 'Stay alive, brother,' he said. 'If Bel is merciful, the next time we meet it will be in Ashur itself.'

'Perhaps.' Rictus rose to his feet as Ardashir bowed to him. Kurun propped him up on one side and on the other he leaned upon a thornwood stick, a black, gnarled length of iron-hard wood polished to a high ebony shine. A parting gift from Corvus, one of many.

'Ardashir.' Rictus called the Kefre back as he was turning to leave.

'Come with me a moment. There is something I want you to see.'

He limped into the antechamber, where his gear had been stowed. His armour, his weapons, the curios and equipment he had hauled halfway across the world. They half-filled the room, hung from the walls and assembled on shelves. It seemed like quite a collection, but it was not much to show for a life.

At the far wall were two black cuirasses, Antimone's Gift, polished and shining in the lamplight. Sometimes they reflected the flames, and sometimes they did not. It was one of the mysteries about them. The two cuirasses were exactly the same; neither had so much as a scratch upon them, though they had both seen hard service. There was no way to guess their age; they were as changeless as the waves of the sea.

'They brought me Fornyx's armour, after they found his body,' Rictus said. 'His is the one on the right, though they can't really be told apart. I've been thinking on it, and it seems to me you should have it. Fornyx would have had it so. After Gaugamesh they policed up a dozen of these from the dead, and I know Druze and Teresian and Demetrius were given them by Corvus. But he never gave one to you, his best friend.'

'Because I am Kufr,' Ardashir breathed. 'Rictus, I am honoured by the thought, I truly am. But I cannot take this thing. It would not be right.'

'Bullshit. If Corvus can wear one, then I'm damned sure you can. You're a marshal of the army – you should be a cursebearer no matter what blood runs through you. Kurun – go get it.'

The boy left Rictus's side and put his hands out to lift the right-hand cuirass off its stand. Then he shrank away. 'I cannot,' he said to Rictus. 'It frightens me.'

Rictus grunted and limped forward himself. He took the cuirass by its wing and lifted it easily with one hand, then tossed it to Ardashir.

The Kefren marshal caught it with an expression of outright fear blazed across his face, as if he expected the touch of it to burn him. He held the armour away from his body in both hands, as one might hold a baby which had soiled itself.

'It won't bite, you damned fool,' Rictus growled. 'Put it on. Kurun – help him, and stop being such a girl about it.'

The snap of the clasps was loud in the room, along with the heavy breathing of the two Kufr. Rictus leaned on his stick and watched while Ardashir clicked down the wings over his shoulders and stood, shocked, as the armour moulded to his shape, extending to fit his long torso.

'Bel's blood – it is alive!'

'No – it's just a piece of craft we don't understand. Men made these things once, but then forgot how.'

'I thought your goddess gifted them to the Macht.'

Rictus shrugged. 'Call me cynical.'

They stood looking at one another. 'What will your people say when they see a Kufr wearing the Curse of God?' Ardashir asked.

'They will get used to it. Times are changing, Ardashir. The army is made up of all three races now. And every man who was at Gaugamesh and the Haneikos knows you have earned the right to wear that armour.'

Ardashir embraced him. 'You have come a long way, my friend,' he said.

'So have we all.'

THE ARMY MARCHED out of its camps two days later, on a bright summer morning in the month the Kufr called *Osh-Nabal*, the time of the high sun. Rictus watched the endless columns filing across the Bekai bridge, Druze and his Igranians already fanning out towards the foothills of the Magron beyond. The shimmering haze of the river-plain blurred the bright sun-caught flashes of bronze and iron on the marching men. A contingent of *hufsan* spearmen marched with them, volunteers who had joined the great adventure to see where it might lead. The army was no longer truly Macht. The empire was no longer entirely Kufr. He wondered if it was for the best, or if it really made any difference at all to the farmers and peasants of the fertile lowlands. They still paid their taxes and saw their sons go off to war as they always had. The more things change...

'Will we follow them?' Kurun asked beside him. The boy was staring at the marching columns with a kind of hunger, the endless curiosity of the young.

'We'll follow them,' Rictus said. 'How could we not?' He set a hand on the boy's shoulder and bent his head to hide the sudden dazzle in his eyes.

TWENTY-TWO
THE STEPS OF THE KING

THEY HAD BEEN gathering people ever since leaving Hamadan, accumulating a ragged tail of leaderless troops, fleeing nobles, masterless slaves. As they came down into the sun-baked lowlands of Asuria, they numbered in their thousands, a cavalcade of remnants looking for a way to become whole again.

At the head of the straggling column Kouros sat upon the big bay Niseian which had carried him clear through the mountains, and reined in at the sight below, his breath caught in his throat at the panorama that opened out before him.

Asuria, the heart of the empire. It was an endless green country which rolled away beyond the edge of sight, gridded with the darker green of irrigation channels, glinting under the sun. In the distance, he could see the grey line of Ashur's walls, the sea of terracotta roofs beyond it, and the two ziggurats, lonely mountains afloat on the haze, the Fane of Bel catching the sun with a brief flash of gold.

Lorka, Archon of the Arakosans, drew up beside him in his kingfisher-blue armour. He touched his forehead and then opened his palm to the sun in thanks to Bel.

'So long as Ashur stands, there is hope,' he said to Kouros. 'You are Great King now – it must be proclaimed. The people must know that the world continues as it did, that all things will one day be the same again.'

Kouros nodded. 'Bring your men into the city – I will see that they are found quarters.'

'And the others?' Lorka gestured to the river of people who were plodding past them, head down and exhausted with the long trek over the Magron.

'They are rabble. Let them find a place where they may. I will ride ahead, Lorka. Make sure that the bullion waggons are within the city walls by nightfall.'

'As you wish, my lord. I will detail a small escort to see you through the gates. Remember me to your mother, and tell her I send my respects and rejoice that I may soon see her again.'

Kouros looked at the Arakosan sharply. 'My mother – yes, of course.'

He kicked his mount savagely, and started down towards the city at a gallop with a skein of Arakosan riders in tow.

They entered the western gates without ceremony or remark. The tall barbican of enamelled tile was the same colour as the Arakosans' armour, and the traffic went in and out of it as though nothing had changed. Farmers still brought their crops to market, merchants still led braying mule-trains, slaves still filed along in chained gangs.

There was one difference, though – there were no Honai on guard, just some leather-clad *hufsan* of the city watch.

Kouros let his horse pick the way through the crowd, massaging his still-stiff torso with one hand. Apart from the magnificence of his steed and his armed escort, there was little to set him apart personally from a thousand other prosperous minor nobles or merchants. His clothing was well made but hard-worn, and he wore no komis; his face was brown and wind-burnt like that of a peasant, and for a weapon he bore nothing more grand than a filthy kitchen-blade of blackened iron. These things would have seemed important to him, once, but no more.

They rode up the Huruma amid the spray of the fountains, the palace ziggurat looming ever closer and taller above them, casting a shadow as large as that of a stormcloud. Only when Kouros set his horse to climb the King's Steps did the guards come awake, and he found himself surrounded by a knot of *hufsan* with whips and scimitars. He thought of the gleaming Honai who should have been there, now dead on the barren plain of Gaugamesh, and something like grief rose in his throat. He did not speak, and let his Arakosans do the talking for him. They cursed and swore at the *hufsan* in common Asurian, the language of the masses, but the *hufsan* guards were adamant; no-one save the Great King himself might mount the Steps on horseback.

Finally, as the Arakosans began to draw their swords, Kouros spoke. In high Kefren he said, 'I am Kouros, son of Ashurnan. My father was Great King of the empire, and I am his heir. The crown is mine; this ziggurat is mine. This city and everything in it belongs to me, as do your lives. If you do not let me pass I will summon my army into the city and have you impaled at this very spot. Will you let me pass, or will you wait here to die?'

Something in his tone stilled them. The guards muttered among themselves, looking at the bright steel in the hands of the Arakosans. They noted the Niseian warhorses, and the effortless confidence of the Black Kefre who spoke to them. Finally they gave way.

Kouros began pacing his horse up the wide-spaced steps that led to the summit of the ziggurat.

This would have been the highlight of my life, once, he thought. Now it is just another road.

THEY HAD WORD of him on the summit before he arrived, so swiftly did the rumour-mill grind in the ziggurat. He dismounted to find an honour guard awaiting him, gaudily armoured Kefren who looked as though they had never held a spear before. There was a disordered flurry, a kind of silent, low-key panic as some sense of ceremony was grasped at. Kouros stood by his patient horse and smiled a little as he saw his mother approach, decked out like a queen in a city's worth of silk and jewels, flanked by Charys, the brutal-faced head eunuch, and little Nurakz, the harem secretary. A train of beautiful young women brought up the rear, as butterfly-like as ever. They blinked in the sunlight and held up little parasols to protect their complexions.

'My son – is it really you?'

She glided up close to him as smoothly as if she ran on wheels, and took Kouros's face in her cold ring-bright hands.

'Bel's blood, your poor face. You are burnt black with the sun.'

'The Mountains will do that to a man. Did you get the despatches?'

'They arrived five days ago. I did not think to find you so close behind them – what are you wearing? Was there no-one to greet you into the city?'

He shook his head free of her hands. 'We must talk.'

'You must bathe.' She clapped her white hands. 'Charys, see to prince Kouros – see that –'

'I am King now, mother. I need no crown for that. I saw my father die, as I saw Rakhsar die. The throne is mine.'

She stared at him for a long, wordless moment, the heavy cosmetics stark in the sunlight, her eyes unreadable. At last she bowed to him, and as she did, so did everyone else in the courtyard.

'My lord King,' she said. 'Tell me what you wish, and it shall be done.'

* * *

THEY CHANGED THE bathwater three times before he got to the end of the dirt ingrained in him. It was his mother's bath in the harem, not that in the royal bedchambers, for the Great King's apartments were being refurbished and aired in readiness for their newest occupant. Kouros did not greatly care. He had not stopped to bathe even at Hamadan, and he had become used to the grime of travel, the smell of woodsmoke, the hard ground for a pillow.

Hufsa slaves as naked as he wiped him down with wooden strigils and applied sweet oils to his abraded skin, combing out the long black hair that fell to his shoulderblades and tying it up in the customary topknot. He stood to be dried and dressed and was too tired to do more than run one hand in absent speculation across the breasts of the prettiest slave. Standing there as they belted the silk robe about his waist, he began to understand his father a little better. He thrust the knife which had killed his brother into the broad sash they wound about his middle. It was an artefact from another world, a world more real than this.

He joined his mother that evening to eat, reclining amid the marble pillars of the harem and lifting ridiculously small dainties from a platter of beaten gold. He had eaten horsemeat in the mountains, and found it not at all bad. In any case, he had little appetite for anything but wine, and this Orsana served him herself in a crystal cup. Kouros held it up to the lamplight and marvelled at the workmanship, the fragility of it in his brown fingers.

'War has made a man of you,' Orsana said from her couch.

'I see things differently now, it's true.'

'I have already sent out a proclamation; the city criers are shouting it all over the streets. Asuria has a new king. My son is alive, and the throne is no longer empty. I will begin preparations for the coronation in the morning.'

'Make it swift, mother. We do not have time to indulge these things any more. The enemy is hard on my heels. He will be in front of our walls before the summer is out.'

She leaned forward. 'So soon?'

'He is a man in a hurry.'

'What did you save out of the wreck, Kouros?'

He thought of the long nights in the mountains, the waystations lost in a sea of refugees, the broken wreckage of a once-mighty army. It had melted away like a late snow. If he had not witnessed it with his own eyes, he would not have deemed it possible.

'A few thousand of the Honai survived. I left them at Hamadan to hold the city, and came on with the Arakosans. Lorka will be within the city walls tonight; he has brought some two thousand horsemen with him, and the contents of Hamadan's treasury. There are thousands more still on the move in the foothills, but they are no more than a common rout.'

The shock sat hard on his mother's face. He almost enjoyed watching her master it.

'Is that all?'

'The Macht did a thorough job. They hunted us all the way to the passes of the mountains. And I have heard that the Juthan have sent an army to join them. There is nothing left beyond the Magron, mother. Asuria is all that remains.'

'And Arakosia,' she said instantly. He tilted his cup to her in agreement.

'We have only the city guard here in Ashur,' she went on, staring into space. 'Five thousand *hufsan* who direct traffic and beat slaves. That is all.'

Kouros lay back on the cushioned couch. It was too soft for him. The weeks in the mountains had accustomed him to the feel of earth and stone under his back.

'I killed Rakhsar with my own hand.' He drew the knife from his sash. 'That, at least, is done.'

'And Roshana?'

'The Macht took her, I think; if she lived. She is immaterial now. The intrigues are over, mother. We must think of gathering more men. We must send to Arakosia, somehow scrape up another levy. These walls must be held.'

She nodded, watching him. She looked upon the blood-grimed blade of the knife he held in fascination and disgust.

'We must meet with Borsanes in the morning,' Orsana told him. 'He commands the city guard. Lorka also. I must talk to him as soon as he gets in. The Arakosans have been coming west for weeks now, but in small numbers. There are perhaps a thousand of them in the city, and more at Hamadan.'

'Enough to stage a palace coup – not enough to

fight off an invading army. You must change your sense of scale, mother.'

Suddenly Kouros hurled the beautiful crystal cup away. It soared through the air and smashed in a shower of glass and wine against the pale Kandassian marble of a nearby pillar, staining the stone. Kouros stood up.

'We are at the end of things here, the finish of everything we have known. Lorka looks to me now; he knows it is I who rule in Ashur. Your intrigues have not prepared you for the waging of war.'

'And running from a battlefield has suddenly transformed you into a general of genius, I suppose!'

Kouros smiled, where once he would have flown into a fury. 'You said yourself; war has made a man of me.'

He strode over to Orsana, where she crouched, cat-like, in a billow of silk, the knife still in his hand. From behind a pillar, he saw Charys, the massive chief eunuch, sidle out, as broad as the pillar himself.

Kouros bent and kissed his mother's cheek, tasting the chalk that whitened it.

'I'm going to bed, to sleep in the chambers of the King where I belong. I will see Borsanes and Lorka in the morning, and I will notify you of events as they occur. Sleep well, mother.'

Her eyes seemed black in the light of the lamps, as cold as stones on a mountainside.

'Do not overreach yourself, Kouros. You stand in my world.'

'Your world is too small,' he retorted. 'You have forgotten what life is like beyond it.'

Then he walked out of the harem, sliding the iron knife back into his sash, and not deigning to give so much as a glance at the glowering eunuch whose eyes followed him all the way to the doors.

THE CITY WAS a changed place the next morning. In the early hours, before even the sun had struck the pinnacles of the ziggurats, the proclamations had gone round with the sprinting, great-lunged city criers. Crowds congested the streets in a feverish hunger for good news. For weeks now, there had been nothing but ominous rumours out of the west. A great battle had been fought, it was generally agreed, but if it had gone well, then the victory tidings would have been spread about without delay. Defeat had been suspected, but never had the high and humble of the imperial capital even dreamed that the Great King himself could be slain in battle. This was the first confirmation they had of the extent of the catastrophe now overtaking the empire. For many, it was the first time they had ever heard Kouros's name spoken.

He rode through the streets at noon that day with an escort of Arakosan cavalry resplendent in their blue armour. A second Royal Standard had been unearthed out of the palace vaults and flew above him in a billow of rich purple and gold, the sigil of the Asurian kings catching the light in a reassuring blaze. Those who were close to the procession as it paraded down the Sacred Way could see that this new king was wind-burnt and thin. He looked like a warrior, not an aristocrat, and they took some comfort in that, and in the white grin with which he received the tossed flowers that carpeted the stones in front of his horse.

Keen observers might also have noticed that the mounts of the Arakosans were not in good flesh, and their riders had dark, tired rings under their eyes which belied the magnificence of their enamelled armour. But the parade reassured the city populace, or at any event it gave them something else to talk about. It took their mind off the storm approaching over the mountains.

In the days that followed, Kouros found he could not rest in the ziggurat – it held too many memories for him, both of his father and his mother, and it was too stiflingly confined by protocol for him to bear, after all the months on campaign. He elected to meet with his officers at the western barbican in a plain room above the gate itself. He wore a diadem now, though he had not been crowned. His father's had been black silk. Kouros chose scarlet, perhaps as a kind of nod to the red-clad men who were now tramping across the empire.

He, Lorka, and Borsanes stood there looking down at a map of the city walls, and flicking through a bundle of tally-sticks representing those available to defend them. Kouros gripped one of these birch-wood counters in his hand as though he could squeeze more out of it.

'It's no good – we must recall the garrison from

Hamadan. There are almost three thousand Honai up there; they will do more good with us than in the hills.'

'Hamadan guards the eastern passes of the Magron,' Lorka said, rubbing the triangular beard upon his chin. Many of the Arakosans were bearded; it was an archaic trait of theirs.

'Those men will not be able to halt a field army. They will merely find themselves besieged. When I left them there, I thought the situation in Ashur was better than it is,' Kouros said. His jaw worked, chewing on the problem.

'If we cannot stop them at Hamadan, we will not stop them here,' Borsanes said. He was a thin, drooping Kefre who reminded Kouros of nothing so much as a wilted sunflower. His head seemed too big for his shoulders, and he had a nose a tapir would have been proud of.

'We will stop them,' Kouros hissed. 'If you lack confidence in our chances, Borsanes, then you should go back to whatever backwater my father dragged you from. You are relieved of your post. Now get out before I decide to make an example of you.'

Borsanes sputtered, eyes wide on either side of his remarkable nose. 'Guards!' Kouros called at once.

Two Arakosan troopers were at the door in a heartbeat.

'Escort this fellow out of the city, as he stands. He is to leave by this very gate. Pass the word about the walls; if he is seen trying to return he is to be killed on the spot.'

The Arakosans took hold of Borsanes with some relish and dragged him, protesting and still sputtering, from the room.

Lorka roared with laughter. 'I do not know if that was your father or your mother I just saw in you, Kouros, but it was worthy of them both.'

'You may address me as *lord*,' Kouros said icily, and Lorka's face went flat.

'Of course. I forgot myself, my lord. Forgive me.'

Kouros was clicking the tally sticks down on the table one by one.

'With the Honai from Hamadan and the drafts of your people who have still to come in, I make it some twelve thousand spears. Those are the real fighters. We can probably round up some of the city low-castes and arm them also to bulk out the numbers.'

'In Arakosia a slave who saves his master's life is considered free by all,' Lorka said. 'There are thousands of imperial slaves in the city, lord. Perhaps they could be made use of. For the right incentive, a slave will fight near as well as a free man.'

Kouros shook his head. 'That is an invitation to chaos. I will not consider it.'

Lorka bowed his head. 'My lord, what of the coronation ceremony, then? It would be a boost to the city's morale.'

'Perhaps. But I do not think we have the time.' Kouros raised his eyes. 'My mother asked you to bring that up.'

Lorka bowed again. 'The lady Orsana is kin to me and mine, as are you, my lord. When she bids me speak to her, I do so.'

'Not any more. From now on, Lorka, if you wish to see the lady Orsana, you will seek my permission first. Are we clear?'

'Very clear, my lord.'

'Good. Now let us go through these tallies once more.'

TRYING TO GET things done in Ashur was like trying to prod an elephant into movement with a needle. So convinced were the population of the city's inviolability that they could barely imagine that it might be attacked, that an enemy could actually enter their gates. The circuit of the walls was in good repair, and fearsomely high, but it stretched for over sixty pasangs, and to defend the perimeter the river Oskus also had to be taken into the equation. It flowed through the eastern quarters of Ashur like a wide brown highway. An inventive attacker might use it to by-pass the walls entirely.

The endless meetings in the audience hall, with Kouros sitting on the throne that had been his father's; the stifling formality of it all, the time wasted on protocol and ceremony, when every moment counted. It threw Kouros into icy rages, which he took out on a succession of unfortunate slave-girls. He did not yet care to inspect his father's concubines, nor would he ever let his mother choose more for him, so slaves were sent up to him from the lower city in a steady stream, and night after night they went back down again, bruised and bleeding. In this, at least, he felt he had some control.

Ten days after his entrance to the city, something new was admitted to the echoing audience hall with its lines of courtiers and scribes. Orsana was there that day, seated to Kouros's right like the queen she was. There was something of a stir as Akanish the chamberlain announced the arrival of Archon Gemeris, a name Kouros knew. He rose from the throne, smiling, as the tall Kefren noble stalked up the length of the hall. He was clad in Honai armour, and the sight of it sent a glad murmur down the walls from the assembled notables and nonentities.

Kouros did not let the man kneel, so glad was he to see him, but took his hand.

'Gemeris – you are well met. So, you made it down from Hamadan in good time – are all your men with you?'

'Yes, lord. Something over three thousand of your bodyguard are now within the city walls.'

'Excellent! We –'

'My lord, listen to me.' Gemeris had marched with Kouros clear across the Magron. He presumed on their acquaintance now, his face stark with urgency. 'I bear bad tidings as well as good. The Macht king is over the Magron Mountains. He has already taken Hamadan; the city opened its gates to him without a fight. Now he is already on the march for Ashur.

'My lord, he will be here in a week or less, and his whole army with him.'

TWENTY-THREE
THE STONE IN THE MOUNTAINS

THE PASSES THROUGH the Magron Mountains were not like those of the Korash to the north-west of the world. Though the Magron were the highest peaks known on Kuf, wide valleys lay between them, linking up to make as good a thoroughfare as any in the homeland of the Macht. Only in the darker half of the year were any of the passes closed, and even then, small bodies of men had been known to win through at some cost, as the imperial couriers had been doing for centuries.

The Imperial Road continued here, not the broad straight highway it was in the Middle Empire, but a meandering track under yearly assault from the elements. It was regularly washed away by meltwater or buried in avalanches, but the empire kept the road open, each waystation along it home to a work-gang of slaves who spent their entire lives labouring in the mountains to this end.

Rictus and his companions left Carchanis some two weeks after the Macht army had departed. They did so in some style, for Corvus had left the forty-six survivors of the Dogsheads behind to provide a kind of honour guard. Under Sycanus of Gost, a short, muscular veteran who had once stood with Rictus upon the walls of Machran, these men now accompanied him east in the wake of the army. Most of them were past the first flush of youth, as seamed and scarred as any old campaigner could be, but there were a few younger men in their ranks too, eager to get across the mountains and view the fabled heartland of the Kufr empire.

They rigged out the blue-roofed caravan once more, though they swapped the horses that drew it for hardier mules, and accompanied by more mules bearing packs, the company left Carchanis behind, following in the rutted track of the main host and marvelling at the views behind them as they clambered higher into the foothills of the Magron.

For Rictus, it was his first time travelling into a region he had never seen before. For the others, it was a relief to leave behind the heat of the lowlands and breathe the cool blue air of the hills.

The waystations were deserted now, their crews having run away at the approach of the Macht army. And they passed abandoned homesteads of stone and heather-thatch close to the road, their doors kicked in, their interiors rifled. It would seem that some of the new recruits were missing the iron hand of old Demetrius.

Not for long, though. They also passed a gibbet hung with three young men, Macht soldiers, their eyes already pecked empty by the crows. Corvus had never shown any mercy to looters, when he had not sanctioned their actions himself.

The company did not hurry, but they still made better time than the army, unconstrained by a vast baggage train. As it was, they passed abandoned waggons on the road, dead mules and horses, and massive stone-built cairns left at regular intervals, as though Corvus were leaving markers for them to follow.

The nights were short, but grew more bitter as they climbed higher into the Mountains. Ragged patches of snow began to appear on the mountainsides close to the road, hardy upland wildflowers springing up beside them, like two seasons living in truce together. It reminded Rictus of the Gosthere Mountains back around his home, or the place he had once called home. There were green glens here with rivers running down them that might have been in the Harukush, and once he caught his breath as they turned a corner on the road and saw, off to one side, a steep-sided valley winding past tree-covered spurs, and a wide, shallow river in the bottom of it, as brown as a trout. In a flash, he was back in Andunnon, building the house with Fornyx and Eunion stone by stone while Aise tended the fire and set barley bannock to baking on a rock griddle. It was so clear in his mind it almost seemed real, and when he came back to himself there was a moment of crushing despair. They were all dead now, every one of them. He was the only person left in the world who still possessed memories of that time and place.

That night, by the fire, he was withdrawn and morose, sitting propped up against a stone with the thornwood stick in his hands, the cold aching in his battered bones. He watched Sycanus and the other Dogsheads around other fires, listening to the timeless banter of soldiers, talk which had been the backdrop to all his adult life. He realised, in that moment, that he was no longer a warrior himself. Rictus of Isca, leader of the Ten Thousand. Who remembered his exploits now, since Corvus had risen like a storm to hurl the world on its head? The boy who had marched beside Jason, who had fought at Kunaksa – he was utterly gone. Even the cursebearer who stood in the front line and held men to his will was no more.

I am old, he thought. I will see Ashur, to sate the dregs of my curiosity, and then my service is over. I owe nothing to any man alive.

Kurun handed him a bowl of steaming goat stew with a smile. Beside him, Roshana was already eating hers with a crude stick-spoon. The three sat apart from the Macht soldiers by choice, whereas once Rictus would have been right at the lip of the centon, in the heart of them.

'Does she know what Corvus has planned for her?' he asked Kurun, nodding at Roshana.

Kurun dropped his eyes. 'She knows. I told her.'

'And how does it sit with her?'

'I will marry him.' To Rictus's astonishment, it

was Roshana who spoke. 'He will be Great King. I will be Queen.'

'I didn't know you spoke our tongue.'

'A little. I learn, for him, for Corvus.'

'You taught her?' Rictus asked Kurun. The boy nodded, stirring his stew with the spoon as though he no longer had any appetite.

'She made me. For marriage.'

He loved her; it was clear in his eyes. But what could a boy-eunuch offer the wife-to-be of a king? Rictus felt a pang of pity for him.

'And you?'

'I stay with her.'

'Even in Ashur?'

He hesitated. 'Even in Ashur.' But the words did not ring true. Rictus realised in that moment that Kurun did not want to return to the imperial capital. Once there, all his dreams would be snuffed out, and the reality of his station would be brought home to him.

Well, we have that in common, Rictus thought.

After ten days on the road they came to the highest point in the passage of the mountains. It was marked by a huge granite monolith, chiselled deep with words in the Kufr language, which Rictus could not read. Of them all, only Roshana could decipher it, and she lacked the skills to render the inscriptions into Machtic, so they passed it in ignorance. It was already a relic from another world. In passing, Corvus had set up a bigger stone, and had carved into it his name and the pasangs marched to this point. Below his name were carved others; those of all his marshals. Ardashir, Druze, Teresian, Demetrius, Parmenios – even Marcan. But Rictus had not been included. Wrapped in his threadbare scarlet cloak, Rictus stood and read the names on the stone over and over again, thinking on it. He realised that Corvus had not forgiven him for staying behind, for becoming old, perhaps. He was no longer part of the adventure.

How Fornyx would have fumed at this, he thought, smiling.

After they passed the stone markers, they were over the divide, and little by little they realised that they were descending again. The high point of the Magron had been crossed, and the rivers ran eastwards now, following their feet. Every stream they crossed was a tributary of the Oskus, far below. The water that ran cold and clear over the stones would soon be coursing in brown channels through the irrigation network of Asuria.

SIXTEEN DAYS OUT of Carchanis, the pass widened until it was no longer a cleft between mountains, but a whole widening country of oblong hills, each the shape of a boiled egg sliced down its length. The air grew warmer – almost overnight they had to pack away their furs and cloaks as the heat of the lowlands returned, edging up into the high places. Summer was waning, but the sunlight still set a shimmer upon the landscape, and out of that shivering haze they saw a city on a hill to the north-east, walls of grey stone rising in ordered terraces to a string of stately towers. Roshana pointed at the city and threw back the folds of her komis, her face alight.

'Hamadan,' she said.

They had come through the Magron, and that night they were able to look down across the sleeping black plains of Asuria and see the lights of Ashur glimmering in the far distance, like a mound of jewels abandoned in the depths of a mine.

TWENTY-FOUR
A MOTHER'S SON

Kouros stood on the high battlements of the western barbican as the sun rose behind him. The city was coming to life under it, and at this hour it almost felt like one vast living beast stirring into wakefulness. Lamps were being lit, fires kindled, and already he could hear the first clamour of the marketplaces as the stallholders set up shop. Another day in the greatest of all cities. Another morning as King of the world.

But not ruler of all he surveyed. He was staring out across the plain at a rival, a rigidly regimented encampment within which the fires were also being lit to meet the dawn. It was so close that he could see the flicker as men walked back and forth in front of the flames. A city in itself, walled in by a wooden stockade and ditch which had ruined the irrigation system for pasangs around. A tented town, harbouring thousands of men and beasts.

He could still not quite believe that it was here, less than two pasangs from where he stood. A Macht army was in Asuria, and now gazed upon the ancient ziggurats of the Asurian Kings.

He looked up and down the walls. They were manned thinly. On this side of the city he had stationed the bulk of Gemeris's Honai, so that the enemy below might see the gleam of their armour upon the walls. Lorka's Arakosans were further north, manning the defences that led up to the Oskus River. Thousands of men, but the endless walls swallowed them up so they were hardly seen. Ashur had never truly been made for defence; it was simply too big. Two million people lived and died within its confines, a population greater than that of many whole kingdoms. The only wars it had seen were murderous private skirmishes on the heights of the palace ziggurat, assassinations and coups fought by small groups of men intent on the deaths of a few nobles. War as the Macht fought it – it did not enter into the equation here, for the city or the people in it.

There must be a way, he thought, tapping his knuckle on the stone of the ramparts. It cannot be the end. We will hold the walls until they tire of attacking. There are not enough of them to besiege this city – they must attack.

'They have been felling trees and building at something in that lumber-yard of theirs for three days now,' Gemeris said beside him.

'These walls are a hundred and fifty feet high,'

Kouros told him. 'No-one can make a ladder that long.'

'They're not making ladders, my lord; that I would swear to. They have a pitchworks and a tannery set up, and half a hundred forges with smiths beating upon iron night and day. You can see the red gleam of them in the dark. The Macht have a genius with machines of war. They are at some devilment to see them over this wall, or through it, or under it.'

'Nothing can bring down this wall, Gemeris. It has survived earthquakes.'

The Honai said nothing, and Kouros felt a rush of anger as he sensed the doubt in the man.

'Send to me if anything changes. I am going to walk the towers and make an inspection.'

'My lord, that is not your place.'

'What?'

Gemeris was white-faced but insistent. 'You are Great King. It is not for you to patrol the walls like a junior officer. Your place is not here. The people expect their king to be where he –'

'Where he belongs?'

'Where tradition has him. Forgive me, lord, but you should be up on the ziggurat, not down in the middle of the fight.'

Kouros simmered. There was something to that.

'We cannot lose another king,' Gemeris said. 'I beg you, my lord, go back to the palace.'

'Very well. But I want a despatch every hour, Gemeris, even if nothing so much as a mouse stirs. You will keep me informed.'

'As you wish, my lord.'

Kouros turned away. As he walked towards the stair that led down to the city below, he realised that a fundamental thing in him had changed since Gaugamesh.

He was no longer a coward.

THE SUN ROSE, the city went about its business much as it had these past four thousand years and more. With one difference. All the western gates were closed now, and the markets on that side of the city were thinly attended. Honai had been marching through the streets these last few days, seizing any man who was young, of low-caste, and who looked fit to hold a spear. The unfortunates had been rounded up in their thousands, hastily equipped from the city arsenals, and then shunted up in droves to man the walls. They stood there now among the Honai and the Arakosans, as out of place as pigeons among a flock of vultures.

They were present to see the labours of the Macht bear fruit. On the morning of the fifth day, the enemy army began to march in thick columns out of its encampments, tens of thousands of troops emerging in bristling phalanxes to take up positions on the plain, trampling the crops and vineyards of the small farms. The trees had long since been hewn down, the irrigation ditches filled in. The fertile country west of the city had been trampled bare and brown, as though the Macht had brought some blight with them out of the west.

And in the midst of the massing enemy formations, great beetle-like shapes moved, crawling titans hauled and pushed by hundreds of the foe. They rolled on crude iron-rimmed wheels, and they were plated with bronze shields which looked from afar like a hide of bright scales. From the front of each poked the gleam of a steel-tipped ram. Two of these monstrosities were trundling to each of the three western gates of the city, and behind them, mule-trains were drawing other machines, angular crane-like contraptions, and great horizontal bows.

The horns of the city watch brayed out in warning and defiance, and the defenders began readying themselves for what was to come. The pitch-cauldrons were filled and the fires below them lit. Sheaves of arrows were heaved up to the Arakosans, and lumps of masonry were set to hand on the tops of the walls, ready to be hurled down upon the attackers.

For a few minutes, in the wake of the horn-calls, the great city came as close to silence as it ever had, and it was in something of a hush that the Honai manning the wall saw the Macht king himself ride out in his horsehair-crested helmet with a cluster of aides. Three of them broke off and galloped right up to the city gates bearing a green branch, and Gemeris stood on the heights of the barbican with Lorka beside him to hear them out.

They were Kefren riders, dressed in red; men of the enemy cavalry known as the Companions. Lorka's face tightened as he saw them. Gemeris stood up on a merlon, a golden statue ablaze in the sun.

'That's far enough. Speak and be quick!'

One rode forward. To the shock of all on the ramparts, they saw that though he was a Kefre of good blood, he wore the black cursed armour of the Macht, a phenomenon never seen before.

'I bring you an offer from my king, Corvus of the Macht, ruler of all the lands west of the Magron Mountains. Open your gates, surrender your city and lay down your arms. If you do this, he will look upon you as friends. Ashur will be spared, and not a man of you will be harmed or dispossessed, save he who calls himself Great King.

'If you do not do this, then we will assault your walls within the hour, and once they are breached, Ashur shall be given over to sack and flame, and the lives of all those who bear arms within your walls shall be forfeit. My king awaits your answer, but be swift, and do not think of any treachery. That is all.'

He raised the green branch in salute, and the three horsemen turned and galloped back the way they had come. The smell of burning pitch drifted along the walls, borne by a hot breeze. Gemeris leapt down from the merlon. 'Get me a good scribe, and a fast runner – quickly!'

'I must go,' Lorka said.

'Do not go far. You'll be needed here soon enough.'

'I know my duty,' the Arakosan snarled. 'Do not presume to teach me it, Honai.'

* * *

THE BALCONY OF the Great King's chambers possessed a view unmatched anywhere else in the world, and it looked west. While standing there, Kouros could survey the grid-pattern of the teeming streets below that was barely discernable when one was walking among them. He could see the grey python of the walls with their punctuating towers, and beyond that, the trampled umber plain which the Macht had made their own.

All things, they destroy, he thought. They come from a land of stone, and reduce to stone and dust everything they touch. They are a pestilence upon this world.

The fine material of the curtains moved inwards as the door to his chambers was opened, though he heard no noise.

'Akanish?' he called, but the chamberlain did not answer.

Kouros turned to pour himself more wine from the decanter on the table at his side, and as he turned his eyes caught a flash of blue.

It was Orsana. His mother stood motionless in a simple robe, azure silk hemmed in black. She had thrown back a komis of snow-white linen from her face, but left the material framing her head. She looked like some stern-faced priestess about to engage in an ancient rite.

'Mother! These are my private chambers. It is not fitting that you be here.'

She was carrying a square of parchment with

a broken seal. 'News from the gates. You should read it.'

He set down the cup and snatched it out of her hand, scanning the seal first.

'Gemeris. This should have come straight to me.'

'Read it.'

The clear hand of a scribe, the ink spattered in his haste. Kouros's jaw worked as he read, chewing on anger.

'I thought I knew what arrogance was; it seems I was mistaken. The barbarian at the gates sees fit to dictate terms to me – to me!' He tossed the parchment aside. 'This has no relevance. But I do want to know why it came to you instead of straight to me, mother.' The anger was still there. He chewed on it like gristle.

His mother was very calm.

'I take it his terms are unacceptable to you.'

'What? Of course they are. Do you think I would ever let that usurping monster into this city without a fight? I killed my own brother to wear the diadem, mother – I will not tamely hand it over. He will see how a son of Ashurnan can fight; I will make him regret the day he ever brought his rabble east of the mountains.'

'That is what I thought you would say.' She hung her head.

'And now you can tell me how you came to break the seal on a despatch meant for the Great King?'

'Kouros, my son – do you not know – have you never even suspected?'

'That your intrigues are unending, that you will

meddle in the affairs of state at every opportunity – that you see conspiracies behind every bush? I do not suspect, mother – I know. I have always known.'

'You know nothing,' she said to him, her voice suddenly rising, like the crack of a whip. 'Do you think I have spent thirty years in the harem polishing my nails? You stupid young fool. I gave up counting the number of times your father tried to have me killed. But he failed. In the end, he had to let me survive, because I made myself essential to him and to the empire. Through me, he had Arakosia, and I made sure that he would have it through me only.

'You think you can give orders to Lorka? He has been my creature since he suckled at his mother's teat. All the high officials of the city, I chose. Marok was mine, but so was Dyarnes – did you suspect that, Great King? All across the empire I have had my ears and eyes planted since before you were born. I killed that Niseian bitch your father would have supplanted me with, but she was only one of many. When a sparrow falls to the ground in Ashur, I know about it.

'This is my city Kouros – mine. I have controlled it for decades. Just because you tied a ribbon about your head does not mean you rule anything at all. I gave birth to you, I had you reared, and I used you to kill Rakhsar. You are my son, my instrument – do not think that you can even begin to take my place.'

She paused, collecting herself.

'I will not see Ashur destroyed to salve your pride. The invader offers terms we must accept. Do you understand me? Your men will not fight. The Arakosans are leaving the walls as we speak. Lorka is sending them back to their homes, on my orders.'

'Gemeris,' Kouros whispered.

'One of mine, ever since he returned from Hamadan. He knows which way the wind blows. Why else do you think he persuaded you to leave the walls? Your father's men all died at Gaugamesh, Kouros. Those that are left serve me. You are alone. You are the last of your father's line.'

'Does that mean nothing to you?' Kouros asked her. 'The Asurian line –'

She drew herself up. 'I am Arakosan,' she said proudly. 'I was a queen before I ever came here, from a bloodline as ancient as that of Asur.'

'You would give it over to him, the last remnant of the empire – you would let him walk in here without raising a hand.'

'He cannot be defeated, not by arms in battle. But that is not the only way to fight, Kouros. I will open the gates to him. I will invite him into these very chambers. I will kneel before him and smile as he dons the diadem. When that is done, I will be patient, as I have always been patient.'

'Rakhsar was right,' Kouros marvelled. 'They all were. You are a poisonous bitch.'

He stepped forward, but as he did there was movement at the door. Charys, the hulking chief eunuch, padded barefoot into the chamber, his face a hairless crag of pink flesh. Behind him came two Arakosan troopers in full armour, scimitars drawn. They closed the doors with a soft boom and then stood waiting.

Kouros stared at them all in some wonder. 'Your own son, Orsana. You would kill me?'

Orsana reached inside her robe. 'I will not have to.' She drew forth the iron knife that Kouros had killed his brother with, and tossed it on the table. It lay black and ugly beside the crystal decanter.

'I said that war had made a man of you. I meant it. And you are my son. There will be no poison, no unseemliness. You will do what you must by your own hand, Kouros. If you do not, then it shall be done for you.'

He stared blindly at the knife.

'I am your son,' he said, and there was a quaver in his voice. He looked at her, and found not one whit of compassion in that hard, white-painted face. He might as well have been looking into the eyes of a snake.

'You are my son, but there is no greatness in you. If this day had not come I would have ruled through you. As things stand, you are an impediment to me, and your stupidity hazards the survival of this city. I leave you an honourable end. If you have courage, you will take it.' She swallowed, and her hands shook a little. She folded them into the bosom of her robe.

He stepped forward and grasped the knife. She retreated from him – one step, two – and the eunuch padded closer; as if the three of them were somehow connected in some absurd little dance.

'Farewell, Kouros,' Orsana said.

'I pray to Mot that I shall haunt your dreams, you unnatural whore.'

She walked away. The Arakosans opened the door for her, and she did not look back before it was closed again.

Kouros looked at the knife, thinking of his brother Kuthra, of Rakhsar, Roshana. His own father, who had died as a man should. They were all gone, and now he would follow. And Orsana would live on to spin her webs and brew her poison. The shock of it brought a laugh into his throat, although it left his lips as a choking sob.

He looked at Charys. The eunuch's eyes were gimlets in that massive, blank face. There was no humanity there.

He heard the horns of the city blowing again, and walked to the balcony to look out upon the majesty of imperial Ashur. There was a roar up by the western gates. He did not know if it was battle or celebration. It was a meaningless sound.

Meaningless.

'I am Kouros, son of Ashurnan, of the line of Asur. I am Great King of the Asurian Empire.'

He chewed angrily on the words. The anger was enough. It had been with him all his life. He thrust the wicked blade into his own chest, stood there wide-eyed with the cold violence he had done himself, and turned to face the men in the chamber.

'I am – I am –'

Then he fell headlong upon the floor, upsetting the wine, his legs drawing up under him. He struggled a moment more, then was still. The knotted jaw relaxed at last.

TWENTY-FIVE
AN OLD MAN'S ADVICE

THEY MET BELOW a canopy of cyan-blue silk, erected a pasang in front of the main western gate. A file of fifty Honai marched out of the city in perfect time, their armour as bright as bronze could be, the sun glinting on their spearheads. From the camp of the Macht came forty-six scarlet-cloaked spearmen, led by a centurion in the Curse of God.

The two companies formed up opposite each other, with the canopy between them. They stood with their shields at their knees, and waited in the growing heat of the morning, looking at each other with frank curiosity. They were professional enough, all of them, to feel no real rancour for their enemy. They had last met at Gaugamesh, in the centre of that great dust-flayed cauldron of mayhem. They had that in common.

As they stood there, the walls of Ashur filled with

people, and the bee-hive mumble of their talk carried clear across the plain. The streets were crowded as though for a festival, and the proceedings were relayed down to the alleyways by those lucky enough to have secured a perch on the battlements far above.

Bronze horns sounding out from the summits of the ziggurats, relayed all the way to the western walls. There was an echoing cheer which rolled out of the east as it was taken up by the crowds.

From the stockaded encampment of the Macht a group of riders emerged, in full armour but without spears. One bore the raven banner, black on scarlet. They were all clad in the Curse of God, and all were magnificently mounted on tall Niseians, save one, an older man who rode a humble bay mare. This company picked its way slowly from the Macht camp towards the canopy of silk and its twin files of spearmen. When it was halfway there, the gates of Ashur swung slowly open again, and emerging from the shadow of the barbican there trooped a knot of horsemen escorting an ornate chariot, over which flew the purple and gold standard of Asuria.

The two groups drew together, and as if by unspoken agreement, they dismounted behind their respective spearmen. Then they joined each other under the twisting, breeze-bulged silk, standing on either side of a long table.

On the Macht side, Corvus, Ardashir, Teresian, Druze, Parmenios, and Rictus.

On the Kefren side, Gemeris, Lorka, and Orsana.

Corvus spoke first. 'I mourn for your loss, lady. No mother should ever have to bear the death of a son.'

Only Orsana's eyes were visible. She wore a black komis to hide her grief.

'I thank you. It has been hard to bear, but when my son saw the odds against him, he decided to spare his people the ordeal of further war. He took his own life and died as he had lived, a brave man.' The eyes above the folds of the komis were bright with tears.

Corvus bowed to her. 'I regret his father's death, and I regret his. Whatever your people might think of me, lady, I do not come to destroy, but to renew. To bring our peoples together.'

'You brought enough of them together at Gaugamesh,' Lorka flashed. 'How did that work out?'

'Peace.' Orsana held up a hand. 'If we speak of nothing but past offences, then we may as well go back to the gates and close them. King Corvus, I am here freely, as the last representative – the last suitable representative – of the imperial family. I come to surrender to you the city of Ashur and its environs, on the terms which you set before us six days ago, when your herald approached our gates. I thank you for your forbearance during the negotiations, and rejoice that we finally meet face to face to finalise this matter. Gemeris.'

The Honai beside her stepped forward and set a gem-studded golden box upon the table. Orsana opened it. Within lay a series of plain iron keys, massive as horseshoes, and ancient-looking.

'These are the keys to the treasury of Ashur. They are yours. I pass my stewardship of the city to you.'

Ardashir took the box, closed it and hefted it under one arm. He bowed to Orsana.

Corvus came round the table, surprising them all. He took Orsana's hand, startling her, and raised it to his lips.

'Lady, know that I value you beyond price for the dignity and wisdom you have shown over the past days. I beg you to remain in the ziggurat, to retain all your wealth and offices. I will treat you as though you were my own mother, and I ask only that you continue to furnish me with your counsel as you have counselled Great Kings before me.'

Orsana collected herself. She grasped Corvus's hand in both her own.

'Nothing would please me more,' she said.

THE ARMY ENTERED the city with the Companion cavalry in the lead, decked out as if for parade, every link and rivet of their armour polished to high brilliance, the Niseians shining and stamping at the sound of the trumpets and the drums. The preparations had been set in hand for days, ever since the death of the unlamented King Kouros had been announced, and now the roadways were strewn with petals, and garlands were hung like banners at every corner. The people of Ashur were overjoyed to finally know that they were to be spared siege and sack and all the horrors of war. They cheered without prompting, and scattered flowers over the heads of Corvus's army as if it were a homecoming and not an invasion.

Corvus took fifteen thousand men, a third of the army, into Ashur. The rest remained outside, and waggons of wine and provisions were sent out to them in endless convoys, the gift of the people of Asuria – though it was Parmenios and Gemeris, working together, who had organised that side of things.

The negotiations had been protracted not by doubts as to their eventual success, but by the protocols attending a Great King's death. The Macht had been halted in the very act of bringing their rams to the gates by hurried riders pleading for more time. The Great King was dead, and the decencies had to be observed, but the Macht terms were broadly acceptable. Could the city not be given a little more time?

Time in which much of the contents of the treasury had been loaded onto swift carts and sent off to Arakosia. Time in which the last surviving officials who had been loyal to Ashurnan were removed from their posts and from their heads.

By the time the terms had finally been agreed, the city was officially over its mourning for a king the people had never known, and the black banners were taken down and laid aside. Preparations were almost complete for the housing of the garrison both sides had agreed was suitable for the Imperial Capital – capital of Corvus's empire now, not of Asuria's. And so the dazed Macht soldiers marched into the greatest city of the world to the music of bronze trumpets, the roar of approving cheers, and a shower of summer flowers. They had never known anything like it.

'Perhaps it was worth it after all,' Ardashir said, grinning. He caught a flower in mid flight and blew a kiss to the *hufsa* girl who had thrown it.

Rictus looked up at the soaring shadow of the ziggurat that lay ahead and blinked in wonder. There were indeed things in the world still worth seeing.

'So this was your home,' he said to Kurun, who was sat on the horse's rump behind him, clinging to his shoulders.

'This was my home,' Kurun said, and he stared up in almost as much awe as the gawping Macht.

The parade continued into the heart of the city and travelled along the Huruma itself. When they came to the fountains, several of the Macht scooped up the sacred water in their helmets and doused themselves with it, and some of the horses drank there, which produced ugly little scenes on the fringes of the crowd. But for the most part the inhabitants of Ashur were as fascinated by the fabled Macht as the conquerors were by what they had conquered.

At the foot of the ziggurat the procession paused. The Honai were drawn up here, stiff as wooden soldiers, and Orsana waited with a cluster of high-born officials, most in Arakosan blue.

Corvus bowed to them from his horse, but he did not dismount. He set his Niseian at the King's Steps and the beast began to climb them. One of the Honai broke ranks with a cry, but was restrained by his fellows. Corvus paused when he was above all their heads, the white horsehair crest of his helm catching the sun, the black Niseian prancing under him, and the Curse of God gleaming ebony on his chest. They saw him grin, happy as a boy. Then he waved at his marshals, gesturing.

They followed him up the steps on their horses. Only Rictus stood his ground, for behind him, Kurun was weeping. 'It is not right,' he was saying. 'This is not right.' The Kefren notables at the foot of the steps stood rigidly in the sun, and Orsana lowered her head in their midst.

The marshals ascended the ziggurat on their horses, and the crowds below watched them in amazed wonder, while the assembled Macht infantry cheered and clashed their spears against their shields, a brazen thunder.

'It is not the way it is done,' Kurun said, wiping his nose.

'What do you care?' Rictus asked, half irritable at the boy's sudden switch in mood. 'It's not your throne.'

'It is my country.'

Up they went. The Honai at the foot of the steps dispersed. One looked up at the disappearing Macht on the ziggurat, and broke his spear over his knee, flinging the fragments away. The Kefren officials fanned out into the Macht formations, seeking the centurions. They bore with them lists and maps, showing where each mora was to be billeted. At once, two full morai began marching off for the Slave-Gate, seeking a humbler entrance to the ziggurat. The crowds, the heat, the noise all rose to a degree which could be equalled only by the midst of battle. Suddenly Rictus wearied of it all.

'Let's give you a view you never had before,' he said to Kurun, and set his own horse at the King's Steps.

'You cannot!'

'Stay on the horse, Kurun. This is a new world we are in, and we've as much right to walk these stones as any other bastard.'

Three thousand steps. They dismounted ere the end to take the weight off their sweating horse, and Rictus walked the last half pasang leaning on Kurun's shoulder and feeling all his old wounds complain bright and loud. But at the top there was a breeze, a coolness like on the side of a mountain in summer, and they caught the smell of growing things, thyme and lavender and honeysuckle, a whole garden in bloom. Kurun's face was running with tears. Looking down at the boy, Rictus remembered that not all bad dreams came from battlefields.

'The world is changed,' he said. 'Whatever happened to you here is over. You are a free man, Kurun.'

'Then, as a free man, I want you to walk with me in the gardens of the King, Rictus, sir.'

'We can walk anywhere you like.'

A STRANGE SYMBIOSIS took place over the following days. Macht spearmen and Kefren Honai stood on guard side by side throughout the palace, mismatched guardians of the new regime. Orsana withdrew to the harem, though Corvus visited her more than once to pay his respects and discuss the running of the city. In the streets below, the Macht mingled with the local population, haggling in the bazaars and making full use of the brothels in the wall-districts. They had the plunder of a continent to spend, and while their ignorance led to a few scuffles, for the most part they were regarded with tolerant curiosity. The city swallowed fifteen thousand of them as though they were a teardrop fallen in a river, and the urban rhythms of Ashur barely changed. The farmers brought their last crop of the year into the markets, the caravans resumed from the east, and imperial slaves still went about their errands bearing the purple-striped tunic of the kings. In the bowels of the ziggurat, thousands still toiled in the dark to see the gardens above watered, the elite of the new empire fed and clothed. Everything had changed, and nothing had.

The lady Roshana was finally escorted into Ashur at the beginning of autumn, borne on a litter and cheered with genuine enthusiasm by the ever-ready rabble of the lower city. She was dressed as an Asurian princess, her eyes painted, a komis of creamy silk masking her face. She was Ashurnan's daughter, and the people turned out to cheer for her in memory of their dead king as much as anything else. She was transported to the summit of the ziggurat and installed in the King's apartments, ready for the great day to come. Corvus was to be crowned with Ashurnan's diadem and married to his daughter in the same ceremony, the one leading to the other. When that happened, his claim on the Asurian Empire would be complete, and an epoch of history would end – or would begin, depending on how one looked at it.

* * *

RICTUS WAS SUMMONED to the King's presence one night, not long before the coronation-wedding. It was *Osh-fallanish*, the month of cool wind. Kurun had taught him that. He had taught him enough Kefren words to greet and bargain at the stalls of the lower city, enough to salute the Honai in their own language, which damped down some of the hostility still in their eyes. He still could not get used to seeing them stand guard over a Macht king.

The chambers of the King had been stripped out of all their luxuries, for Corvus had never been in any sense a sybarite. Rictus had to smile as he saw the humble camp furniture from Corvus's campaign tent arranged in the vast echoing emptiness of the Great King's apartments. He touched the plain brass lamp which stood there with its four dangling wicks, thinking on the nights it had lit up the map table on campaign with them all bent over it, following Corvus's finger across the features of the world.

He had a bigger table now, marble-topped, with curling legs of pure gold. There were papers heaped across it, and the wooden scroll cupboard sat to one side, a battered contraption that had been with Corvus longer than Rictus had.

The King was not alone. He sat by the balcony in a plain wooden chair with a cup of wine in his lap, and opposite him sat Orsana, wife and mother to two dead kings. She had lowered her komis and her white face turned to Rictus as he limped towards them, his thornwood cane clicking on the floor.

Rictus came to a halt and bowed, at a loss how to proceed.

'So this is Rictus,' Orsana said. She spoke in Machtic, her accent light and sibilant, but the words perfectly clear.

'He is an old man. But then it is thirty years since the coming of the Ten Thousand.' She stood up and spoke to Corvus in Kefren. There was a fluid exchange between them in the language, informal, affectionate. She offered her cheek and Corvus kissed it. Rictus bowed again as she glided past him. The doors boomed out of time with each other as she left the room, the Honai and Macht guards having not yet synchronised their efforts.

'How is the leg?' Corvus asked him.

'It keeps me upright.'

'Well, sit, and give it a rest.'

A breeze billowed up the gauze curtains. They sat silent a moment, looking out at the city below, a thousand lights still burning in the darkness, Phobos rising over the Magron like a leering head. It was indeed a view fit for kings.

'We have not spoken in a long time,' Corvus said. 'That is my fault. I felt you blamed me for Fornyx's death, for the destruction of the Dogsheads.'

'They were a military resource. You used them to great effect.' Rictus's voice was cold.

'I went too far. Perhaps I expected too much. Rictus, I was wrong – I know that now. You must forgive me for this.'

'Forgive you?' Rictus tapped his stick on the floor. 'We're soldiers, Corvus. We don the scarlet and we take our chances. Gaugamesh was a victory, and it cost a lot of blood, as victories do. There is no more to be said.'

Corvus stared into his wine. 'Ardashir tells me you intend to leave.'

'Ardashir talks too much – he's damn near as bad as Fornyx was.'

'Will you not stay to see me crowned?'

'I have already seen you crowned, Corvus. Do you remember, the night before you were made high King of the Macht? Fornyx and I were with you then, and it was that night you put on Antimone's Gift for the first time.'

'How could I forget? You were like a father to me, Rictus.'

'I know. But the son outgrows the father, as you have. I have nothing left to teach you, Corvus.'

'That is not quite true. You did one thing before we left Carchanis that taught me a lesson beyond price.'

'Oh?'

'You gave Fornyx's cuirass to Ardashir. You allowed a Kufr to wear the Curse of God.'

'So?' Rictus growled. 'He deserved it. He is one of us, whether he is Macht or no.'

'No other man could have made that gesture but you. The army would not have stood for it. But because it was Rictus, they knew it had to be the right thing. With that single act, you changed the way they thought of the Kufr. You made me look at the empire itself differently. For that, I will always be in your debt.'

'There is no debt. You owe me nothing, and nor does any man. I know why you asked me here, Corvus, and it will not work. I am not some kind of talisman, or mascot that you must keep by you. My time in the scarlet is over.'

'Then stay for just a little while more, as a friend. See me crowned Great King. See me marry Roshana.'

Rictus shifted uncomfortably in his chair. He tapped the floor with his stick again, an old man's tic which he hated. He had caught himself doing it time after time.

'Look after her, Corvus. She is a fine young woman, and she is not so strong as she thinks.'

'I suppose she reminds you of your daughter,' Corvus said with a smile.

'No... not my daughter.' Rictus grimaced, stamping down on the unbidden memories.

'Protect her. I do not trust Ashurnan's widow, this Orsana. The woman came over to you too easily. There is no bitterness. I would feel happier if she hated you a little.'

'You think my charm worked too well?'

'I think your charm may have met its match. When I got your father killed, all those years ago, your mother hated me. I offered to protect her, and the child she carried, but she walked away into the unknown. She despised me and all the Macht.'

'I know,' Corvus said quietly. 'But as I grew up, she talked of you often. She knew my father loved you like a brother. As the years passed, she grew less bitter. You were very young, she said, and it was something you would have to carry with you for the rest of your life.'

They were silent again, looking out at the vast foreign city, remembering a time long past, their minds full of the faces of the dead.

'Orsana will put the diadem on my head,' Corvus said at last. 'I need her goodwill, Rictus. But I will listen to this last advice from you. I will be careful – and nothing shall touch Roshana. You have my word on it.'

'Then I'll stay to see the Great King crowned, if only to honour the memory of his mother.'

Corvus inclined his head. 'There is one more thing – Roshana has no kin left in Ashur, nor anyone she was close to in her life here. She has asked that you stand for her at our wedding, that you give her into my hand.'

Rictus kept staring at the spangled darkness beyond the balcony.

'I should be proud to,' he said at last.

TWENTY-SIX
KINGS OF MORNING

THE LONG HOT zenith of the year was past, and the first of the autumn rains were sweeping across the city like scentless smoke. They soaked the tented pavilions which had been erected in every public space, and the wind tugged down the flower-chains decorating the length of the Sacred Way.

Orsana placed a black diadem on Corvus's head, and the high priest of Bel anointed him with water from the Huruma, and gave him of it to drink. Another priest then placed in his hand a compound bow of ancient make, its string long withered, the grain of the wood replaced by minutely engraved ebony. In his other had was set a horse's rein.

The horse, the bow, the truth. The trinity of the Asurian Kings.

Corvus stood wrapped in the purple and gold robes of royalty and acknowledged the cheers of the

Macht thousands with a grave nod. His marshals stood all about him, mingled with high officers of the Honai and representatives from all over the empire. He took his place on the ancient throne with the cheers still echoing from the high walls of the audience-chamber.

In that moment, he looked wholly like some high-born Kefre of the ancient nobility, and it seemed that there was nothing of the Macht left about him at all.

Roshana was led to him moments later, on the arm of Rictus. As she passed Orsana the two women glanced at one another with a brief, intense gleam of enmity.

She squeezed Rictus's arm as he brought her to the Great King, and in perfect Machtic, she said '*Thank you*' to him. He nodded, and moved away. Kurun joined him, setting the thornwood stick in his hand to lean upon. The boy had eyes only for Roshana, but she never looked at him once.

The high priest thumbed scented oil across their foreheads, and then Corvus undid Roshana's komis, letting the white silk fall from her mouth. He kissed her, and a murmur of approval rippled down the hall.

The Empire had a Great King once more, and a Queen of Asurian blood as his consort.

THE BANQUETING HALL seated five hundred, and it was overflowing, bright with lamplight, hot and close with the heat of the crowds and the flames. From the kitchens below, endless courses were transported up on the serving platforms, and the purple-striped slaves of the lower city were everywhere, two for every guest. Macht and Kufr ate and drank side by side, talking in their own languages and making an effort at each other's. The palace had not seen such an animated throng since the days of Anurman.

Rictus stood by the wall, watching, wiping the sweat from his face. Corvus and his new bride were talking away to each other, oblivious to the rest of the room. The Great King was holding his Queen's hand. He looked flushed and eager as a boy.

Three seats down, Orsana sat like a graven statue, only her eyes moving. Her wine was untouched, and as Rictus watched, one of the slaves bent and whispered in her ear.

Oh, Fornyx, Rictus thought, you would so have enjoyed this.

He thought their departure from the hall went unnoticed, but Ardashir and Druze ambushed him as he and Kurun were making their way down the passageway beyond.

'Would you leave without a farewell, brother?' Ardashir asked, and there were vine-leaves in his hair and a sadness in his smile.

'There is no need for soldiers to say goodbye,' Rictus told him. 'In the end, we will all meet again in the same place.'

'Hell,' Druze said with his dark grin. The Igranian had a wine-jar by the neck and a wedding-garland was hanging from one ear.

'He wants you to stay – he's as much as begged you to,' Ardashir said gravely.

'I am of no further use to man nor beast, Ardashir. I will not stay here to sit and drool in front of a fire, to be wheeled out on great occasions. And besides, the climate does not suit me.'

The three laughed together while Kurun looked on, eyes wide and solemn.

'Is this a protégé?' Druze asked Rictus. 'Or is he just along to keep you warm at night?'

'He's free to come and go as he chooses,' Rictus said. 'For the moment, his road leads with me.'

'And what is that road, Rictus?' Ardashir asked. 'Where are you going to?'

Rictus tilted his head to one side and closed one eye.

'I have a yearning to see my own mountains again, brothers. It seems to me that a man near the end of his life often feels most comfortable where he started it. I have family in the Harukush. I shall be less worried about drooling before them; that is what grandfathers do.'

The humour faded from Ardashir and Druze's faces. They knew Rictus's family history.

'Corvus would give you a kingdom to rule, if you but asked him,' Druze said. 'Of us all, you deserve it most.'

'I am not made of the stuff of kings, brother. Once upon a time, a long while ago, I led the Ten Thousand. To have done that is enough, for any man's life.'

'Parmenios is writing a history,' Ardashir said. 'He begins with the sack of Isca. He says that the seeds of a new world were sown that day.'

Rictus thought back on it. He had been eighteen years old, a boy waiting to die by the shores of a grey sea.

'Good luck to him,' he said with a smile. 'I hope he remembers it better than I do. Come, Kurun; let's be on our way before more of these bastards chance across us.'

Druze held up the jar. 'A last drink, Rictus. To see you out the door. Come, brother.'

They drank from the jar one after another, even Kurun. When they were done only a trickle remained. Rictus poured it out onto the floor.

'For absent friends,' he said. And he tossed the empty jar back to Druze with a smile.

Then he turned and limped away down the passageway, leaning now on the stick, now on the slender frame of the boy beside him. Ardashir and Druze watched him go, the stick clicking on the marble floor, his shadow passing along the walls until he was round the corner and out of sight.

GLOSSARY

Aichme: A spearhead, generally of iron but sometimes of bronze. The spearhead is usually some nine inches in length, of which four inches is the blade.

Anande: The Kefren name for the moon known as Haukos; in their tongue it means *patience*.

Antimone: The veiled goddess, protector and guardian of the Macht. Exiled from heaven for creating the black Macht armour, she is the goddess of pity, of mercy, and of sadness. Her veil separates life from death.

Antimone's Gift/the Curse of God: Black, indestructible armour given to the Macht in the legendary past by the goddess Antimone, created by the smith-god himself out of woven darkness. There are some five to six thousand sets of this armour extant upon the world of Kuf, and the Macht will fight to the death to prevent it falling into the hands of the Kufr.

Apsos: God of beasts. A shadowy figure in the Macht pantheon, reputed to be a goat-like creature who will avenge the ill-treatment of animals and sometimes transform men into beasts in revenge or as a jest.

Araian: The Sun, wife of Gaenion the smith.

Archon: A Kufr term for a military officer of high rank, a general of a wing or corps.

Bel: The all-powerful and creative god who looks over the Kufr world. Roughly equivalent to the Macht 'God,' but gentler and less vindictive.

Carnifex: An army physician.

Centon: Traditionally the number of men who could be fed from a single *centos*, the black cauldron mercenaries eat from. Approximately one hundred men.

Chamlys: A short cloak, commonly reaching to mid-thigh.

Chiton: A short-sleeved tunic open at the throat, reaching to the knee. The female version is longer.

Drepana: A heavy, curved slashing sword associated with the lowland peoples of the Macht.

Firghe: The Kefren name for the moon Phobos, meaning *anger*.

Gaenion: The smith-god of the Macht, who created the Curse of God for Antimone, who wrought the stars and much of the fabric of Kuf itself. He is married to Araian, the sun, and his forges are reputed to be upon the summit of Mount Panjaeos in the Harukush.

Goatherder tribes: Less sophisticated Macht who do not dwell in cities, but are nomadic hill-people. They possess no written language, but have a large hoard of oral culture.

Goatmen: Degenerate savages who belong to no city, and live in a state of brutish filth. They wear goatskins by and large, and keep to the higher mountain-country of the Macht lands.

Hell: The far side of the Veil. Not hell in the Christian sense, but an afterlife whose nature is wholly unknowable.

Himation: A long, fine cloak, sometimes worn ceremonially.

Honai: Traditionally, a Kefren word meaning *finest*. It is a term used to describe the best troops in a king's entourage, not only his bodyguards, but the well-drilled professional soldiers of the Great King's household guard.

Hufsan/Hufsa**:** Male and female terms for the lower-caste inhabitants of the Empire, traditionally mountain-folk of the Magron, the Adranos and the Korash. They are smaller and darker than the Kefren, but hardier, more primitive, and less cultured, preferring to preserve their records through storytelling rather than script.

Isca: A Macht city, destroyed by a combination of her neighbours in the year before the Battle of Kunaksa. The men of Isca were semi-professional warriors who trained incessantly for war and had a habit of attacking their neighbours. Legend has it the founder of Isca, Isarion, was a protégé of the god Phobos.

Kefren: The peoples of the Asurian heartland, who led the resistance to the Macht in the semi-legendary past, and then established an Empire on the back of that achievement. Throughout the Empire, they are a favoured race, and have become a caste of rulers and administrators.

Kerusia: In Machtic, the word denotes a council, and is used to designate the leaders of a community. In mercenary circles it can also refer to a gathering of generals, sometimes but not always elected by common consent.

Komis: The linen head-dress worn by the nobility of the Asurian Empire. It can be pulled up around the head so that only the eyes are visible, or can be loosed to reveal the entire face.

Kuf: The world, the earth, the place of life set amid the stars under the gaze of God and his minions.

Kufr: A derogatory Macht term for all the inhabitants of Kuf who are not of their own race.

Mora: A formation of ten centons, or approximately one thousand men.

Mot: The Kufr god of barren soil, and thus of death.

Niseian: A breed of horse from the plains of Niseia, reputedly the best warhorses in the world, and certainly the greatest in stature. Mostly black or bay, and over sixteen hands in height, they are the mounts of kings and Kefren nobility, and are rarely seen outside the Asurian heartland.

Obol: A coin, made of bronze, silver, or gold.

***Ostrakr*:** The tem used for those unfortunates who have no city as their own, either because they have been exiled, their city has been destroyed, or they have taken up with mercenaries.

Othismos: The name given to the heart of hand-to-hand battle, when two bodies of heavy infantry meet.

Paean: A hymn, usually sung upon the occasion of a death. The Macht sing their Paean going into battle, to prepare themselves for their own demise.

Panoply: The name given for a full set of heavy infantry accoutrements; including a helm, a cuirass, a shield and a spear.

Pasang: One thousand single paces. Historically, one mile is a thousand double-paces of a Roman Legionary; thus, a pasang is half a mile.

Peplos: A woman's garment, very like a cloak but generally finer and lighter.

Phobos and Haukos: The two moons of Kuf. Phobos is the larger, and is pale in colour. Haukos is smaller and pink or pale red in colour. Also, the two sons of the goddess Antimone. Phobos is the god of fear, and Haukos the god of hope.

Qaf: A mysterious race native to the mountains of the Korash. They are very tall and broad and seem to be a strange kind of amalgam of Kufr and ape. They are reputed to have their own language, but appear as immensely powerful beasts that haunt the snows of the high passes.

Rimarch: An archaic term for a file-closer, the last man in the eight-man file of a phalanx, and second-in-command of the file itself.

Sauroter: The lizard-sticker. The counterweight to the aichme, at the butt of the spear, generally a four-sided spike somewhat heavier than the spearhead so the spear can be grasped past the middle and still retain its balance. It is used to stick the spear upright in the ground, and also to finish off prone enemies. If the aichme is broken off in combat, the sauroter is often used as a substitute.

Sigils: The letters of the Macht alphabet. Usually, each city adopts one as its badge and has it painted upon the shields of its warriors.

Silverfin, Horrin: Silverfin roughly correspond to a kind of ocean bass, and horrin to mackerel.

Strawhead: A derogatory term used among the Macht for those who hail from the high mountain settlements. These folk tend to be taller and fairer in colouring than the Macht from the lowlands, hence the name.

Taenon: The amount of land required for one man to live and raise a family. It varies according to the country and the soil quality, a taenon in the hills being larger than in the lowlands, but in general it equates to about five acres.

Vorine: A canine predator, mid-way between a wolf and a jackal in size.

THE MACHT TRILOGY

BOOK ONE

THE TEN THOUSAND

UK: 978 1 84416 647 3 • £7.99
US: 978 1 84416 573 5 • $7.99

The Macht are a mystery, a people of extraordinary ferocity whose prowess on the battlefield is the stuff of legend. For centuries they have remained within the remote fastnesses of the Harukush Mountains.

Beyond lie the teeming peoples of the Asurian Empire, which rules the world, and is invincible. The Great King of Asuria can call up whole nations to the battlefield. His word is law.

But now the Great King's brother means to take the throne by force, and has called on the legend, marching ten thousand warriors of the Macht into the heart of the Empire.

"A bold, strong new voice in fantasy."
– Robert Silverberg

BOOK TWO

CORVUS

UK: 978 1 906735 76 0 • £7.99
US: 978 1 906735 77 7 • $7.99

Twenty-three years after leading a Macht army home from the heart of the Asurian Empire, Rictus is now a hard-bitten mercenary captain, aging and tired. He wants nothing more than to lay down his spear and become the farmer that his father was. But fate has different ideas.

A young war-leader has risen to challenge the order of things in the very heartlands of the Macht, taking cities and reigning over them as king. His name is Corvus, and they say that he is not even fully human. He means to be ruler of all the Macht, and he wants Rictus to help him.

"One of the best writers working in fantasy."
– SciFi.com

THE MONARCHIES OF GOD SERIES

VOLUME ONE

HAWKWOOD AND THE KINGS

UK: 978 1 906735 70 8 • £8.99
US: 978 1 906735 71 5 • $9.99

For Richard Hawkwood and his crew, a desperate venture to carry refugees to the uncharted land across the Great Western Ocean offers the only chance of escape from the Inceptines' pyres.

In the East, Lofantyr, Abeleyn and Mark – three of the five Ramusian Kings – have defied the cruel pontiff's purge and must fight to hold their thrones through excommunication, intrigue and civil war.

In the quiet monastery city of Charibon, two humble monks make a discovery that will change the whole world...

"One of the best fantasy works in ages."
– SFX

VOLUME TWO

CENTURY OF THE SOLDIER

UK: 978 1 907519 08 6 • £8.99
US: 978 1 907519 09 3 • $9.99

Hebrion's young King Abeleyn lies in a coma, his capital in ruins and his former lover conniving for the throne. Corfe Cear-Inaf is given a ragtag command of savages and sent on a mission he cannot hope to succeed. Richard Hawkwood finally returns to the Monarchies of God, bearing news of a wild new continent.

In the West the Himerian Church is extending its reach, while in the East the fortress of Ormann Dyke stands ready to fall to the Merduk horde. These are terrible times, and call for extraordinary people...

"Simply the best fantasy series I've read in years and years."
– Steven Erikson, author of the *Malazan Book of the Fallen*

WWW.SOLARISBOOKS.COM

Follow us on Twitter! www.twitter.com/solarisbooks

THE CHRONICLES OF THE NECROMANCER

BOOK ONE

THE SUMMONER

978 1 84416 468 4 • £7.99/$7.99

The world of Prince Martris Drayke is thrown into sudden chaos when his brother murders their father and seizes the throne. Forced to flee, with only a handful of loyal friends to support him, Martris must seek retribution and restore his father's honour. But if the living are arrayed against him, Martris must learn to harness his burgeoning magical powers to call on different sets of allies: the ranks of the dead.

The Summoner is an epic, engrossing tale of loss and revenge, of life and afterlife – and the thin line between them.

"Attractive characters and an imaginative setting."

– David Drake, author of *The Lord of the Isles*

BOOK TWO

THE BLOOD KING

978 1 84416 531 5 • £7.99/$7.99

Having narrowly escaped being murdered by his evil brother, Jared, Prince Martris Drayke must take control of his magical abilities to summon the dead, and gather an army big enough to claim back the throne of his dead father.

But it isn't merely Jared that Tris must combat. The dark mage, Foor Arontala, has schemes to cause an inbalance in the currents of magic and raise the Obsidian King...

"A fantasy adventure with whole-hearted passion."

– Sandy Auden, *SFX*

WWW.SOLARISBOOKS.COM

Follow us on Twitter! www.twitter.com/solarisbooks

THE CHRONICLES OF THE NECROMANCER

BOOK THREE

DARK HAVEN

UK: 978 1 84416 708 1 • £7.99
US: 978 1 84416 598 8 • $7.99

The kingdom of Margolan lies in ruin. Martris Drayke, the new king, must rebuild his country in the aftermath of battle, while a new war looms on the horizon. Meanwhile Jonmarc Vahanian is now the Lord of Dark Haven, and there is defiance from the vampires of the *Vayash Moru* at the prospect of a mortal leader.

But can he earn their trust, and at what cost?

"A fast-paced tale laced with plenty of action."
– SF Site

BOOK FOUR

DARK LADY'S CHOSEN

UK: 978 1 84416 830 9 • £7.99
US: 978 1 84416 831 6 • $7.99

Treachery and blood magic threaten King Martris Drayke's hold on the throne he risked everything to win. As the battle against a traitor lord comes to its final days, war, plague and betrayal bring Margolan to the brink of destruction. Civil war looms in Isencroft. And in Dark Haven, Lord Jonmarc Vahanian has bargained his soul for vengeance as he leads the *vayash moru* against a dangerous rogue who would usher in a future drenched in blood.

"Just when you think you know where things are heading, Martin pulls another ace from her sleeve."
– A. J. Hartley, author of *The Mask of Atraeus*

WWW.SOLARISBOOKS.COM

Follow us on Twitter! www.twitter.com/solarisbooks